Jesus, Mary & Lucifer

VERSUS

Paul of Tarsus

& the Evil of his Church

Book 2. Paul

By

John E. Hunt

As the old saw says well: every end does not appear together with it's beginning.
Herodotus

All characters appearing in this work are fictitious. Any resemblance to real persons, living or dead, is purely coincidental.

TABLE OF CONTENTS

CHAPTER 1. A SURPRISE

Goth Girl and Lungorthin walked in, late for dinner, and quickly sat down. Goth Girl was the focus of careful side-glances from all because she was, well, just different. She was bigger, stronger; her movements were more confident. The appraising looks became less carefully hidden as Goth Girl happily filled one plate, and then another, with food. The others dropped all pretenses and stared as Lungorthin reached for another empty plate for her.

Cali, who thought that she was eating a lot, glanced at her full plate, which was the equal of Hal's plate. Then she stared at Goth Girl's two plates, each of which had twice the food on them that Cali's plate had on it and then stared at Goth Girl holding her new, empty plate, contemplating what to put on it.

Goth Girl looked up and noticed the stares. She blushed, but looked excited at the same time. She glanced at Lungorthin.

Lungorthin carefully put his arm around her, slowly, like holding a crystal goblet.

"It seems," Goth Girl confessed, taking another quick glance at Lungorthin for support, "I'm eating for two. Well, we think so." She bit her lip, uncertain. "The pregnancy tests, well, they are giving rather confused results. We're having a hard time finding a gynecologist who has any experience with mythological creatures, so we don't have any third-party verification. You'd think someone would have something in their Yellow Pages ad, but no. But I think so."

Everyone stared, astonished, and then smiled and offered quick congratulations.

Hal laughed and walked over to Lungorthin. He carefully slapped Lungorthin on the back.

"You old dog you, I didn't think you had it in you," Hal grinned. "No one gives the males the respect they deserve for their part in all this."

Lungorthin laughed and grumbled something.

"Tell me about it," Hal replied. "Like it's our fault they get sick in the morning." Hal looked up and Cali and Goth girl were staring at him with fixed expressions.

"Ah, well, perhaps we had something to do with it," Hal mumbled.

"If you males are done celebrating your reproductive prowess now, perhaps you could get us some more food," Cali teased.

Hal immediately rushed for more food, followed by Lungorthin, who had caught a look from Goth Girl.

Mary stood up and walked over to Goth Girl. "Well, let's see what we have here. I'm a bit of an expert on these things, including mythological creatures." Mary reached down and carefully put her hands on Goth Girl's slightly bulging belly.

Goth Girl stared, very worried, as Mary gently moved her hands.

Then Mary stepped back and put her hands on Goth Girl's shoulders. "Healthy," Mary assured. "Healthy and strong."

Goth Girl beamed.

"Both of them," Mary added, smiling as she walked back to her seat.

Goth Girl gasped. "Two? Are you sure?" she stammered.

"Fertility goddess here," pointing at herself. "I know these things."

Cali jumped up, rushed over, and embraced Goth Girl, who was staring at Mary, stunned.

"Will...well...will it be okay?" Goth Girl pleaded, staring intently at Mary

"It will be fine," Mary promised, smiling. "More than fine, I think."

Cali and Goth Girl hugged.

"Beast feeding might be a problem," Mary observed. "His children will have teeth."

Goth Girl blushed.

Lungorthin came back with several bowls of food and set them on the table.

"It is good?" he rumbled to Mary.

"Very good, my friend," Mary replied.

Hal set fresh food on the table. "Does this meet with your approval, my queen?" he offered, bowing to Cali.

"Better," Cali replied, giving Goth Girl a final hug. She walked back to her seat. Cali sat down and enthusiastically filled her plate. "I'd never realized what hungry was, before this."

Jesus stood up and slowly walked over to Lungorthin and Goth Girl. He put his arms around both of them. Mary and Lucifer watched, amused.

"What a wonderful event," Jesus declared, standing over Lungorthin and Goth Girl. "I couldn't be happier! But I was wondering," studying Lungorthin. "Are you going to do the right thing by my little girl?"

The entire table sat motionless. Goth Girl's mouth was frozen open, the food on her fork falling off.

"Ah...I had arranged for your birthmark to be hidden," Jesus continued. "I'd lost so many children over the years. I thought you'd have a better chance of survival that way."

Lungorthin sat open-mouthed, staring first at Jesus and then at Goth

Girl and back to Jesus. Goth Girl just stared at Jesus.

Hal covered his mouth to hide his laugher until Cali elbowed him and he gasped.

Lucifer turned away, snickering.

"My lord," Lungorthin rumbled. "I'd never have, well, had I known, I'd have asked...well..." He looked helplessly at Goth Girl, who laughed.

"There is a sight," she teased. "The mighty Lord of the Night, speechless. You were never speechless with me." She stood up and wrapped her arms around him.

"I could not be more pleased," Jesus vowed. "Our oldest, best friend. Something new in this world, after all the long years." He looked doubtfully at the full plates in front of Lungorthin and Goth Girl. "Hmm...I think you are going to have to buy a grocery store. I don't know how else you can get enough food. And two babies? Maybe two grocery stores. Still, this will work." He beamed at them.

Cali elbowed Hal in the ribs again.

"Oof!" Hal gasped, moving his arms to protect his ribs. "You enjoy doing that."

"I think we should go into the other room, watch a little TV, and let them talk," Cali suggested loudly, looking around the table.

"A wonderful idea," Lucifer agreed, standing. He walked over and clapped Lungorthin on the back. "Ouch," Lucifer groaned, rubbing his hand. "I have to be careful doing that. I forget how solid you are. Welcome to the family, Lord of the Night. And you also, my dear." He bent over and kissed Goth Girl on the forehead. "Beyond our hopes to have more children with us."

"And you," Lucifer laughed, clapping Jesus on the back. "I knew you were up to something."

"Everyone out," Cali remarked, standing up and grabbing food. "Here, you can carry those for me, if you would, my prince?"

"Your pack animal hears and obeys, my lady," Hal replied, grabbing everything he could.

"Here," Mary ordered. "We have servants for that." She motioned, and servants started carrying food into the living room.

In a few minutes, most of the group had decamped into the living room.

Jesus, Lungorthin, and Goth Girl sat around the table, touching and talking with happy smiles.

Cali and Goth Girl were talking the next day, sitting on the beach and exchanging early pregnancy experiences.

"No, I don't want to top that one," Cali mumbled, shaking her head. "You win."

"Just another little surprise, one of a long list of things no one talks about," Goth Girl sighed. "Like, have there ever been any children of mixed species like my mine will be? What is my labor going to be like? That's something I think about occasionally. What was Lungorthin's birth weight? Not something I get a good feeling thinking about. Or like our brothers and sisters over the eons who don't seem to exist."

"Yeah, Hal and I talk about that," Cali agreed.

They sat for a few minutes.

"I think Mary knows," Goth Girl guessed. "She seems to know everything."

"She does," Cali replied. "I'm glad she wasn't my mother when I was a teenager. Can you imagine rebelling against a fertility-goddess mother? Or trying to live up to a fertility-goddess mother? Neither seems like a workable plan. Then, trying to deceive her? Not a chance. Not that I, of course, ever deceived at all."

Goth Girl laughed.

The next day, another marriage on the beach, a joyous day.

CHAPTER 2. A NEW LIFE

It's about eighteen months later. Cali had a baby girl, Maria. Goth Girl had twins: a boy, Durion and a girl, Cinnamon. Hal, Cali, Goth Girl, and Lungorthin live in a converted warehouse in New York in an old industrial part of the town.

THE COMET

He jumped out of the water, the sky burning bright, and saw the fireball high in the sky. He jumped again and again, the pod swimming with him but with each jump the fireball was closer and closer, blotting out the sky, and then it hit. The oceans rose into miles-high walls of water, which swept towards him and the pod. They frantically swam away. Just before the wall reached him, he dove, but the water was so powerful that it pulled him back up, and he twisted and shook as it pulled him high, high, the enormous power of the water threw him...

"Damn!" sitting up and holding his head. He looked over, and Cali was sitting up also, shaking.

"The comet hitting all those eons ago?" Cali asked.

"I think so. I thought a dolphin could handle it better than that."

"An eight-foot wave is pretty powerful. A mile-high wave? Not so good."

"That does it," Hal ordered. "No pizza with extra spicy sausage before bed."

"Admit it, honey," wrapping her arms around him. "You were reading poetry last night after I went to sleep. I told you, no poetry readings again!"

"A shape with lion body and the head of a man, A gaze blank and pitiless as the sun, Is moving its slow thighs, while all about it..." turning to Cali and starting to move his thighs.

"Really? Do you think sex solves everything?" Cali teased.

"Well, yeah! Guy here."

"You sweet-tongued tempter," Cali whispered, pulling him down to her. "I'm always open to a good idea."

WATCHING THE NEWS

"So what's up?" Cali asked, walking into the community kitchen.

Hal was sitting on a bar stool, watching the TV grid array. "This is good," flicking the control so the scene was spread across the nine monitors. The glass church in California was blowing apart in slow motion, again and again. "It turns out that there were some distant surveillance cameras. Fortunately, they were far enough away that we don't show up."

"That was pane-full," Cali observed, watching the glass shards catching and reflecting the leaping flames as the shards were blown high into the sky.

"They got their glass handed to them, no question."

"And today, the church rebuilt," the voice over solemnly announced, the camera pulling back to a panoramic view of the new glass church, jarringly out of place against the neighboring big-box retail stores.

"They destroyed what good soil there was when they bulldozed everything for that strip mall," Cali complained. "Once land goes to desert, the ecology changes, and it's almost impossible to get it back to fertile soil."

"Out of this stony rubbish? Son of man,
You cannot say, or guess, for you know only
A heap of broken images, where the sun beats,
And the dead tree gives no shelter, the cricket no relief,
And the dry stone no sound of water...[1]"

Hal muttered quietly to the TV.

Cali glanced at Hal, surprised. "Eliot?"

"You'd be amazed what they have redone as a comic book."

"Not my favorite poem," Cali admitted. "I've seen and felt far too much wasteland. And I don't like that guy." She leaned towards the TV, watching as the new minister smiled into the camera.

"Tied to Paul. I've been doing some checking. Notice the very attractive but carefully sad blonde woman?" pointing at the screen. "She's the late Reverend Ostein's wife. The minister who died in the explosion at the church."

"Was it true he was drugging his parishioners?" Cali asked. "The rumors that came out later were nasty."

"Lots of juicy rumors! There was more interest in discrediting him than I would have expected. I'm thinking that while he was clearly no hero, the whispers were setting up the next group to be supermen. This is interesting, though. Doesn't Mrs. Ostein seem rather tense?"

They peered intently at the screen while the woman gave her speech, carefully watching her expressions and movements.

"Definitely stressed, far more than I would have expected," Cali agreed. "I'd guess she expected them to make her an offer, but maybe the offer was one that could not be refused. "

"My thoughts exactly. I'm sure there's a lot more going on there than this pleasant and placid play indicates."

"What do you hear about the new cartel boss?" Cali asked.

"The Major? Competent, dangerous. Government trained, then

turned. And there is more," Hal added. "He's Paul's chosen person, high in their organization."

They sipped their coffee, watching as the TV droned on about the terrorists who destroyed the first church, who had not yet been found—but new leads were developing daily. Then the announcer solemnly trumpeted the redoubled strength of the congregation, how adversity had tempered and toughened them and how the devil's work could not destroy their faith.

"More true than they would know," Cali sighed, shaking her head. "Faith in a false minister and empty theology—nope, couldn't dent it a bit."

With a flourish, the announcer introduced the new Minister, who calmly stepped to the podium, smiling as he acknowledged the clapping and cheers of the audience.

"Trust is the currency people use to take stuff from you," Hal declared cheerfully to the TV.

Suddenly, a loud furious cry split the air. Cali ran quickly into the other room. In a few minutes, she came back carrying Maria, whose little face was bright red—what face could be seen around the open, howling mouth.

"Good lungs," Hal commented, cringing. "That's what the doctor said. I think they put 'wear earplugs when examining' on her medical chart."

Goth Girl came in behind Cali, pushing a baby carriage with both of her children inside. They were screaming at the top of their lungs also.

"That's not a scream, technically," Hal contended, wincing and covering his ears. "That's at least a bellow."

The nanny rushed in, followed closely by Hal's mother.

"A moment's rest," his mother grumbled, but she brightened when she saw the group.

"What?" Hal shouted. "I can't hear you. I think a tornado siren went off in here."

The nanny and Hal's mother quickly went into action. In a few minutes, the kids had bottles and pacifiers poking out of mouths and their color was subsiding back to a normal pink.

"Here, we'll take them," the nanny ordered, bustling around with the kids. "You rest!" waving her finger at Goth Girl.

Goth Girl collapsed on the sofa, weakly smiling but clearly exhausted.

"I there anything I can do to help?" Cali asked, worried.

"No, I'll be Ok," Goth Girl sighed. "At least the throwing up stage passes pretty quickly. Got to crash, though." She melted info the sofa.

The kids were wheeled/carried into another room and were already making cute child noises as they left.

"At least their moods pass quickly at that age," Cali noted. "I'm dreading teenagers."

"Why?" Hal asked. "Weren't you the vision of happiness and jollity at thirteen? Frolicking through the meadows, not a care in the world? That's what you told me."

Goth Girl choked, she was laughing so hard at Cali's expression.

"Umm, that was me, no question," Cali nodded. "But I'm a little worried about your components in the mix."

"Moi?" Hal offered. "Sullen, hostile, defensive, and withdrawn. Other than that, a joy to live with."

"And when did that change?" Cali inquired. "Or did I miss the transition?"

"You just remember me in class," Hal smiled. "The professor didn't bring out the best in me."

They listened to the nanny fussing with the kids, teasing them.

"She is so wonderful," Goth Girl sighed, stretching her legs. "She's the only person, other than their dad, that they will listen to."

"I'd listen to her, too," Hal advised. "She does have bigger teeth than they do. Fortunately the kids don't know what she really can do or they'd be terrified. No monsters in the closets for the kids! The monsters would run from the nanny before she could eat them."

They watched the church dedication for a few more minutes.

"Cali, how is your mom doing?" Goth Girl asked.

"She's angry," Cali replied. "She's been traveling a lot. I asked a few questions and she started getting that Kali look, so I backed out of the room and decided to wait for her to talk."

"Angry is going to be bad for someone," Hal observed. "My dad has been the same. I see him occasionally. He pops up and says hi and then runs off. They are both really frustrated, and I'm seeing flashes in the news about what he's doing."

"Like this? Goth Girl exclaimed, pointing at the TV.

"The ambitious plans of several European countries and China for mining critical minerals from the deep ocean have been set back," the newsman announced. "Another mining ship has sunk in the north Atlantic, following two that sank off the China coast. There is no clear explanation for what has happened; all the sinking's are blamed on equipment failures. Several environmental groups, while expressing regret over the loss of the crews of the boats, have said that the mining was a terrible idea and should be banned until a complete analysis of the effects can be completed."

"Yeah, like that," Hal agreed, frowning at the TV.

"Lungorthin has been gone a lot," Goth Girl complained. "But he seems happy that something is finally happening."

"Obviously not gone all the time," Cali teased.

"No," Goth Girl laughed, actually blushing. "Well, he works hard, and I want him to feel welcomed at home."

Cali bent to her and whispered. They snickered.

"It's really helpful that he changed his appearance," Hal admitted. "Now we can go out on the streets without any real problems. Other than walking next to a seven-foot-tall football linebacker, which draws a little attention. People do back away carefully. My dad says that's all your doing, Goth. You brought him out of, well, his shell, which had never happened before. Dad was impressed."

"Oh, I was as surprised as anyone. My dad said the same thing" She frowned. "It's good to see Dad happy about something! He's so frustrated."

"Is he going to be back here soon?" Hal asked. "We miss him! And he is the best at dealing with the press and publicity."

"I'm not sure, but I think he'll be here this week. He does enjoy standing up there and talking to people. And they eat it up; he has a gift. Still, doing the liaison work around the globe is tiring. He is the public face, since the others are taking more direct action, and it bothers him to not be actually helping them."

"He's helping more than he realizes," Hal argued. "Getting all these people and structures doing something useful is critical. Without his work, there wouldn't be any resources to put to direct action."

Goth Girl gazed up at the ceiling, thirty feet away. "I love this old warehouse! "Cleaned up, it's beautiful. And it's huge, and private!"

"It has come down well," Hal agreed. "Gives us the privacy we need, because at night, most people are happy to get away from this block. Seems that there are rumors of strange creatures at night. And people have gone missing, I have heard. Like the people who tried to break in just after we moved here. So all that helps keep the curious away. And, I can't see Lungorthin in a twelve-hundred-square-foot condo on the forty-third floor."

Goth Girl laughed. "I'm not sure he'd fit in the elevator."

Cali picked up her head, the shouting starting again. "Time to help." She quickly kissed Hal, and then walked rapidly towards the noise.

"Everyone is so wonderful," Goth Girl mumbled. "I'm just so tired..." She closed her eyes and fell asleep on the sofa in moments.

Hal smiled and turned back to the monitor screens. He carefully moved his hands over the controller and the screens changed, each screen showing a different live feed. He watched for a while, making notes.

"Enough of that," the caretaker declared and Hal ducked—but not quickly enough. The wood cudgel lightly hit him between the shoulder blades. "More sword-fighting practice is obviously needed."

"Got it," Hal agreed, turning the monitor screens off. "Where's Cali? She so enjoys our little sessions of beating me with a stick."

"She's meeting us down there," the caretaker promised.

THE GLASS CHURCH

The TV cameras were on platforms spaced around the edges of the carefully manicured garden; absurdly incongruous plopped in the middle of a desert.

"And here we have the new Minister!" an announcer whooped, in his best Hollywood professional 'excited' tone. There was enthusiastic clapping as the Minister stepped up to the podium.

"Thank you for letting me help with God's calling here in this Garden of Eden. This," waving his hand at the rebuilt church, "is a triumph over the terrorists and their godless ways." He rambled on; making some subtle pitches for the building fund and all the new activities that would be starting. "We're getting started on our very exciting Christmas plans," winding up. "It's only a month away, and we have a lot to do to celebrate the Birth of our Lord."

Jesus was lying on a hotel bed in São Paulo, Brazil, watching the television ceremony. "Seems to me my birthday was in March?" he mused to the TV. "But I was pretty small then. Horus, Adonis, it all mixes together over the years. Still, celebrating the winter solstice is always a happy thing."

"Let's go over here," the reporter began walking, and the camera followed him. "This is a mini-museum, a record of the old church and its terrible destruction. Mrs. Ostein will take us through it and tell us what all the items are." The reporter stood next to Mrs. Ostein. She was elegantly dressed with her smiling teenage daughters standing next to her, crying softly as appropriate times—a well-rehearsed performance.

"This is dedicated to the heroic struggle and death of Reverend Ostein, who died to protect his flock, fighting the godless terrorists. He was working alone in the church and was cowardly ambushed by an overwhelming force," she announced tearfully.

Watching Mrs. Ostein, the Minister reflected on how hard it had been to keep the other bodies out of the news and the police reports. Silver or Lead was the offer and almost everyone grasped the concept. Those who didn't were out there in desert, somewhere.

The Cardinal and a large delegation from the Catholic Church were attending the dedication, along with many other ministers, making it an interdenominational celebration. When the speeches ended, they all shuffled into the cool air of the church, pulling hats and heavy vestments off, soaked with sweat from the merciless sun.

"So good of all of you to come," the Minister declared to the perspiring group standing in the nave of the church, the glass soaring high above them. "There is food and drink in the hospitality room. If you will, please let the young ladies be your guides. I can promise they are more enjoyable company than I!"

The group split up and moved off, each minister paired with an enthusiastic young woman guide who had been tutored on the fine points of that minister's theology. The Cardinal held back as the group wandered off, politely excusing himself from his young guide and then glancing at the Minister. The Minister nodded and walked to another stairway. There was a quick, fifteen-minute conference in a small conference room and then the Cardinal took his leave, his guard spread out around him as he strode toward the exit.

AT SEA

Lucifer and Mary were on a small trawler, far out at sea. It was a deceptively run-down boat. Underneath the worn exterior, it had all the latest electronics and engines. It was carefully designed to be unsinkable and held a variety of equipment that incorporated weapons-grade technology. That explained several of the mining ship sinking's, which self-destructed when their electronics went haywire. Other sinking's were tied to crewmen, now on the trawler, who had been on the mining ships before those ships experienced disastrous structural failures.

Mary sat on deck, reading aloud. Lucifer sat near her in a chair, listening.

"While I knew that the citizens of the sea tend to have three main goals in life—to find or produce food, to avoid being eaten, and to reproduce—I never realized the extent of the strange sex going on in the oceans. The instinct undersea to procreate is strong, and creatures have evolved many intriguing strategies to attract mates, copulate, and improve the likelihood that their progeny will be born and survive. Group sex and partner switching are common, while monogamy and fidelity are rare. Some marine organisms can be both sexes at once, while others change gender when the need arises— they are transgender on call. In some species, the difference between the sexes is extreme and mating habits are somewhat unusual, to say the least. While coupling, organisms in the oceans have to contend with changing conditions, sinking, and predators. Sometimes, even in the middle of the action, their own partners are a threat. Marine organisms are often outfitted with accouterments designed specifically for sex, and some are especially well endowed. Below the waves, cloning, seduction, and competition among rivals are rampant. And some creatures must literally give it their all in mating or in the incubation of their offspring, as breeding is a precursor to life's end. The oceans are a den of strange sexual relations that enable life to exist and genes to pass from one generation to the next.[2]"

"I love this book," Mary remarked to Lucifer. "It's all about sex—it makes a fertility goddess feel right at home. Humans are so boring on the whole topic."

"All of the great apes are pretty boring on that," Lucifer agreed. "Except the Bonobos. They have a more relaxed attitude."

"Here's a description of the mining people's best friends. Along with their gruesome propensity to feed on the dead, hagfishes are well known for their slime, lots of slime. If a hagfish, alias slime monster or slime hag, is threatened or injured, it releases mucus from hundreds of glands along its body. In just minutes, one hagfish can fill seven buckets with slime. The glands of the hagfish actually release a thick white fluid containing vesicles of mucus and bundles of thread-like cells. Like balls of string uncoiling, the threads unwrap; they then tangle, combine with the mucus, absorb seawater, and expand into massive amounts of sticky, slimy hagfish goo. Hagfishes use their slime to deter predators and facilitate escape. However, if a hagfish gets caught in its own slime, it can suffocate and endure a most unpleasant fate—death by goo.[3]"

"I can't believe they are disrupting the habitat of their closest friends," Lucifer admitted. "Just proves they have no morals at all."

"Do you remember these creatures?" Mary asked. "Sea cucumbers are real-life shape-shifters; if predators are near they can morph their skin from hard and lumpy into something a bit less appetizing akin to a gelatinous slime. When danger looms they literally turn to mush! Sea cucumbers have another very effective and rather disgusting means to deter predators: they eviscerate, readily expelling their insides as a decoy or trap. Some sea cucumbers eject a sticky spaghetti of white tubules, while others release their actual internal organs. A predator such as a fish or sea star may become entangled in the slimy mass or be distracted long enough for the sea cucumber to slowly crawl away.[4]"

"As for their sex life, it is active and free of gender issues. Many pteropods start as males, mate male-to-male, and then turn into females. During mating, male pteropods exchange capsules of sperm, which they store for later use as females. The deed itself is a tricky mid-water endeavor, given their propensity to sink. Pteropods sometimes float, often swim, and may hold on to each other as they mate. And they have different position preferences—some like to do it back-to-back, while others prefer a more traditional face-to-face arrangement. After mating, a pteropod's male organs are reabsorbed into its body and female parts develop. Then, with sperm already in hand (or body as the case may be) and the right equipment now in place, most pteropods lay thousands of fertilized eggs within long, floating ribbons. A few pteropods brood their eggs, releasing a smaller number of more mature offspring. In several of the shell-less pteropods, their private parts are adorned with spines and they have a suckered, tentacle-like appendage to aid in copulation. Some of these winged creatures may function as males and females at the same time, and pairs have been observed in endurance-testing embraces lasting for up to four hours. It is an energy-sapping process as they slowly beat their fins to stay afloat. Imagine an intimate encounter that lasts for hours and all the while, you and your partner must tread water. To stay fueled up, pteropods may continue to feed while mating, like grabbing a sandwich on the side during the action.[5]"

"They'd fit right in at a fraternity," Lucifer concluded. "Pizza, beer, and sex."

"Here's an idea," Mary argued. "The cone snails that preferentially hunt shellfish use their venom to induce paralysis, which makes it much easier to pry their prey out of its shell. Researchers have discovered that cone snails have a tremendous variety of venoms and, amazingly, individual organisms can even change the composition of their toxins between strikes. Their at-the-ready harpoon-like teeth and array of varying and potent venoms more than make up for these snails' lack of speed and agility.[6]"

"Maybe we could distill their venom and use it on the mining ships?" Lucifer asked.

"Better yet, put it in the corporate offices," Mary replied. "Strike to the heart of the matter. They waste the easy resources and then try and destroy what's left of the oceans by tearing up the critical deep waters. They don't even run the right calculations on the energy and other inputs required to do all this mining, they just run berserk because the governments are behind them with promises to pay anything needed."

"You know," Lucifer mused, "I'm thinking that your comment about the attacks on the corporate headquarters should be our next goal. Fat decision-makers in suits, far from the devastation they cause, need to be brought up to speed about the effects of their choices."

Mary stared out over the open ocean for a few minutes, contemplating, and then eyed Lucifer. "I'll tell the captain. We've slowed them out here, and now we'll stop them from the top."

NEW YORK, THE WAREHOUSE

Cali crept quietly into the room, peeking at Goth Girl sleeping on the sofa.

"The war is under control?" Hal whispered.

"Peaceful for the moment," Cali whispered back. "They are just starting to get lively, my mother tells me. I think she says that just to enjoy the look of despair on my face. You know, that moment of excitement at the thought of a new child, rapidly turned reality by lust/desire and action? There should be a thirty-page disclosure statement listing the side effects, including no sleep, no rest, and no sanity for the next twenty years. We'd all ignore it anyhow, but at least we'd be on notice. Hey, did you see the work I did on the

21

new project?"

"Yeah. I loved it! Your work is so good that people are going to get their noses out of joint because they didn't figure it out themselves."

"'Not invented here' runs rampant. There are some things I don't miss about not being in an office," Cali replied. "All those nice interpersonal conflicts, for example."

A loud and annoyed "meow" came from behind them, and Cali turned. "Oh, it's the cat overlord, making an appearance." The cat jumped up on Cali, regally rolling over on her lap. She carefully scratched the cat under her chin. The cat gave Hal a look that clearly said that he could be doing something useful also. Hal laughed and scratched the cat, which closed her eyes and purred.

"I was so glad she was saved from Ann Arbor," Cali mumbled. "Something salvaged from the chaos. I wonder sometimes..." She looked sad. "...whether Maria will hold onto a few things that she got from us. I wonder whether we'll live to see her grow up?"

Hal was silent for a moment. "I've had the same thoughts. When we honored the anniversaries of our parents', well, adoptive parents' deaths, I worried about that. It's not good that there are no other children who have survived. Or grandchildren, as far as I can tell. Still, we're here, and full of fight."

"The one who lacks courage to be a hammer comes off in the role of the anvil," Cali vowed.

"You absolutely have to find some lighter reading. Aren't there any pithy sayings in the fuzzy bunny book you've been reading Maria?"

"Nothing that really has much to do with the world," Cali frowned. "The book has the lamb and the lion lying down together as friends. Later, she'll discover it's a power lunch, but for now, it's something. And she likes to touch the little fur inserts. Just this week, she held the book and pointed out what I was to touch."

"Strong minded, she is." Hal acknowledged. "I wonder where she got that?"

"Not from me," Cali teased. "Sweetness and light, as I happily trip through the flowered meadow; that's me, the elf mother. Must be from you, with all those serious looks and that powerful elf warrior image."

"I've got to grow my hair longer, to get the elf warrior look, no question about it. Speaking of warriors, at least the truce is something. We can go out to the deli for food, and not worry about it being poisoned. Well, not poisoned by our enemies. There are the usual New York sanitation issues, or lack thereof, but we're developing antibodies against run-of-the-mill food poisoning."

"In all truth, without the protection of Lungorthin and others, I doubt we'd be here today," Cali murmured, snuggling up to Hal. "Even with a powerful elf warrior protector, it's good to have friends."

Hal gazed out the window for a minute. "You're right. Sadly, the truce won't last. Too many old angers, and too many reasons for people to wish us gone, but it's here for a while."

"Oh, petty reasons, like the money we took, the computer networks we destroyed, Don Cortes' death..." Cali was counting up on her fingers. "Then there was..." She stared at her hands. "I'm running out of fingers."

"Little things that would bother only small-minded people. Trifles. Before the truce, I heard what they were offering as a bounty for us and I was trying to figure out how we could get a part of it. It was a meaningful number, let me tell you."

"Take it as flattery," Cali offered. "It's nice to be wanted."

"In fourteen countries, twenty four states, and thirteen counties? Maybe a little too much!

"Lungorthin has his people, well, creatures watching," Cali observed. "That helps a lot. Remember, people think that there are strange things on this block, so the curious—and the wise—stay away. Makes it a lot easier to monitor what's going on."

She said nothing for a few minutes. "I think of the wall when I fear. It makes me feel alive again. And," snuggling closer to him, "when I feel alive, well..."

"Wow, it's late," Hal declared, grabbing her by the hand. "Time to turn in." They quietly walked upstairs.

A TRUCE

"So it's a truce?" Lucifer asked, sitting down at the coffee shop. "Peace in our time, and all that?"

"Not the way I'd phrase it," the Cardinal countered, smiling despite himself. "This a document from Paul. I am only an emissary in this matter. Truly," catching Lucifer's look. "Nothing of my work."

"Why would that be?" Lucifer observed. "Hypothetically, as you are the strong right arm of Paul."

"Strong left arm, I'd say," the Cardinal remarked. "Grendel still lurks."

"Yes, of course," Lucifer sighed. "Who could forget him? As much as I wish I could some days. He sat back and contemplated the Cardinal for a moment. "This really is not your work?" Lucifer queried.

"No," the Cardinal insisted. "This is my home turf. I should have been consulted. I was not, and my guarantees were not requested. Or provided," the Cardinal continued, idly doodling on a piece of scrap paper. "My fingerprints are not on this. This is not a part of me—no representations or warranties provided."

Lucifer leaned forward, studying the Cardinal carefully. "I'll remember that. And I appreciate your honesty."

"I represent what I can do," the Cardinal replied. "We all have our own standards of honor, different as they may be from others."

"Essentially, everyone leaves everyone alone," Lucifer summarized as he read quickly through the document. "That's thoughtful. We killed Don Cortes; took several hundred million dollars from his organization; destroyed his computer network; pulled a great deal of private information off the network before destroying it; and unleashed that rather nasty surprise that Paul had rigged up with the government to control anyone he wanted. But he's willing to let bygones be bygones? That's large of him, I have to say. Perhaps he's mellowed with the years?"

"Perhaps," the Cardinal remarked. "Only Paul knows his mind. And," glancing at his watch, "I regret that I have an appointment across town. I leave this with you. Thank you for taking the time to meet with me."

"Honored, as always, Your Eminence," Lucifer replied, standing.

"Another day, perhaps, Sir Jonathan," and the Cardinal left. His guard surrounded him as he stepped out on the sidewalk and escorted him to his limo.

Lucifer sat back down, staring unhappily at the truce document. Jesus walked over, pulled out a chair and sat down, picking up the document. He quickly read over it.

Jesus tossed the truce back on the table. "It stinks," Jesus complained. "It reeks of *The Art of War*, chapter and verse on deception."

"I know," Lucifer agreed. "But it gives us a little time. How little, I don't know. The enemy that talks is planning to strike, so we'll have to watch carefully. *The Art of War* calls for strength before an attack and I don't see any of that in town. Still, we'll increase security and warn Lungorthin and Hal. It's all we can do."

"As the alternative is all-out warfare on the streets, I agree," Jesus conceded.

"That's the problem," Lucifer admitted. "They are easy targets. If you knew who was coming after you, you could take steps. But there are so many possibilities! That cartel has many allies and gunmen are cheap. All these little groups that come out of nowhere—there's no way of guarding against them. So a truce is something, little as it may be."

They thought for a few minutes in silence. "Peace in our time?" Lucifer mused. "He had an odd reaction to that, which worries me." He put his coffee down and left a tip. "Time to do our work, I guess." They stood up and left.

NEW YORK. LUCRETIA'S EVENING

Lucretia, sighing with relief, stepped out of the private elevator that opened directly into her condo, a heavy briefcase in one hand, her oversized purse on the other shoulder. Peace, she rejoiced, stepping into the foyer. She looked up, smiling, and saw her mother leaning against the wall for support.

"Your son has been throwing up," her mother mumbled. "Your daughter fell at day care and has a big bruise, which they said was her fault. I'm feeling rather sick myself." Her mother made a run for the bathroom.

"Ah, pizza tonight, anyone?" Lucretia offered gamely to the chaos unfolding around her.

It was a couple of hours later. Everyone had been fed and cleaned, some several times each.

Lucretia was holding her daughter, curled up in Lucretia's lap. "I think she's asleep," Lucretia whispered to her mother, who was lying on the sofa, pale.

Her mother glanced at her and nodded slowly.

Lucretia carefully stood up, trying not to disturb her daughter, and shushed Jose, who, despite his earlier sickness, wanted more pizza and was dashing around the apartment. She carried her daughter carefully to her room, got the girl settled in her bed, and then backed slowly out of the room, closing the door.

Suddenly her mother ran by her, slamming the bathroom door as she bolted in. Her daughter started crying. Lucretia slumped. I'm thinking of crying myself! Resolutely, she stood up straight and went back into her daughter's room.

LUCRETIA'S OFFICE

Lucretia stood, pushing her office chair back. That morning coffee is pretty expensive based on the actual time you rent it, she calculated.

She walked down the hallway and carefully opened the women's bathroom door an inch. Then she loudly said something to a non-existent someone down the hall.

The conversation in the bathroom immediately hushed and then changed tone. In a moment, three women swept by her, smiling as they passed her, graciously greeting her.

I'm liking the imaginary employees a lot more than the real ones, Lucretia told herself as she walked into the bathroom. Wow, that must really be good gossip. Their level of niceness to me is inversely related to the viciousness and depravity of the day's gossip about me. They were all sweetness and light, so I wonder if I'm killing children on the witches Sabbath again? She shook her head and went into a stall.

COLDMEN SACKING. A CONFERENCE ROOM.

"Those numbers suck," Lucretia concluded, standing and pointing to the display screen. "They are outside all of the parameters we set at the last meeting and accomplish none of the goals. Why did you generate this nonsense?" She sat down to a dark silence. Okay, swami knows all, sees all and here's what he will say, she told herself. First, all my ideas are not perfect, so none of them are any good.

"Lucretia," the man replied, standing up, "I considered your ideas and they didn't cover all of the possibilities. Sure, your ideas did include a lot of issues, but they just were not a complete solution. So I looked at other ideas."

Check. Now, he'll reject my ideas because there are only two choices. No compromises or other possibilities allowed.

"And," he continued, "We have to make a decision here. We can't pick through alternatives all afternoon. It's these two or nothing."

"Because you can only hold two thoughts in your mind?" Lucretia snapped despite herself.

"Really? Is sarcasm going to help here?" a junior partner interrupted, trying to cover.

"I hide behind sarcasm because telling you to go fuck yourself is considered rude in most social situations," Lucretia snarled. "And I'm a senior partner, so you can all go sit on it. Look, you've all made up your minds, and you don't need—or want—my opinions."

"Don't be so hard on him, Lucretia," another junior partner urged. "It's an interesting idea."

"So is breathing in outer space," she remarked, "but it doesn't work. And neither will this." She glanced at her watch. "I've got another meeting in Midtown. Thank you, gentlemen." She walked out, smiling at all the men, who smiled at her beauty despite themselves. It ain't what a man don't know that makes him a fool, but what he does know that ain't so—but I'm not telling them again, she thought.

Get the door shut fast, she told herself, before the remarks start. Men, at least, are not catty. Vicious and physically humiliating in their descriptions and opinions, but not catty. And I don't like animals, regardless of what they say. They are all so boring and repetitive in their fantasies.

Riding down the elevator, she decided that I'm adding this to hiring evaluation: a level of creativity sufficient to at least generate some new evil attributes for the VP of darkness, Lucretia Liancol. Glancing at her watch again, she scowled. Shit, I'm late. She dashed out of the elevator, rushing through the lobby, then stared down the street, waiving her arm for a cab. "What am I complaining about? It pays the bills," she muttered to herself. A dirty cab ground to a halt in front of her. She pulled the door open, standing, disgusted, for a moment to let the breeze air out the cab, then sighing, she climbed into the cab.

LUCRETIA PACKING

Lucretia is at home, packing for a critical trip to Switzerland.

"I'm worried," she told her mother. "They are finally bringing me into the inner circle, whether I want to be in or not. These are powerful and dangerous people. Old world? No, ancient world. I don't understand them at all. Hell," tossing her underwear into the suitcase, frustrated, "I don't understand the secretaries at work or the investment people either, but they don't have any real power. And vicious as the investment bankers are, they don't actually kill for pleasure. So I guess you could say I'm not comfortable with these people I'm going to meet."

"You're right to be worried! You should listen to your feelings. You're the one who's so smart and thinks so much, except about these people, who are probably the most important thing you should think about. You're the one who always wants to look outside the box and here you are in a box now—the tightest box you could be in."

"That's supposed to make me feel better? I go to you for emotional support and you tell me it's twice as bad as I think? I'm not sure it's that bad, Mom," Lucretia responded. "They pay well."

"That Mother Superior isn't the devil herself, because the devil has mercy and understanding. She has none. She's a predator—the worst I've ever seen. So you be careful! They are more dangerous than you think. I know danger," her mother warned. "I was in a dangerous line of work, but it's nothing compared to what you've fallen into."

CALI & GOTH GIRL

"This truce isn't going to last," Cali sighed to Goth Girl as they watched Maria and Goth Girl's children play.

"No, it won't," Goth Girl acknowledged, frowning. "Lungorthin says the same."

"Hal gave me this long list of things to practice doing, told me where the weapons are and told me what we should anticipate. Hal's been practicing more with the caretaker, and they have been bringing in trainers to practice against."

"Does he really picture them using swords?" Goth Girl asked. "How quaint! But, having watched Lungorthin with a sword, it's as efficient a killing tool as anything made."

"Well, I don't think he really expects swords. But it's reactions and response, Hal told me. And you never can tell. In a small space, a knife and a sword are still the best."

"Lungorthin pictures a commando squad," Goth Girl advised. "He's been explaining what to do. They are planning escape tunnels and safe rooms, but it's a slow process. It's New York and hiding construction from the inspectors is tough, even with bribes. Obviously, we can't put the plans with the city or there's no point in building the escape routes, so it's just going to take time."

"How long?" Cali asked. "Hal wouldn't say."

"Maybe two, maybe three months," Goth Girl guessed. "Maybe longer? We'll know soon enough, I'm afraid."

"We've got the nanny, we've got Lucifer's and Lungorthin's creatures." Cali was counting up on her fingers "We've got the guards, strong walls, and weapons. All pluses." She studied all the fingers standing up, encouraged.

"Hal's mom—that's a minus," Goth Girl countered. "Sweet, strong, but not a fighter."

"And there are people on the staff who are on the other side," putting fingers down for the negatives, frowning. "That's what Hal thinks, but they can't figure out who."

"I've noticed the caretaker watching everyone closely," Goth Girl remarked. "I can't figure out who it could be, either. And here I am, moving slowly, like a cow. Moooo. I won't be a lot of help if it gets rough."

"That's not a problem," Cali assured her. "Then you can watch the kids and let me focus on defense, if it has to happen."

"What's going to happen when the kids are older?" Goth Girl mumbled, biting her lip. "My kids are not going to fit in anywhere. A few minutes with them and it's obvious that they are not quite human. Savage, vicious, and dangerous, but not quite human."

"They'll be ready for junior high school," Cali promised. "Naturals. Run the school for sure."

Goth Girl laughed. "It's kindergarten I'm worried about. They might eat the teacher."

"Everything I learned in kindergarten was wrong. So that might work out too. And Maria? She looks human, but she's so bright and, well, different. Young and old at the same time, like they say elves were. She won't fit in well. Kind of like Wednesday Addams, I'm afraid."

"There was an old man dying," Goth Girl cautioned, "who said his life was full of problems that never happened. Let's get through potty training before we worry about schooling."

Dinner at the Cardinal's Mansion.

A liveried servant ushered the Minister into the dining room, bowed, and backed out of the room.

"Beautiful!" the Minister exclaimed as he glanced around, almost dazed. "Exquisite taste. Money beyond measure."

"Almost beyond measure," the Cardinal replied. "Living well is the best revenge. So what did you think of the young lady at Coldmen Sacking?"

"Remarkably competent," the Minister answered. "I don't think, frankly, that she thought much of me. My work is quite different from hers. Many of the things you can count don't count. Many of the things you can't count really count and financial people generally miss that."

"I doubt that she missed anything," the Cardinal advised. "You'd be surprised at her background."

"She did have an excellent plan for the church," the Minister admitted. "She had detailed calculations about the various funds and ideas for increasing returns."

"Perhaps you could give them to your accountant," the Cardinal suggested, testing the Minister. "He has considerable ability."

"That's a pirate crew," the Minister declared, not noticing the Cardinal's careful gaze. "The administrative team was brought forward at your request. And they are good. They just have to be kept in a back room, and not let out. But they do their jobs."

He stared at the table for a minute, collecting his thoughts. "Which ones," the Minister inquired, "know of the control drugs that the late, unlamented Reverend Ostein was using? As ordered, I have begun the special services again, with the help of the advisor you sent."

"The accountant and the collector know everything," the Cardinal replied. "You have nothing to fear about them telling anyone. Not that you have nothing to fear from them. They are actually dangerous people. Seeing them in their work context shouldn't fool you. That insurance adjuster who saw too much? That was a timely, unfortunate accident. The collector's specialty, I understand."

The Minister was discomforted for a moment, and then shrugged. "The drug does work. I prefer my old-fashioned methods. But I accept the necessity for the new methods," he quickly added, noticing the Cardinals expression.

"I realize this is a difficult step for you. You were very successful before this. You will be far more successful as part of our group. You will do more good, for more people, than you ever could have before. But you must manipulate them. Cold, calculating, heartless manipulation. For their own good, of course. But can you see yourself pure and doing this?"

The Minister was silent, reflecting. "You know, far better than anyone, that my history is far from pure. I originally came into contact with your people because of, well, indiscretions of mine. This is different. I'd be the first to confess that I've sat up late into the night, questioning what I'm doing."

"Confession is good for the soul," the Cardinal remarked, idly making the sign of the cross. "Tell me of your sins, my child."

The Minister flushed but looked down, suddenly serious. "I ask myself whether what I'm doing is really for their good, or for my own power and glory."

"And?" the Cardinal inquired, thoughtfully studying the Minister.

"It's for my power and glory," the Minister confessed. He stared at the Cardinal. "I can fool them, but I can't fool myself. I accept it. I don't like it. I cursed my actions, and cursed myself, but I want it. And I cursed you for offering me the chance."

"Do you fear me?" the Cardinal inquired, amused.

"Yes, I fear you, Your Eminence," the Minister answered, blankly staring at the floor. He was silent for a moment and then glanced up at the Cardinal. "I also hate you."

"I love you, my son," the Cardinal replied, smiling. "Even when you fail, as you did with the last drug test. But you will do better, I know."

The Cardinal toyed with his wine glass for a minute before motioning to the servant to refill it. "That Mrs. Ostein," he grimaced. "She can't have any real role in the church. No power, no authority, and no contact with money. She cannot be relied upon. Her husband was weak and she never saw it; she, wrapped in the good that she believed they were doing, saw only the picture she wanted to see. That kind of blindness has no place in our organization."

"Many people in the congregation love her," the Minister objected.

"And that is good," the Cardinal advised. "Make her a mouthpiece, a figurehead. Have her do something with children that will reflect well on the church. The accountant and the collector—they will weave a web to ensnare her daughters, to ensure our control. I've been informed that certain documents, concealed by the prior administration, but happily discovered by the accountant, would reflect poorly on her if revealed. In a criminal way, I've been told. You must make those things clear to her, and yet retain her enthusiasm."

"I am overwhelmed by your faith in my abilities," the Minister sighed, thinking about the difficulty of the task.

"Do not fail, my son," the Cardinal ordered. "This is important." He glanced past the Minister, at a servant. "Ah, another guest," the Cardinal announced, rising. "Minister, I do not believe you have met Mother Superior?"

"Not in person," the Minister stammered, paling slightly. "I have, well, heard certain stories."

"All false," Mother Superior promised, smiling viciously. "The true stories are usually much darker than the rumors. The rumors leave out the details." She sat down, ignoring the Minister's expression.

They talked business and gossip for two hours while the Cardinal's staff served a superb dinner. Then the Minister was escorted to his hotel by several of the Cardinal's retainers.

"He'll not be in a meeting with two such dangerous predators again for a long time," the Cardinal observed, sipping the last of his wine from the fine crystal goblet.

"If he does, it will not be a meeting he'll survive," Mother Superior replied. "He's got potential, I think. He'd not survive the chalice, but he can fill an important role. I'll watch carefully."

"Good," the Cardinal agreed. "We should retire, as we leave early tomorrow for Switzerland. I'm looking forward to a pleasant vacation at the chateau. Your staff has been made comfortable in their rooms, and wait for you to join them."

"Your Eminence," Mother Superior stood and bowed. "Until the morning." She walked out, the servants hastening to hold the door for her.

The Cardinal gazed out the window for some time, contrasting the lights of the city with Constantinople as he had known it before its capture by the Arabs. And before that, with Rome in its glory, when it was the center of the empire.

"A guest, my lord," a servant announced.

The elderly man who was head of the government secret agency that didn't exist was escorted into the room. The Cardinal rose, shook his hand respectfully, and they sat and talked.

CHAPTER 3. IT'S A LIVING

THE DAILY ROUTINE

The warehouse wasn't far from the office, but was still a half-hour trip in the heavy morning traffic. In the spring and fall, it was a pleasant walk. In December, it was far too cold—a vicious wind whipping down the concrete canyons practically tore one's skin off. Having a driver was a blessing, Hal thought. The guard sitting next to the driver—that was new in the last month.

It was sunny, and the bright, blue sky peeked between the towers. Large, yellow ball in sky—what could that be? Where is the gloomy, overcast, oppressive grey of the last month? Really, why don't we move to a warm, sunny climate?

The car drove past the gatehouse into the underground parking lot. As the driver slowed to stop as near to the elevators as possible, the security guards had already moved into position—one in back of the car, one on the way to the elevator, and a third in the elevator.

Hal absently studied the flashing numbers as the elevator rose. So much for the truce! Sign a truce and double the guard, which is probably the correct approach.

Hal stepped out onto the top floor. It was a relatively low building by New York standards. The fifteenth floor looked out over Central Park, high enough to enjoy the view but low enough for some semblance of human scale. His office was at the end of the floor. Not exactly the corner, because corner offices were too hard to secure. The security people had started talking about heavy rifle fire from adjoining buildings, and Hal was happy to have them build a wall there that was supposed to stop anything. Anything, Hal reflected, that wouldn't otherwise take the building down. His view over the park had the advantage that any facing buildings were a long, long way away. He knew that weapons technology was capable of many things people didn't suspect, but the longer the range, the harder the shot. Finally, high tech eavesdropping, variations of bouncing lasers off glass to capture the words being said within, was impossible here. Between the double, special glass, the distance and the wind outside shaking the building, he could enjoy the view and not be watched or overheard.

His work area was carved up into several different spaces. His main work area was a stand-up desk with an array of monitors carefully arranged along the back. Then he had a regular desk with another array of monitors and finally a conference table, casual and informal, near the windows. He powered up the computers, thinking that he could heat the building just from my office. On cold days, it actually felt good to warm his hands near the monitors.

"Good morning," Aliston bubbled. The executive secretary for

Francisco d'Plata had been assigned to Hal while Francisco was traveling. Hal suspected she had been assigned to him to make sure that Hal didn't do anything too foolish. Given that Aliston knew everything—where all the skeletons were buried and all the little rumors that couldn't be written down but were critical to make decisions—Hal couldn't be happier. She was beyond beautiful, so overwhelming that Hal thought of her as a statue that walked and talked. Cali had approved, which Aliston found surprising, but Cali actually liked Aliston. Aliston had her own makeup person on staff because her image was the image of the corporation that visitors took away with them, and the makeup fooled people about her abilities. She was ex-Israeli army, held a master's in psychology, and was so bright that she tested off the charts.

"Here's today's list of meetings," Aliston announced, handing him the list.

"I appreciate you taking the time to go over this," Hal admitted. "What you know about all these people, their histories and their real interests and needs can't be put in an e-mail, is what makes all the difference in dealing with them."

She smiled. "This person," pointing to the 10:00 appointment, "has another agenda besides the meeting topic. There was a problem..." She outlined it briefly. "...and he doesn't know how to deal with it. And this person," pointing to the 3:00 meeting, "was referred by Sir Jonathan. There was some friction between their companies in the past, but the people on their end who were caused the problems seem to have vanished in the harbor. Their handiwork, actually. So they now believe the past can be smoothed over in today's meeting. It's important because he's a supplier to the drug subsidiary in Hong Kong and has important connections."

They talked for a while longer about the meetings, the unwritten agendas, and the issues involved.

"Tomorrow is the big meeting regarding the new business plan," Aliston commented, worried. "Sir Jonathan and Francisco unanimously voted for you to carry the weight. They agree you are right—they are just happy to let you give people the news."

"I'm good with that," Hal replied. "It was my plan. I might as well take the blame."

Aliston glanced at the clock. "And your first appointment is here. I'll bring him in."

THE ORGANIZATION ISN'T

The next morning, bright and early, the big meeting started in the conference room. People arrived, were greeted, browsed the goodies and drinks and finally were shown to their seats. There were slightly over thirty senior corporate officers at the main table and all of them had assistants and flunkies sitting behind them. So it was a big crowd, who were at least physically comfortable in the plush chairs. A few smiled cheerfully as they talked, a few looked bored, and the remainder appeared politely annoyed to be there.

Well, it's Showtime, Hal told himself, and walked in. Smiling, he ignored their doubtful looks. Fine, I'm half their age. New blood and all that. Hopefully not soon to be spilled on the carpet.

"All of you have been generous with your time and your staffs' time over the past few months," Hal announced, standing at the front of the room. "I know that the time you spent on this project was valuable time; time you could have spent elsewhere dealing with the host of other responsibilities you face."

There were a few nods. People caught themselves quickly and stopped. Hal smiled to himself.

"I know that I've been annoying—it's a personality strength of mine. And just to prove my last statement, here is the key idea for this meeting. Each day, you are the end point for a flow of information from all over your company. That information is carefully gathered, reviewed, summarized, and passed up the chain of command to your desk so that you can make critical decisions about what to do next. Said decisions are then passed back down the chain of command. Your future, your employees' futures, the business's future, the suppliers' futures, and your competitors' futures are in those binders sitting there in front of you. You are the critical link between the past and the future, and everyone's future is your responsibility.

"What if the information in the binders is useless? What if the only function of the chain of information going up and going down is to keep everyone busy in a structure that can be evaluated and controlled? What if that process of evaluation and control throws out anything that challenges the central concept, the central 'story' of the business you run?" Hal asked.

Hal stopped and took a sip of water. Progress, he thought. There are now NO happy faces in the room.

"I started this process because I have a sense of unease about our business structures and our plans for the future. It seemed to me that many of the plans were based on stories laid down a long time ago. Stories that said that the business we are in is 'X' business, which is defined in a certain, limited way. Stories that assumed certain types of competition, stories that assumed certain available resources, certain possible choices. Stories freeze solid over time and perpetuate themselves. Most business failures, engineering disasters, product malfunctions, and the like occur because the stories retreated into a make-believe world.

"When you read bedtime stories to your children, you laugh to yourself at the silly stories. The newspapers are full of sad events, which, if analyzed, go back to silly stories that people believed with all their hearts and souls.

Sadly, their hearts and souls is what they paid for their mistaken beliefs. For example, my wife tells me that my career plan to be an inspirational speaker is poorly considered. Her opinion is that my plan is based on an internal story of mine that the outside world doesn't seem to think is realistic and I'd suspect you all pretty much agree with her at this point." Hal was relieved to see at least a few smiles from the group.

"Now, disasters of all kinds are almost always preceded by near misses. Close calls that, had it not been for chance, would have been worse. We all know people who live their lives as a constant 'Wow, almost got it that time,' and then are shocked when they finally don't skate. We laugh at them, but we close our eyes to our near misses because we're human. None of us likes questioning the stories that we run our lives by. We all and I mean all of us, think of our stories like that advertising campaign for watches: It takes a lickin' and keeps on tickin'. A rough spot only means that the story is working, we tell ourselves. Any story can only deal with part of reality, and so the story is going to take hits.

"Here's a key point. On one hand, there is the story that is going to take hits, and may be looking a little tattered, but the core story is correct and undamaged. On the other, there is the story that is looking okay because it's been patched up but is actually leaking badly under the waterline. Errors of omission and commission. One error is not using the tattered but correct story, judging that it is failing because of the superficial damage. The other error is using the pretty story that's actually sinking fast because it looks good and because it's so important to all of us.

"Both of those mistakes can lead to disaster, but generally it's that second story that sinks the company and careers." Hal smiled, noticing the sudden attention when he said "careers." "It's the near misses that managers often misinterpret. People don't, or won't, see the warning signs because we are all blinded by our hidden biases. We pass off the near misses as proof that the system is working. 'Wow, look what the system caught that time!' we breath a sigh of relief, and leave it at that. Or the near misses are just off our radar. That semi truck filling the space on the road you occupied a few seconds ago that you didn't see coming, for example.

"There is a cartoon I saw. This little old lady is sitting on a park bench. A mugger runs up, takes her purse, and starts to run away. He slips on loose gravel, falls, and knocks himself out. As the police take the mugger away, the old lady proclaims, "Well, see! The system works."

There was more laughter than Hal had expected. That's a good sign, he thought.

"Why do we not notice the near misses, the close calls? Because it's a big world and you can't watch for everything. So one collects limited feedback about events. And let's be realistic; information coming back that says key stories are not working is nothing but trouble. If you are too low in

35

the group to control the story, then you're a troublemaker. If you are high enough to have control over the story, then you've invested time, effort, and perhaps your career into making that story a star. Admissions that your star story is leaking reflect poorly on you. Maybe the story isn't leaking, maybe it is a random event, and we were taught that the boy who cried wolf was punished for his actions.

"Now, it's easy to forget that we are not paid for hard work. I don't care, Sir Jonathan doesn't care, and Francisco doesn't care if you work twenty hours or eighty hours a week, IF you are making money like gangbusters. You are paid to solve problems, and making money like gangbusters means that you are solving problems. It's too easy to fall into an employee evaluation, and a self-evaluation, based on hours and 'stuff done' when that's not looking at the real problems. 'There is nothing so useless as doing efficiently that which should not be done at all,' Peter Drucker, the master.

"What I've tried to do, with your help, is move the Japanese Kanban system concept, which works very well on a factory floor, to a higher-level analysis. By and large, mistakes are the fault of the system, not the people. With the Kanban system, shouting about problems popping up as stuff is being manufactured is rewarded, and pushing problems away and hoping things will work is punished. Now, that's a lot harder to do with information flows than with physical products, but at least the goal is clear.

"So, some ideas. What's a meeting without slogans? Seven stars and seven stones, to see far away," Hal offered. He noticed the blank looks. "Hmm, no *Lord of the Rings* fans here? Okay. How about seven strategies to recognize/learn from near misses? Boring, simple ideas that we all have heard, but don't use. As you all know, it's hard to remember that the goal was to drain the swamp when you are up to your ass in alligators.

"So, these ideas:

o When time or cost pressures are high there will be problems ignored, nay, more than ignored-problems will be magically wished away. They will come back, and at the worst time, because the wishing fairy has a sense of humor. Deal with the problems when they show up, or at least memo them so they can be handled when there is time.

o Watch for deviations from the norm, which means we have to first explicitly define the norm, and secondly think about what could vary. And then expect trouble, not hide from it.

o Uncover the deviations' root causes—not an easy or short task, because the trail steps on others' domains. Remember, it's the system to blame for errors, not the individuals.

o Establish who is accountable for near misses and not just for blame. Who really had the power to keep that train on the track? What in the system prevented action? Throwing the closest body off the train as a sacrifice is emotionally rewarding but destructive to the group on many planes.

o Envision worst-case scenarios as a real planning tool, not as a device to make the last disaster look 'not as bad' as it was.

o Look for near misses masquerading as successes, which is emotionally and mentally hard to do, but less embarrassing before that big blowup than after.

o Finally, let's make better mistakes tomorrow by rewarding people for exposing near misses, which runs counter to almost everything taught from kindergarten on."

"All of these are just variations on not believing that the information in the folder on your desk is all, or even any, of the relevant information you need. We hire brains. You are expected to use those brains, to define what your work is. Information in the past flowed from the bottom up, and orders flowed from the top down. Structures ossify, slip into a bureaucratic process, and people do what's expected, work on the stuff people push in front of them. That's 'hard work'—people seeing you after hours pushing papers around. Working on the key stuff that you define and looking at the end goals—that's what matters. I know how easy it is to do the little jobs, the stuff in front of you, because those are knowns. The process has been done before and walked through, and the success goals and criteria are clear; measurable. We all avoid the hard things that don't measure well—the stuff that we are not sure about or frankly don't know how to do. I know I do, especially when I am tired, and I have to assume that everyone does."

"We've arranged for five managers to give presentations on near misses that they caught, and how almost-disasters changed their goals and the stories they work by. The stories are embarrassing, even humiliating in some ways, for the people involved. The directors of the corporation appreciate their willingness to disclose what they've run into. All of these managers were promoted after these problems were handled, and they have led their divisions to considerable profit and budget improvements."

Hal sat down, far in the back, and paid polite attention to the presentations, which he'd seen at least three times before. He'd delegated responses to various people, so his job was to be a lump. I like this job, he thought.

He reflected on his speech, and a line from a movie popped into his head: "We are building a fighting force of extraordinary magnitude. We forge our tradition in the spirit of our ancestors. You have our gratitude." He muffled a laugh with a cough. No, can't say that one at this meeting. They wouldn't get it. He started doodling on some ideas he'd been working on. How do you build stories that encourage change, not shut it down? Even when you turn the structure upside down, it won't change. After the revolution, the prior security apparatus is now the new security apparatus, only the names have changed from Czar's Minister of Security to Comrade in Charge of Political Correctness. Tortures remain the same. Don't want that.

One of his aides made a polite noise, and Hal suddenly came out of his thoughts to see everyone staring at him. He glanced at the note in front of him and the slide on the screen.

"That's actually what I was in la-la-land thinking about," Hal admitted, standing up. "How, out of all the random events flowing at and by you, do you get the important stuff to pop up? Really, the key question is, 'What should I be thinking about?'" He started pacing.

"Don't you wish there was a program that, each morning, would give you a printed report, with gold stars and red highlights, and which would tell you, oh, by the way, one, the mysterious liquid on the floor of the garage is going to cause four thousand dollars in engine damage today unless you do something quick and two, your wife's distracted smile is based on your failure to remember the fourteenth anniversary of the time you went to a special place shortly after you met, and three, four, etc. All those things that are little, easy to ignore, but have huge consequences down the road. As opposed to the obvious problems that look important but that work themselves out. Williams Randolph Hearst was reputed to not bother to answer letters because they eventually answered themselves. Sometimes yes, sometimes no. It's spotting the difference between ripples in a pond caused by an acorn falling from an overhanging tree and the small ripples an alligator makes as it moves carefully towards you.

"How about this? It is better to be hurt by the raw truth than to be comfortably deceived, because all deceptions have an alligator waiting at the end. So, is this boring?" Hal asked the group, not really looking at anyone, almost dreading the response. "What we're after is hard to measure and hard to control. A company strategy of, well, 'It isn't clear and we're not sure.' Not really a warm feeling to leave with, is it?"

"If you want a warm feeling, peeing your pants in a dark suit always works," one of the senior managers observed. "And it gives you what all warm feelings give—temporary comfort and considerable embarrassment down the road."

Hal laughed. "And with that inspirational thought, which actually captures conceptually the key issues, we'll adjourn. Thank you all for coming."

They actually clapped for a few minutes. Hal was shocked, but kept smiling, shaking hands until they were all gone.

Setting the Foxes Loose

Hal sat in his office afterwards, staring out the window. Trees and forests, foreground and background alternating. But what about when it's the background definition that's the problem? When the definition frames the problem in a way that really isn't the problem? Memo to the file. Watch more Looney Tunes reruns. Nonsense is good for the mind.

"We are building a fighting force of extraordinary magnitude. We forge our tradition in the spirit of our ancestors. You have our gratitude," Aliston remarked.

Hal stared at her for a second and then laughed, happy and relaxed. "I'd never have suspected your misspent youth," when he could talk again.

"That went well," Aliston reported. "I watched. Oh, from behind the mirror. If I walk in, every male in the room will be running on testosterone all meeting. And the females will be running on envy and anger, so I hide. But it went well. I've seen Francisco trying to make the same points, over and over, and you've come further than he did."

"Thanks," Hal replied, surprised. "I wasn't feeling all that good about the meeting."

"Of course," Aliston pointed out, "the cartel has a different background. The illegal side—they pretty much weed out their mistakes because the pressures of the business make the errors so clear and the consequences so severe. It's a lot harder with a legal business and a bunch of high-priced egos sitting there. Men who come to the top over the bodies of the fallen are a lot less complacent about their abilities and plans."

"There's a thought. But internships in the peripheral parts of the business probably would be hard to arrange and a security nightmare. That's the terrifying part about the drug cartels and the international drug business that the governments and the news ignore. Those businesses evolve rapidly. Problems? They adjust, move around. They're quick, boots on the ground, rewards and punishments clear and rapidly applied. Governments trying to catch them? They're slow, inefficient, obsessed with infighting and status. It's the difference between evolution and Intelligent Design, and it's pretty clear who's winning."

"Every year, the Columbians provide cocaine at a higher quality and a lower price than the year before," Aliston observed. "I keep thinking that they should hire them to run the medical system, which every year comes at a higher price and lower quality than the year before."

"I'm not sure I want the Columbians doing my colonoscopy," Hal objected. "They might leave things in there and view it as a new distribution system. Still, they are brutally efficient." He gazed out the window for a moment, and, turning to Aliston, smiled: an odd, cheerful smile.

"This is not good, kemosabe," Aliston warned. "That look is trouble."

"I have a new idea, that will be less popular than any of my ideas to date."

"That would be quite an achievement," Aliston admitted. "What, electric buzzers in the executive chairs?"

"That's a better idea than mine," Hal mused. "I'll make a note. No, I'm thinking that we need to get—what's that buzzword—'creative destruction' churning away inside the company. New little companies that we own tearing the old ones apart. We need to stop waiting for the brash new competitors in sleazy offices to eat our business as we sit in gilded towers, confident in our power."

"So, I'll bite," Aliston sighed. "What specifically are you suggesting?"

"Look at Microsoft. They resisted the split-up of the company, and what happened? Free from competition, the operating system became bloated, a mass of patches and major security holes popped up on such a regular basis that it wasn't even news anymore. Then the application programs, fat and happy knowing that they were tied to the really secret inside wiring of the operating system, lost track of the needs of the users and instead the programs were designed to enhance the power of the division heads. You ended up with the equivalent of fins on a Cadillac—useless padding. The stock price dumped. Had they split up the companies and let them tear into each other, they'd have a group of companies making top-notch stuff. Like the Soviet Union, they got so caught inside their own world that they forgot the bigger world they were supposed to be serving."

"So you want to split up the bigger companies and set up little tigers to tear each other apart?" Aliston asked. "You are going to be popular."

"I'd rather be hated for who I am than loved for who I'm not," Hal declared cheerfully.

"We'll have to double security," Aliston grimaced.

"Again?"

"Again," Aliston acknowledged, worried. "Things, well, they seem weird. Little, odd things are happening. So we took your advice and are trying to adjust to them."

"And you have my fervent thanks!" Hal stood up and started pacing. "The formal stories-prime example, a company mission statement-are useless because those are pretty stories, not the real stories people believe. The stories people really believe and act on have emotion and desire in them, not the selflessness of the publicly allowed stories. If you put a pretty, but empty, story on the wall, you're not going to reach anyone. Meetings are the same—full of words we 'should' be saying, not real words we'll act on. The problem is that having a 'word' as a name for something doesn't mean that the 'thing' the word represents exists at all, or exists in the way you think it does. Create a workgroup, and they produce grammatically correct sentences that are wishful social fantasies, warm feelings and bright pictures. Nothing that refers to the outside world in a useful way."

"You talk like this at dinner?" Aliston questioned. "And your wife puts up with it? You chose well."

"Cali talks like this at dinner," Hal replied. "She is a planning freak. She says so herself."

Hal sat on the corner of the desk, staring out the window, scowling. "We hire this hotshot to come in, and what does he say? The consultant stands up, and with a serious expression, says that the key ability for the tribal chief of the future is foresight—to be able to forecast what is going to grow and what will be fashionable next. Once Swami sees all, knows all, then this person must have the decision-making ability to execute the forecast. Miracles abound with this person, loaves and fishes filling the break room, as this person then motivates the whole organization with their swift execution of their decisions. And, although this person is the font of all knowledge, the father/mother that all come to for guidance, this person must also maintain an environment that can generate useful information and ideas, even though the only one with ideas is the leader. Plato's philosopher king holding court in the corner office! Drucker wrote that trying to predict the future is like driving down a country road at night with no lights while looking out the back window. That's why philosopher kings don't come through in the clutch, because that critical ability to see the future doesn't exist. What's the option? Set up a bunch of foxes and let them tear the prey apart as best they can. Winner moves to the tiger trials."

Hal glanced at Aliston. "I had a dream the other night that I was in jail. It was okay, it wasn't a bad place, and then I realized that I shouldn't be in jail. There was no reason I should be there. I just hadn't taken the steps to not be there. Then I recognized that I'd put myself in my own jail and I could let myself out. It's getting people to see that and let themselves out, and justify the salaries we pay them—that is the hard part."

"So, how are you going to sell this to the Board?" Aliston asked. "You're taking profitable entities and tearing them up with no guarantees about what they will be able to do. That's a hard sell."

"You're dead right about that. Every meeting with the directors is always the same. 'How much is this going to cost?' 'I don't know' isn't the winning answer. If you assume tomorrow is today, then any change costs too much. It's spending $10,000 to make $50,000 that gets people's attention. Spending $10,000 by itself, well, that's money out the door."

"One of the best studies was that corporate boards spend a lot LESS time considering proposals over $10,000,000 than on proposals under $10,000,000," Aliston commented. "Now, that was an old study, so it's probably $100,000,000 and up now. But it's because people just can't grasp zeroes to the left of the decimal point. No one really has an emotional feel for numbers that large, so there is no emotional attachment to the big dollars as they run out the door. One of the mutual-fund managers was quoted as saying that people really don't emotionally connect with anything over

$139.00. Larger than that, it's all zeroes, no emotions. If you want to get killed, steal $20 from someone, because that means something to them. Steal $10,000? It's annoying, embarrassing, but not as emotionally charged as that twenty in your pocket is."

"I don't have a clue what the future profit numbers would be," Hal complained, "but I can promise that the profits will go to zero if we don't change our processes. Look at the changes coming. The newspapers are talking about networks of up to one trillion sensors that will cover the world and can deliver data to anybody who needs them, from carmakers to municipal governments. Note, that those are the networks that the government will allow access to. Figure in another trillion sensors run by the various militaries. A company planning to function based on a controlled information flow from the bottom, carefully filtered up through the hierarchy, isn't even in the right geologic era."

"You took this job because...?" Aliston wondered, looking at him appraisingly.

"I was foolish enough to be spouting off to Sir Jonathan about these ideas, pointing out various stupid things the companies had done. So he told me, 'Then you do it,' and here I am. I'd be happier playing with the computers."

"No good deed goes unpunished," Aliston advised.

"And it will be punished," Hal promised. "Look at this," handing her an elaborate diagram. This is my idea for splitting up the various companies and divisions and getting life back into them."

"Has anyone seen this?" Aliston gasped, biting her lip as she went down the list. "Ah, 'There is nothing more difficult to take in hand, more perilous to conduct, more uncertain in its success, than to take the lead in the introduction of a new order of things.'[7] Let's make that triple security."

"That popular, you think? Nice to know I'm still overachieving. Cali has seen this, and some of the info tech people must suspect, because I've thrown out odd questions about sharing information between companies, except those companies don't exist yet. The info people are pretty good with this because they are used to people's constant attacks and sneaky behavior. And they hate the VPs because the VPs don't recognize the importance of the info tech people."

"Perhaps they would if the tech people recognized how the small niceties, like bathing occasionally, affect other people," Aliston countered, grimacing. "There was a petition circulating to isolate tech support in another building, but we couldn't figure out who would fix the computers. Not that anyone understands their explanations anyhow."

"They are open to change...well, change other than their personal habits. I know, I used to be a hacker. With computers, it's all change. You plan

—

42

and plan and then someone plants a virus on your machine that takes over and pops up a detailed middle finger waving at you on the screen before trashing the hard drive and network. A few times cycling through that, and you learn to plan for disaster and anticipate change. I've created a few of those myself, and gotten hit with a bunch of them.

"I have a meeting with Francisco and Sir Jonathan next week. If they like it, then a meeting with the directors. If they buy in, the shit hits the fan fast, because the rumors run wild once the directors see anything."

"Look at this," pointing to the computer screen. He quickly typed in several keystrokes and a program started to run. "For the meeting preparation, I was playing with little programs, simple equations that run and produce outputs. Wolfram wrote an entire book about the idea. Sometimes they run and then settle into an equilibrium quickly, for all eternity. Like a traditional steel company, for example. Sometimes they run completely randomly forever, but that's pretty unusual. It's the ones that somehow grow and improve we want, but that's really, really rare. That's the key model we want—continued evolution as a structural process. What we have now is case one: equilibrium into a dusty grave. See, they make some really neat visuals, in bright colors."

"I don't care what Cali's background is," Aliston insisted. "If she listens to this at dinner, you really owe her a nice meal somewhere. A very nice dinner, with flowers."

"Probably, but she'd think that so odd as to be suspicious," Hal replied doubtfully.

"Never," Aliston promised. "Always take a nice dinner with flowers. It's in bold print in the secret book for girls. Take my word for it."

CHAPTER 4. PAUL

NEW YORK TO SWITZERLAND.

Lucretia was whisked through security in New York to the large private jet. No strip searches? No keeping my pictures in their offices? This is living. She settled down happily into the plush seat. Almost a suite! Really, this is the way to travel. The quiet host and hostesses fussed around her, taking her order for lunch and offering drinks, snacks, and blankets. There were several others on the plane, but they kept to themselves.

More like a European train, she thought. It's private and public at the same time. No, that isn't quite right, but this is so much better than the red-eye cattle cars that interns take. There is really no comparison. It's the ear tags that you have to wear that are the worst, she recalled. No respect at all. Mooo!

She read and actually dozed off for a while, it was so comfortable. The attendant carefully woke her up twenty minutes before landing. This is nicer than Coldmen Sacking's partners' jet, and I didn't think that could be done. She stood up and an attendant quickly grabbed her bags. This is heaven, she concluded, as she strode out of the plane. Normally I'm balancing three bags, holding one strap in my mouth, tottering on high heels down the aisles. No, I'm flying like this from now on. At the end of the walkway from the plane, there was a uniformed guard waiting for her. He took the bags from the plane attendant. The guard escorted her through the airline terminal, and she was waved through security without a glance. I guess they don't suspect me of smuggling watches into Switzerland? Outside, a driver opened the door of a vintage Rolls Royce, and she settled into the back seat. Like a pig in clover! I could get used to this. F. Scott Fitzgerald was right; the very rich are different from you and me.

She relaxed as the driver pulled into traffic, peering at the town as it briskly darted by. So clean and orderly, she noted. Then she let her mind go, idly gazing at the scenery along the winding roads as the driver left Zurich, heading south. She gasped at the beauty of Lake Lucerne and the beautiful homes surrounding it. There is money, and then there are giant shit piles of it. These are really, really giant shit piles of it. Beautiful, but she knew what it took to grab and hold that much money. The driver turned onto a private road, and she saw a huge chateau looming behind high stonewalls. Okay, this is the summer cottage? I don't think I went to a school as large as this. The Rolls stopped for a second and the guards at the gate waved him through. As they drove through the grounds towards the chateau, she noticed guards on the walls and guards patrolling the grounds.

So he doesn't play nicely with people. People feel hurt after they do business with him. At least the people he leaves alive, that is. Large piles of money do not accumulate by themselves. Pearls have to be pried out of the oysters, and the oysters are eaten afterwards. Ironically, the pearls are created by the oyster to remove an irritation, and inadvertently, at least from the point of view of the oyster, they become the cause of destruction. That's too deep for today, she decides.

The Rolls pulled up to the front entrance. Servants rushed out. One held the car door and offered his hand to balance her as she stepped out of the deep leather seat. Memo! No short skirts, as there is no graceful way out. You expect to make an appearance, and more appears than you expected. Standing up and quickly yanking her skirt down, she smiled at the servants as they carefully put her luggage on the trolley. They smiled back mechanically, impersonally, at her. Well, being friends with the guests probably is dangerous here. Wow, liveried servants. She followed a guard into the chateau, a train of servants behind her with her bags. Did I change time periods and not just time zones? She was escorted to her room. It was a long walk down lavish hallways. Her room was elegant. Like a penthouse at the Ritz, she thought, awed. She just stood there, gawking, and finally the woman servant coughed discretely. Lucretia turned to face her.

"The funeral will be at seven," the woman announced.

"Funeral?" Lucretia exclaimed.

"Yes," the woman replied. "Only a few honored guests have been invited. The Butler will tell you more."

Whatever. "May I walk around?" Lucretia asked. "I've been sitting for quite a while."

"If I may, I'd suggest you be cautious near the guards. They can be touchy," the servant advised. "The Butler can give you a pass to walk around with, which I'd recommend."

"Thank you."

The woman bowed deeply and slowly backed up, her eyes staring at the floor. She backed through the door and then shut it behind her.

Disrespectful to turn and show your back? No, I haven't gone back centuries. Millennia, that's what I've gone back.

Lucretia changed into something more comfortable to walk about in and set off to find the Butler. Her natural inclination to not ask for help worked against her, as the chateau was enormous—a confusing mass of dark hallways and rooms. She accidentally wandered into the kitchens, which triggered a full-scale panic by the kitchen help. Security immediately showed up. Not a flexible organization, Lucretia reflected, as the kitchen staff stared at her, whispering to each other. Or what they expect to happen when things don't go right is so serious that they can't improvise. Security was not happy, but they were polite, and their English was perfect. Security made a few quick calls as the kitchen went back to its work, the staff snickering at her discomfort. Lucretia was terrified of the casually carried firepower of the security guards. Machine guns with silencers! Military weapons, and I think they're loaded. She smiled brightly at the guards, who regarded her with polite caution.

"You need a guide, I think, my dear," the Cardinal announced, appearing at the door. "Here, this is my daughter, Dominique. She will show you around our little slice of paradise."

"Please, let me be your guide," Dominique declared to Lucretia. "Father has told me such wonderful things about you, and I'd hate to see you shot before we have a chance to get to know each other."

"I'm in agreement with that," Lucretia stammered.

"It is fine," Dominique dismissively told the guards, waving them away. When they didn't immediately move, she glared at them. Then they moved quickly.

Lucretia heard little clicks as the guards backed away. Safeties going back on, she realized. They were standing around me with loaded machine guns with the safeties off? No, I'm not walking around by myself again.

"Here, come with me," Dominique told Lucretia, taking her hand. "For your safety. The guards are, well, touchy here."

"Touchy is irritable," Lucretia retorted. "Loaded machine guns ready to fire—that's PMS."

Dominique laughed.

They walked out the front entrance and past the bustling servants escorting new guests in. They went through the beautifully kept grounds. Dominique is distant, formal, almost like royalty, Lucretia thought. Should I curtsy? As they walked, Lucretia was very glad that she had a guide. There were heavily armed guards everywhere. Lucretia, surprised, realized that Dominique had her own retinue of guards following her in bright uniforms. She looked around more carefully and noticed that there were a variety of guard uniforms. That really is like the old days. Old, old days. I'm thinking the ones in the black on black are the chateau guards, as there are more of them.

"Now, look, but don't look at them directly," Dominique whispered. "Those guards, to the left—don't look and linger."

Lucretia looked to the left, willing herself to be casual, which didn't work. She quickly forced herself to look past them and forced a calm expression back onto her face.

"They're rather odd," Lucretia stammered, when she had her breath back.

"That's a polite statement," Dominique replied. "And they are as touchy as they are strange. You thought the guards in the kitchen were touchy? Those guards are far more dangerous."

"They look fair and feel foul," Lucretia offered. "That's a bad sign." She quickly raised her arm to push her hair back off her face, the light wind having blown it out of place. Out of the corner of her eye she saw the guards moving into position, watching her intently as she played with her hair. She slowly brought her hand back down to her hip, carefully leaving her hand open and in full view. The guards relaxed.

"You're catching on," Dominique smiled.

"Such a beautiful place, but so many guards," Lucretia observed. "It's like being a guest at Jabba the Hutt's castle. Especially with those last guards! I knew I should have brought a lightsaber."

"Jabba the Hutt?" Dominique laughed. "I like that. People are usually so impressed by this place that they don't allow themselves to recognize what they have walked into."

"Ladies," a silky male voice purred behind them.

The hairs on the back of Lucretia's neck rose. It just gets better, she realized.

They turned and a man, seemingly middle-aged but somehow older and younger at the same time, stood there, smiling at them, surrounded by his retinue.

"I was told that a new, charming woman was touring the grounds. The description was completely inadequate, I see," he remarked politely—but with an undertone of contempt at the same time.

"Have we met?" Lucretia inquired, detesting the man on sight.

"I don't think so," the man replied, puzzled.

"Cairo! Were you there in March?" Lucretia demanded, snapping her fingers and smiling.

"Not that I recall," the man answered, shaking his head.

"Well, that's it," Lucretia announced confidently. "I wasn't either."

Dominique laughed.

The man froze, his face furious.

"Now, now," Dominique warned, quickly stepping in front of Lucretia. "She was just jesting with you, Cesare. She thought you were the court fool, and now that I think about it, well...she's right." Dominique smiled brightly at the man, who was enraged.

"I wouldn't do that," Dominique added as the man reached into his jacket

Lucretia, shocked, saw that Dominique suddenly had a knife in her hand. The various retainers quickly moved into position, hands going under jackets and cloaks.

"Really," Lucretia stammered, "this seems overdone. Just a joke, nothing to be offended about. Right?" She looked around, smiling at them all.

"I would agree," a voice declared behind her. She could hear rapidly marching feet, and a troop of guards in the black-on-black uniforms quickly surrounded the group. "This is a solemn occasion, a day for quiet and contemplation," the Captain of the Guards carefully advised. "Your father gave very strict orders, my Lord."

The man nodded, controlling himself. "Of course," he snarled. "I was only testing her." He forced a smile, and, snapping his fingers, walked away. His retainers followed him, backing away carefully from Dominique's guards and the chateau guards before turning and falling in behind the man.

"Brave you are," the Captain observed to Lucretia. "You should watch yourself." He motioned, and the chateau guards followed him as he walked away.

"Okay, I'm not liking this place as much as I did," Lucretia concluded, staring after the guards, worried.

"You've made an enemy," Dominique warned, taking Lucretia's hand. "But also a friend—moi! Anyone who can talk back to him like that is on my side. But you must now be careful, mon ami! That was Paul's son, Cesare, and his temper does not improve with age. Your long-ago ancestor, Lucretia, also knew him. He killed her because of an offhanded remark. He's just like that."

"He killed her?" Lucretia gasped. "Then he must be hundreds of years old! Another one, like the Cardinal?"

"Yes. I saw him kill her, but I couldn't stop him. As you may be beginning to grasp, this is a very strange place. Like medieval Europe in many ways. No, more like the Assyrian court. I fear you cannot imagine what you have stepped into here." She looked troubled for a moment. "Beware of Cesare. I'll arrange for guards for you from now on. He is dangerous and twisted. My serving maidens go missing every so often, and only pieces show up—just one of his little games. Not a nice person at all."

"That's awful," Lucretia gulped, horrified. She mentally made an inventory of her parts and was relieved they were all still attached.

"Well, then I have to kidnap one of his guards and send back the guards private parts. It keeps him respectful," Dominique replied as she sheathed her dagger and slid it down between her breasts. "Call me an old-fashioned girl, but it's always good to have a weapon near. Now, I understand you like alligators—tell me all about it!"

Lucretia laughed and told her the story about the cartel meeting as they wandered carefully around.

"Nice people you work for," Dominique commented. "Remember that the people here are the same, but they have had hundreds of years of practice."

"That's supposed to make me feel better?" Lucretia replied. "Ah, you wouldn't have another dagger I could borrow, would you?"

"No, my dear. The penalty for carrying a weapon on the grounds without explicit permission is quite severe. And, I while I don't doubt you have the will, you have not the skill to handle such a weapon. I'll have guards around. Oh, and do watch what you eat and drink here. Cesare loves his little poisons, and now he has all these new drugs! Even though we are somewhat resistant because of the chalice, don't test it. Especially with prince uncharming there—he does some really astonishing and awful things with his little toys. You see, he prefers the devious and the twisted to the open fight. It's just him."

"I'll remember," Lucretia promised. "The fraternities had their tricks in college, but this is levels past that."

"With fraternity boys, at least you wake up in the morning," Dominique explained. "Not with Cesare. By the way, you are the first in a long time to pass the ordeal. I'm very impressed."

A young woman rushed up to Dominique and whispered in her ear.

"Mon Dieu!" Dominique exclaimed. "It's nearly time for the funeral, and we must change first. It's very bad form to be late. It shows disrespect, and that is serious around here."

"I don't really understand the funeral," Lucretia complained.

"You'll understand afterwards," Dominique assured her, and they rushed back to the chateau.

A FUNERAL AT THE CHATEAU

The large, formal room was somber, draped in black crepe paper, and soft requiems played in the background as the mourners shuffled in. There were black candles flickering in the corners of the room, casting deep shadows.

Lying in a casket was the body of a very old man. The room filled with those coming to pay their respects. Powerful, feared, hated—many would have vied for the honor of having killed him. The chateau was not heavily guarded for no reason. Only those who would have truly mourned his passing stood in the room. A football stadium might have been too small to hold those who vied for the honor of helping him into the great beyond. Certainly a football stadium would be too small to hold those that the man had helped into the great beyond.

Sitting quietly in the room were the Cardinal, Mother Superior, Lucretia, Dominique, Cesare, and perhaps sixty others.

The service began. A priest stood, reading from the service for the dead. Then a strong, healthy, middle-aged man gave the eulogy. There's something weird about this, Lucretia mused. He's enjoying himself too much,

49

and there are too many smiles on the guests' faces.

After the service, guards carried the body out. The mourners formed a line behind the pallbearers and followed them through the grounds. Lucretia watched, astonished, as the guards laid the casket on a large fire pit. Gasoline was sprinkled on the casket, and the middle-aged man who gave the eulogy tossed a torch onto the casket, an odd smile playing on his face. The fire engulfed the casket. The mourners stood quietly as the pyre was consumed. As the mourners turned to leave, Lucretia noticed the guards carefully collecting the ashes. Then the mourners filed into the formal room again and sat, silent.

Beyond weird, Lucretia concluded, but she couldn't ask Dominique anything. It's clear that this is quiet time. I hated quiet time in kindergarten. I'm bored.

The middle-aged man who had lit the fire sat alone on the stage. His hand moved slightly, and the servants bustled out, closing the doors behind them. It was absolutely silent in the room for a moment.

The man stood up. "Thank you for coming to my funeral. As it turns out, reports of my death were greatly exaggerated."

There was careful laughter, which quieted quickly.

"A necessary fiction in today's world, which tracks these things more carefully than ancient times," the man observed. "Still, I understand there are advantages to this charade. All the necessary conveyances have been made?" He studied carefully an older man in the room, who was expensively dressed in a perfectly fitting suit.

"Yes, my Lord," the attorney replied. "And there were even significant tax advantages to the plan, which included..."

"Thank you," Paul waved the attorney silent. "I'm sure you have done well. Our attorneys," He gestured at the man. "The finest in the world. Now, was it Dewey, Cheatem, and Howe? Or Catchem and Skinem? No? A prior affiliation, I assume?" The man flushed, but smiled.

The crowd laughed.

"It's always nice to enjoy your own funeral," Paul remarked. "Beautiful flowers! And a peaceful passing, not like on the fields of war, as many of you remember from our past. Well, what was it Samuel Goldwyn said? You know, the reason so many people showed up at his funeral is that they wanted to be sure he was dead."

There were more laughs from the mourners.

"So, we have our property, our power, and a believable story for the world," Paul summarized, gazing thoughtfully at the group. "And we have this very strong group of friends to help. Some are new friends: please, stand. Lucretia, who survived the chalice, the first to do so in many, many years.

There, The Major, the new head of the cartel, taking over after the tragic death of Don Cortes, who shall be missed. The Professor, who is heading up our drug research. Finally, the Minister, who has taken over that church in California after the death of the weakling. That church is a very powerful tool to increase our influence and control. Please, welcome our new associates and partners."

The other guests clapped. Lucretia stood, embarrassed, until Paul motioned for them to sit back down.

"We shall have a wonderful dinner today—a wake, to be traditional. It's important to follow the formalities. There are others here you will meet tonight and over the next few nights. This sad event gives us a chance to meet together as a group, so rare for us. As we have ample guards, and I understand that our adversaries are in the United States at present, concerned with their problems, we have nothing to worry about from them."

Paul paced on the stage for a moment, as the guests intently watched him. "But I think they have much to worry about from us. I've come to the conclusion that Don Cortes had the right idea," standing still and studying the guests. "We have fought all these thousands of years with no resolution. But now, with the new science, with the new developments, we can reveal ourselves to what is left of the world after all of the changes coming. It will be a world again under our control! Then there will be no more need for these sham funerals."

"And you, my dear," Paul declared, looking directly at Lucretia. "I understand that you have a child, a daughter, by the good Don. We thank you for preserving his line and his strength. Added to your strength, which I've been told is considerable, your child will be fearsome to her enemies."

"Thank you, my lord," Lucretia stammered, not sure if she was really supposed to say anything. Evidently she had done the right thing, because Paul nodded to her.

"Shall we go?" Paul asked, raising his arms. All the guests stood up and walked out.

An Elegant Dinner

Lucretia was escorted back to her room by Dominique, who left several of her guards with her. Lucretia tried to make conversation with the woman guard, but gave up after several minutes of inarticulate responses. I guess you get used to the lack of privacy, Lucretia concluded as the guard sat in a corner of the room. Is there a class royalty takes? Well, here is my dress, and I have a short time to make myself beautiful. She set to work.

An hour later, there was a knock on the door. The guard jumped up and carefully opened the door, her pistol at the ready in her hand.

Really, this is a nice place, Lucretia decided. A good place to raise children? Not.

Dominique swept into the room. "You look radiant," she told Lucretia. "And we're on time. Fashionably late is unwise here." Dominique took Lucretia's arm and they walked out, proceeding down the hallway arm in arm, surrounded by Dominique's guards.

The elaborately dressed servants escorted them into the formal dining room.

Who has the cleaning concession? Lucretia wondered. There's a fortune right there. She examined the servant's uniform as they were led to her table. How would you even clean that? I guess it's the peasant in me to even consider the issue.

"I love your dress," Dominique observed to Lucretia as they walked.

"It's real Paris designer," Lucretia marveled, gently stroking the fabric of her dress. "Well, to you it isn't such a big deal," acknowledging Dominique's look. "But this is a long way for me!"

"Do you want to ask how they knew exactly what size you are so that it could be custom made for you?" Dominique inquired dryly.

"No." Lucretia suddenly realized that the fit was perfect. And also the underwear that came with it, such little as it was. "I can't just assume they figured I was a size six off the rack? No, I guess not," as Dominique shook her head no.

"Now I feel so dirty."

"Exposed, technically," Dominique corrected.

"That makes me feel better? No," I don't need to know to whom and to where the pictures went. I'll just play pretend."

"Pretend is the favorite game around here," Dominique acknowledged. "You'll fit right in."

The obsequious servant showed Lucretia to her seat, her name beautifully printed on the heavy parchment card. Lucretia stood uncertainly by her chair. The servant bowed to Dominique and pointed politely towards where Dominique's table was. "Please, if you would be so good as to follow me, my Lady," the servant begged.

"No," Dominique commanded. "Lucretia and I sit together. I'll have someone to talk to, finally, at one of these affairs. And you need a guard," whispering to Lucretia. "Non," she announced to the servant. "I will sit here," pointing at the seat next to Lucretia.

The servant was furious for a brief second, then put a polite, obedient expression back on, bowed, and backed away. Guests around them gossiped, clearly enjoying the scene. In a minute, the servant came back, followed by the Butler.

The Butler smiled, his best accommodating smile. "Please, Dominique," the Butler pleaded. "The table seating was arrived at through long discussion, and your father signed off on it."

"Then he can sign off again," Dominique replied pleasantly. "Or you'd rather I lose my temper? I've had a long day today. Many frustrations are building up. Like a volcano, you know." She smiled, teeth showing.

Not a nice smile, Lucretia noted. And she carries a knife. I'd run if I were he.

"Please, my lady, no. There is no need for that," the Butler begged, quickly wiping his forehead with a cloth, physically slumping for a moment. "I'd really rather not have that. So," he growled at the servant, "either we move this person," peering at the card next to Lucretia, "or we move someone over there..." He waved at another table. "...where this lady, " he muttered, giving Lucretia a look that politely said that she was considerably less than a lady, "could sit."

"I'm sitting here," Dominique ordered the Butler, relishing his anger. "Right here," regally pointing to the seat next to Lucretia. "Move that person. And move that person also," she commanded cheerfully, pointing to another seat. "Move my lady-in -waiting there. The guests who were to sit here—they will be honored to be at a front table, I'm sure."

The Butler's face flushed red, but he gulped, breathing carefully, and then very politely replied, "As you wish, my lady." He bowed, and, motioning to the other servants, stiffly walked away.

"His underlings will have a rough half hour," Dominique laughed. "After a bad day at work, a man goes home and yells at his wife, his wife yells at the kids, the kids yell at the dog, and the dog chases the cat. Well, I try and spread a little joy into every life I touch as I go through life. Just merrily frolicking through the fields."

Lucretia laughed, picturing Dominique frolicking through a meadow.

Dominique grinned at Lucretia. "And I'll bet my good name is being slandered. If I wasn't the Cardinal's bastard daughter—well, some would say technically it's 'bitch' instead of bastard—the mother of at least ten children in wedlock, the unwed mother of several more children, and the shameless widow of my last three husbands, I'd be offended." She caught Lucretia's look. "You have children over the centuries, you lose track after a while."

"The widow of your last three husbands?" Lucretia asked. "Do you have a temper?"

"I do," Dominique replied, "but it isn't that bad. Well, generally, anyway. No, unexpected and unfortunate accidents took my poor, beloved husbands. When people lose their value to Paul, the retirement plan is quite, well, final. Truthfully, an inheritance is better than a divorce settlement, and besides, we are all good Catholics here. Divorce is a sin! In truth, they were marriages of convenience to toads. I wasn't that sorry. I'm thinking of asking for a punch card from the florist, though."

"This place reminds me of the firm I work for," Lucretia commented. "Coldmen Sacking. A name they live up to as best they can."

"I like that," Dominique replied. "But I've seen real war and sacking. It's worse, believe me."

Dominique's lady-in-waiting bustled over to the table, quietly laughing at the outraged Butler.

Another servant escorted the people who were supposed to sit on either side of Lucretia to the table. They stood there, confused, as the servants hurriedly conferred.

"You will take my seats," Dominique told them. "Thank you so much for being understanding. It's important that I be with my friend. My father, the Cardinal, would think favorably of you if you would grant me this small favor. And you will sit at a front table! See, the one up there, with Mother Superior and her friends."

The people paled and then recovered, gushing their happiness to Dominique, Lucretia, and the servant as they were led away.

"I like this better," Dominique concluded. She looked around, smiling at people she knew. "We can talk more, farther from Paul's table. And the listening devices will be all confused now."

Lucretia studied at table, half expecting to see microphones.

"You don't know our little world, do you, my dear? Remember your dress size? That's just a fraction of what they know," Dominique advised. "Wait, I think it's almost Showtime." She pointed to the entry.

The guests milled around the tables for a few moments, uncertain, watching the entry. They are all tense, apprehensive, Lucretia realized. All forced smiles. The hum of conversation faded away as everyone stood, staring at the door.

Ten men walked in, guards in ceremonial uniforms with trumpets. They lined up on each side of the red carpet, raising their trumpets, and blew a flourish. Then they snapped the trumpets down to their sides like weapons and stood at attention as ten more brightly uniformed guards marched into the room. Paul walked behind them, wearing a dark suit and a black mock turtleneck, smiling at the group, who immediately began applauding.

Dominique nudged Lucretia, who started applauding as well. Worse than a school play, she sighed. I never could get the timing right on those, either. She stopped applauding for a second, shocked, staring at the others following Paul into the room, but started clapping after an elbow in the ribs from Dominique.

A semi-human followed Paul into the room: huge, hulking, but moving quickly and easily. Behind him, there were several smaller versions of the semi-human and then more guards.

Paul stood at the head table before his seat (a small throne, Lucretia realized) and then he smiled and motioned for all to sit, which they quickly did. The semi-human sat and his oversized chair creaked with his weight.

"Let us be comfortable here," Paul announced to the crowd. "Here, the wicked cease their troubling, and there the weary repose. Relax and enjoy!" He sat down.

"Do not stare at Grendel!" Dominique ordered, in a small, frightened whisper. "Whatever you do, do not annoy him! It—whatever you call the creature. It's dangerous, more than you can imagine. You don't want to know what he feasts on. Even Paul's son is afraid of Grendel."

Lucretia was shocked, but was careful to look quickly away from the creature. Then she noticed the fabulous wealth of the room. She had not had time to look at the room between the process of being escorted in, the whole drama of the seating changes and finally the grand entry of Paul. And I thought the Cardinal's penthouse was fabulous! she marveled. This is what, fifteenth century? Sixteenth century? The works of the masters themselves, not copies.

Dominique elbowed her gently, and Lucretia, surprised, looked up at the waiter. "Ah, what she's having." She smiled uncertainly at the waiter and pointed to Dominique. The waiter's facade of obedient respect became contempt for only a moment, and then he smiled respectfully at the next guest.

"This is a fun place," Lucretia offered. "A vacation paradise, relaxing and comfortable. Warm, supportive, kind, and caring people fill the rooms. Remind me to not book a long stay here."

Dominique snickered. "That's a pretty good assessment. Don't say it too loudly, though. Paul likes his formalities. They used to be more elaborate. You're not likely to be invited to the palace in North Africa. You are the wrong sex, my dear, for what they do there. Women are not guests there, they are entertainment. The very, very old style of entertainment—what Xerxes liked when he was alive, I'm told. My father told me to never, never go there, under any circumstances. Mother Superior and her guard are the only women I know of that go and return. She is reputed to enjoy it, if that gives you a feeling for what it is like."

Lucretia shuddered, trying not to imagine what Mother Superior would enjoy.

There was a string ensemble playing in the back.

"They are superb," Lucretia declared, listening carefully. "Absolutely wonderful."

"They are usually first string from some major symphony," Dominique replied, peering at the ensemble. "Paul pays well. People who refuse his money? They often find themselves in debt to him and forced to serve him.

Truthfully, he prefers the control. Once an emperor, always an emperor."

The waiters expertly served the dinner, course after course of elegant and beautifully prepared food.

"Wonderful," Lucretia sighed. "I try and push it away, but it's so incredibly good I can't deny myself."

"It's beyond world class," Dominique agreed. "If I were invited here more often, I'd lose my girlish figure."

"So, you live...?" Lucretia asked, trying not to pry too obviously.

"A villa outside Nice," Dominique answered. "Overlooking the Mediterranean. Perhaps you could come there sometime? It would be a vacation."

"I can cancel everything on my schedule and be there tomorrow," Lucretia offered. "If that isn't too eager."

Dominique laughed. "Paul has plans for you, I've been told. After those are done, you must come and see me." She put her arm around Lucretia. "Now, chit chat," she whispered.

Lucretia nodded and asked about her dress.

Dinner ended with a wonderful, extravagant dessert carefully carried out by the almost exhausted servants and waiters.

Lucretia leaned back, pushing her half-finished torte reluctantly away. "I cannot," sadly eying the dessert. "I'll have no clothes to go home in. As it is, I'll have to diet for a week, but that was wonderful."

"I agree!" Dominique pushed her unfinished dessert away also. "Now, the speech. There always has to be a speech. Look alert, attentive, and smile. Nodding is good. Clap when others do, but only when others do, and just as hard as others do. No more, no less. All around us there are watchers, and our fellow guests take notes for favors to trade later. The court is like Stalin's Russia: just good comrades here who are tested every minute. The Gulag is in the basement for those who fail. The meat grinders and processors in the kitchen can grind anything, I've been told."

Lucretia's eyes widened. "Okay, as hard, no harder, no softer, and only when others do, but don't be obvious looking at others to copy them. Got it. Well, at least my metabolism has revved up a bit to burn off some of that dinner."

"There's a friend of yours," Dominique pointed at the front table she was to have sat at. "The one and only Mother Superior, and she looks as though she's in a good mood. That's going to be bad news for someone."

"I wouldn't say 'friend,'" Lucretia countered. "But we've met."

"You challenged her and you're still alive," Dominique commented. "If nothing else you had done was exceptional, that alone would merit a gold star. There, sitting next to her, is Jacques Fournier. At least, that's a name he used to use. I lose track of what he calls himself now."

"Who?"

"He was a Grand Inquisitor a long time ago. He became a Pope because he slaughtered anyone who voted against him. A heartless sadist, all in the name of the good, of course. Now he's a gun runner and drug merchant—he keeps himself busy. Can you see the ring on his finger? Paul's special gift to his favorites. You should be very, very careful around people with that ring," Dominique whispered. "You wouldn't want to know what they did to earn it."

Dominique pointed out several other people, outlining their histories briefly. Lucretia became increasingly worried. These people are really dangerous! Way outside my world. I have gone back millennia and fallen into the Assyrian court. How did they like blonde women back then? Roasted, I think. Not a good thing.

The string ensemble suddenly stopped playing and the room immediately hushed.

Paul stood up, his arms outstretched. "A wonderful dinner? Yes?" "The chef has outdone himself again."

Cries of "Yes, wonderful!" filled the room.

Paul smiled and the crowd immediately quieted. "The problem with German food is that, no matter how much you eat, an hour later you're hungry for power," and the crowd laughed.

"Well, this is a wonderful opportunity for us all to be together. It happens so rarely in today's world. We've had many huge successes since we were last here, mixed with a few failures. The computer program—that child pornography program we created to control politicians and many others—was exposed, as it were, and ruined. Still, we got a lot of use out of it, and still have strings in many places. The people who caused us the problems? They will pay in time. Revenge is a dish best tasted cold, a saying that is still true today."

"I think of a friend of ours, unfortunately killed by the small-minded politicians who took his money and then ran for cover. He was a wise man who built an empire from nothing with only his determination and his own hands. A powerful man, strong-minded and focused. Many parts of the organization he created continue today, and we are honored to be associated with some of them. He became too famous, too notorious, and eventually the governments hit the nail that stands up. This is something we all have to remember for ourselves; while the governments are slow and stupid, they have armed police and standing armies. The last time I spoke to him, the end was approaching. I remember he told me: 'The difference between a good man and a bad man is and will always be the one who does not get caught.' In his memory, we shall endeavor to be good men."

The crowd smiled and nodded.

"The world is changing," Paul commanded, suddenly serious, his face animated, his eyes flashing. "This democracy nonsense, this fantasy of the equality of all men, it will end when the cheap energy ends. When life becomes hard again, the people will cry for strong leadership. You who have been with me over the eons know that all empires are created with blood and fire. All of you who are with me shall be well rewarded when the new world comes. You shall be Dukes, Lords—the titled nobility again, and the peasants will kneel when we ride past. The old world will come back, and we will be ready."

The crowd cheered, pounding the tables in their excitement.

Paul smiled regally. "I thank you again, my friends, for coming to this wake. A true Irish wake, where the deceased ate and partied with you! Now, there will be aperitifs and music in the grand ballroom. I must beg off, as I have much business to attend to, but I want all of you to relax and enjoy yourselves. We all shall have much hard work in the coming time. This pleasant night will be a good memory."

Thunderous applause broke out as the guests leaped to their feet.

Paul waved as a king does, acknowledging their cheers and applause, and then strode off, the emperor in his element.

People started to mill about after he left, slowly working their way out to the grand ballroom.

"Do not leave my side," Dominique whispered into Lucretia's ear. "Paul's son is casting glances your way. We must be good friends tonight." She clutched Lucretia's hand tightly. "Or...you shall not see the morning, I fear. He does so love his little amusements, you see."

Lucretia paled and squeezed Dominique's hand. They went slowly into the grand ballroom, and the music and drinks lasted for hours. Lucretia danced with a few men, ones that Dominique picked out, and guards were carefully near her when she was on the dance floor. When they left, Dominique quickly assigned several of her guards, and for good measure, several of the Cardinal's guards, to Lucretia. One slept in the room with her, and the others guarded the door all night.

Lucretia's Audience

In the morning, Lucretia woke up, the bright sun flooding into her eyes. She stumbled out of the bed and into the bathroom. How to look today? Ravishing? Serious? Nun-ish? There will be none-ish of that! She laughed to herself. But serious it is.

A little later, there was a knock on the door. One of the chateau guards was there, waiting to escort her to her audience with Paul. She followed behind the guard, Dominique's guards following, watching for tricks.

How does anything get done around here? Lucretia wondered. All these petty murders have to be hard on productivity. The guard led her to the audience chamber. The chamber door was opened by two chateau guards and Lucretia cautiously walked in. Dominique's guards stayed outside the room, waiting for her.

As soon as she was in the room, a grim woman pointed to a seat, which Lucretia quickly walked to and sat down at. Like in the nuns' office at the school, she thought. She looked around, curious. There were many people in the room. Some were seated in the chairs lining the back, and others paced nervously, waiting for their moment. Paul sits on what is really a throne, she noted. Well, duh! She felt she knew the scene, but couldn't place it. A few minutes went by, and she suddenly remembered a movie, with a scene in Xerxes' throne room. This is it, updated to the modern and simple. There were guards around the dais, and some sultry young women not dressed or acting as secretaries. The ancient world disguised in modern clothes, but the old behaviors.

Lucretia waited and waited. People who came in after her met with Paul first. She sat there, trying not to look unhappy or fidget. Perhaps I shouldn't have insulted his son, she wondered. But having Cesare touch me? Ugh! Little could be worse than that. She had been warned not to take notes, not to review her notes, or read anything at all. She was to sit and wait for her Lord's command. Like an ancient court, it's almost hypnotic, idly watching servants and supplicants bustling about, constant motion. It's the Barbary Coast—the king on his throne, the room full of cruel slave traders and merchants seeking audience and favors, heavily armed guards, hostile and vicious, like pit bulls on a tight leash. I've been an intern, Lucretia challenged them. You can't make me feel lower than Coldmen Sacking did. Although it's a good try, she conceded after a couple of hours. The chairs could be padded.

She studied a carving on one wall. It was dark, and hard to make out, but finally she remembered the scene from a book. The enemy was on his knees; the pharaoh had a hold on the enemy's top knot and was about to strike the man dead. Conquering people! There's nothing in here about getting along and working together.

Lulled into a trance by the soft sounds and movements around her, the pain in her bottom fading as it grew numb, Lucretia suddenly realized that her name had been called. She stood up, her legs stiff, and almost stumbled over a chair. Elegant, she sighed to herself as she limped up to the dais, her head bowed, her eyes down. She'd memorized the routine after seeing several punished for their failure to follow the ritual absolutely perfectly. They were hauled away summarily, screaming for forgiveness. She elected not to wonder about what was going to happen to them. Worse than a salary review, which I didn't think possible. They use real chains here.

Reaching the dais, she knelt down on the steps, waiting for Paul's command. Ouch, she thought. A part of my body that didn't hurt is now chiming in. Bony knees on hard stone, but, knee pads probably wouldn't show the proper respect.

Paul motioned and a nondescript man in a blue suit stood at the side of the dais and started reading. The man was discussing Aeternalis, GmbH, a company she had never heard of. Lucretia had the oddest vision, looking at the man, of him in a toga, reciting the same dull figures off a papyrus scroll. She pushed the vision away, and frantically tried to squirrel away information in her head without a pad of paper or anything to take notes with. How does anything ever get done right? This violates all the rules for an effective meeting. But it's worked for three thousand years, she remembered. If I fail, I die, and they find another, so I doubt they are too concerned about my problems.

Paul gestured and the man immediately fell silent and stepped back from the dais.

"So," Paul commanded. "I need information that this company has. Aeternalis, GmbH is an eternal thorn in my side, certainly. I need financial leverage over them, ideally theft of their intellectual property. I need this information very badly and I need it soon. We, perhaps, have some people in the company, but they have been checkmated, unable to provide me anything useful. They pass rumors to us, but that's as far as we have gotten."

Paul idly toyed with something on the arm of his throne for a minute. "I've sent many people out to get information over the years. Few of them came back, well, as neatly assembled as they went."

Paul stroked his chin and looked at Lucretia for the first time. "I'm told you have many abilities that we can use. I've been told you're strong, you are brilliant regarding financial matters, you have a science background, and you have computer abilities. All the abilities we need for the new world."

He brooded for a moment, then suddenly leaned forward. "Fourteen days," Paul ordered. "I need results by then. You will be leaving after lunch to start." He waved his hand to dismiss her and turned his attention to the man in the suit.

"Ah, thank you, ah, my lord," Lucretia stammered, but Paul did not pay any attention to her. She carefully backed up as she had seen others do, silently cursing her high heels, and then was ushered out of the audience chamber by the chateau guards. She was so humiliated by her treatment that she kept her head down, fearing the contempt of the others waiting until she saw a few that were frankly terrified to be in the room. Then she forgot her feelings, glad to not be them. A little shame is nothing to what they are facing, she realized.

Paul motioned to an aide after Lucretia left.

"There is something about that young woman," Paul remarked,

frowning. "Perhaps there is more in her past than we have turned up. Please look into it. Do we really know her family? Blood tests—I think we need to know where she really came from, what her history really is."

The man nodded and quickly conferred with several other people while Paul went back to meeting with the supplicants waiting for his favor.

Dominique's guards quickly escorted Lucretia to Dominique's room.

As Lucretia walked in, Dominique rose, and, smiling, came to greet her. They kissed. "You are leaving immediately after lunch," Dominique announced. "Now, I've made some small changes to Paul's plans. We have some fine-sounding reason to tell him, but he will know it is his son. It's always Cesare. Paul humors him. So, let's have lunch right here, where we can talk."

They walked onto the balcony overlooking the lake, where lunch had been laid out.

"I spoke to my father about you," Dominique told her. "You knew I would. I gave him quite a good report. Normally, the new hires are just thugs and goons, savage people. You are so refreshing, and so bright. You may survive. The thugs don't, which is some blessing. Here, try the sandwiches—they are excellent. Prepared by my cook. I'm not careless enough to let the chateau staff cook for me."

Lucretia had been staring doubtfully at the food, but then ate with gusto. That awful wait in the audience chamber had pushed her appetite away, but she realized she was starved.

"My father will arrange for some security in New York," Dominique promised. "Cesare usually doesn't pursue his petty vendettas. He has so many that he loses track of them, but it never hurts. If you see people acting strangely, well, more strangely than normal around a beautiful blonde woman, here is someone you can contact." She handed her a phone number. "Not unless you need it," Dominique cautioned. "Father will help, but there is no point in stepping on toes unless it's necessary."

"Understood," Lucretia agreed. "I'm, well, going to be glad to get home. This place is rather wearing."

They chatted over lunch, which was quickly over. "The time!" Dominique exclaimed. "You must rush. Your luggage is here, and you must do exactly as my servants tell you. Understand?"

Lucretia nodded, they embraced, and Lucretia was rushed out into a waiting car.

It wasn't a flight back on the private jet, but at least her seat was in first class. The next day, Lucretia was told that on the plane Lucretia was to have taken, the woman who sat in the seat reserved for Lucretia somehow acquired a terrible illness and died. They were guessing that there must have been something related to her seat that had something to do with it, because the woman jumped up, screaming in pain, as soon as she sat down. After she landed, the illness struck. A later examination of the seat had yielded no pin or other evidence, so the case was closed.

Lucretia felt sick. *The firm is ugly, but I've moved to a new level of savageness.* Rather, she corrected herself, *a very old level.*

Paul's Yacht. Paul, the Professor & the Major

The yacht was huge, really a small ocean liner. There were many decks and passenger cabins, a heliport, and all the modern conveniences and devices. There were more guards with heavy weapons than normal for a private yacht, unless one were, say, carrying the Israeli prime minister on vacation. And perhaps not even then.

The Professor and the Major were sitting on a private deck, relaxing under the warm sun, and enjoying the view of the water.

Paul walked onto the deck and waved away his guard. "Thank you for coming, gentlemen. Here, sit, please," he ordered. They had jumped up when he entered. "I trust that everything is to your satisfaction?"

"It's incredible," the Professor replied. "Absolutely amazing."

The Major nodded his agreement.

"Well, business," Paul advised, sitting down. "It's time for a new era in drugs. We need to think about what people really want and give that to them. It's a new world, and we need to change with it. The drugs we sell now have all these side effects. Some are awful, some are not so bad, and in all truth, usually there are not as many side effects as the legal drugs the international drug company's push.

"One of the legal drugs," the Professor interrupted, "lists explosive diarrhea and projectile vomiting as side effects. Those side effects are what people take drugs to stop, not cause."

"Why can't we give people their high, their lusts, and make them stronger physically?" Paul demanded. "Make the women more shapely, the men more muscled, and high as a kite at the same time. A drug like a Red-Court vampire venom? Then the victims love the drug, and they willingly give up their lives and power. We need a drug for lust, a drug like the touch of a White-Court vampire. At the vampire's caress, people's lusts and desires make them forget everything else in their lives. Let's give them a pill that can do that. Let's get some sin back into these people's lives. What do you say? It's just a matter of rearranging the pleasure/pain receptors, isn't it?"

The Professor was intently making notes, but quickly nodded his head 'yes'.

"Good. We've been too small-minded. We're in the drug business, and there is a story that we think of as 'the drug business.' That story has become too small. We're stuck in the same story that our competitors believe in. We need to rewrite our story, make it a bigger story, because that's the only way to reach the future we dream of. We have to ask ourselves what's missing today, what would make something, anything better, and how can we do that? What did that that philosopher Russell say? People preach one life and practice another? We want to give them the life they dream of practicing via our pills.

"The more they practice the life they are ashamed to preach, the weaker the governments and the other social structures get. The governments are frozen, reacting to the wrong stimuli, spending their resources the wrong ways. They can't find a way to deal with the fact that while perhaps bad people sell drugs, nice people use them. Shouting about the supply from the bad people and ignoring the demand from the nice people plays into our hands. The more they lash out against us, the stronger we become. They artificially raise the price levels for us by restricting supply, increasing our profits. Pass laws to stop us? Now we can control them by using the laws against them, because now everyone can be convicted of a crime. So we own them! We, the people that their laws were supposed to protect them against. There was a book, oh, title was roughly 'everyone in America commits three felonies a day'. I think that is probably an understatement, based on our attorney's opinion. We own the people who use our drugs because we can cut them off, or burn them, or give them extra if we want. We own the enforcers because we can set them up. We give drugs to security people and we know everything about everyone. And we have control over the police and prosecutors because we can make them money. Real money, so they can give up that fucking day job. Or they can be burned into one of their hellhole jails if we set them up because they won't work with us. Or maybe they vanish into the desert. Missing people don't count in the crime statistics—an interesting omission."

Paul sat and looked out over the water, thinking. "It's a sick joke," he mused. "I've seen this before—the over-legalization of the system, frantically trying to keep control when the foundations are breaking up. Reminds me of Rome at the end. Well, that's another set of stories. Another day."

The Major and the Professor glanced at each other, then back at Paul.

"Then, we have all these little countries fighting with each other, all over the world. Dictators seeking power, and the weapons to create and hold power. We provide weapons; we provide financial advice and set up protective structures for them. We help them milk their country for their retirements and by our control over their banking systems we have cover for what we want to do. Give them a piece of the action, and we can import stuff where necessary, manufacture where we want—no one can stop us. We just need better drugs. Once we have the drugs, our attorneys are setting up a host of nonprofit corporations all over the world to hide behind. If we run into problems with one, we shift to another. They can't track them across jurisdictions and countries."

"This is good," the Major agreed. "It's what I saw happening when I was with the police. It's why I changed sides."

"I understand," Paul commented, studying them, "that you have continued in Don Cortes' path regarding Santa Muerte? I didn't think either of you were especially religious."

"Well, I guess I never understood religion before," the Major smirked.

"It's was unexpected, but surprisingly gratifying," the Professor observed.

Paul leaned towards the Major. "Now, with all respect, because I embrace violence myself, I must ask you to please control your killings a bit. I know," Paul added, raising his hands, "it strengthens your reputation. But it draws attention from those whores in the media. Just a little less drama, okay?"

The Major looked skeptical.

"We've got it made," Paul declared, "like I've never seen before. The governments can't accept the individual demands/desires and don't can't respond effectively. Drugs fill desires that people have only dreamed of, that only we can give them. And governments, by carrying on their 'war on drugs,' a useless set of actions that only increases our profits, hand the cartels power and money."

"This Lucretia," the Major interrupted. "She had a child by Don Cortes. Some of my men still respect him; too much, in my opinion. Keeping his memory alive is a challenge to my authority. Is there anything that can be done about this?"

Paul examined the Major thoughtfully. "I have assigned the young woman an almost impossible task. If she survives and brings back good information, I will assign her another impossible task. With the exception of Mother Superior....."

The Major crossed himself at the sound of her name.

".... I do not like having women in the inner circle," Paul commented. "I think that this problem will resolve itself over time. Once she is gone, well, the child will be friendless in the world. But wait!" Paul bent close again to the Major. "Wait until the right time. When I give the signal."

"My Lord," the Major acknowledged. "I await your command."

Cross Lucretia at your peril, the Professor thought. But this isn't my battle.

"What about this young man who caused us so much trouble?" Paul asked the Professor. "You knew him? Had run-ins with him before?"

"I don't really know him," the Professor replied. "I actually arranged for the family to be killed years before, and I had been told he had died when his parents died. It turned out they were his adoptive parents, a surprise to me *and* to him. Then, when I discovered he was still alive and attending the university, I thought I'd found an opportunity to get rid of him. As we all know, that went really, really badly. Astonishingly badly, for a number of reasons."

"You must wish him dead," Paul inquired, studying the Professor carefully.

The Professor sat back and looked out at the water, gathering his thoughts. "Yes," he replied, "but no."

"Why?" Paul pounced. "I'm curious. He's humiliated you, devastated your academic career, his adoptive parents almost destroyed you, and he's a sworn enemy that would kill you in a moment. And no?"

"Because he's lucky," the Professor argued, looking intently at Paul. "More than lucky. Everyone who took a swing at him was paid off for the effort. I think I got off lucky with my skin, and I don't care to take another shot at him. It's just bad luck. A feeling, but yeah, that's how I feel."

"Are you afraid of him?" the Major demanded.

"I'm not afraid of him as a person," the Professor replied. "Listen to me. He's protected. I don't understand it, but I don't stand in front of trucks, and that's what he is. Okay, it's just superstition, but that's what I think."

"Well, I want him dead," the Major growled. "He embarrassed us. He took a great deal of money and killed my people, including Don Cortes. I want him dead. Dismembered would be nice, but dead for sure."

Paul sat back and gazed out over the water. "He will be dead," Paul promised. "But the Professor has made a good point. I will take more extensive precautions when the time comes than I would have before. I'm superstitious also." He studied the Professor. "Listen to those little discomforts—they are telling you important things. I've taken shots at people only to have them rebound. Good. That is helpful to know."

Paul leaned back. "So, you have drugs in the works for what I want?"

"I do," the Professor blurted out, excited. "I have these five." He held out sheets of paper. "They can do these things..."

They talked for another hour, and Paul left, pleased.

PAUL'S YACHT. PAUL, THE MINISTER, & THE TRUTH

The Minister was alone on a private deck, high up on the yacht. He was sitting in an elegant teak deck chair, sipping a cold drink. There was a plate of fresh fruit on the small table next to him, partly eaten. He seemed happy.

Paul stood behind the sliding glass door, watching the Minister, assembling his thoughts before he walked out to talk to him. This is important. People say they want the truth, but they can't handle it. Still, he must be completely with us, or nothing.

"So how do you like your church?" Paul asked, pushing open the door and walking out onto the deck.

"Very much!" the Minister replied, jumping up to show respect. Don't shake hands with Paul, he remembered in time. You don't touch the emperor. "You have given me an incredible opportunity. After my indiscretions, I thought I was ruined. Your people covered it all for me and made the problems go away."

"A trifle for a friend," Paul remarked. "After all, what are friends for? Here, let's sit."

They settled into their deck chairs. For a moment they were quiet, looking out over the water at the land in the far distance, slowly coming closer.

"You'll be happy to know that this yacht is a nonprofit corporation," Paul commented. "A needed resource for many charities; it delivers supplies, carries orphans and the sick, and other wonderful things."

"Really? A tax deduction?"

"And it also delivers drugs and weapons," Paul added. "Cash, diamonds, and gold, too. Steals from them two ways."

The Minister laughed. "I never liked paying taxes very much. Never liked nosy auditors much, either."

"The attorneys have a host of new nonprofits set up for your work," Paul told him. "They can funnel the drugs through those entities. If problems show up, they can be stopped at the corporate level, and new corporations will be set up. Then all the problems are deflected."

"Thank you, my lord." He thought for a moment, frowning. "One of those new drugs has been giving me problems," he reported. "The one that increases religious fervor? It does that, but sometimes too much. Out of, say, two hundred and fifty people we've tested it on, I think five have died, and another fifteen really never recovered. The ones that died, died shouting the name of God and begging for paradise. Really rather scary, actually. I don't dare use that drug in a large setting because I can't risk the publicity. In a small setting, it can be handled. We can separate the people having problems from the rest before the others realize what is going on, and have not had any issues. The ones who are damaged but don't die? Well, they donate much more than they did before. But that drug—it isn't ready for the big time."

"Let's test it further under different conditions," Paul advised. "Some overseas testing...perhaps we can get it to be more controllable. I'll have people test the manufacturing, also. That's helpful to know. I'm glad you told me that.

"Now, when we dock, there will be a media event for you. You are visiting various sad events. Famine, sickness, and poverty give us a stage to show your strengths. You will tour the hospitals, orphanages, and other facilities that we have built to help them, handing out large checks as you go. You will meet with various local religious groups and have your picture taken. It's very good publicity and will be televised. There will be reporters from major newspapers there, along with many ambassadors and other dignitaries. And important contacts from the African countries who are receiving the bulk of the charity money. All real charity, by the way," reading the Minister's flicker of expression. "Oh, it's a cost of doing business. It comes out of the various drug manufacturing and processing activities in the countries, the arms trade, and the money laundering. I haven't gone soft in my old age—don't worry. But if you do nice things, people don't look past them. They forget that just because a person does good deeds doesn't mean they are a good person. Never forget that, especially in your line of work. Then, after all your good works, you will meet us at the palace in the desert. Rest and relaxation is good for the spirit."

"Wonderful," the Minister declared, surprised. "I didn't dream I'd be asked."

"It's an experience not to be missed," Paul laughed. "Even after all the years, I still enjoy it. Now, is your drink good? Refill on the fruit bowl?"

"This is fine," the Minister answered, holding up his drink. "And the fruit is wonderful!"

Paul leaned back in the deck chair, looking appraisingly at the Minister. Showtime!

"I've read a number of your sermons," Paul began. "Did you know I've had a lot of experience with sermons? I know a good sermon when I read it. I'm glad to see that you can keep things straight. Most people writing a sermon get all mixed up between what they need to say to others to motivate them and what they need to say to themselves to motivate themselves. Those are two quite different messages.

"Well...there is something you should know," I enjoy this part, he thought. It's nice to drop the deception. "What I'm going to tell you, I promise that you will find it hard to believe, but it's true. Think about all the wealth you have seen, at the chateau and here. All the connections, all the power that I have. Do you think that was accumulated in one short lifetime? I'm older than Methuselah. I was Paul of Tarsus, all those long years ago. I hijacked the message of Jesus for my own purposes. I turned the message upside down and made it serve me, my church, and my friends."

The Minister choked on his drink, but he caught himself before he said anything.

Paul studied him, smiled knowingly, and continued. "Look, remember the story I told you when I hired you? Foe, the Chinese teacher, had a remarkably effective method for controlling the common people. He taught them, first, that there is a real difference between good and evil; that there is justice and injustice. Second, he taught them that there was another life in which one would be punished or rewarded for what one does in this one. Third, he taught them that happiness could be attained by means of thirty-two figures and eighty qualities. Finally, and most importantly, he taught them that he was a deity and the savior to mankind; that he was born out of love for them, that he expiated their sins, and that by this expiation they would obtain salvation after death and would be reborn happier in another world."

The Minister nodded.

"Now, Foe said that the interior doctrine can never be revealed to the common people because they must fear hell to be kept in their place. The inner doctrine is that there is nothing; that our parents came forth from the vacuum and they returned to the vacuum. Dust to dust—no new ticket to life in the beyond. I've had many who couldn't keep it straight. They start believing themselves, for their own needs, and then become confused. The front office and the back office for any business are not the same. The people who write the ads are not the people who make the loans. You can't have the lenders believing the ads, or they start making mistakes."

The Minister held his drink, motionless, and stared out over the water.

"Would you like to know how all this started?" Paul asked. "Well, it's a nice day, and we have some time. I was wandering around the Middle East, down on my luck. There were these people speaking, and I listened to them. Actually, in all truth, I had taken a position with the Roman authorities, helping them keep watch on subversives. They used different terms back then, but that was the concept. So I sat in this meeting. What they said was interesting, and I started thinking. You've got to get people by their emotional hooks. There are lots of authorized stories, thousands over the centuries. People have emotional hooks, and if you can sink enough of the emotional hooks into people, you can get away with, well, logical weaknesses in the authorized stories. A myth, a religion, doesn't have to make sense. It has to be comfortable. That's the key. The human animal is driven by emotion.

"One night, I re-imagined the religion. Oh, it sounds pompous, but it's true. That storied trip from Damascus? Jesus was a Jew, speaking to Jews. He had some very good ideas, and he meant well. But it was a skeptical audience in that part of the world. Those were lively times—many religions clashing with each other, people arguing all the time about theological issues. There were looming economic and political catastrophes everywhere, ominous dark omens and signs of the end and the beginning. Many of the people were actually quite intellectually sophisticated, but emotionally empty, and they needed something. And something is what they got. Never blithely assume that the message you clutch to fulfill your needs is the complete message.

You'll find, eventually, that the complete message changes the message you thought you understood into something vastly different, but usually it's too late when you find that out.

"St. Paul's great insight on the road to Damascus was that the death of Jesus Christ on the cross could be integrated into the mystery religion's understanding of the death and the resurrection of the savior. That's what the books say, and they are right. I integrated some key ideas into the message and claimed the title of Apostle to the Gentiles. Oh, the others preached to the Gentiles, but effective marketing means making your brand predominant. I, as Paul, claimed a special commission from the risen Jesus, separate from the Great Commission given to the Twelve. Well, why not?" Paul asked the water. "It wasn't like there was going to be a burning bush in the center of the coliseum in Rome telling everyone I was wrong. I pulled in elements from mystery cults, long gone and forgotten. The image of Isis holding Horus became Mary and Jesus because that's a strong emotional hook that people liked and had already accepted. Then I made it an accounting religion. The principal of retributive justice was key, and it all revolved around whether you wanted to live forever or not. Now, THAT is an effective emotional hook. You've got to hook the fish before you can reel it in."

The Minister had put his drink down and sat, frozen.

"In seminary school, when you actually thought about all of this, did you ever ask yourself how the sophisticated intellectuals of the ancient world, schooled in the deep rivers of philosophy that had grown in depth of thought over a millennium, could suddenly abandon all of their doubts and turn to a universal belief in an anthropomorphic God? Before, the philosophers denied the possibility of change in a God. The philosophers and the Jews rejected the idea of a god with a biography, an image: a face, a mother, a handshake, and a style of speech. And suddenly here was God, made man. The message of Jesus was a leap of belief. The invitation to believe that the kingdom of God had come; belief in the miracles, belief in the predictions, and belief in the forgiveness of sins. People jumped off that diving board, believing, because I re-imagined the religion based on the magic of resurrection and the life everlasting.

"Re-imagined, God was so connected with the afterlife that Jesus' miracles were symbols, tokens, for the one great miracle: he was going to save humanity from death. Now, under the old religions, before people were offered eternal life through Jesus, there were all kinds of mixed ideas about death and whether there was life afterwards. Would you just rot? Or be a ghostly shade in Hades? Maybe serve the Pharaoh carrying heavy stones for eternity? Not now! Jesus' death and resurrection became the center of the new religion. Not only did you live again forever, but you answered to God only, not the lords and kings that made your life miserable here on earth.

Who wouldn't a bit suffer on this world for that better world to come?"

They sat quietly on the deck for a few minutes, watching the gulls wheel in the sky. The minister slowly sipped his drink.

"I was impressed," Paul remarked, "at how well it worked. Did you know that my old adversaries, Jesus, Mary, and Lucifer..."

The Minister spat out his drink and stared at Paul.

"Yes, there is a Lucifer. A great warrior, and a fearsome leader. Not, of course, quite as I marketed him, but dangerous enough. Anyhow, they never knew what hit them. I worked and worked, building a stronger and stronger group. I adopted the religion for the empire when I was Constantine because, politically, it worked well. A religion for kings, designed to control the people. There was a king in heaven, and a king on earth. And rebellion, well, you know what happened to the rebels.

"The church? Corrupt to the core. An ancient version of the Nazi Brown Shirts, thugs and grifters with a seasoning of idealists to front and write. Later the core became, well, an SS. The true believers got out of control, mixing the message of what they needed with the message that the people wanted. The Inquisition brought the house down. Slowly, over centuries, the rot worked in, damaging the simple faith of the people that the huge edifice is built on. Still, it worked well for a long time. Surprising, in that it denied all that is human and alive for a phantom future cobbled together from worn platonic ideals and ancient court protocol. Over time, the platonic concepts were dumbed down, and the only thing the priests really grasped was the platonic love for small boys.

"Do I shock you?" Paul asked, glancing at the Minister. "Here I am, reminiscing like an old man. Well, I am an old man—the oldest you'll ever meet."

"No," the Minister stammered, actually shocked to his core.

"I know better," Paul laughed. "People are always shocked when I tell them the truth. And you should be. A lifetime of teaching and beating the story into you, and POW! The story isn't the real story—it's just a story to control people. I ask you: would God create life to turn his/her back on it? No way, but it's a story that has grabbed and held the emotional hooks over the centuries. Oh, there have been many failures, but I have adapted."

They sat quiet for a moment.

"Tell me—have you ever bought a fake picture?" Paul asked.

"I, ah, well, sold a couple once," the Minister answered, defensively. "I was an art major in college, and, well, one thing led to another."

"You'll find that the more you pay for it, the less inclined you are to doubt its authenticity," Paul declared. "That's kept the church going all these years."

"Man made the gods in his own image, but that's not God's image," the Minister mused. "I think everyone knows that in their heart."

"Only the ones who think," Paul replied, "and that is a small, small subset of the world. I've seen them come and go—take my word for it. In Ecclesiastes, the priests set up an impossible question that you can only come back to me/the priests to solve. And we tie your place in the social structure and your emotional well being to the question! It's slick, and it wasn't my idea. I was the king of a small land, a long time ago, and the priests outflanked me with that trick. They tried to throw me off the throne and take over for themselves. I crucified each and every one of them, and was more careful after that." He sipped his drink for a few moments.

"And the soul?" Paul snickered. "How slick was that! This thing that you can't touch, you can't see, but the priests can. And this thing that only the priests can see, it controls your eternal life, everything that really matters, which you only have because they know about it. Sometimes you pay the most for the things you get for nothing. When you commit a fraud, you have to have a way of heading off questions. Plausible denial, it's called in accounting. The soul is the best I've found. Ask about your soul, and you've damaged it already, and only the priests can fix it. And the priests will only fix it if you don't ask any more. If you ask a lot, you get burned-really burned, here and now. There were always lots of people willing to take on the enforcement jobs. The enforcers didn't seem to care about the theology all that much, but they did enjoy their work.

"And the priests and their magical powers? Does anyone really think—if you step back for a second—that God really cares about the fancy puppet in their colorful vestments, covered with symbols, making secret signs with their hands and standing in front of you telling what you should think and do? No. But I fenced out doubt in the theology so the question couldn't be asked. Doubt, and you've already fallen. If you set up hot buttons in people's heads, they jump right past the weak spots in the theology. Now, people like to think, so I turned doubt on its head. You were to doubt whether you could believe enough, so I sent the dogs off chasing the wrong fox. And again, burn the really annoying people. No, what that person in the robes is shouting about is clearly a social behavior. The tie the priest asserts to the larger world doesn't exist.

"Foe, the Chinese teacher, was wrong, however," Paul added. "The world is complex beyond our understanding. Kant argued, essentially, that our perceptions are so flawed that we can't grasp the world. He remained religious. And why did he remain religious? Because there is a little voice inside each of us that feels something. People in the church, people against the church, wild savages in the Amazon. They feel something. What I did was hijack that for the building fund and social control. Once you have an organization rolling, it takes care of itself. With the control drugs, we're just adding a little spice to the mix. Take my word for it—most of your people would happily take those pills and be told what to do with their lives if they had a choice. The number of people willing to think about their lives and choices is pretty damn small."

Paul sat back and nursed his drink, thinking about the past and smiling to himself. "The real beauty of it is that they are all in my box. "Devout believer, agnostic, atheist—all in my box, fighting within the structure. They don't step outside the box, and as long as they are in the box, I've got them, because the hooks are set deep.

"Now, Montaigne actually had it right. Custom and law are what define religion, not some inner knowledge of truth or any rational argument for truth. Sense experience can tell us nothing of God, and reason is a tool that without empirical verification is worse than useless. If we cannot know anything about God through reason, then we cannot know anything about religion either. So we should simply believe, because we must for ourselves. The feeling of transcendence, something greater, is a hard-wired emotional basic, deny it as we will. So how do we live in such a situation? We cannot trust our senses or believe the world to be as we perceive it. But we can accept things as they come to us and simply enjoy them 'Receive things thankfully,' said the Preacher, 'in the aspect and taste that they are offered to thee, from day to day; the rest is beyond thy knowledge.'"

Paul contemplated the Minister. "You have a pulpit and a message. You have our backing and our money. You should not be afraid of greatness, my child. Some are born to greatness, some achieve greatness, and some have greatness thrust upon them."

The Minister sat stunned, his mind whirling. Well, hell, it's a nice day, a great boat, and a good drink. Why not enjoy it all?

PAUL'S YACHT. PAUL & THE CARDINAL

"My good friend," Paul declared, walking onto the deck where the Cardinal sat, a drink in his hand, two exceptionally healthy young women fawning over him. "Do I interrupt?" Paul asked, smiling as the women jumped up.

"Not at all," the Cardinal assumed. "These young ladies wanted to go downstairs and get a quick lunch. I've kept them up here past lunchtime— really thoughtless of me. Go, go," he ordered them, making shooing motions with his hands. "I'll call for you later."

They smiled, kissed him on the forehead, and wiggled down the stairs.

"It's a great life," the Cardinal laughed, watching the women vanish.

"One can hardly argue with that," Paul agreed. "Do they know what is coming at the palace?"

"I sincerely doubt it," the Cardinal replied, sipping on his drink. "It will be my little surprise. But, my Lord, what is on your mind? You have that look."

"I'm thinking of a new plan," Paul mused. "You know we've talked about the world going to hell, and it seems to be accelerating. Just look at the water as we pass through. The water is sick, full of dead fish, and the omnipresent plastic debris—it seems every trip it's worse. I can hardly get a decent meal out of the Mediterranean anymore. And it's all because there are too many people."

"Hard to argue with," the Cardinal agreed. "The first recorded work of literature, say roughly 3500 BC, lamented the collapse in morals of the young and the coming downfall of their society. And their society did fall, actually. Things are always crashing."

"It's too many people," Paul insisted. "They are eating up the seed corn—my seed corn—that I need for the future. I've seen this a thousand times in small villages. Those oil wells are being sucked dry, and for what? For fat people to drive to stores for food they don't need. Fine." He glanced at the Cardinal and shrugged. "Rationalization, isn't that the new word? But they are draining the wells that we could use for another four thousand years...if there were less people. A lot less people."

"I tried leading the Mongols across Europe," the Cardinal recalled. "Oh, it cut back the population for a while, but they snapped back. World War II, they kill fifty million and it doesn't even slow them down. They just reproduce like rabbits. War isn't working to keep the population down. I'm assuming we don't want the crash to reach the famine stage, because then we don't have food either. Disease? It's so, well, uncontrollable. The Black Death really exploited defects in their lifestyles as much as the disease bacteria."

"True enough," Paul agreed. "But we have all these drugs now. We have research, we have manufacturing, we have crazies willing to use things if they think it will make their lives better—now or in the afterworld, as they see it. Oh, we're not quite ready, but I'm seeing real possibilities here."

"Is there something I should be doing?" the Cardinal inquired. "Or am I a sounding board?"

"A sounding board, my friend, I've sent the young lady you found in New York to make a run at Aeternalis, GmbH. It would be enormously helpful if we could get anything."

"My daughter took a liking to her," the Cardinal noted. "Dominique felt that she has real potential."

"My son took a dislike to her. She was flippant with him."

"She was, wasn't she?" the Cardinal commented. "Well, that's a point in her favor, for sure."

Paul glanced at him.

"Cesare has no sense," the Cardinal advised. "He's dangerous because he's filled with random hatred, flitting from one target to another. I know he's your son, but truth is truth."

Paul sat back, frowning. "You're right. We all indulge our children. I'll make sure his little plans don't get in my way. I'll call off his thugs and let her have a fair chance at the difficult task I assigned her. Dominique has excellent judgment, so the girl may be worth more than I estimated. If she brings back anything from that company, she will have passed a major hurdle. Well, we shall see."

Paul snapped his fingers and a waiter appeared. "Another drink" he commanded, gesturing at his half-empty glass. "And for you, Your Eminence?"

"Another drink, thank you," the Cardinal told the waiter, who vanished.

They reminisced for hours, until the boat docked at twilight.

NORTH AFRICA.

The yacht docked at a private dock on the northern African coast. Everyone, except for a skeleton crew to guard the yacht, left for a very private, ancient castle.

It was a several-hour trip to the castle, far out in the desert wastelands. A caravan of armored personal carriers, courtesy of the local military, carried the guests. There were guards in front, back and on motorcycles running interference.

Finally, the vehicles roared through the castle entrance, past the tall, stonewalls, and stopped in the courtyard. The guests spilled out. There had been an abundance of alcohol and any drug desired, so the guests were jovial, approaching incoherence. They stumbled into the castle, laughing and shouting.

Accompanying the guests were an abundance of young, healthy men and women, cheerful and happy. The party picked up steam. Plied with food, drugs, wine, beer and hard liquor and any type of entertainment a person could wish for, they partied through the night and collapsed when exhausted.

The next morning, there was a late breakfast/lunch. Some very tired-looking men held their heads. After a little food, they boarded the personal carriers and went back to the yacht. Mother Superior and her guards transported the remains of the formerly young, healthy men and women to the desert, where the sun and the vultures would rapidly dispose of them. Some had been sacrificed to the old gods in the ancient ways. Some were killed as witches or wizards after their confessions, very surprised at the Inquisition they faced. Few realized that the Inquisition is technically still theologically defensible. "Of course, you have to have the right friends for the paperwork," commented the Archbishop who signed the warrants for their deaths.

"Like old times," the Cardinal muttered to Paul.

"To the victor go the spoils," Paul mumbled, carefully holding his head.

"Xerxes' court was the best," the Cardinal recalled. "Those damn Greeks! All those manly men who loved to nobly fight with each other. We offered them good deals, but no. They just loved to fight."

"There is a god—or gods," Paul mused, sitting back. "I've worshiped and sacrificed to hundreds over the last four thousand years. The gods are different from the stories we make about them. We make stories about them for our small, human purposes, to control and manipulate each other. What the gods think of this is probably better not known. Maybe they don't care. The universe is so vast and huge, they probably don't really notice."

"What did the Minister think of the truth?" the Cardinal asked.

"He was so shocked that he could barely finish his drink after I talked to him on the yacht," Paul laughed. "Still, he seems to have accepted things well."

"The events last night lock him into the organization, in many ways," the Cardinal observed. "He enjoyed himself, more than he would have expected. His behavior would not play well in today's world of equality."

"The church fathers thought little of women. Less than little, if you read the words as they were meant. Or read the writings that are pushed away now into musty corners of the libraries. They were more than scathing in their hatred of women, they truly detested them. The whole story of Eve, set up for the sin of man, and more. I never really understood," Paul mused, "why women liked the church so much when it hated them so much. Let's see. What did they say?

"St. Clement of Alexandria, the Greek Father of the Church, wrote that for a woman, 'the consciousness of their own nature must evoke feelings of shame...For exercise, a woman should fetch from the pantry things that we need.' Tertullian, the African Father of the Church, called women 'the devil's gateway, you desecrated that fatal tree, you first betrayed the law of God.' St. Gregory of Nazianzum said, 'fierce is the dragon and cunning the asp; but woman have the malice of both.' Simon Peter said to Jesus, 'Make Mary leave us, for females don't deserve life.' And these are some of the nicer ones. The writings go on and on, and then there were the Inquisition witch-hunts. But when it comes down to who is in church, it's the women who answer the call. Odd, it is. There are things I still don't understand about women after all these centuries. Probably never will understand, actually. Oh, well."

They rode in silence for a while.

"You met with Lucifer regarding the truce?" Paul asked.

"I did," the Cardinal replied. "I provided him with the document and the conditions. He seemed agreeable, although he did make a pointed remark about peace in our time."

"I'd have expected that. And he's right. He knows in his heart it's a ruse and a trap, but he wants to believe that it isn't. This should give us enough time to clean out that nest of vipers. It will be Jericho. They should remember what they wrote all those centuries ago. They may have softened, but I have not. The little children are taught that they marched around the town and the walls came tumbling down. Then the children laugh and sing."

The Cardinal quoted, "'When the trumpets sounded, the army shouted, and at the sound of the trumpet, when the men gave a loud shout, the wall collapsed; so everyone charged straight in, and they took the city. They devoted the city to the LORD and destroyed with the sword every living thing in it—men and women, young and old, cattle, sheep and donkeys.' I don't think they teach that part to the children. Or to the adults, who should remember what life is really like."

Paul smiled, savoring the memories.

"'Successful crime is called virtue.' Seneca, I think," the Cardinal recalled.

CONFERENCES

The yacht docked and the passengers went back to their lives. There was a rush of private jets headed across the wide world from Rome's airport. Paul continued on to the home on Lake Lucerne with his guards. He had a quiet dinner, a string quartet playing quietly in the background, footmen and guards quietly waiting for his orders.

He walked upstairs after dinner, thinking about the events of the past few days. There's nothing like death to make you appreciate life, noticing the black crepe still in place from the funeral. "All that," he ordered the Butler, pointing to the crepe, "can be removed."

"As you command, my lord," the Butler replied. The Butler stopped, turned to his staff following him and started issuing orders.

Paul walked towards his rooms, down the dark but elegant hallway, alone except for his guards. At his bedroom, one of the guards opened the door. Paul didn't even notice the action, or the man's existence, but simply walked into the room. The guard closed the door behind him, and then the guards took up their positions in the hallway for the night.

Paul's bedroom was enormous, a large apartment fitted into the chateau. It included a study, a bedroom, a luxurious bathroom, and two balconies overlooking the lake, facing the sunset. Scattered around the room, subtly displayed in finely wrought bookcases, were small trophies, souvenirs collected over the centuries. The value of the trinkets in some of the bookcases easily surpassed the value of the chateau. The room was everything that could be done and bought, at least in the modern world. It is bare and simple compared to some of my palaces in the past, he thought, but comfortable for me.

He changed into the uniform of an Assyrian king, still more comfortable in that than any other clothing. Then he sat on the balcony, looking out at the dark lake. He thought about the lake over the centuries; the conquests, the building, the changes. His mind wandered.

"Everyone's gone?" a voice called out. "Come out, come out, wherever you are," it called.

"Ah, a long day," Constantine commented, sitting on the chair. "All this paperwork. Better to lead the legions into battle. More satisfying."

"Or heavily armed men against savages," Cortés asserted, standing by the wall. "What's the point of a fair fight? Slaughter, that's where it's at."

"'Man's highest joy is in victory: to conquer one's enemies; to pursue them; to deprive them of their possessions; to make their beloved weep; to ride on their horses; and to embrace their wives and daughters,'" Tamburlaine quoted, poking at the fish in the tank.

"I'm never sure," Paul mused, "whether you are all real." He turned his gaze from the lake to the men in the room. "That's the problem with being all those people over all those years."

"Look at it this way—it multiplies the consciousness's attention span," Constantine offered. "We've been over this."

"I like your plan," a deep voice boomed, and the others snapped to attention. Xerxes stood in the room, the master. "The plan is bold, creative, forward looking. Taking advantage of new opportunities."

"And slaughter," Cortés added. "Lots of that."

"Pyramids of skulls," Tamburlaine growled. "Like the old times." His eyes glittered.

"There is that," Xerxes acknowledged, stroking his beard and smiling. "Far too many of these arrogant scum infest the world today. Weed them out until they kneel down to the great emperor. Yes, the old days. And get back to palace that is a palace," critically examining the room. "This is a summer cottage, hardly a palace."

"We're all agreed," Paul announced. "Now we just need to get rid of Leonidas. Lucifer and his little band—they've been a thorn in our sides far too long."

"And they are multiplying," Cortés worried. "The children are competent, dangerous. They can work this modern world and its trickery. Yes, they must die."

"Too bad it isn't the old days," Xerxes declared. "Down in the dungeons, they could slowly wither. Well, perhaps those times will come again."

"You think so?" A shadowy figure came slowly out of the blackness filling a corner of the study and stopped in the middle of the room.

"From whence you came?" Paul asked, carefully using the formula. Magic formulas for control, he thought to himself.

The Adversary answered Paul, "From roaming the earth and walking about in it."

"Always against our plans," Tamburlaine grumbled. "What foolish pap presented as wisdom do you waste our time with today?"

"Your vision is so small," the Adversary complained. "Always playing in these human games, humoring your urges. Why act so hastily? You have power and money, and all this research and technology is running in your direction. You will have overwhelming power in a few years, so why act now? In other words, idiots, why are you invading Russia in the fall? The same mistake, over and over."

"Who can say what will happen in the years to come?" Tamburlaine countered. "Lucifer, Mary, Jesus—they are not standing still. They may grasp the opportunity that all this technology offers before us. Those accursed children of theirs have proved their ability already, and they are still gaining strength. With each year that goes by, the masses use up the resources we need."

"From each according to my need," Xerxes commanded, "and to each, according to my desire. Too long, the peasants have lived by foolish slogans that make them think highly of themselves. Time for the ancient laws to apply again."

"Look," the Adversary argued. "You're making all the usual mistakes. You've anchored the decision around their 'now.' This whole elaborate structure they have built up—it's an aberration. Nothing like the past three hundred years has ever existed. These complex social structures will crash and burn on their own. We should be waiting in the bowels of the earth, ready for conquest, not tempting fate trying to ride the whirlwind."

"But look at the situation!" Constantine demanded. "They are sucking down the resources so fast. A little push, and the structures crumple, and then there will be more for us."

"You're only looking at what you want for your argument," the Adversary objected. "When there are only a billion, perhaps less, of them, the resources will stretch for thousands of years. There are many other possibilities. Look, you're framing the problem wrong. Frame the problem wrong, and you've picked the wrong problem to address. Go after the wrong problem, and all the decisions that flow from that mistake are garbage."

There was silence in the room. Paul studied the Adversary. "We must act," Paul declared. "Life is action. Perhaps you are right, but where is your proof? We don't have the luxury of multiple universes to experiment in.

Counseling waiting, prudence, over caution—that is also a trap. You do not propose a plan, you propose we rust. How many times have I waited and plotted when action would have cleared the way for success?"

The others nodded their heads in agreement.

"Then it's upon your heads," the Adversary replied. "Time shall reveal all."

Cortés laughed. "Speaking of revealing, what did you think of that blonde wench from Sweden at the castle last night?"

The others hooted their approval, and they talked about the night as the Adversary withdrew into the dark with a goblet of fine red wine. He sat, watching the others' glee with a thoughtful expression.

Finally, Paul waved his hand. "I'm tired," he muttered to the group. "I can't think any more. I can hear your words, but they mean nothing. Let's sleep, and you can run on the oceans of the unconscious."

"Let's watch the world burn," Cortés suggested, "like so many towns in the past."

Paul stumbled into bed, and slept.

AN OMEN

Paul slept. He dreamed of old hunts. He was out in a field, a king of an ancient, lost kingdom, hunting game. His falcon flew off his arm after the doves and drove toward a dove that had veered off from the flock. Paul laughed, delighted, anticipating the kill. The falcon, his creature and his will, streaked to the kill, diving on the dove, which fluttered in confusion. He was shocked when the falcon suddenly veered off, ignoring the dove, and flew up, away from Paul.

Paul shouted at the bird and ran through the field, cursing it. Finally he stopped and threw down his leather glove as the bird vanished into the distance. He stomped back through the field, but he was uneasy. His power, his control, suddenly was like the wind, blowing through his fingers, nothing to grasp onto.

With a start, he woke up in a cold sweat. He sat up in bed, fearful. Omens! In the old days, the priest would read the entrails of a sheep, reverently pronouncing the message of the omens. Now, bright young people with MBAs prepare long reports. Both equally useless, but I liked the priests better. At least you ended up with mutton. Maybe I'll have the MBAs disemboweled and they can read their own entrails? Couldn't be any worse than the advice I've been getting from them, and it would be a lot more entertaining. And it would decrease the retirement plan funding obligations. Hmmm.

He gazed out and saw the shadows of the birds wheeling overhead, far above the lake. Again, the same dream, coming more often. Why?

It all started after that damn Yeats poem. What had it been? Not quite a hundred years, a blink of an eye. Now, how did it go? Suddenly, he was happy. Actually, gleeful. He clapped his hands in joy.

"Things fall apart; the center cannot hold;
Mere anarchy is loosed upon the world,[8]"

How could I have been so blind? This is a foretelling of my plan. The falcon had to run free before my plan could come to fruition.

He jumped out of bed, stretched, and walked out onto the balcony. He drank in the beauty of the scene, humming an ancient Persian hymn to the Gods. Then he pulled the cord for his Butler. This is the dawn of a new day, indeed.

PAUL & GRENDEL

'This young woman at the party, who was sitting with the Cardinal's daughter," Paul commented. 'She is doing some work for us in New York. I don't trust her."

"Since when do you trust anyone?" the creature rumbled.

"None except you, my friend," Paul promised. "Watch her. This truce won't last, so be ready to act on my command. I understand that Lungorthin is there with them. Perhaps you can pay him back for those scars he gave you when you last met?"

"I've been dreaming of it," the creature hissed.

"But wait!" Paul ordered. "Wait for my command. No improvisation. Capice?"

The creature nodded his agreement, reluctant but obedient.

CHAPTER 5. CAT AND MOUSE

A WARNING

"So, is there a plan?" Mother Superior demanded, sitting across the desk from Lucretia. "You have, I think, eleven more days, if I count correctly," and Mother Superior smiles.

Her smile, Lucretia thinks. It's the hungry animal savoring its prey. I wonder if she cooks them, or eats them raw. "You are right on the number of days, and there is a plan," forcing a smile. "I have some methods that your prior people didn't have."

Mother Superior stood up, and casually walked over to the display case. "Like these fine computer toys you are so proud of?" she asked casually, stroking a glass vase.

"Yes. That's where the power is today."

Mother Superior dropped the vase, and watched, pleased, as it shattered into a thousand pieces. "That's the power of your computer toy's," she announced. "Nothing at all."

Mother Superior strode to Lucretia, who was still staring, shocked, at the shards of very expensive crystal all over the floor. Mother Superior leaned over the desk, right into Lucretia's face. "The power is between your legs, Blondie," she snarled. "And you'd better use it soon and well. Termination from the group is, well, permanent." She stood up, smiled, carefully arranging her hair, looking at her reflection in the glass walls. "I'll be waiting," and she walked out.

Lucretia slumped in her chair. At least she's honest, she thought. Better than the men in the meetings, and they say the same things. Shit.

She buzzed her secretary, who popped her head in the door.

"Ah, please get maintenance in here. And then no interruptions, please for two hours," Lucretia ordered.

"You have a meeting in an hour with the senior partner," her secretary replied, puzzled. "Didn't you remember?"

Lucretia scowled. "True, but it's cancelled. Be so good as to say something that will cover."

The secretary examined her skeptically, and shrugged. "I hear and obey, my lady," and closed the door.

It will be more insinuations about my reproductive organs, Lucretia thought. I wonder if I'm pregnant again or just woman problems. Well, if I don't solve this problem, I won't have to worry about much of anything, least of all, the senior partner's opinions.

"So," she declared to the broken shards of crystal, "I have to get this information. Something in their database, something that can either weaken the company financially, and/or get patent and research information. That won't be easy."

A shout down the corridor distracted her. I'm out of here, she decided, and packed up her computer and notebook. She walked out, interrupting a whispered conversation between her secretary and several other women from the department, who looked quickly up at her and smiled.

"I'll be back later," Lucretia told them. "My phone is turned off. I'll call you."

Her secretary raised her eyebrows, but just nodded. Lucretia smiled at the women as she walked past them, and they gave her respectful looks, that turned into glares when she passed them.

Lucretia settled into her favorite coffee shop, four blocks from the office, that had a sweeping view of the river. I'll become a pirate! Then I can make the swabs walk the plank. She visualized the office women dropping into the ocean, complaining about their hair being messed up and the salt water damaging their expensive dresses, and it made her feel better.

So, what do I need to know? I'm supposed to be the best. Focus.

A couple of hours later, she had pages of doodles and few solid ideas. It's the pressure, it's getting to me. If I fail Paul, what will my family do? Worse, what will he do to my family? Should I send my mother and the kids away? As if there was a place they couldn't find them? There is no place, she knew. Their power runs through the world. She stared at the river. This is your life and it's ending one minute at a time. No, that's not helping.

She doodled again. Well, this worked in the past, she mused. Is it really right for this situation? I can't think of anything else, but it doesn't feel quite right. Hell, I can make this work. Improvise. It's worked before and it will work again. It has to, actually. She spent the next hour filling in ideas, and then closed the notebook and went home.

LUCRETIA & HER MOTHER TALK

"You're home early," her mother demanded.

"I can't think at work," Lucretia sighed. "I have this special project, and I can't clear my mind."

Her mother turned on the TV and the radio at the same time. Satisfied that there was enough background sound to cover their conversation, the turned back to Lucretia. "From your trip?" her mother asked, worried.

"Yes. An opportunity, but one that has been failed at before by many other people. Succeed, and they will be impressed."

"Fail, and you are fish food," her mother retorted. "Nice people! They are monsters in human faces with no sympathy."

"Not all of them have human faces," Lucretia commented without thinking. "It was an interesting place."

Her mother sat down next to her, and they were silent for a few minutes.

"I know people," her mother observed. "A whore has to make snap judgments about people, or they'll find you in a ditch the next morning. Most people are relatively harmless. Perhaps a little wild when drunk, when the lust is on them. Take away the lust, and they go to sleep like puppies. Not these people. They are wolves. Worse than wolves, hyenas—roaming the plains and tearing apart the weak." Her mother glanced at Lucretia. "You're not defending them?"

"No, I agree with you, unfortunately. The trip there was eye-opening. A world out of the past, savage beyond anything I've seen. Like opening a romance novel set on the Barbary Coast and realizing that the pirate ship bearing down on you isn't a fantasy that goes away when you close the book. A bodice-ripping novel isn't as much fun when it's your bodice about to be ripped."

"Hmmm. Well, since we're in the stew, let's make the best of it. So what has to be done?"

Lucretia started talking randomly about the assignment and her ideas. Two hours later, they had some clear plans.

How?

"Okay," she mumbled to herself, sitting in the coffee shop the next morning. She'd called into the office, telling them that she couldn't come in for a few days, but that she would call for messages.

Her secretary was gone, but the temporary secretary was polite and promised she would tell the necessary people.

Where has my secretary gone? Lucretia wondered. She's a vicious bitch, but I'd rather know where she is. Who was it, the Godfather? 'Keep friends close but enemies closer?' Who knows who she is talking to? I wonder if she's got her resume updated for a shift to another position in the company? She probably figures I'm a goner. She may be right, but for the wrong reasons.

Lucretia spent the morning writing and re-writing, furiously crossing out her brilliant perceptions and making more notes. It's no good, she thought, frustrated. As I intensely pore over this, I become more insecure and uncertain about the whole mess. Then, for control, I focus on each tiny, minute detail, a parody of a detailed planning process. The longer I fuss, poking and prodding the details, the further away is that evil day of action. Which actually is the whole idea—to avoid the real problem.

Paul was wise to set a tight deadline, or even I would never have acted. It's such a big problem and it's hard to get my mind around it. She threw away all her scribbles and started doodling on a blank sheet. I need to start with the critical question: What is success? What will it look like when I am done? I have this critical information in my finely manicured fingers. Paul and Mother Superior are kneeling at my feet, awed at the wonder of my abilities. Scratch that—Paul would be looking up my skirt. Probably Mother Superior, too. Anyhow, I need certain facts about that company.

So I need information. Does the information exist? I think so, and more importantly, Paul thinks so. It would have to exist, because that company is in certain businesses and those business processes are dependent on that information. As it's important to them, it isn't public information. Because it isn't public, it's guarded, and access is controlled by a limited number of people. I'm not exactly sure who knows what. So I need to know who the players are at that company. Now, the people at that company are local. They have lives, families, friends the usual overlapping social webs, outside of their work. Church's, clubs, bars, shared interests with others. Each person has a big circle around them encompassing everything in their life, which overlaps with other people's circles. Somewhere there is an overlap, like one of those annoying Venn diagrams and there is the information I want. So, they are full of information. Full of it, actually. They know lots of stuff. What I want to know, they may consider critical information in their world, or not really all that important to them. Regardless of what they think about the information I need, I need full, correct, and open disclosure.

Actually, the information isn't really held by the people; it's access to the computers and files that have the information that's key. Better, because people don't realize they gave something. They might realize they gave access, but computer access, with the right passwords, is like sneaking in on little cat feet. If someone tracks back to what I looked at, well, at least I got the information and passed it on.

What are the possibilities? The good fairy could make them happy to tell me by tapping her little wand on their heads. Or by putting them in the dungeons at Paul's, tapping their little heads with a club. A tempting thought, but hard to arrange. If I had time, I could blackmail them, because everyone is hiding something(s). Or I can pay people. I fill their pockets, and they open their minds to me. Finally, I can trick them, and they open their minds to me without knowing what I took.

Okay—I never had much luck with the good fairy before, I don't have a dungeon, blackmail takes time, and paying people doesn't seem to work. First, paying people fails because then they realize what they have done and run to confess. I need them to give me the information without knowing or thinking about what they did. Secondly, paying them takes more money than I have. So, it's down to tricking them.

Too bad, because I like the good fairy idea. Okay. I need to trick people, which makes me the bad fairy. How do I do that? First, people don't estimate risks well. The danger of the risks shouted on the news are overestimated, and the little, daily risks are underestimated. It's driving to the airport, not the flight, which is dangerous. So what is a risk people overestimate and overreact to, and what is a risk people underestimate and so don't think about what they are doing? I need information from strangers, and for them to freely and gladly share with me that which they should know better than to do. More: that which they are sternly ordered to not share.

One possibility is to engage them in a rebellion against their oppressors. People are happy to do what they are not supposed to do. It's a kind of freedom, proving their power—they can't be bossed around. It's the remorse the next day one has to watch. How to handle that remorse? Mother Superior has methods that are not right here. Perhaps not right anywhere, anytime, but that's another issue. So people who don't remember their next day's actions are the best. That usually requires down-and-dirty action, hands on, as it were. Fine! Mother Superior, with her insinuations regarding my lack of moral character—she should talk!—and my willingness to sacrifice the sanctity of my body for my work, my life, and my family, is right about me, and that's probably what's going to be required here. They are priests, she told herself. They can re-sanctify me. I can flit through the office hallways dressed in white, with flowers in my hair. Mother Superior's style would be black with thigh-high hobnailed high heels. I kind of like that look myself, actually. She doodled a dress for a minute on the page. Maybe later. She crossed it out. Now, I liked that part in The Three Musketeers where M'lady had the warrant from the cardinal. "For the good of France, and by my order, the bearer has done what they have done." Clean conscience and clean hands at the same time.

So, it's geeks in a bar, she sighed. Ugh. That is something I do know how to make work. Maybe I can just get them drunk and they can fantasize afterwards.

But I don't even know who in the company is worth stalking in a bar. Back to people. First I have to acquire a target, and time is short. She jotted some notes and did some research. There are lots of documents out there, and it's hard to hide on the Internet. She worked up her requirements and e-mailed them to the research department at Coldmen Sacking. They are always sticking those noses into other people's business, that it doesn't look odd at all—not as odd as it would look for little old me snooping around.

She kept working, and the reports came back quickly. Being known as the evil queen has some advantages. Perhaps I could become Mother Not-So-Superior, but above average. Probably a bad idea. My kids would have terrible rebellions in their teen years. As if they won't anyway, my mother cheerfully hints? Move on, focus. She kept reading. Yes, this is useful. She made notes, poring over the pages. After a couple of hours, she had ideas. This person, and this person? They might be useful leads.

Okay, second step. What happens rarely in an office? It's the rare things that people stumble over. If I call and ask for your computer login password—everyone knows better than that. Well, not that intern we had to fire who opened the database to that hacker, but almost anyone who doesn't have an MBA knows better. Keeping your password secure is a situation that is addressed all the time. But a technical question, posed in a non-threatening way, and an answer that gives me something to work with—that can work. It has worked before.

On the bright side, people hate security, they create simple and boring passwords that they put in their wallets, and leave files open on the network because it's a hassle to close things. So how do they run things there? Who, in their info tech department, would know that? Lucretia thought, and smiled. I know people in that world, and they owe me favors.

A long lunch later, during which she pried useful information out of several people who never looked above her low-cut blouse, and she had some clear targets. A gift! A tech convention, and one of their people is speaking. It's local. What's the luck on that? So several of their people will be there. And it's at this hotel. She quickly made more notes. She registered using a little company with a technical name, creating an identity for herself. That's two days from now. It runs a day, so I'll have seven days to get inside and get information. Doable.

She made some rough organizational drawings, but that didn't tell her much. Not enough information! I got nothing useful from Paul. I know nothing about the small, practical stuff: like doors, guards, types of passes, how big the company is, do people know each other, are there outsiders there a lot or never?

Most decisions make themselves if you just gather data. A picture will form in your mind. So, where's the picture, what is the unconscious thinking? Lucretia doodled. It's just black. Ravens in a coal mine. Okay. We use heuristics, unconscious routines to cope with the complexity inherent in most decisions. That stupid prof at Harvard, going on and on, and the only decision he had to make was what beach house to buy, and which PhD students to abuse and steal research results from. I could have gotten a PhD and lorded it over the undergraduates, but no, I had to go for the gold. Well, that was a choice made in the past.

I'm just not seeing the whole picture here. I'm doing what I've done before, and this is different somehow. But what are my choices? Social engineering is playing with people. What can I do? The first and most important rule: the only people who can rob you blind are people you trust. So, I'm creating trust. There are many ways to create trust, but my options are limited because I don't have time. One possibility is posing as an employee of a vendor—a partner company—or a law-enforcement official. If I do that, there is a trail that can be easily proven false. Not so good.

Or, I can pose as a consultant who can solve a problem for them. It has to be an important, urgent problem, and it has to be a problem I can solve. Post hoc ego prompt hoc, or something like that means that it has to be a problem I created and put inside their system. Nothing really awful, but a real problem for someone who will let me in to fix it. Best if it's fixed on the sly, so their boss doesn't know about the issue, as it would reflect on their competence/career. To do that, I need to get close—very close— to someone on their staff. But that really can work.

So what is this seminar about? Lucretia reviewed the topics and groaned. Maybe Mother Superior in the dungeon would have been easier, but she went to a bookstore for some technical books. She spent the next day working through the books so she would be ready for the seminar.

She sat at her desk the night before the seminar. I can't think! There is just too much going on. There is something not right here, but it's not coming to me. Still, it's the best plan I can think of-any port in a storm.

She slept poorly that night. She went to the seminar, carefully dressing down as far as she could, minimizing her makeup and wearing the tackiest, most boring glasses she could find. She still glowed in the mostly-male geek setting, but she didn't want to overwhelm. The little birds will run away, she knew. Flock with sparrows, be a sparrow. Draw them in. Leave a trail of seed corn for them to follow. Or is it offering them the chance to leave a trail of seed corn? These nature analogies get confusing.

PUZZLE PIECES

She reflected on the ride home from the seminar. Okay, that was fun. A day of chattering with poorly groomed geeks about network routers. Boiling in oil would be easier. Which is what Cesare has in mind if I fail, she reminded herself. Perhaps not easier?

Now, sketching out ideas, once inside I can have fun. Capturing keystrokes, drop a document or file at the company mailroom for interoffice delivery, load Trojan horses, all the good stuff. But I've got to get inside. That guy at the seminar—it was clear that access from the Internet isn't going to work. He was so proud of their security measures. His chief of security would love to hear what he said.

Actually, this is weird. The quality of the security here is far, far higher than it should be. Higher than the investment bank, and I thought they were the gold standard. No wonder they have lost people trying to get in! But Paul's probably right— there is gold in there. You don't put up a really, really big wall if there isn't something important to protect behind it.

The financial stuff that Coldmen Sacking came up with—there's nothing to work with there, she thought as she threw it aside. The company seems to be privately held through a very confusing ownership structure. Key parts are held by companies in countries that don't require-nay, allow-information disclosures. There are many subsidiaries and spinoff companies, but the overall financial strength is astonishing. No loans to purchase from banks to get an edge. No chance of getting control of the stock. Maybe one could go after a distant, partially held subsidiary, gain control over that, and then sue for information, but that would take years. Its interesting how they have setup little companies all over the place. I can make a nice map of that information, but that would be an extra to give to Paul, not the main course. He doesn't want dessert. That's my function if I don't perform.

I have made real progress-I have names, and an idea of the structure of their company. She worked up a diagram of the technical staff based on what she heard at the seminar. Who did what, which operating systems and protocols, and who was responsible for what. There were lots of empty boxes on her drawing, but a structure formed in her mind. Definite progress, she thought. What I need is that idiot from Ann Arbor who trashed the cartel's network. I'm storming the palace with a toothbrush, so it would be nice to have some resources. And speaking of resources, there was talk about a bar that some of them liked. The sun is over the yardarm-hopefully not the one that Paul is planning to hang me from. So it's time for after-work cocktails. Mother Superior would be so proud: it's over the wall, I guess.

At home, she quickly redid her makeup, changed her clothing, and became a bright bird, flying out to the bar. Shortly thereafter, Lucretia was sitting on a barstool. She'd bribed the bartender to be her ally, and he told her who was who. Sloppy work on my part, she thought, but who'd follow that trail back? Watching people drift in, she recognized some of the men from the seminar. She managed to drop something, a gawking tech picked it up, and a conversation started. She held her breath for a moment, but they didn't recognize her. That's because they are not looking at my face, she thought, relieved. She was soon sitting with five of them, and the drinks were coming in pretty fast for a weeknight.

This is working, she thought, stumbling a bit as she left the bar, falling a bit on the tech, letting him help her walk. Helping himself, she growled to herself, but kept smiling. Remember, work into the key information. Another two or three questions, a little chat. Two or three pieces of information might be all it takes to mount an effective impersonation. She sighed as they reached his apartment. But the memory of Mother Superior's firm belief in the value of down and dirty drove her through the door.

In the morning, she had employee names and numbers, phone numbers, scans, RFT captures of the badges, and a drawing of the information technology department's personnel structure. And, a solution for the problem that is going to pop up on the network when he plugs his ID into the equipment in the morning. Nothing that they had seen before, but something her company could handle, something she'd talked about, over and over, with the group last night. She had passed her card to all of them several times. She owed the Professor for that—he had sent her toys without asking any questions.

INFORMATION OVERLOAD

There's too much stuff to track, Hal thought, staring dejectedly at the piles of paper taking over his office. Worse, the e-mails are stacking up faster than I can review and toss them. He gave up and idly watched the number of unread e-mails increase by the minute. It's like playing Whack-A-Mole, but my hammer broke.

He started pacing. The world is too complex to monitor everything, clearly. A pile of paper shoved on a corner desk decided to slowly cascade down to the floor. "Thank you," he told the pile on the floor, "for accenting my point." And, I only see what I'm looking for anyhow. So the important stuff, the stuff I should be thinking about, should be watching for, is hiding from me in plain sight. By the time it's in the newspapers, it's too late. So how to see that little stuff before it gets big?

Driving in fog and rain has always called for caution as well as a clear sense of destination. Nice slogan, but useless. He sat on the corner of his desk and stared out the window. So, I have to learn to see what I'm not looking for, to see the subtle emerging. Another useless slogan! I'm beginning to sound like the caretaker— it's all Zen. What is the sound of an unsent e-mail?

How can I see the crucial gaps in what I know? He doodled on a piece of paper. First, doubt what I know. Gaps are obvious if I can recognize an absence of something. That's really, really hard to do, because the mind hates not knowing, not being sure. Indecision and uncertainly are no fun, not even for the systems-obsessed of us. It's too easy to just slide past the odd parts, the puzzle parts that don't fit. We all have a box somewhere that the extra parts get shoved into and forgotten. Basics: it's a system out there, interacting with itself, and the story format we all use doesn't handle random events well. We all use analogies that may or may not be right, and there are delayed consequences and multiple causations all over the place. Argh. 'Fifteen men on a dead man's chest, yo ho ho and a bottle of rum. Drink and the devil have done for the rest, yo ho ho and a bottle of rum.' No, the sun isn't over the yardarm yet; the bar hasn't opened. Not a solution set.

It's the odd parts that are key, he realized, excited. That's how I caught that problem at the San Francisco plant. And the Paris problem—that was an oddity. Something didn't reconcile with what it should have. A type of fraud against the assumed story, I guess. Catching the peripheral, marginal signals that are the early warning signs of threats and opportunities. The near misses and the close calls I talked about at the seminar, but making them the center of attention. Like noticing when Cali isn't really smiling, which means I forgot something. That article I read contrasted passive versus active scanners of our environment. Active scanning still requires attention on something, a focus, but setting up structured, open-ended questions? Could work.

Use the creature. The mind processes all the time, and consciousness just gets in the way. Relaxation, visualization. What I'm thinking about will pop up. When I'm uncertain, undecided, I'm trying to tell myself something. The phone rang. When I get a f*cking moment to think, that is. He controlled his breathing and picked up the phone. Twenty minutes later, the small group left his office, smiling.

Hal sat there stewing. There was a cartoon I remember: the guy answers the phone "And on that day you will feel my wrath with the heat of a thousand suns! You will recede into the depths of hell and you will bear witness to my fury!" Yeah, that's the recording I'd like to put on the phone to weed out calls. That meeting was useless. The dance of indecision. I've got to start pushing the responsibilities down further. I don't want to help them make decisions. That's what they are paid for. I just need to see what the decisions are coming out as.

So, back to how to think? Risk is the margin, where it matters. And we all overestimate risks for things that are out of our control and that people talk about at the water cooler. We underestimate risks for things that are mundane and ordinary. It's that little drip we ignore that is the warning sign of the flood.

DINNER & IDEAS

Hal and Cali were having dinner at a nice Italian restaurant near the warehouse. Hal's mother was taking on the terror that was Maria for a few hours.

"If it's written down, it's too late," Hal complained. "By the time I see it, it's just piles of stuff to sign off on."

"The real problem with focusing on anomalies is that you are then outside the social consensus," Cali observed, buttering the hot bread the waiter had just brought them. "No one, well, except anti-social, systems-obsessed men..."

"Who are exceptionally well-endowed physically," Hal interrupted.

"...want to be outside the social consensus," Cali continued, ignoring his remark. "You talk about watching the edges, what's wrong—it makes people uncomfortable, uneasy. You're asking them to peek into the abyss and they don't like that. There's stuff moving in there! Anomalies are thinking different things, looking for different things, finding different things. That is a constant challenge to others in many ways that disturbs their worldview and their sense of self. So people don't do it. Now, if you do focus on anomalies, the group won't be happy, but you're right—it works a lot better for reading the real world."

"That makes me feel better. I've played with anomalies as an orienting response, but I didn't follow them up in a structured way because there wasn't a lot of reinforcement. Even geeks appreciate a little social approval occasionally. Now it's clear why that approach is rejected and denied by people and society. So it wasn't my unwashed clothes all those years?"

"No, it was the unwashed clothes," Cali countered. "Shallow surface appearances mean a lot in bars."

"Actually, shallow surface appearances mean a lot everywhere. "People can just act without thinking, using the usual symbols that people wear to judge them. That's what produces all those useless reports, measured by weight instead of quality. What was that ad campaign that advocated men buying an ultra-expensive automobile because women would then give them hand jobs? I think the campaign was pulled because it was deemed too crass or too truthful—one of those."

"Mind on the table, out of the gutter. As if a woman would have to do anything so gauche to control a male," Cali sniffed. "So how do we use anomalies to truly understand Sun Tzu? 'To lift an autumn hair is no sign of great strength; to see sun and moon is no sign of sharp sight; to hear the noise of thunder is no sign of a quick ear.'"

"That is the complete question! "Answer that question, and you have the key to *The Art of War*, and probably life, too."

"So, bringing it back to a practical level—we're trying to head off disasters of all kinds before they become too big to fix," Cali mused. "It's like an airplane. Every minute it's off course, but it's constantly correcting to get to the airport."

"I like flying less and less."

"It's knowing where you are headed that makes it possible to course correct. There's a lot of good stuff on how to make decisions when you know what you are facing, when you know what the goal is."

"Management by objective works, if you know the objectives. Ninety percent of the time you don't," Hal quoted. "Gospel from Drucker, the master himself."

"Where you know your objectives might be more than ten percent. "But that's the key. It's when you don't know what you're facing, what the hidden gaps are, which unexpected feedback is out there that is showing up randomly as noise. The surprises that the world has out there, how the world just doesn't want to follow the storylines that each of us, in our infinite wisdom, have laid down for the world to obey."

"There are lots of good slogans," Hal growled, poking at his salad. "Never fall in love with your decisions, remember that everything is fluid. Be constantly aware of and subtly adjust your feelings. Yeah, what does that mean? And as high as I am in the organization, if I just sit at my desk and stare blankly into space, people start to talk. Oh, less since I put that plank in and walked a few of the malcontents off the fifteenth floor, but they still whisper."

"It's the immeasurable feedback that drives you crazy," sketching ideas on the tablecloth. "Whoops, this is cloth, not paper. Hal, leave a bigger tip. Humm, maybe a lot bigger. An event is something in, something out. If we don't notice the event, then the chance to head off what is coming is gone. If we are missing the real inputs and outputs, then what we are measuring is useless. Worse than useless, actually. Solving the wrong problem, with all the disaster that brings. What about that article on luck you found in that magazine? Good luck is finding what works for you—that's what it was driving at."

Hal did a quick search and popped up the article on his laptop. "Yeah, this one." He scooted his chair over, and turned the screen so Cali could see it also.

"Hands on the computer, please," she ordered. "That won't help you to get lucky." She kissed him.

"Lucky is focus," Hal replied. "Always keep trying. Okay, it's these ideas. Pay attention to your surroundings; you won't spot good luck unless you look for it."

"Yeah," Cali replied, doubtfully. "Being awake is good. But awake to what?"

"Idea. Strike up conversations with strangers. You might meet the love of your life or make an important business contact."

"No love-of-life conversations," Cali declared. "Not allowed. That's already been found. Skip the conversations with wicked-looking women."

"Can't argue with that," Hal agreed, "but I'll take another kiss. Okay, back to the list of ideas"

"Idea. Vary your routine every day. Walk on the other side of the street or try a new lunch spot. Never a bad idea," Hal mused. "But if you're the kind of person who goes for new stuff, that's different from the fixed person. Maybe we put that on the job interview questions? People who vary their inputs keep more alive. I'll make a note. How about this? Be aggressive about making the changes you want. Keep thinking about moving cross-country? Just go already."

"Let's not," Cali demurred. "I don't want to pack all this stuff. And if you get any more aggressive about making changes at work, they will throw you out a window."

"Angry mobs with torches...And the wind was a torrent of darkness upon the gusty trees, the moon was a ghostly galleon tossed upon cloudy seas...running across the dark moors[9]," Hal murmured. "Yeah, that's how I want to go."

Cali studied him carefully. "See, I was right, you are really weird."

"Too many graphic novels in college. They love that stuff. Hey, if you're going to go, make it dramatic," Hal advised. "Otherwise, the people at your funeral have nothing to talk about. They get bored and go through your pockets for loose change."

"Moving on," Cali declared. "Idea. Follow your hunches and gut feelings and treat nagging doubt as alarm bells; they're often right, even if you can't pinpoint the reason."

"That's also Moscow rules," Hal added. "Never go against your gut—it's your operational antenna."

"That's critical," Cali agreed. "Remember how we detoured to look at the wall in Ann Arbor? We'd have walked into crossing rifle fire if we hadn't. Of course, my nagging doubts about your suitability as a stable, solid, providing mate had some basis, actually."

"Ah, you fell into the confirming evidence trap! We seek out information supporting our existing predictions. You made judgments based on my poor attitude in class, my failure to wash my clothes often, my unkempt hair, and my scurvy friends. Only the exterior shadows of my true self, as it turned out."

Cali eyed him doubtfully. "I reference my prior remarks, Senator."

"Perhaps we should move on here. Idea. Expect good fortune! If you think something's going to happen, you'll be more likely to spot it when it does. So you expected good things in college, and there I was," Hal asserted, ducking the roll that came flying towards him.

"Ah, sorry," Cali apologized, smiling sweetly at the couple in back of Hal.

"Not a problem," the woman laughed. "I usually throw knives." The man she was with smiled, but didn't look happy.

"You throw like a girl," Hal snickered. "Oof!" The next roll hit him in the head.

"I am a girl," Cali pointed out, "and if I get close enough, it doesn't matter how I throw."

"I'm thinking a really, really big tip might get us back into this restaurant," Hal sighed, "but I'm doubtful. Hey, and if you get close enough," moving his chair right next to Cali, "then that's when lucky starts. So how about this idea? Idea. Smile. People will smile back, and suddenly you're off to a good start."

"Or they will wonder what you've been up to—or are planning. Your smiles in class, for example, usually meant something awful was going to be said to the professor. Which wasn't a bad thing, truthfully. I used to enjoy his red-faced outbursts. Aliston tells me that when you smile, she's learned to double security because something bad is coming."

"It's going to be wall-to-wall guards there at this rate."

"So what's the concept? Intellectual, that is, please!" she protested as Hal started kissing her neck.

"What is all this really saying? That lucky is holding out your hand, and what you want drops into it, out of the confusion and noise of life. Except that lucky is a continued focus, staying out of the daily rut and paying attention to the outside world. Actually, that's probably the essence of all the little sayings—they just try and take small bites of the apple. In control is too controlled, and out of control raises opportunities. Or this: go for walks. Read a lot. Go outside your comfort zone. Stay interested. Daydream?"

"It's clear it's the anomalies," Cali agreed. "Catching the oddities— that the stories are going sideways, or a new story is opening up. First, people hate anomalies because they love their stories just the way they are, and you are already ahead of them simply by noticing the differences. Second, the anomalies do the heavy lifting of changing your focus. Notice the oddity, ask questions, and your focus moves to the problem that you didn't suspect. And it's the anomalies that the gut spots first."

"The voyage of the Starship Hal: to seek anomalies that destroy/void plans?" Hal mused. "I like that. Maybe I can get a soundtrack to go along with it? At least a guy with a saxophone to follow me around, anyhow. Where is the disaster, where could there be a disaster—and be open to those little things. It's a plan. And speaking of a plan, I have a plan, and I'm feeling lucky tonight."

"Oh, you are?" Cali teased. "Well, maybe I'm feeling lucky too. But after dinner! How about dessert?"

"I'm good with that," Hal promised. "I'll bring the whipped cream."

LISTEN TO YOUR OWN SPEECHES

Hal met with the information technology officer and his staff the next morning. He was talking about close calls, near misses, and spotting the edge problems, but the underlying goal was to get information from them to see if his ideas about splitting the companies could work, without really talking about splitting up the companies. He thought that they suspected, but were playing along. They talked for a while.

Later that day, Hal was glumly staring at his e-mail, watching the little messages flock in. That many?? I'm not sure this is really communication. He scanned through them, deleting with glee. Take that, and that! Out, damned HR! He almost deleted one from an information staff tech, thanking him for the pep talk about looking around the edges and how it had helped him catch a problem that the tech briefly outlined. It was just his luck that he'd met someone who could handle that exact problem a few days before. His boss had already taken the preliminary steps to hire the contractor.

That's nice, Hal thought. I miss the old days playing with computers.

He moved to delete the message, then stopped. But odd, that is. That's not a problem that happens on its own. As a matter of fact, I know how that problem happens because I've caused it for people. How did it get inside? He almost fired an e-mail back.

Pay attention to your surroundings; you won't spot good luck unless you look for it, that's what we went over last night. Well, among other things. So, here is someone thanking me for helping them be alert to a problem, but it's a problem that shouldn't be. They spotted, solved and moved on, but they skipped the important step. Why did it pop up? That's the vague shape looming behind the anomaly. The real story isn't that surface problem, it's whether the problem's appearance is someone maneuvering to get inside from the outside. The problem existing, as described here, means, to me, that someone got something inside already. The next step, hiring a body to solve a computer problem, means opening up the network to access, which we completely forbid, or someone waltzing in the door and putting their dirty physical hands on the keyboards. He thought for a minute.

"Aliston, do you know where this person is, physically in this building?" he asked.

"He's in this office," she replied, writing the room number on a piece of paper. "Down, deep in the bowels of the building, as far away from us as we can bury the info people. Why?"

"I had a thought."

"Worrisome, that is," Aliston smirked.

"These lunches of yours with Cali are having a subtle effect," Hal commented, shaking his head. "But I'm curious about something, and I need to ask him some questions in a casual, off-the-cuff manner. No department heads or formality. Is there any way you can see if he's there?"

"Got it," Aliston replied. She picked up the phone and started asking questions.

Hal went back into his office and examined the e-mail again, making some notes. No, he thought, that's not a problem that should be here.

"He's in," Aliston called out, "doing disgusting geek things. He's not expecting you."

"Thanks! I'll be back in a bit."

"So what is this?" she asked.

"I'm not sure if someone is getting ready to storm the castle," Hal observed. "It's odd, just a little thing."

"A mote it is to trouble the mind's eye, in the most high and palmy state of Rome[10]," Aliston quoted.

"If you see any sheeted dead, call the zombie disposal squad," Hal ordered as he walked to the elevator.

He went down, far down into the bowels of the building. He stepped out in the sub-basement. Even smells like the game shop, he sniffed, happily. He walked casually down the hallways, carefully not looking at people's screens in their offices. Why make trouble? If they are doing what they are supposed to be doing, they are probably not competent.

Hal knocked on the tech's door, gave him a moment, and then walked in. "Thanks for the e-mail," Hal told him. "It's nice to get some positive feedback. So tell me more. I'd like to use this story as an example of how things work right."

The tech, like most people, was happy to talk about what he was doing and why he needed better equipment, among other things. They talked for twenty minutes. The tech was surprised at Hal's grasp of the issues, but kept it to himself. Finally, the tech started talking about the magic help person.

"You know we don't let just anyone in the door. So, what did you think? Worthwhile? We're always looking for competent contractors," Hal asked, pretending interest in the computer display.

"Yeah they knew what they were talking about," the tech replied, "And a woman, which is really rare. Pretty voice, a teaser," the tech added, and he reddened. "Well, not many women know or care about these kinds of networks. She walked me through a temporary fix, but she insisted she needs to sit down here to work on it, since we can't open up the network."

"Really? I can understand that. Sometimes it's complex to get the problems fine-tuned. Did she have a schedule?"

"She was pretty flexible," the tech answered. "I want her in as soon as possible. Little glitches turn into big ones sometimes if they are not fixed. I'm almost afraid to have her come in—she'll be three hundred pounds and that would ruin my fantasies," he laughed.

As they were talking, several other techs wandered in. Hal had tried to keep some contact with the techs—memories of his college days. He didn't share those memories of his misspent youth with them, but he missed the hacking.

"I had a conversation with a person at a seminar a few days before about this vendor," one of the techs volunteered. "A brunette, talked with an accent. She mentioned she had used that company when she had this kind of a problem."

Hal started to ask a question, but all the techs started shouting down the hallway.

"And there he is, Mr. Lucky," they jeered as another tech wandered in.

"This guy met this blonde at a bar, two nights ago," a tech told Hal. "What a knockout! Why she'd waste her time with you, we can't imagine."

"It's my, well, disproportionate physical attributes," the tech bragged, and ducked as people threw things at him. "I don't remember much of that night. I was pretty wasted—woke up in my bed with a headache and a nice note. Lipstick in odd places, which is encouraging."

"Your fantasies are way out of control," the others scoffed.

Hal listened intently as the tech talked about how charming and knowledgeable the woman was. She understood the acronyms. "Heck, she explained some network things to me. Never met anyone like that."

Why would she be so attracted to him? Hal reflected, examining the tech. He meets her, and the problem started the next day. Hal slapped the tech on the back, congratulated him as the others laughed and quietly left.

Back in his office, he worked the puzzle backwards. Yeah, those passwords and ID would get this mystery person to X. And you could get this problem in like this, because I've done it before. I remember the time I planted that little surprise in the university network. They never did figure out how that PhD was awarded to the head cook at the dorm. They were too embarrassed to take it back, and the person became an extremely competent teacher. Who was to know?

Okay. Let's create the question map to go fishing in unknown territory. I put a topic in a center circle and then generate questions about that topic. Then I create "know" and "need to know" lists. What is it I know, and what is it I need to know? Then question the "I know" maps. He played with the lines on the paper for a while, linking things, and then sat back, thinking.

Then he walked out to Aliston's office. "If I wanted some investigation done, who would be the best?"

"About what?" she asked. "The tech?"

"Not directly," Hal answered. "But kind of."

"I'll send some people in."

An hour later, three men in nondescript suits walked into Hal's office. Aliston carefully shut the door so they could talk in complete privacy.

POKING AT THE PROBLEM

The next morning, Hal reviewed the reports from the investigators. Yeah, that's what I thought. It's what I would have done. That was my specialty at the accounting firm. So...this type of contact is next, so I need to have it routed to me. Who do I talk to in the company to arrange that? I don't want to ruffle any feathers or make people curious. He thought, and then casually walked into the information technology manager's office.

After a few minutes of the usual idle chit-chat, Hal got to the point. "I was wondering. One of the techs thanked me for alerting him to a problem, but now I'm curious about it. I don't want the tech to know of my interest, because what he did was the right thing, but there is no reason for him to stay involved in this. So when a phone call comes back from this vender that he talked to, could you pass it to me in a way that isn't obvious? And only to me, but as if I were a lowly tech?"

The managers cheerful expression faded as he connected the dots. "That blonde at the bar?"

"Who knows?" Hal commented. "Say nothing—nothing!—to that tech. Perhaps he just got lucky, but I wonder. He's done us a favor, because if it is her, she was sloppy. There are a lot of ways into any company that wouldn't be as obvious. Besides, he was off work, and we don't know if he said anything. After a few drinks, she could have gone through his computer, his wallet, who knows. Not his fault at all."

"Got it. I agree, but my predecessor would have done it differently."

"Oh, yeah, him," Hal observed. "Well, your predecessor seems preoccupied running the new office in Delhi, India. It's been a tough experience, I understand. He's been plagued by power blackouts, critical parts go missing and his staff has very poor English skills. Actually, 'poor' would imply that they speak or write English at all. It seems that there was some kind of problem with the job descriptions that HR created and once the staff was hired, well, there they were! Some kind of tax incentive or something like that, they couldn't be terminated. Sadly, it seems that he is stuck with them. On top of all that, I've heard that the air conditioning in his office isn't working, and they can't seem to get it fixed. Odd, because other buildings in the complex seem to have no problems. And the toilets didn't seem to work all that well, either. Maybe we'll have to use a different rental agent next time. Or maybe not."

"Perhaps there is justice in the world," the manager offered, trying to hide his surprise. Damn, this guy is connected! "Ah, any chance he could get dysentery too? Just want him to get the complete third-world experience, that's all."

"It's a thought," Hal replied, nodding thoughtfully. "Shit is about all he ever produced anyway."

The network administrator coughed to cut off his laugh. "I'll make sure that contact comes to you. Not a problem."

"That's wonderful! I appreciate your help." He went to walk out and then stopped at the doorway. "You've been doing good work down here. It's been noticed by the powers that be."

"Thanks," smiling as Hal vanished down the hallway. Powers that be? Powers in front of me. He carefully crafted hell on earth for my predecessor, which is pull from the very top. But he didn't push his power in my face, which is the normal corporate game. That's more worrisome, actually, because it says he doesn't have to. I'll handle this little matter he wants myself. The manager stood up and walked out of his office.

LUCRETIA SETS THE HOOK

Lucretia called the company to follow up on the computer problem she had created and to set an appointment to fix this security problem. She asked for Kyle and was on hold for a few minutes. What's wrong? her stomach churning. It went perfectly the other day. Then a new voice came on the line.

"Hi, I'm Hal," an uncertain male voice mumbled. There was a pencil tapping and pounding techno music in the background. She quickly noted that the band was an old one, faded away from most playlists.

"I'm Sally. I'd talked to Kyle," Lucretia advised. "I was able to help him temporarily fix this problem he'd been having with the network."

"Yeah," Hal replied, "he told me. It seems that, well, that area is really my problem. My little area of the world, actually, so he passed it over to me."

"So, I've got experience with this kind of problem. I can fix it if you let me log in."

"No can do," Hal replied. "Absolutely not. The powers that be cut off parts of a person's anatomy for that. Need to keep what I've got."

Such as it would be, Lucretia thought scathingly. That last geek was disappointing in so many ways. She smiled to put the perk back in her voice. "Well, if I've got to go on-site, let me check my calendar. Humm, I'm pretty busy, but this really needs to be fixed. I can open up some time tomorrow?" Lucretia offered, moving in for the close

"Well, I've got to talk to my boss," Hal whined, sounding uncertain and small. "We all have to answer to people and I've got to make sure I cover myself."

"Not a problem," Lucretia remarked, getting ready to pounce. He's perfect, she thought. "It's always good to get clearance and to stay within the rules. Especially given the extent of the security breach here. I'm surprised it hasn't been caught before. This breach actually endangers the whole company. I'd hate to be the person who was responsible for creating this if the full story came out."

"You know," Hal stammered, his voice trembling. "last week my boss told me he didn't want to be bothered with these kinds of small things. We can meet at, oh, say, ten tomorrow? I'll meet you at the front door and get you through security. I'll make sure there are no problems. Oh, and if you call back, just ask for me. There is no reason to involve others in this problem. This is just between us, okay?"

"Ten o'clock," Lucretia agreed. She could hear his pencil tapping frantically in the background. "Got it. See you then. Bye." When you close the deal, Lucretia told herself, get up and walk out.

"Hasta la vista, baby," Hal quoted to the dial tone. He smiled. Hook, line, and sinker. We see what we look for. So what did I miss? She's going where I'd go, Hal reflected. Get in here, and it's all gold after that. She'll have credentials in case things go wrong.

NEW YORK. DINNER AT THE WAREHOUSE

"I've got a situation at work," Hal complained. "One of Paul's people is making a run at the company computer system. A very bright person—actually with Coldmen Sacking. Not the person I'd use for what they seem to be after, but it is what it is."

"Who is it?" Lucifer asked, about to take a bite of spaghetti.

"Lucretia Liancol is her name. Very competent. Very cold. Very aggressive and hard driving. The alligator woman, actually."

Lucifer stopped chewing and glanced quickly at Mary.

"Alligator woman?" Cali questioned, staring at Hal. "What?"

"Oh, a couple of years ago, a delegation from Coldmen Sacking flew down to a meeting with Don Cortes at his hacienda in the mountains. In their wisdom, the Coldmen Sacking people managed to have lost most of the money he had invested with them. They went to the meeting, not to express any remorse about the losses, but with the express intention of asking for more money."

"That showed nerve," Cali admitted.

"They made a slight error of judgment," Hal laughed. "They read that mark completely wrong. Rumor has it that Don Cortes pointed out to them that they had stolen his money through a set of slick paper transactions, and that stealing from drug lords was different than stealing from pension funds. He gave them a brief but cogent explanation on how to accurately assess risks, and then he fed them to the alligators, one by one, to emphasize the point. I heard it was quite the scene, the investment people screaming and his men laughing and placing bets. Lucretia, rumor has it, was brought to the meeting to be the sacrificial lamb/blonde play-toy, and it turned out that she was the only one who came back. It's reported that she stood there, laughing and cursing the Coldmen Sacking partner as he was chewed up, and then she killed one of Don Cortes' thugs when he insulted her. Finally she essentially told Don Cortes to go to hell and throw her in if he wanted to. He liked her attitude, and when she figured out how to get all his money back they became fast friends. The firm gave her all of the cartel's financial work after she came back, as well as a promotion to senior partner. And there are rumors that money from various Catholic Church funds were assigned to her as investment manager."

"And she's Paul's servant," Lucifer added. "She took the chalice—well, what they have, anyhow—and lived. The first in a long time. She's tough. But she's an outsider to them, so she has to prove herself. They recently had a large gathering at Paul's chateau, and she was introduced to him then. Her taking a run at our company has to be Paul's direct order, as a test. He knows that it's been done over and over with no results. Usually the person doesn't come back, actually." He sipped his coffee. "Well, not as neatly assembled as they went in, anyhow. Odd that he'd waste a person of her talents on a job like this."

"Maybe that's what she deserves," Cali snapped. "Sounds like she'd be better in the water with the alligators—heck, she's one herself."

"There's something you should know," Mary commented. "She has never married, but she has two children."

"What does she do?" Cali snickered. "Eat the men like a black widow spider after mating?"

"People have hard lives sometimes," Mary mused. "Her son's father was your adopted brother, Jose."

Cali gasped. "He had a girlfriend in college. I remember that it ended badly. He was angry and he never wanted to talk about it. But I know he never said anything about a child."

"She never told him," Mary replied. "She's a strong woman, determined and proud."

"What would that be like? Gosh, I don't know any of those," Hal observed, carefully stirring his coffee. He smiled to himself as he ignored the withering looks directed at him.

"Can I contact her?" Cali exclaimed. "She is family, and I didn't think I had any of that family left."

"She is, as they would say, a servant of the enemy. If they knew that you are connected to her son, it would be bad for her—and for the boy," Mary advised. "Very bad. They'd use him as bait, or worse. And I heard there were some blood tests ordered, as Paul is suspicious of something about her. So any connection to us would be a sudden death for her and her family. It's bad enough that she's a woman, which is probably why Paul gave her this impossible task. Paul doesn't like women as part of the group. He's still Xerxes at heart."

"Her other child was fathered by Don Cortes," Lucifer added. "A little girl. That one will be strong minded! Lucretia's mother stays with her and helps raise the children. You can't imagine the hard life she has had. Her father divorced her mother, threw her out. He was a powerful, vengeful man, and forced the mother to whore to make a living. Lucretia grew up as the oldest daughter of the village whore, protecting her mother, her sisters, and herself. She fought her way out, went to Harvard, rose to the top. She doesn't know the meaning of surrender."

"Her mother lives with her?" Cali wondered. "Having lived that kind of a life? People usually try and, well, distance themselves."

"Not Lucretia!" Lucifer countered. "Lucretia is fiercely protective of her mother. She stood up to Mother Superior, in fact, defending her."

"You're kidding," Mary gasped. "I hadn't heard that story. And she lived— that's what's unusual."

"Who is Mother Superior?" Cali asked.

"More of a 'what,' actually. Another servant of Paul's," Mary answered. "A vicious serpent of a woman. An ancient priestess who still prefers live sacrifices. Very tough."

"Are there any of these people you know who are close to what we used to believe were normal human personalities?" Cali blurted out.

"Not really," Lucifer replied. "These are ancient people, from hard times. They're Old Testament people, and they like it that way. I grant that there was a certain simplicity and clarity to the old methods."

"Well, all that makes it damn near impossible," Hal protested. "So I can't just trap her and have her arrested. I can't let her get information on the company—she's too competent for that. And I can't stop her cold, because her people will turn on her, and she's family."

"All you have to do, honey, is draw her in, trap her, tell her that she's family, and then let her go with enough information to protect her from her people," Cali bubbled. "Burn and Turn. Piece of cake."

"Chocolate with white frosting?" Hal inquired. "And your feminine intuition tells you how I should do this balancing act, maneuvering between precipices every second?" He looked glum. "Playing people games is not really my thing. And burning is always a hazard. Some people get heroic and others roll over immediately. Burning can bring out the stubbornness in people."

"Let me think," Cali admitted. "Mary, Goth, and I can talk. What's she trying to do, actually?"

"It's classic social engineering. Competent work, not excellent. A bit rushed, actually, now that I think about it. A rigid, textbook approach, not being very creative. She's pretending to be people, collecting passwords and names, trying to worm her way in. She went to a seminar in disguise. Met some of our people, later showed up as a blonde at a bar. Rumored seduction, but I tend to discount the source. Not that he wouldn't have been agreeable. I suspect the tech drank too much, passed out, and she went through his apartment. She planted a toy, probably on his ID, and now is the magic solution to this problem that popped up. She tried very hard to get something she could access online, but I forced her to come into the building, where I can control events. She's meeting with me in my disguise as a lowly tech."

"I always thought the rising corporate executive was the disguise," Cali commented, "but that's just the wife in me talking."

"No man is a hero to his wife," Hal sighed. "Even the winged shoes I put on in the morning to fly to the office don't impress her."

"Focus, people," Lucifer ordered. "I agree completely with Cali's plan. We will need to block her communications. If I know Paul, he's tapping everything she does. He just enjoys that kind of thing. So we need her in the building, those transmissions cut off, and controlled. She's very bright and competent and would be a major asset for us if you could turn her."

"Sounds good," Cali replied. "We'll think about the social mechanics and get back to you."

"She's coming in at ten tomorrow. She's charging in like a bull, so we have little time to plan. She is obviously under pressure-her reputation is formidable, and she should be more competent than this. She's showing all the signs of a facing a deadline, and people don't think as clearly at the margins then. They freeze, stick with a pattern."

"Knowing Paul, I'd say a 'deadline' is an accurate description," Mary pointed out.

"'Hence the skillful fighter puts himself into a position that makes defeat impossible, and does not miss the moment for defeating the enemy,'" Hal quoted. "We have her coming to our office, under our control. We know her game, and we believe she does not know our game. Check there. Pithy saying two: 'Thus it is in war the victorious strategist only seeks battle after the victory has been won, whereas he who is destined to defeat first fights and afterwards looks for victory.' That's your part, Cali, to figure out the strategy once I spring the trap. *The Art of War* was a great comic book, full of busty Asian wenches carrying swords," Hal offered, noting Cali's skeptical look. "So tell me, my beautiful and all-knowing consort, what is the Empress's plan under heaven for victory? Guide me into the mysteries of the female psyche, I pray you."

"Beseech me," Cali teased. "I love that part."

"That requires...well, a private discussion," Hal grinned. "Later?"

"Opportunities multiply as they are seized," Lucifer laughed.

"Better you use a Chinese accent, my lord Sun Tzu," Mary remarked. "We girls will talk, and come up with ideas."

"I really do need help with this," Hal admitted, frowning. "I have a pretty good idea of the known knows, and known unknowns. I don't know the unknown unknowns, such as how much pressure she is under and exactly what she has to bring back to be a success—or at least survive. Calculating people's emotions and drives by their actions is really a projection of our selves into them. The greatest danger we have in dealing with her isn't our ignorance, it's our illusion of knowledge; what we think she thinks we think, and so on."

"And to think you got through college reading comic books," Cali sighed. "There is no hope for the educational system. Mary, Goth, and I will talk and come back with ideas."

She looked at the table for a minute, drawing little diagrams with her finger. "Oh, and let's not have any kids popping up like Jose's just did," she announced, smiling sweetly at Hal.

"You know, a guy forces himself to go through the grinding boredom of mating with some busty tramp, suffering through cheap hotel rooms and bad booze, just trying to save his beloved the rigors of pregnancy and the pain of labor. But does a guy get any thanks? Not a chance," Hal complained.

Mary laughed out loud, and Lucifer snickered at Cali's expression.

"No sale," Cali declared.

A GIFT

Lucretia was sitting in her office, going over her notes.

"How kind of you to come by," Lucretia declared to Mother Superior, who walked past Lucretia's temporary secretary without any acknowledgement of the woman's existence. Mother Superior closed the door and sat down across from Lucretia.

"I understand you took my advice," Mother Superior laughed. "Men are such easy marks. Good. You are resourceful and committed. I was glad to see it."

Lucretia was shocked for a moment. Watched, all the time. Dominique had told her so. "I bowed to your knowledge of the world," Lucretia admitted. "And it helped."

"I wouldn't say bowed—maybe more like knelt," Mother Superior observed. "Remember, you have five days, my dear. I'm eagerly looking forward to positive results. First, it would show your ability, and as I recommended you, it would reflect well on me. Secondly, and this is just between us, Paul really has contempt for women. It would be nice to have a woman show him up and do something that all the men he sent couldn't do."

"There's a lot of that attitude out there," Lucretia observed. "People seem to have lost their perspective on the whole sitting versus standing to pee issue."

"Yes, but like most things about Paul, it's more serious. And Paul doesn't like something about you. He's been checking into your family history. He's like that."

"I should have been nice to his son," Lucretia mused. "But Cesare is just an asshole."

"Your opinion of his son shows judgment and taste. Even Paul doesn't trust Cesare. However, Cesare would be the first to volunteer to discuss your failure with you if this doesn't work out well."

"There's a cheerful thought. I was worried I'd have to date him."

Mother Superior stood up and walked to the windows. Facing the windows, she asked, "Do you like the substitute secretary?" She turned around with a strange look of excitement on her face, examining Lucretia.

"She seems competent," Lucretia answered, puzzled. "My regular secretary went out of town? I didn't get a clear story."

"Your regular secretary was a noisy fool," Mother Superior sneered. "She hated you and slandered you at every opportunity. She has moved, actually, to another state. Of existence. Treat it as a favor to you if you succeed, and a warning if you do not. Well, you have important things to do, my child, so I'll leave." She stood up and walked to the door, pausing with her hand on the handle. "I can send you the recording of your secretary's, ah, transfiguration, if you should want. Quite entertaining. My work is quality, from long practice. Give it some thought." She smiled and walked out.

Lucretia sat, stunned. I hated that bitch, she thought, but killing her? They'll probably find my jewelry next to body. That would be the way Mother Superior works. I have learned from them, she realized. We shall double our efforts, Lord Vader! I don't want the Emperor showing up unhappy. Forgiving, I am sure he is not.

That night, Lucretia sat at home, playing a game with her son. She hummed "You Were Mine for the Taking," reminiscing about Jose in college as she looked at her son. She was happy for a moment and then sadly wondered how it went so wrong.

Her mother understood her look and walked over, putting her arm around Lucretia. Lucretia rested her head on her mother's shoulder as she held her son.

10:00, AT THE CORPORATION HEADQUARTERS.

Hal met Lucretia at the main building entrance. There was a little confusion with security and Lucretia's heart went into her throat for a moment, but then the disgusted guards waved her through, contemptuously telling Hal that he should learn something about the way the company operated. The security guards continued their sarcastic remarks about Hal and geeks in general as he walked Lucretia to the elevators.

"It's down into the bowels of the building," Hal warned her, pushing the button for the sub sub-basement.

Figures, Lucretia thought. I just hope it doesn't smell.

The elevator opened to a worn hallway. It smells, she thought. Of course it would.

They walked down the hall, past messy offices with geeky guys staring at multiple computer monitors. Lucretia noticed some images on the displays that definitely were not work related, and quickly looked away.

Finally, they reached Hal's office. It was the farthest down the hallway from the elevator, near a humming closet of equipment.

"Home, such as it is," Hal laughed, waving at the office and sitting down. "Oh, you can sit here." He quickly picked up a pile of papers from the only other chair.

Lucretia noticed that there seemed to be pictures in the pile and looked away again. Dirty. My skin is puckering up just standing here. Please tell me that chair doesn't have anything awful on it. I won't look. She sat down, smiling at Hal.

Several of the geeks had followed them and were joking with Hal, trying to get Lucretia to respond to them. Hal shooed them out, and they stood down the hallway, making jokes. Hal finally closed the door.

"Sorry," Hal apologized. "They don't see many real women. We don't monitor the network down here because, well, we don't want to know what they are thinking. Hormones raging, I'm afraid."

Lucretia had carefully dressed down, her hair a dark red, and she wore thick-lensed, black, round glasses. What if they connect me with the blonde? she had worried. But given that none of them ever looked above my bust line, this should work.

Hal sat in his chair and awkwardly smiled at her. "So, Sally, you are an expert in this problem? This is really embarrassing for me! I've got to tell you that my position in the company would be in danger if, well, certain people knew about this. So I appreciate you coming by. Can you fix this thing?" Hal smiled nervously, tapping furiously on his desk.

"I need to input into the system." Don't be too eager, she thought, but I can't have him type for me.

"Got it," he quickly logged in. "Here, you pull up to the keyboard." He pushed his chair back.

Lucretia maneuvered her chair so she was in front of the keyboard and started typing, Cheerfully bantering with Hal, and subtly letting her blouse slip down as she bent over the keyboard, she was confident he would notice nothing-at least nothing that she was doing on his computer.

After fifteen minutes, the problem seemed to have been eliminated. At the same time, certain information was transferred to various places without Hal seeming to have noticed. And she knew how to install surprises onto the network, if she could just have a few moments alone with the machine. She was very happy—happy enough to be nice to the geek.

"This is great!" Hal exclaimed, leaning over to look at the screen. "Really great." He let his eyes drop to her blouse. "Ah, you told me you needed to run some confirmation tests. While you're doing that, I'll check on that other information you asked about. I don't have the security clearance for that, but I'll see if I can get you to someone higher up." He rested his hand on her shoulder. "Ah, remember that this problem is, well, it's our little secret." He winked at her, and then he wandered out.

Lucretia nodded, and waited until he was gone to choke back a laugh. That wink! It wouldn't have worked in the sixth grade. Geeks. She pulled her blouse back up to a more respectable level. *He'll probably be in the bathroom for a few minutes amusing himself. Still, if I could get to that information, it would be incredible. What I've grabbed is great, but that's the key to what is really hidden. Why is it that they never suspect women?* She looked at her credentials quickly. *Okay, what's the backup if it goes south? Always be prepared—the Girl Scout motto.*

"Let's get going," she murmured. She'd taped him typing his higher level password, a camera in the brooch slightly above her left breast. *No male is going to stare long enough at that,* she snickered, *to catch the camera in it. They are so easy. So, here's a toy.* She held the flash drive. *Hmmm,* she thought, studying the computer. *Nice, easy inputs? That's odd for the tight security they have. Maybe if you get this far in, they don't worry as much?* She pushed the drive in and started typing.

How thoughtful! He even has a compiler program on this machine. It's possible to create a backdoor without modifying the source code of a program. So I can recompile this little program after changing the computer's date to something less obvious. Then the new code just hides in there until I call it. Fun and games. The backdoor pops up, and into the system I go. And it's a program they won't pay a lot of attention to, but is actually the key to the whole system. Nice. Technically, it's computationally intractable to detect the presence of an asymmetric backdoor—too much computer time required—so it's safe that way, too. She hummed cheerfully to herself as she typed. The actual changes took only a couple of minutes. She carefully logged out, and then sat, waiting for Hal to return. Almost ten minutes went by. She had started to examine the office, and after a few minutes decided she really didn't want to know any more about his life than she already did. *Where did he get those magazines? I had understood that disgusting bookshops were all out of business in the modern world.*

"Hi," Hal stammered. He was obviously drying his hands off on a paper towel as he walked in, which he then dropped in the wastebasket.

Lucretia cringed, willing her mind to not go there.

"I talked to the powers that be, and you get to meet with more important people than me. Here, it's down this hallway."

Lucretia stood up, and he touched her arm for a second with his still-damp hand. She almost flinched away, but caught herself.

They went back down the dirty hallway and waited for the elevator. She ignored the heads poking out of the offices, watching her. *Where's my whack-a-mole hammer?* she thought, flexing her fingers.

"Only a few elevators come down this far," Hal apologized. "Sorry it's so slow." Finally, one came, and it took them to the fifteenth floor. They stepped out into a beautiful hallway with marble floors and wood-paneled walls. An astonishingly beautiful woman greeted them, perfectly dressed and made up, who looked at Hal with, well...disdain is too light a word, Lucretia realized—perhaps total contempt wasn't even strong enough. Lucretia agreed with her, thinking that the woman didn't even know about the pictures in his office. That office, ugh. Lucretia floated off for a second, dreaming about the bath she would soon take to wash off the stain of being in the same room with Hal for forty-five minutes.

"Would you please come with me?" the beautiful woman asked Lucretia, smiling cheerfully. "Not you," she snarled at Hal. "You, back to your lair!" She turned back to Lucretia, pretending Hal didn't exist. "Please," gesturing to Lucretia, "this way."

Lucretia caught a glimpse of Hal in the mirrored doors as he slumped into the elevator, looking out of place and lost.

"Geeks," Lucretia sniffed.

"Can't live with them, can't shoot them," the beautiful woman sighed. They chatted as they walked down the hallway, and then the woman showed Lucretia into a large executive office.

"The director of information security will meet with you in a few minutes. Please, have a seat. Can I bring you a coffee, Coke, or water?"

"Water would be good. Can I sit over here, at that table?"

"Make yourself comfortable, please. I'll be back with your water in a minute."

Lucretia sat down and gazed out at the wonderful view over Central Park. This location, this view? This is serious money!

A MEETING ON THE 15TH FLOOR

She heard the door open and turned, expecting to see the woman with her water. Shocked, she stood, her mouth hanging open as she saw Hal walk in, carrying her water, wearing a tailored English suit. The beautiful woman walked behind him, no longer smiling at Lucretia.

"Hi, Lucretia, here is your water. No? I'll just put it on the desk here."

She stood, frozen.

"Genuine Swiss bottled water," Hal added. "Fresh from the mountains. I understand this is a favorite around Lake Lucerne."

Lucretia held her purse like a shield, her hands shaking just a bit.

"Miss McGowan is ex-Israeli intelligence," Hal advised. "Her father was Scotch, so don't be confused by the name. She worked for their counterintelligence. I'd not care to argue with her, and while you are many wonderful things, you'd not wish to argue with her either. And some of Paul's people hurt her family, so she doesn't like Paul or his associates."

"I wish to speak to my lawyer," Lucretia stammered, trying to control her voice.

Hal sat down behind his desk, ignoring Lucretia's comment, and quietly organized some papers. He opened a notebook and looked at a page intently, writing for a moment.

Lucretia stared at Hal and then glanced around, taking inventory of the room. The secretary, without being obvious, had positioned herself between the door and Lucretia. And there were suddenly two people in the doorway—a man in a suit and a woman in a blue jacket and skirt who were clearly not office staff. Hands in pockets and purses, at the ready, Lucretia numbly concluded. What had Paul mentioned about people being returned disassembled?

"Please, sit," Hal asked Lucretia, motioning to the chair.

Lucretia looked at him, bit her lip, and sat down in the chair in front of his desk.

"You are Lucretia Liancol, a senior partner in the investment firm Coldmen Sacking?" Hal stated, in a calm, bored voice. He didn't look at her, but picked up a piece of paper from his desk, examined it, and put the paper in his notebook.

Lucretia said nothing, trying to keep her mouth angry, but her lips twisted out of her control. She clamped them shut.

"Yes?" Hal inquired, glancing at Lucretia for a moment and then looking back down at the notebook, bored.

"I am Sally Eastblock," Lucretia snapped, breathing carefully, projecting control. "I believe that you have mistaken me for someone else. I am being held here against my will and I will file a report with the police, unless you allow to leave immediately."

"My information has been carefully checked," Hal commented, as if the questions were merely a formality and Lucretia's responses of little consequence.

"Who are you?" Lucretia hissed. "You think you are a commissar? You have no power over me! I have important business this afternoon and you will make me late."

Hal slowly turned the pages in his notebook, indifferent to Lucretia's angry response.

"Ms. Liancol, I must ask you to study the photographs that I am going to lay on the table."

"Photographs? Why should I study any photographs?" Lucretia demanded, her rage mixed with panic.

Hal, ignoring her outburst, calmly stood and then walked slowly to the table, carefully laying out the photographs, his back to her, paying no attention to her.

"I demand to telephone my attorney and the police immediately!" Lucretia shouted, her voice starting to break.

"I would suggest that it would be in your best interest to review these photographs first. Afterwards, you are free to telephone anyone you want. If you could start at the left, please, as they are arranged left to right." Hal gestured to show the progression and stepped back, wordlessly waiting for her. "Please."

Lucretia stood up, straightened her skirt, and then forced herself to walk to the table, head up and shoulders back. She bent her head over the photographs.

First, a photograph of Lucretia at the seminar, a brunette sparrow in big glasses and a serious suit, talking to the techs.

Next, a photograph of Lucretia at the bar, bright blonde in a blazing red dress, laughing with the techs. A smaller picture, paper clipped to the larger picture, showing her leaving with the lucky tech.

The New York Identification provided to the security guard at the door when she entered the office building earlier.

Several photographs from a recent financial magazine profiling her as a rising star at Coldmen Sacking, a rare woman in a man's world.

A photograph of Lucretia typing on the computer after Hal had left the room. Next to the photograph was a transcript of the keystrokes.

A photograph of two men watching her walk into the office building, taken from behind her. Paul's men, she thought.

Finally, a picture of Lucretia, her mother, and her children in the park, with two men circled in the background. The same men who had followed her to the office building.

Hal had mentally arranged the pictures while waiting outside his office in the sub-basement when Lucretia was sitting inside, typing frantically into Hal's computer. He had imagined, trying to see them in Lucretia's mind, a cascading succession of disasters. Her whole plan revealed, the contradictory identities and documents sticking to her like glue, deny them away as she might. And finally, her family, all that she had to lose, along with proof that Paul was watching them, his hand outstretched to grab them at any moment.

A blackmailed person is any of us caught, desperately struggling in the jaws of the trap, Hal mused as he watched Lucretia stand stiffly before the table. She slowly moved from picture to picture, touching them for a second and then pushing them away as if that would make them vanish. She is not merely a person found out, Hal knew. Her vision of her life, her goals, had suddenly imploded. She will be a public failure, a fool for all to see. Worst: her family, all that she cared about, facing the fate she had done everything she could to guard them from. And she stood tall, looking carefully at the pictures. She's tough.

Lucretia stood, staring at the picture in the park, her eyes flickering back and forth to the picture of her walking into the building, testing that the men were the same men.

"Please, sit," Hal asked, carefully and calmly. "Please."

Lucretia came out of her nightmare with a start and stared at Hal for a moment as he motioned for her to sit. Then she walked back to her chair and sat down.

"Please consider the effect these photographs, transcripts and the related documents that would accompany them would have on your world. First, on state and federal authorities. Forgery of official identification documents; theft of intellectual secrets; planting a computer virus; destruction of computer code and programs. Seriously illegal acts under state and federal statutes. Felonies. Then, because you are a partner in an investment firm, holding several federal licenses, your actions are separate crimes under the statutes that control those licenses." Hal never looked up at her, reading in a dull voice. He stopped for a minute and made a note on the page.

"Then, at your investment firm. You would be dismissed immediately, your pension and other benefits forfeited. Your financial life destroyed, your assets frozen. Your reputation destroyed, and all the people who had hailed you would be the first to throw stones or other materials," Hal continued, still bored, not looking at her.

"But," Hal advised, lifting his eyes from his notebook for a moment to study Lucretia, and then looking back down at his notebook, "we have the effect of these photographs on your real employer. Paul had his watchers follow you to this office today, as you can see in the photographs. Paul seems to have misrepresented to you some of what little they knew about our security and operating procedures, which is interesting. And, as we know, his penalty for failure is quick and absolute."

Lucretia's shoulders slumped despite herself, and she looked at the floor, her hands twisting.

"May I ask what time you told your staff that you would be done with the work at our office?" Hal inquired, without looking at her. His voice and manner was that of the relentless bureaucratic messenger of the inevitable, an officious steamroller looming over her.

Lucretia could no longer sit still. She jumped up and quickly looked around. The secretary moved slightly and the two guards at the door tensed. Lucretia slumped, and sat down. "I anticipated being back by two, but my schedule was not fixed." With that statement, she surrendered. They have me, she knew. If it weren't for my family, I'd be safer with them. Or if they just kill me, as Paul remarked they did to the others before me, my family will get the insurance money, I hope.

"So, do you still wish to speak to your lawyer?" Hal inquired. "Perhaps we can just talk for a few minutes? Perhaps we can find a solution to this problem that we both can live with."

Lucretia forced a smile. "I'm always willing to talk. A woman's life in these parts often depends on a mere scrap of information."

"I always loved that movie," Hal replied, abandoning the dull tone of voice. "The man with no name, always watching for anomalies. It's what isn't quite right but looks right that tells you more than anything else about where the problems are. You have to think, ask yourself where disasters could come from, not sit and wait for them. It's hard to do, and actually, results tend to be somewhat accidental. My catching you, for example, was somewhat random. What you did was good work. A bit rushed, a bit too structured, but good work."

"That's good to know," Lucretia sighed. "I'll think about that in jail."

"Let's talk," Hal offered. "Miss McGowan, if you could give us a moment?" The woman smiled pleasantly at Hal and nodded, then gave Lucretia a different smile, a toothy smile of predator spotting prey, and then walked out, closing the door behind her.

"She's really quite vicious," Hal remarked casually. "I've heard stories."

"So cut the crap!" Lucretia snarled.

"That's what I thought you'd say." Hal leaned back against the desk. "This corporate formal politeness is a nuisance. Look, I recognized the toy you planted the other day, and I set this trap. You waltzed right in under false pretenses after having planted the bug that caused the problem you just fixed. It was just your bad luck that the bug created a problem that I'd done to others. You grabbed a bunch of information in our little session downstairs and opened a nice back door into the network. I was impressed. It was good, competent work, done right in front of me, and I'd not have noticed except I knew what you would do, because it was what I would have done. Now, I did lock that computer and you away from the real network, because you may be trickier than I anticipated. One should never underestimate your opponent, a rule I try to remember."

He stood up and walked over to the window. "It was, of course, hopelessly illegal. All videotaped, keystrokes recorded and then there is the flash drive in your purse that you used while I was outside the office. Desperate times require desperate measures, but there are downsides."

"So are you calling the police?" Lucretia demanded, sitting up straight. "Then I am demanding to speak to my attorney immediately!"

"No, I'm not calling the police," Hal answered, leaning against the conference table and studying her. "No attorneys, and I know you are bluffing anyhow. You don't want your people to know about this because they are serious people who treat failure as moral weakness. Their penalty for moral weakness is death, I know-I've dealt with them before. And you really can't leave without my permission, because Miss McGowan is waiting outside with friends."

"Then, what?" Lucretia mumbled, slumping. "Do you kill me here?"

"No. Far from it, actually. No, we have a situation here that I only just discovered the other day. You will find it a surprise, I can promise."

"And it would be?" Lucretia blurted out, frantically trying to connect the dots.

"More pictures, I'm afraid." He opened a folder and pulled out a large picture, which he handed to Lucretia. "He was my wife's brother," Hal murmured sadly. "Well, technically, her adopted brother."

Lucretia stared at the completely unexpected picture of Jose standing on the beach with Cali, alive, happy, and smiling. She held the picture in her trembling hands, gaping at it.

"Here is Cali now, with our daughter." He handed another picture to Lucretia. Lucretia stared blankly at the pictures for a moment and then she put her head on the table and cried.

Hal looked away, not really sure what to do or say. Under conditions of complete uncertainty, he told himself, sit and shut up.

"Here I am crying," Lucretia apologized, after a few minutes had passed. She quickly dabbed at her face, grimacing at the mess on the tissues. "You must think I'm just a weak little woman."

"Not a bit. The female is the more dangerous of the species, but please don't tell Cali I said that. She has a temper. And there is no weapon as dangerous as a woman's tears."

"I remember Jose talking about his sister," Lucretia murmured, half to herself. "He loved her, told me how sweet she was, except when she was angry. And then, even he was afraid of her! And he was afraid of nothing."

"Look," Hal declared. "I'm really not good at all this intrigue, which is probably your conclusion anyhow. I know that your son's father was Jose. Cali didn't know until a few days ago. She wanted to see you and your son, but I told her how dangerous that would be. You agree?"

Lucretia nodded yes.

"Now, it gets more complex," Hal grimaced.

"That's really not possible, is it?" Lucretia exclaimed, despairingly.

"Au contraire, mon ami," Hal countered, shaking his head. "I can hardly follow all this myself. You see, a while ago, Cali's real mother, Mary, was kidnapped by Don Cortes. I know Don Cortes is the father of your daughter. Mary killed Don Cortes in a duel, a fair fight. I helped with the organization and the structure of the attack, so I'm at least partly responsible, and I have no regrets, because the alternative was Mary's death. There was no choice, and it was not a battle I started, but I was there. So you'll have to decide how you want to deal with that. So, yes, I'm family to you, but I also helped kill someone close to you, who would have killed family. People who are actually family to you also."

Lucretia stared blankly at him, flashes of anger and amazement going over her face, and then she looked away, gazing out the window, her lips moving wordlessly.

They sat silently for ten minutes.

"The people watching you are going to wonder where you are. They will want to know what happened all this time, and you need to have a cover story. They are not the trusting type."

"How do you know all this?" Lucretia complained, confused. He can't know that much, she thought. Is he watching me too? Why not just put my sad excuse for a life on cable?

"Your people are watching you. There was a team monitoring you on the way down—that picture on the table—and there will be one on the way back. I'm afraid it isn't the nature of Paul to trust. He verifies instead. You may have had an inkling that they were watching, but no real idea of the extent. Everything you do, everywhere you go, is broadcast on your phone, all the time. If I were you, I'd flush the toilet really loud from now on."

"Who are you?" Lucretia shouted, standing up, facing Hal with her fists doubled. "What do you want with me?"

The door quickly opened and Miss McGowan stood there, poised for action with a cane in her hand.

"It's okay," Hal told her and the door closed again.

Hal studied Lucretia for a moment. "I am a person who respects you, Lucretia. And your people would not think we should be friends. I, ah, pretty much destroyed their computer network a couple of years ago and took a bunch of their money."

"You!" Lucretia yelled. "Now I remember you. And your girlfriend? She's Jose's sister?"

"Adopted sister," Hal answered. "She didn't know she was adopted until everything fell apart. Until just before Don Cortes ordered Jose and his parents killed. Cali was to have been killed, too, except that fate intervened. You didn't know that?"

Lucretia sat, staring open-mouthed at Hal, shocked and frozen. She looked down at her hands because she had to focus on something.

Hal pulled a flash drive from the pocket of his suit coat. "This has a lot of very good, valuable information on it. Now, it's dross, really. It isn't gold. But your people will think it's gold, and they will be very happy with you. It's far better than anything they have ever captured on this company. Only you and I know it is dross."

Hal put the flash drive on the table near Lucretia, and then he walked over to the windows.

"All the activity downstairs has been erased—it just never happened. No recordings, no keystrokes, no nothing. The back door into the network is still there because you might need to show people you set it up. It won't go far, and is actually a reverse trap. If you open it, it will pull information from the network you are attached to, but your people won't know that. I used to love that kind of game in college," Hal sighed wistfully.

Hal turned to her. "So, you can walk out of here anytime. You can take the flash drive that you made downstairs and represent that you got bits and pieces, and couldn't get more. You walk out of here and take your chances with Paul. Or, you can take the flash drive on the table and your people will think you got gold. The first person to do that, actually. As I understand it, the first one to leave walking, also. The others left in pieces, I'm told. All that was before my time. I'd bet you can come up with a good reason why you can't go back into this company again, that the bridges were burned. Now, you know that if you take my flash drive, you and I are partners. At least, your people would think that if they knew. I could force us to be partners, but as you are family, it seems inappropriate. Besides, you are a brilliant person, and I don't want to worry about you plotting against me. I'd like your friendship, odd as that may seem."

Lucretia was still staring at her hands, which were twisting in her lap.

"Tell you what," Hal offered. "I'll have Miss McGowan's makeup assistant come in and fix you back to normal."

Lucretia glanced up at Hal, puzzled.

"Yeah, she has her own makeup assistant. She's actually the personal secretary for Francisco d'Plata. You walked into far more than you anticipated. Paul suspected all this, and they still let you come. Nice people you work for! They value you highly."

Hal left and a young woman bustled into the office. In a few minutes, Lucretia was restored to a state of radiant beauty.

Hal walked back in. "Wow," he commented. "That's wonderful work."

"And you don't say anything," the woman ordered, wagging her finger. "I don't want this damaged."

Hal smiled and the woman walked out.

"It's been a pleasure meeting with you," Hal observed.

Lucretia grimaced. "Thank you for having me. It's been wonderful being had."

Hal laughed. "I like that. Oh, here is your phone," handing it back to her. "I practice my pickpocket skills occasionally." He smiled. "I took the liberty of putting an application on there. Should you wish, you can call me and it can't be traced. So if you ever need to get ahold of me, there it is. Once we are done here, security will escort you out of the building as an honored contract worker. Oh, and the windows are tinted from the outside. No one could see you standing there looking out. I just thought you'd want to know."

Lucretia sat dazed, her emotions running wild. Finally, she fought her emotions down and smiled at him. "Well, it's nice to know there is family out there. Unexpected, this is."

"Yoda, this is a good look you have now. I'd keep it. But you don't know the power of the dark side," Hal laughed. Then his smile vanished. "You will, though, if you don't get back out there soon and have a good story when your people show up. Oh, speaking of that—here's a plastic bag to put that flash drive in." He noticed Lucretia's sudden look of contempt.

"This was suggested by Cali, who pointed out that your people are not going to just believe you waltzed out of here with a flash drive in your purse," Hal added. "I have a dirty mind, which is a source of great comfort to me, but this didn't occur to me. It's more technical than dirty, actually."

"Thoughtful," Lucretia snapped. "I may have made some plans myself, but thoughtful."

"Well, this conversation is rapidly going downhill. Let's move back to a higher plane. Ah...there are some people I want you to meet, as long as you are my guest. Here, I'll go and bring them in."

Hal walked out, giving Lucretia a moment to compose herself, and then Hal came back in with two men. One man was older, with salt-and-pepper hair and bright blue eyes, and the other was a little younger, perhaps forty. "This is Sir Jonathan," indicating the older man. "He has a significant ownership interest in the firm. Your investigations didn't show that, I know—it's rather carefully hidden. And this is Francisco d'Plata, president of Groupe Heroico GmbH."

Lucretia stared at them for a second, astonished. "I'm sorry," she mumbled, shaking her head. "I forget my manners." She stood up and shook hands, smiling.

They talked for a few minutes, saying the usual polite things, and then Sir Jonathan and Francisco d'Plata excused themselves.

"So, that's it," Hal remarked. "Oh, and I've given you something important. Your people don't know I'm here, doing all this. They have no good feelings for me. Actually, that isn't completely true. They would love to have me roasted in a wine sauce. So the exchange hasn't been all one way.

You now have information on me that Paul would desperately like to know."

Lucretia glanced at him, and then stared down at the floor. She bitterly muttered, "How can you trust me? You know I work for Paul, that I've deceived, lied, and tricked my way in here to damage you."

"What are a few felonies between family?" Hal smiled. "That would be small minded of me."

Lucretia laughed. "I didn't think I'd ever laugh again," she admitted, shaking her head.

"One of my favorite Monty Python scenes was in the Holy Grail, where, after Lancelot has killed half of the wedding party, the father of the groom introduces him to the angry crowd. "Please, please! This is supposed to be a happy occasion! Let's not bicker about who killed who."

Lucretia laughed again. "I'd forgotten that. Paul's people don't seem to like Monty Python, for some reason."

"If that isn't a sign you're on the wrong side, I don't know what would be," Hal replied. "But you need to go back to your world now."

Lucretia nodded quickly and started to walk out. She stopped, took a couple of deep breaths, and then said to the wall, "Perhaps Cali could see my son sometime."

"That would mean a great deal to her. But the risk to you, and to your son, would be enormous. Perhaps someday? Your people would NOT be happy to find out that you are related to her. Not a bit. You know what they would do."

"Hal," Lucretia declared, turning to look at him. "Ah, they have people in your company. This is what they told me." She went over the little that she had been told. "It isn't much, but I thought you should know."

"Thanks! You didn't have to do that and I appreciate it. And that's enough to back into who they are. That is a gift."

Lucretia smiled, and then walked out.

Hal sat down behind his desk and absently gazed out the window for a few minutes.

Francisco d'Plata and Lucifer walked in and sat down.

"So, thoughts?" Hal asked.

"She's good," Francisco d'Plata admitted. "That was a lot to dump on her at once."

Sir Jonathan stared out the window, his face hard, not noticed by the others.

"She had little choice, I'd say. She had a clear deadline, and with them it is a 'dead' line. Do and win, or die—a hard set of choices," Hal admitted. "So she was given little time, with a mandate to discover a lot, to protect her family and herself. I doubt, actually, that if it was only her life at risk, that she'd be doing some of what she did. So she's going back to her people with gold, when I didn't have to give her anything. I laid out who was on what side, and who did what, and there was a lot that she didn't know. Now she'll have to think."

"I wouldn't want to be in her position," Lucifer acknowledged. "Cesare and Mother Superior would fight over who got the honor of slowly killing her if they even suspected. But before she died, they would kill her family in front of her, in slow, creative ways." He shook his head.

"And now she walks on a knife edge," Hal concluded. "We threw her a lifeline with no obligations. No threats, no control. We offered friendship and protection. But she knows that I've sent her out to work against her master— no help for that. She knows there isn't any neutral ground. We can only wait to see what she does. Still, there's something about her," Hal muttered, almost talking to himself. "Something else under there."

Delivering the Goods

Lucretia walked confidently out of the building and hailed a cab. This is a day to remember, she thought. Well, let's get some pleasure out of the day. I've certainly paid for it!

The cab let her out at the Cardinal's building. She went straight to Mother Superior's office, buried in the back of the Cardinal's offices. Mother Superior was busy and so Lucretia sat and waited, actually enjoying being there. This may be a first, she thought, contemplating the room. No one has ever wanted to be here.

Finally, a young nun came to the door and called out Lucretia's name. Lucretia stood, and the young nun escorted her into Mother Superior's office, carefully closing the door behind her.

Mother Superior sat behind her desk, an ancient, elaborately carved masterpiece. She studied Lucretia. "Two days left," Mother Superior announced, tapping a knife on the desktop. "Do you ask for more time?"

Lucretia put the flash drive, still in the plastic bag, on Mother Superior's desk. "There is information in there I think Paul will be pleased with," Lucretia declared in her best professional manner.

Surprised, Mother Superior stared at Lucretia, and then smiled. "Good, my child." She snapped her fingers, and the young nun dashed into the room.

"Take this, very carefully, to the technical people," Mother Superior ordered. "Carry it as if your life depended on it, which it does, actually."

The young woman paled, carefully picked up the flash drive with trembling hands, and went out of the room.

"Very, very good," Mother Superior admitted, leaning back and contemplating Lucretia. "Well, perhaps you should go back to the firm now. I'll make a call, and all will be forgiven there. That's what I do, isn't it?" She smiled wryly.

"I, ah, met some other people at that firm," Lucretia added. "I happened to be in a room, and some of the officers came through. Everyone wants to meet the pretty girl, so I shook hands with people. One of them was a very senior officer, they said. I think his name was, what was that? Sir Jonathan, yes, that's it—an odd name."

Mother Superior, stunned, quickly made the sign of the evil eye. "He's the most dangerous, the adversary!" she hissed. "Had he known of our connection, you would never have left that room alive."

"Well, then this has been my lucky day," Lucretia declared. She stood up, smiled, bowed, and left the room. As she walked down the street, she was astonished that Mother Superior was terrified of Sir Jonathan. She's never been afraid of anything, Lucretia thought.

RECAP

Tinker, Tailor, Soldier, Spy. George Smiley, with his Russian dolls. You open one and another puzzle doll stares solemnly at you. That's who he was, Lucretia thought bitterly. George Smiley, quiet, efficient, carefully reeling me in. And what does that make me? Karla, the spymaster killer without a conscience, whose life and family were chaos? Yeah, that's who it makes me. "This wasn't my career aspiration," she glumly muttered.

She hummed to herself. "Sitting on an angry chair...stomach hurts and I don't care..." Lucretia sat in a coffee shop, doodling. I can't even draw at the office or the house. The watchers are everywhere. She drew a sloppy circle on the page, studying it. That's what I look for. It's the gestalt that I see, and I don't see outside the lines. No one can see everything all the time. The mind weeds stuff out. How many investment seminars and stock offering meetings have I sat through where everyone around me was so focused on the information on the pages they were given that they didn't ask: what's supposed to be on the page, but isn't? What's the logical extrapolation of the story being presented, which isn't there? The dog that didn't bark, Holmes said. The mind is always happy to weed something out. The dog was sick, it was asleep, out hunting, so it didn't bark. The guard dog, one hundred and forty pounds of vicious malice, didn't bark. The dog didn't bark BECAUSE NO ONE BROKE IN. And we dance on, happy with the story we are telling ourselves.

In life, the missing numbers and information are more important than the carefully prepared words and numbers on the page in front of us, all that carefully arranged flotsam and jetsam given surface relevance. That's why the information is missing. That information is so important to someone that they carefully crafted the smoke and mirrors to hide them. The errors of commission are often easy to spot, holes in the story we expect. It is the errors of omission, outside the story we are reading from, that constantly bedevil us. So, Hal beat me good, spotting what I didn't see.

What else am I missing? Oh, the fact that Paul intends to get rid of me. Why? A lack of rapport? Maybe I could buy him drinks at a bar and we could watch the football game. Not promising—I'd doubt if we back the same team. It's because I'm female, and that doesn't meet his specifications. I can't ride a big horse and carry a big sword. Women don't have upper body strength? Try carrying two small children through a mall sometime, and see who has upper body strength. Oh well. I'm not going to change his mind without becoming Mother Superior. Ugh, there's an ugly thought. Maybe you have to be born like her, I hope. Is this where I see a hall of mirrors, with my possible futures for myself reflected in the flickering candles, and I'm supposed to choose between dark, light, or fashionably dressed? I don't have any candles. No, I don't want the future with the flying monkeys, I'm sure of that. Flying monkeys shit on everything. Nope, don't want them. I mean, how can I be the personification of evil rampant in the world if I have to spend all my time cleaning up monkey shit?

Hal didn't burn me. Oh, he could have. He could have had me as a puppet on strings if he had just reached out his hand. Instead, I'm in a new country, the implied offer of a new world, my choice. Now, he's sent me to work against my master. Heh, heh, heh, evil master. If I wasn't in public, I'd do my hunchback imitation. Jose laughs every time. Oh, Hal didn't do it in so many words, not obviously, but what choice would I have? On legal, ethical, moral, practical grounds, no other choice. That was good of him to make it my choice. He even offered friendship! Paul would have locked me down tight, and then tightened the ropes just a little more for the sheer joy of it all. Maybe taken fingernails as trophies. Hal's offered me an out if I need one. Now, the opposite of a bad situation isn't always a good situation, but it's an out. Any port in a storm—that's the old expression.

Lucretia left the coffee shop and walked through the park, taking the long way back to the office. The little information I did get from Paul was false, Lucretia brooded. I still can't believe it! Set up. They didn't want me to succeed. Testing is one thing, but handicapping for failure is a bad sign. Expecting to get me back in a box in pieces, that's not sporting at all. What is it that they say? When someone does something wrong, don't assume it's the only thing wrong. Of course, what haven't they done wrong, if I list all the things that I know about?

And Sir Jonathan and Hal seemed more than employer-employee to me, she realized, surprised at the thought. There was a level of comfort there past simple work relationships. No, Hal had Sir Jonathan's backing, and Francisco d'Plata was along for the ride. They must be family. More family? It's been just mom and I since my sisters detest me, and now there is family coming out of the woodwork. That's something to think about—all these new relationships. If they are family, then no wonder Hal is so dangerous. He played me like a fish. I never even suspected for a moment! But I'm still taking that long bath tonight. Yuck—that office! If Mother Superior is frightened of Sir Jonathan, and he and Hal are related, then perhaps I do have a shelter to run to.

And Don Cortes and Cali's mother? What the hell am I supposed to think about that? He was hasty and violent. And it was a fair fight, from everything I've heard back. He did start it, and he fought and died. They gave him a chance to fight instead of simply killing him, which was honorable. But he was fair to me when others were terrible. I'm going to have to let that simmer for a while.

Mother always gives good advice, and a sounding board is what I need. But when and how? casually observing the person walking behind her in the reflected glass of a store. That person was ahead of me earlier, and, yes, that person ahead of me was behind me. Hal was right about the watchers. Dominique told me the same thing. I just didn't think I was really all that important. Maybe I'm flattered? Not!, she sighed.

THE WATCHERS

Lucretia decided to prepare a business case on the watchers. That professor in business school argued you could start with any event/ transaction and back into a huge company's structure because things have to follow in certain patterns. So, let's play the game. First, how extensive is the surveillance? Do they watch everything? Is it just me, or mom and I, or the whole family? If it's all the time, then that's extra people, and if there are no extra people, then there must be breaks or inefficiencies when watchers are tired. To figure out how many people are involved, start counting the ones I see: who, when, and where. So, how many people are involved?

She tested them cautiously, not wanting to let them know that she knew they knew she knew... "My head hurts when I start thinking like that," she mumbled quietly to herself. Over the next few weeks, Lucretia confirmed that her phone was tapped, her apartment was wired, and she was following constantly. She thought of a final test. She mentioned something small, human, gossipy outside the office, with parents at Jose's school, and her secretary slipped a few days later and said something.

Lucretia quickly switched the subject, talked about other things for a few minutes, and was sure the secretary didn't catch her mistake. Based on the bodies she had counted watching her, she worked up a calculation of the cost of all the watchers. First, the watchers she saw, and then backing into the hidden bodies required for support, transport, and administrative, including people who prepared reports, and she was impressed. I would never have thought the little details of my life were so important, she thought wryly. Why don't they just pay me instead? I'll give reports.

"Subject looked like hell walking into the bathroom in the morning. Subject used facilities, took a long shower. Came out radiant. Subject chanted hymns praising the power and glory of Paul for ten minutes before work; needs better choreographed dance steps." I could retire ten years earlier. She shrugged, carefully drew lines over her thoughts on the papers she had been doodling on, and threw them away. As she crossed the street, she caught a glimpse of someone digging in the trash. An original signed Lucretia. Who would have known how valuable they would become? Do I have to cut my ear off? Maybe breast enlargement could count towards the required suffering? Although an artist's work is only valuable after their death, she reminded herself. That does takes the fun out of it.

It's nicer at work now. She'd forgotten what it was like to not have to steel your soul before walking in each day, and she actually enjoyed the new regime. Rumors flying through the office about her secretary's abrupt disappearance had defanged the wolves. Turned them into sheep, actually. They were so sweet to her now that it almost made her sick some mornings.

The problem is, she thought, it isn't a bad day, it's a bad life.

Jose's Soccer Game

Lucretia and her mother were at one of Jose's soccer games. Jose was thrilled to have her there—it was so rare for his mother to be able to come to a game. Her mother gave her an appraising look as Lucretia stood on the sidelines, shouting encouragement.

"Wrong game," her mother offered helpfully. "That's a different game's moves. A scrum is rugby. Verboten in soccer."

"Oh?" Lucretia replied, looking confused. "All these kids' games look the same. A lot of wild running around after some little ball. Soccer, rugby, football, kickball—they blur together."

The other parents looked away as Lucretia glanced around.

"Fine, I'm a bad mother," Lucretia laughed. "It's nice to be snubbed again! The office staff has become so sweet that I'm worried about developing diabetes."

"They are small, boring people," her mother commented. "I suffer through the coffee and donuts before the games for Jose's sake, but you're not missing a thing."

"Turns out I've been missing a bunch," Lucretia whispered to her mother. "All the watchers. Everywhere. I knew there were some, but not as many as there are."

"I've seen them. It's force of habit, trying to stay alert. I could spot undercover police at one hundred yards when I was younger."

Lucretia glanced at her, raising her eyebrows.

"My eyes were stronger then," her mother advised, shrugging. "Now, these glasses don't work like they should. Are there more than I have seen?"

There was wild cheering. Someone got a goal.

"Everywhere," Lucretia declared under the crowd roar. "House, car, walks, office. Microphones, cameras, live watchers. It's Paul's signature style, and there's something else. He doesn't like me. Doesn't trust me."

Her mother bit her lip. I've told her that, she thought. No good saying it again. "And all the good work you do for them," her mother asserted. "That many watching? Maybe I can get on the payroll too. I could use some extra money."

"I was thinking the same thing myself," Lucretia agreed. "We would have that place on the beach years faster. No, there seems to be a union involved, and we don't have the connections. I'm wondering if I get royalties on the clips of me in the shower on the Internet. I haven't seen any checks. Have you been hiding them?"

"Oh, the grocery money?" her mother smiled. "Didn't I tell you? Sorry. Nice full breasts you have, that's the general comment. Well, that's the politest general comment."

"I love it," Lucretia laughed. "That explains some of these parents' side glances at me, now that I think about it."

Lucretia shouted more encouragement to Jose, this time using the right terms for soccer.

Another goal, and a lot of shouting.

"Nothing to be done?" her mother whispered.

"Nothing I know of," Lucretia muttered. "Smile and be cheerful. We wait and see." She started clapping as the buzzer sounded, and they followed the other parents onto the field.

"Your friend?" her mother asked, staring at the ground so her lips couldn't be read. "They could have done far more to you, but they didn't. That's worth something. And your people hate them—that's worth a lot. I've had years to think. My life was ruined when I did what I should have, rather than what I felt."

"I met someone important," Lucretia whispered. "At that company. I was telling Mother Superior. A man named Sir Jonathan."

Her mother looked quickly away, shading her eyes with her hand as she watched the kids celebrating. "And?"

"Mother Superior was terrified of him," Lucretia smiled. "I didn't think it was possible." Lucretia was watching Jose, not her mother and missed her mother's quick smile.

"I had a feeling," Lucretia whispered, kneeling to tie her shoe. Her mother bent over, rearranging the stuff in Jose's bag, very close to Lucretia.

"A feeling that Hal and this Sir Jonathan are related. Just the way they acted together. Just a hunch."

"Then you may have friends," her mother replied, in an odd tone. "Life isn't always lemons and making lemonade. Sometimes life hands you iced lemonade with a straw in a frosted glass on a hot day. Sometimes you just take the damn drink and don't ask questions."

Lucretia glanced, confused, at her mother, and then Jose ran over to them with several friends and their parents.

"Quality work!" Lucretia told him, jumping up and embracing Jose. "Food now?"

"Food it is," another parents agreed.

"We generally go to the pizza place afterwards," one of the mothers sniffed, with just the right intonation to make it clear that Lucretia wasn't usually there.

"And you can come, mother?" Jose pleaded.

"I can," Lucretia promised. "The pirates will have to sack and loot without their leader today." She smiled, teeth showing, at the catty woman, who, startled, quickly walked away.

Jose ran ahead with his friends as Lucretia picked up her daughter and walked to the car with her mother.

CHAPTER 6. THE NEW WORLD

HONG KONG

The Professor sat in an elegant office, bored, staring out the floor-to-ceiling windows. The office was at the top of a skyscraper in Hong Kong. Outside, the light rain was misting on the windows. It was cool in the building, only a few feet from the sweltering humid heat.

"We have an agreement," the lawyer stammered, walking into the room. "Here is the order form." He handed it to the Professor. "It is as we discussed, with the monies in the bank under the control of a neutral party."

"Nasty stuff," the Professor complained, studying the order. "That strong a control drug has unpredictable and undesired side effects."

"They know that," the lawyer replied politely. They buy what they buy, he thought. Get this over with.

"That will be all," the liaison dismissed the lawyer.

The lawyer nodded, bowed slightly to show respect and walked out. He wiped his face after he closed the door. Is the mansion worth this? he thought. Or is there any choice? Once in, there is no out. With that happy thought, he stomped down to yell at the support staff for some typing errors he had found.

"The side effects are not our concern," the local liaison advised. "You know, negative opinions are not always appreciated. Not part of the team."

"I've seen teamwork," the Professor answered, studying the liaison. "Without feedback, the group goes happily over the cliff. You need my skills? You get my opinions. I'll make it, and it will work. But it will do more than the specifications. It always does."

"The government of that country starves and shoots anyone they don't like, which is most of their population," the liaison commented, shrugging. "A few dropping off from side effects is small change. It might actually be a favorable result, from their point of view." The liaison thought for a moment, gazing out the window before looking back at the Professor. " Look, I actually appreciate a man who will tell me more than what I want to hear. Not everyone does."

"Just putting in my two cents," the Professor replied. "I can promise that there will be an angry message about the side effects in a month or so, and at least you'll know it's coming."

The liaison reflected for a minute and nodded his head. "I'll explain what will happen to them. Maybe head off that problem. Maybe they will buy more when they know all that the drug will do. Odd that they hate their own people more than anyone else, but I guess they know them better than anyone else. But now—a party! The leader of the triad we work with is putting on a show for us. It would be impolite to not come."

"I have some special party favors to give them," the Professor declared. "This is a good opportunity to show our customers what we have coming in the pipeline. They will be excited, if they can remember afterwards."

Another party, the Professor thought, sitting in a comfortable chair at the beautiful mansion. He was in a corner, professionally evaluating the results of his drugs and he was satisfied. Naked bodies were scattered around the huge room, some still moving, many drugged out. I must be getting old, he thought, slowly sipping his wine. He held the wine glass a foot away, carefully inspecting the wine. This is good wine! Much better than I usually buy. He picked up the bottle, read the label and quickly wrote down the details.

Sitting back, he scrutinized the room, professionally evaluating the effects of his drugs. Lust and desire—that one works. What is the Chinese name for that? Something cute. I can't remember. The ideogram is better—an arrow entering a circle, which seems to express the idea quite well. He glanced at another group. Now the pain/pleasure. That is having a stronger effect than I'd estimated. It's so weight dependent, and they tend to be rather crude in doling out the dose. Given that they are semi-comatose, it's surprising they can measure anything. These girls tend to be smaller than American women. Maybe we'll have to package these differently here. Maybe sell a lower strength so they actually have to think a little as they pass them out. There will be some very happy deaths tonight, but they can clean up the mess.

"A man's world, drug dealing," a deep voice rumbled next to him.

"You honor me with your presence," the Professor replied, hastily standing to show his respect. It was the head of the triad who had brokered the large drug sale. A burly, grizzled, middle-aged man with a long face scar, legendary for his ruthlessness. Tonight, he was all cheerful host.

"Please, sit," the man ordered, waving his guards away. "All those stories about my demand for respect, well, those are only partially true. And I respect you, my good Professor, and your work. You have created far better products than I'd ever imagined, and some of them are actually legal! I may end my life a respectable man, the honored head of a major pharmaceutical firm. A better end than my predecessor had, crushed in an auto salvage yard. Or so I'm told."

"It's a rough business," the Professor agreed as he sat down. "But it has its rewards."

"True. It tests a man. You have to pick a goal. You have to think for yourself. The clarity of a man's world, a hunter's world. If you succeed, you gain respect, power, luxury, and women. Fail, and, well, failure has a quick and simple price."

"All true," the Professor offered. "And the business is getting bigger and bigger. We have surprises coming that you'll be excited about. Not my place to tell you, but you won't be disappointed."

"Good. I'm glad that you became part of the organization. Good to have some people who think. Too many killers, too many quick solutions that turn bad over time. Well, that's enough thinking for now. Would you honor me?" he asked, waving his right hand. His guards quickly escorted over a beautiful young woman whose eyes were wide with drugs and fear.

"A treat, a rare prize. For you, my honored friend."

"You do honor me," the Professor declared, looking carefully at the woman. "Truly exceptional. I thank you."

"Your room is prepared. "Here." He pointed to one of the guards. "He will show you to your room."

As the Professor and the woman followed the guard down the luxurious hallway, occasional moans came from behind the doors they passed, mixed with occasional frantic screams. The woman looked straight ahead, ignoring the sounds.

"Your room," the guard advised, bowing, and pushed the door open.

The Professor and the woman walked into an incredibly luxurious room. "Wonderful!" the Professor exclaimed, glancing around. "Did you know I used to be a professor? I never had hotel rooms like this." He turned to the woman, "Or company as charming as yourself."

"Everyone wants to be a drug lord," she replied in perfect English. "How could you not? The lifestyle is exciting. It's all power and money. You don't have to be nice to people you don't like."

"That's probably the best perk," the Professor agreed. "No faculty meetings and small but vicious power struggles. At least in this business, the power struggles are about something worthwhile."

The woman smiled. "And people here consider you valuable. Very valuable. Very happy with you. I am your slave." She knelt. "The Lord's concubine," she offered, gazing up at him and smiling. "Nothing but your pleasure. Just a lowly woman, waiting."

The Professor contemplated her carefully. "Beautiful and bright. Sophisticated. Let's talk, but afterwards."

AFGHANISTAN.

The tribal elder was pacing in front of the buyer, furious. "You can't be serious. You offer this for our crop? It is a fraction of just last year, which was less than the year before," he shouted. He was livid, stomping as he talked.

Puffs of dirt rose as he marched around the room.

The other men from the tribe were nodding their heads in agreement and angrily staring at the buyer as they sat cross-legged on the ground.

"It's all I am authorized to offer," the buyer protested. "There isn't the demand anymore. The new drugs have pushed out the old ones. The long supply chain for the old drugs is too difficult to manage, transport is too expensive, and the bribes to the officials are too high. The new drugs can be made anywhere and are easier on the people who use them. We continue buying these for a dwindling base of addicts."

"My village will starve," the elder growled.

The buyer moved his fingers just a little and his guard moved into defense mode.

The tribesmen carefully moved their hands away from their weapons.

"I have known you and your families for a long time," the buyer declared sadly. "My father bought from your father. There is nothing I can do. I have begged the company to pay more. They thoughtfully didn't shoot me for my disrespect, but took the time to explain exactly what the problems are. Their hands are tied also. They can only pay what they can sell the product for and make a profit."

The tribal elder glanced around at the other tribesmen, who stared at the ground, not meeting his eyes. The elder's shoulders slumped and he nodded. They quickly completed their business, and the buyer and his men drove into the night.

YEMEN.[11]

More than half of Yemen's scarce water was used to feed an addiction. Despite the drought killing Yemen's crops, farmers in villages all over the country were abandoning other crops to grow a thirsty plant called qat. Addictive, the qat leaves were chewed every day by most Yemeni men and some women for their mild narcotic effect. The farmers had little choice because qat was the only way to make a profit.

Meanwhile, the water wells were running dry. Deep, ominous cracks were opening in the parched earth, some of them hundreds of yards long.

"They tell us the cracks are appearing because the water table is sinking so fast," a tired-looking farmer complained. "I've lost two-thirds of my peach trees to drought in the past two years. What can I do? It takes years to regrow the trees, and what can I sell in the meantime? Every year we have to drill deeper and deeper to get water. What will happen when the water is gone?"

MEXICO.

The Major, the Professor, and a buyer sat on the veranda outside the hacienda in the mountains. Another hot day. The air conditioning was running overtime to cool the shaded table outside.

"People want the drugs," the Major argued. "I can't even believe it sometimes myself. Want is a small word for their lust, actually. They fight for these."

"These are good work," the Russian admitted. "Russians have never seen anything like this. These are wonderful. It makes their lives bearable. The leaders don't like the drugs? Without the drugs to tranquilize the people, they'd have people rampaging in the streets. The leaders should think of how good they have it. I do more to keep them in power than the police do."

They sat in the outside courtyard, where years before the Professor had watched Don Cortes feed the Coldmen Sacking people to the alligators. Some things don't change, the Professor thought as the suspected traitors the Russian had brought with him finally sank into the bloodstained water, the alligators fighting over bodies as they pulled them under.

BIG GAME HUNTING

The Professor was hunting in Africa with the President of the country. A formerly rich land, now impoverished because of the actions of the President.

President? The Professor mused. A warlord, looting and killing for his pleasure. And why not? In his mind, the country is his, and they all deserve it. Perhaps they do, if they let him run roughshod over them.

"There!" the guide shouted, stabbing his finger frantically towards the moving grass.

The Professor aimed his rife, waiting. The lion appeared for a second. The Professor fired, killing the lion at one hundred yards with a single shot.

"Excellent shot!" the President commented, impressed despite himself.

"I cheat," the Professor admitted. "This rifle is computer assisted, and it practically makes the shot for you. Would you honor me by trying it?" The Professor carefully offered the weapon to the President.

The President eagerly grasped the gun. "A real target," he demanded, and his troops pushed several men out of a truck, shouting at them. The men ran, terrified, out into the Savannah and kept running.

"How does this work?" the President asked, puzzled, studying the rifle.

"Look through the scope," the Professor advised, carefully showing respect. "In the scope, there is a red dot. Line up the red dot with the target, and the computer will lock in and track. Pull the trigger and see what happens."

The President was doubtful, but he raised the gun, tracked a running man and pulled the trigger. The man collapsed and lay twitching into the dust. The other men shouted at each other and ran faster.

"Let them run," the Professor suggested. "Test the gun."

In a few minutes, all the men were dead.

"The gun tracked them perfectly," the President declared. "An amazing weapon."

"The bullets are actually more like little missiles," the Professor explained. "They can make little course corrections as they fly towards the target. This is our gift to you, if you would honor us by accepting it. A small token of our appreciation for your help."

The President laughed and pumped the rifle over his head.

The traditional sign of power, the Professor thought, carefully not letting his thoughts affect his expression. Humans have changed little over the eons.

"These men, they are our friends," the President shouted to his entourage, and they cheered. "They bring us money and these toys!" The President pumped the rifle over his head again. "We all make more money than before." The President stared at his aide. "Do we have more targets?"

"Yes," the aide assured. Over the next half hour, the trucks were emptied, and the savannah was littered with the bodies.

I'm glad I brought extra rounds, the Professor thought. There—those offerings to the lions offset the loss of the one that I killed.

"The ones in that truck—just push them out and leave them here," the President laughed. The guards quickly pushed the women and children out of the truck, and the prisoners stood on the ground, terrified, watching the predators that had been scavenging the dead bodies start to move slowly toward them.

"It's one thing for a man to consider losing his life challenging me," the President told the Professor. "It's another for him to consider losing his family's lives. Make sure that you take pictures of this," the President ordered his aide.

The aide nodded quickly and shouted at some other men.

"Well, time for dinner. Here, ride with me," the President told the Professor. They walked to the personnel carrier and climbed in.

"The latest American equipment," the President boasted. "Air conditioned and everything."

"It's very nice," the Professor agreed, settling into the comfortable leather seat. As the personnel carrier pulled away, it left behind the first screams of the women as the hyenas ran laughing at them.

"The first man I shot was the former head of the banking regulators," the President commented. "The others were busybodies associated with him. It seems we need new banking regulators."

"Fortunately, I have just the men for you. Legal backgrounds, excellent credentials, with ties to banks all over the world—very experienced in moving money and making it come up clean. 'Pecunia non olet,' or, roughly, 'Money has no odor' is their motto. Foreign governments are happy to take the money and never ask questions about where it came from. So, should you ever wish to leave here and settle in Paris, well, the money will be there."

"Always a good plan," the President laughed. "Life is so uncertain, and I like Paris. And this new drug you have developed—the potential is large? It must be something risky for you to bring it out here."

"I've been following the extensive work on vaccines against cocaine and other drugs. I've been duplicating the studies, with a twist. It turns out that it's easy to turn the vaccine on itself and create a really hopeless addiction. People doing the research are blinded, you see, by what they want to accomplish. So they did the heavy lifting for us, and now we have this nice new product."

"Amazing," the President remarked, shaking his head. "Are those governments really so stupid that they don't see anything beyond their pretty pictures? The little people, trying to pay their mortgages and bills, don't look above at what they could have. Well, there are few men of vision such as ourselves," he announced, clapping the Professor on the back.

"Men of vision such as yourself," the Professor replied respectfully to the President, being very careful not to move his arm toward the other man. He's a god in his mind, the Professor remembered. Gods don't like being touched. "Your vision for your country has turned it around." Around the corner and off a cliff, the Professor concluded, but it's their country. Their train wreck. Not my business.

After dark, the party stopped at a retreat built for the President's hunting expeditions.

The Professor sat on a cot in the hut far out in the bush as a ravishing young African woman was led in.

"A daughter of the late banking regulator," the guard declared. "With the President's compliments."

It's a life, the Professor thought wryly.

SHINING GOALS OR PROFITS?

The standing arms of society—the police, the prosecutors, the judicial system, the legislatures, and the executive branches—hold charters with proud goals and bright ideas. Down in the trenches, the shining ideas and bright goals are confusing to apply, and it is easy to slip away from what 'should be' to what the particular group trying up uphold the goals and ideas 'can do'. Because the standing arms of society hold the weapons and the keys to the jails, their adherence to the right for the society, instead of the possible for the group, is critical.

The corruption of the standing arms of the society is thus the most destructive event possible. Because it takes money to act in this world, and there are always many hands out for money, the standing arms of society have to fight for their money. It's always popular to take money from the 'wrong', and give to the 'good', thus forcing the 'wrong' to fund the 'right'. The problem is that any time any situation is profitized, the focus of the structure will always become the profit. Perhaps slowly, perhaps dragging it's feet, perhaps kicking against the pressure, but eventually.

So where the criminal justice system is profitized so that it makes more money from some choices than from others, it will, inevitably, choose the actions that bring profits. In the name of the right at first, because those actions that bring in money give resources to further the bright ideas and goals on the charter. Later, the structure will maximize profits because profits are easy to measure, and bright goals and ideas are difficult to measure, so the structure looks best by bringing in money. And finally, the structure will focus on profitable actions because the leaders discover that their status grew with the greater resources. Then the nature of the organization changes from bright ideas for the society to what the structure thinks will perpetuate itself.

Structures will thus expand profitable possibilities because the system rewarded profits. Police who collected large sums from wrongdoers could then leverage their power to collect more and more—in the name of right and justice, of course. Eventually, it would create new categories of wrongdoers after a while. For good reasons, and for justice, of course, and because the police were on a budget and always needed more money.

Speed traps were a common but trivial example. The blatant abuses on nonresidents were legendary. The new traffic cameras, which were for the "good" of the people and brought in more and more money, were just an extrapolation of the past.

Much more serious abuses were seen in cases such as the prison unions in California, who were behind the "Three Strikes" law, which put people behind bars for life. The more people behind bars, the more power the union had. A union like that, tied intimately to both sides of the law, was especially dangerous because who knew what they really knew? Who knew what whispered threats legislators received late in the night before important legislation was up for a vote? All in the name of the good, of course. Controlling the flow of information and publicity, the power of the unions was enormous.

And where local police could keep the proceeds from drug seizures and other law violations, who watched over the natural tendency to abuse? Who could afford to defend charges filed against them, crushed under a welter of federal, state, and local charges, many of which required no criminal intent and marginal direct involvement? People recognized the different attitude of the police on the street, and the basic respect for the law turned into a fear of enforcement by the law-abiding. The end game is when the enforcers, already far down the profitization path, the bright goals distant, could be bought off, and were.

THE MIDDLE EAST.

The cartel agent was sitting in the Arab bank. From the air-conditioned jet to the air-conditioned limo to the air-conditioned bank, he'd hardly noticed the burning sun and blazing heat of the desert.

The vice president of the bank sat across from him, smiling and making little jokes as his staff rushed back and forth with receipts and transaction printouts.

This heretic, the vice president contemptuously thought, smiling politely at the cartel agent. He does more damage to his countries and their false religions with his drugs than any terrorist could. I wage holy war on them from an air-conditioned office and I am paid millions for it. This is better than that cave in Pakistan I used to work out of.

The vice president's chief assistant walked up to him, holding a final printout.

The vice president took the printout, glanced over it, and nodded his head. He then handed the printout to the cartel agent. "As you requested, sir," the vice president advised, his words dripping honey. "The money has been transferred to all of these places, and they have confirmed receipt. All of the deposits have gone to clean companies, who will transfer them on, across jurisdictions, so that there can be tracing of the funds. Within a month, the funds will be back here, clean and ready to be invested into anything you wish."

"Well worth the ten percent processing fee," the cartel agent agreed. "We have come a long way from Pablo Escobar and loose piles of money in a barn. He used to figure he lost ten percent a year from the rats gnawing on the bills."

And so you don't mind the ten percent we rats gnaw away, the vice president thought. "Times change, and life is as god wishes..." The phrases rolled from the vice president without thought, smoothly and pleasantly.

"Thank you again," the cartel agent declared, standing up and shaking hands with the vice president. "I must travel on. I still have far to go today."

"Your limo is waiting," the assistant advised. "Please." He ushered the cartel agent out into the waiting car. There were three cars in the caravan—guards in front, guards in back, and the agent in the limo. They roared off towards the airport.

They think this doesn't affect them, the cartel agent thought, smiling at the new city built in the desert. They are so happy to destroy the western world that created this city and the toys they now live by. I know that vice president's past and his plans. But he doesn't know the new drug pipelines into his country that we are planning. Perhaps, fool that he is, when he does find out he'll just want his cut. He can't imagine the effect the drugs will have.

CHAPTER 7. MRS. OSTEIN

Mrs. Ostein put the phone down and stared absently at the kitchen cabinets.

"Ah, mom?" her younger daughter asked, worried. "Is there something wrong?"

"No," Mrs. Ostein replied. "It's just another meeting at the church this afternoon. It's just that they are quite insistent—much more than normal. Well, who knows? Probably another marketing study on the ideal color of the choir robes." She smiled at her daughter. "You get to school—you'll be late! You know those disgusting photographers wait in ambush to get something on both of you."

"It's such crap, what we have to pretend to be," the older daughter grumbled. "When dad was here, I could at least pretend it was for something. Now, for these people?"

"Hush! The food on the table comes from them. Now, go!"

The girls grabbed their bags and went out. In a minute, she heard them driving away. She tapped her fingers on the counter. Grimacing, she realized her daughter was right. She picked up the car keys. I've got two hours before the meeting, I might as well get some shopping done first.

Mrs. Ostein walked into the private administrative room in the basement of the church. She had rarely gone there even when her husband ran the church because she detested the administrative staff. Her husband was insistent about keeping them, but they revolted her. She'd wondered for a long time if things were off track somewhere, but so many of the parishioners were happy—well, maybe it was right. Doing right was being right, she'd thought.

Waiting in the room were the Minister, the disgusting Collector, and the Chief Accountant, who was almost as disgusting as the collector. Then she noticed another figure—a tall, stern-looking man who stood away from the others, in the corner. She suddenly shivered, but controlled herself.

"Gentlemen?" she asked, sitting down.

"You have been asking questions," the Minister shouted, furious. "I told you not to do that! You've been going over the church's private records, making copies, and reading e-mails when you should not have been."

"I'm an officer in this church," she stammered. "I have responsibilities."

"You are nothing," the Accountant rasped.

She stared at him, shocked.

"You were foolish," the Minister hissed. "All of the copies you made vanished from your house and the secret storage facility today. All your notes, your computer—everything. So you have no proof of anything at all. No cards in your hand."

She stared at the table, terrified. She knew what the men had done to others, which was why she had forced herself to try and assemble something to protect her and her daughters. Now it had turned completely against her.

"Now, you may not know this," the Minister advised, leaning over her, "but your late husband beat to death—while violently raping—that choir woman. No, she wasn't killed by her husband. We have complete tapes of the whole scene. He laughed while killing her. Very sick, actually. And it was well known that you hated that woman. We have affidavits from people who recalled they heard you demanding that he terminate her shortly before her death."

"Very poor choice of words, in retrospect," the Accountant observed, smiling.

She gasped, staring at the Minister.

"It turns out," the Accountant added, leering at her, "that your late husband also used church funds for personal uses. We have copies of many checks signed by you. Checks to clothing boutiques, hair salons, and payments for clearly personal travel—all of which were deducted as business expenses. And then there is the private bank account he had, siphoning funds away for personal use. We have checks drawn on that account by you, for your personal pleasure. Won't look good to people after all your high-minded speeches, but it's more than a moral and ethical problem. These are crimes. State and federal crimes. We have stacks of records and solid affidavits. I find it doubtful that the police would hesitate for long should we provided them with this information."

"What?" she screamed. "None of this is true!"

"Shut up," the Minister growled. "Not that you would go to trial. You'd be a tragic suicide, found out and unable to face the truth coming out."

Stunned, she stared at him. The rumors were true. All of them.

"And your daughters," the Collector chuckled. "They were arrested this afternoon. Your older daughter—can you believe that she stole jewelry from a store and then attacked the guards when they tried to stop her? She must have been stealing to pay for the drugs in her purse. Heroin, actually. It's expensive. Her blood test was positive, by the way."

Mrs. Ostein stared blankly at the Collector, denying in her mind that this was happening.

"And your younger daughter?" the Accountant added. "She was

arrested for money laundering and drug possession. The police found over a pound of cocaine in her car, and her accomplices confessed. Hard to believe a nice young woman like that would have tattooed gang members as best friends, but we have pictures. This is very serious. Years, perhaps life in jail, assuming she lives to go to trial. They usually don't, you know."

Mrs. Ostein began to beg, helpless.

"Quiet!" the man in the corner ordered. "My name is Archleon, but I am called the Sandman. I put people to sleep. But not slowly—more like that odd character in those kids' horror movies."

She shook to see his face in the light. Handsome, but wrong. Just wrong. Fair but foul, she frantically thought.

"All of these events never happened-yet-as far as the news or the prosecutor knows," the Sandman announced. "But they are all written down, and the evidence is clear. Any, and I mean any problems from you, and terrible things will happen to your family. Are we completely clear on that?"

"Yes," Mrs. Ostein cried. "Yes."

"Good," the Sandman commented. "Oh, and if your younger daughter should say that anything happened to her today, some little misunderstood event between the Collector and herself, you tell her about our little meeting here. And that event is just a small taste—bitter, I grant—of what will happen to her—and you—should you, or they, cause any more problems. Do you understand?

"Yes," Mrs. Ostein growled, fury over the attack on her daughter pushing aside her terror.

"We will be watching," the Sandman promised. "We know everything." He stepped to the door and then stopped, turning and looking at her. Smiling, he added, "Should we ever meet again, I will be the last thing you ever see on this earth. After having watched your daughters' horrible deaths." He walked out of the room, closing the door behind him.

Mrs. Ostein stared at the door and then glanced back at the Minister, the Collector, and the Accountant. She realized that they were as terrified of the Sandman as she was, that oddly gave her strength.

"You listen!" the Minister screamed at her, his face transfixed with rage. "Don't act up! You don't want him back, and I don't want him back."

"Who is he?" she forced herself to ask.

"More of a what, you might say. A liaison with the mother church," the Collector stammered, not looking at her. "A man...well, a man shape...who handles trouble. Very final handling. You should go home," he told her, gazing at her in an almost friendly manner. "You may not appreciate it, but usually people are not given a warning. Usually the judgment is pronounced before the meeting, and the meeting is only to execute the sentence."

The Collector reached his hand out to help her up and she actually took it.

"You may think me disgusting," the Collector admitted. "All do—I accept it. But we," waving his hand at the people in the room, "are small creatures of the dark. We are the mice, perhaps the rats, coming after the remains of the prey. That creature...man ...is the predator who kills for pleasure. Don't forget my words."

She numbly nodded and fled the room.

Somehow, she was able to drive herself home. She remembered nothing of the trip, but when she looked at the car she didn't see that she had hit anything on the way. Slowly, she walked into the kitchen through the breezeway door. She walked into an emotional maelstrom.

Her daughters came running at her, screaming about their days.

"Shut up," she shouted. "Shut up. I know everything."

"It's all false," her older daughter wailed.

"And he molested me!" the younger daughter whined, staring helplessly at her mother. "No one did anything or listened to me. The police called me a liar! They wanted to arrest me! They called me a whore!"

"Listen to me!" Mrs. Ostein snarled. "No one will do anything. No one is on our side. I've been told clearly that our only choice is between providing our devout help at the church or our deaths. Quite probably a fate worse than death, actually."

The girls stared at her.

"This is our situation," and she told the girls about the meeting she had come from at the church.

It was a quiet dinner at their house that night.

Mrs. Ostein & the Minister talk

Mrs. Ostein sat in the private chapel at the church the next Monday. There was no one else in there. There rarely is, she thought. We've trained them to follow, not think.

The Minister walked in. She ignored him.

"You did well," the Minister observed, sitting down next to her. "You and your daughters were perfect. Better than ever, actually. You brought tears to my eyes, and everyone else's."

"Tell me," she snapped. "Where have you been hiding all my life—and why didn't you stay there?"

"You are so funny," the Minister replied. "You should try the open mic at the comedy club. When you do, please tell me so I can bring tomatoes. Nice green ones, solid and hard. I understand stoning was once a traditional approach. Perhaps we can use unripened tomatoes in today's world. A green alternative."

She glowered at him. "We understand the rules. We're not stupid. I'm just trying to reconcile...my faith...with what has happened."

"The front office and the back office for any business are not the same," the Minister answered, staring at the wall. "The people who write the ads are not the people who make the loans. John Wycliffe, who died, oh, roughly 1384, wrote that all the hierarchy from the pope down was accursed by reason of their greed, simony, cruelty, lust for power, and evil lives. The popes of the period were the Antichrist and not to be obeyed; their decrees were as naught and their excommunications to be disregarded. The *Canterbury Tales*, set a century before that, broadly tarred the clergy as corrupt thieves and molesters. At the edge of contact between the real world and the fancy ideas in the books, the fancy ideas somehow get twisted to give people what they desire in their loins. Not the pretty story we teach in Sunday School, is it?"

Mrs. Ostein was speechless. She held onto the richly carved pew for support.

"You embraced a church that has nothing but contempt for women and their problems, and you expected differently?" the Minister demanded. "A theology that said a woman is not human, a woman is nothing in the eyes of the Lord, according to the exact letter of the old scriptures? You are Eve, the cause of our fall. In the writings of the Holy Fathers, really—I'm not making it up. Suffering was prescribed for a woman. You should thank me."

"You mock my pain," she shouted. "My faith is genuine! My father was a preacher of the gospel. Not this fancy stuff we do today—the old, simple religion. I believed, and I can't reconcile this."

"Your father was a fool," the Minister scoffed.

"He was loyal and honorable, and in a shifting world, he held fast to his beliefs," Mrs. Ostein replied. "So, yes, he was a fool, in your world."

"You listen, but you do not hear," the Minister sighed. "A heaven modeled on the nightmare of an Assyrian court? A hell like the dungeons under the palace? The Accountant was talking about fraud and how frauds are structured. It's key that a workable fraud has an alibi—what he called a plausible denial—for what happened to keep people from looking into the lies and catching the fraud. The best plausible denial is first, one that can't ever be checked, and second, one that you will be punished for even asking about. Think about that, bitter as it may seem."

She stared at him, open-mouthed. "Heresy! You!"

"Oh, grow up," the Minister replied, leaning back against a pew. "What the church does have are enemies. We certainly deserve them, but we deny that anyone who means well could be an enemy of the church. So we create enemies that are supposed to be tempting the faithful constantly.

Look, if the devil opened up an office to buy souls, the line the first morning would run across the state. I don't think people need nearly the encouragement from the forces of darkness to be tempted to do the things they are not supposed to do, as my sermons would suggest. Legions of demons are not needed. I think, actually, the legions of demons got jobs at the check-cashing companies because they wanted something really evil to do.

"Be that as it may, we perform certain functions," as he stood up and starting to pace. "Some of the things we do are authentically good, by any standard, and we do help people. That a large chunk of the foundation is built on lies—that's part of life. This isn't the public sermon, but I need you to do things for me and for the church, and I don't need you to throw a faith crisis on TV. How about if you take the position as the liaison with the national child groups? They really do help many weak and vulnerable children. So you can do some real good for people's lives, knowing you're participating in a fraud, or you can walk away from those people who need your help because you are too righteous to dirty your hands in the real world. Are you in or out?"

She stared at the floor for a while, and then glanced at the crucified Jesus hanging on the wall.

"Yes," she promised, "I'll do it. I'll do it better than you think I can."

"Good," the Minister replied. "Look, I'm sorry about the shock treatment. The problem is that any crisis brings the Sandman back. You don't want that, and I don't want to have to deal with the mess afterwards. There's always a lot of paperwork, as well as assorted body parts to clean up."

He walked over to the door, then turned and looked at her. "And I'm not joking. I've seen his work. He is like something out of a nightmare. Even the Collector felt sorry about the situation you're in."

Mrs. Ostein shook at that thought. What kind of horror could make the Collector sympathetic to her? That was a place she couldn't force her mind to go to.

ROAD TRIP

It's a couple of weeks later, after life had settled back into an uneasy routine.

"Road-trip time," she told her daughters one Tuesday morning. "The hell with school and routine. We need a break."

"Hard to deny," her oldest daughter agreed.

"So pack some clothes. Not much—a couple of days in the desert. Let's just get away."

"Whatever," the youngest daughter mumbled.

They drove for hours, far out into the desert. Mrs. Ostein finally pulled into a dusty parking lot. An old man came out of a weathered shed, and she gave him the keys.

"This way," she ordered the girls as she shouldered her backpack.

"Mom!" her younger daughter whined.

"The cabin is a long way away. Save your breath. It's a long walk, and it's hot. Or stay with Mr. Refugee from a slasher movie." She pointed at the old man peeking at them from his shed.

"Ah, got it," and the girls quickly pulled their backpacks out of the car.

They walked away, the girls nervously glancing back at the weathered shed.

"He isn't as bad as he looks," she told them. "And I brought help." She showed them the pistol in her belt.

"Bad as he looks? He's a ringer for that guy in that slasher movie that hung the girls on thorn trees!" the older daughter exclaimed.

"No," the younger daughter disagreed. "He's the one that kept the scorpions."

The girls argued about horror movies for the next half hour as they trudged down the dusty path.

> Here is no water but only rock
> Rock and no water and the sandy road
> The road winding above among the mountains
> Which are mountains of rock without water
> If there was water we should stop and drink
> Amongst the rock one cannot stop or think
> Sweat is dry and feet are in the sand
> If there were only water amongst the rock[12].

She spoke quietly, almost to herself.

"Ah, mom, I don't think that is helping," her older daughter grumbled.

"I think I'd rather have the slasher," the younger daughter complained. "At least he'd have some weed."

Mrs. Ostein glanced at them, shook her head, and walked on. They reached the cabin hours later, and sat, exhausted, on the front porch. An hour later, they had recovered enough to make some dinner.

"Here's the deal," Mrs. Ostein announced. They were sitting outside. The stars were bright; the sky pitch black. The world was quiet—there were a few animal noises, and an occasional jet far overhead.

"We're out here so the watchers can't hear us. Everything is recorded at the house. The car, the house, your cell phones—everything. Probably your underwear.

"Shit," the younger daughter snarled. "I just hope there isn't a live

Internet feed going somewhere."

"The Minister, the Collector, the Accountant and the others—they worked for your father. Turns out they hated him, but they did good work, at least by their lights. They are disgusting people in lots of ways. But they are in league with—no, really more under the control of—people who are worse than I ever imagined. I've never been so shaken. The people they work for are more like the Enemy that my father preached against than anything I ever hoped to meet. They have us tied up fourteen different ways, and there is nothing we can do. We're caught in their web. There are all these terrible things going on that you need to know about, but you can neither tell anyone nor do anything about them. All we can do is help ourselves."

"Mom, isn't that against what you always told us?" the younger daughter asked. "You insisted that we should help others and tell the truth."

"If we tell or do anything, all that will be found of us is separated body parts," her mother sighed, staring into the fire. "I'm absolutely confident about that. And the body parts will be separated while we are still alive, or at least they will start that way."

The daughters started to cry. No one said anything for a long time.

"So, this is it. This is what we are going to do..."

THE MINSTER

It was late Sunday night, after all the services and the meetings.

The Minister sat in his study, peering out at the desert. The separation of the lush green grass around the church and the dry empty desert was like a knife's edge, sharp and clean. And my job, he knew, is to keep their little minds in the green grass, artificial as it is, and from straying into the desert. The real world would just confuse them. Lord knows it confuses me a lot of the time.

Wasn't there something about blind, vaulting ambition? he recalled. What doesn't kill you makes you stronger, I guess. Times have improved. I collect from the faithful my ten percent. Perhaps these drugs help a bit, but what I do is nothing compared to what the mother church did.

He opened an article he'd found, from Kamen, "The Spanish Inquisition". He still couldn't believe it as he read it.

It was widely accepted that the Inquisition existed only to rob people. They openly affirmed that truth and worked it into the justice they pretended to enforce. Rich and poor knew that it was the rich who were most at risk. The Inquisition had profitized itself, funding itself from the property it confiscated. The goals rapidly focused on more collections, which meant in practice that it burned people on commission. Individual inquisitors also funded themselves, acquiring great wealth during their careers. Corruption follows the usual paths, fabricated evidence used to extort money from victims, but even when the false evidence was discovered there was no punishment. How could there be? They had done what they had done for the good of the church. If people were wrongly punished, well, they were justly punished for things that had not been caught before. The inquisitor's staff— the familiars— committed crimes without fear of punishment by the secular courts. Amazingly, after 1518, this was formalized. Familiars enjoyed immunity from prosecution similar to the benefits of clergy or modern diplomatic immunity. On top of their exemption from taxation, this was another cause for popular scandal.

But what can be done when you accuse the accusers, who have the whips, the guns, and the prisons? Little, actually. What isn't amazing is the eventual protests, he thought. What's amazing is how long it took. And how many continued, and still continue, to buy in, heart and soul, as it were, into the stories. That article is a historical judgment from people safe from those bands of inquisitors. The inquisitors, so sure of themselves, kept detailed records to prove their devotion to the cause. That's part of the problem. They were in a race. If they didn't perform, didn't raise money, they became suspect. With enemies everywhere against them, all they could do was accuse others first; prove their devotion with greater violence and more money collected.

People with good intentions usually have few qualms about pursing their goals, which are socially blessed. The conviction that our intentions are unquestionably good may sanctify the most questionable means, and they are eventually sanctified. The church could not have committed the evil it did had not so many cared so fervently about the good.

Well, enough of that, the Minister decided. So I've rationalized that what I do is for their own good, and far better than was done in the past. And that the Cardinal and the Sandman were the Inquisition, and are never to be crossed in any manner.

Chapter 8. Christmas

Switzerland. Lucretia Reports

Lucretia knelt before the dais in Paul's audience chamber. She had given a full report of her activities at the company, and had been vigorously questioned. Cross-examined? Interrogated? Closer to the process, she thought. I'm hoping they don't pull out the whips. Her knees hurt on the stone, but she knew to say nothing. It's like those old churches. You are supposed to suffer.

She listened to Paul's staff as they gave him a detailed report on what was on the flash drive. Wow!, Hal was reeling them in. There's stuff on there that sounds really good. From what I know of Hal, it's either out of date or carries poisoned gifts with it, but I'm my lips are sealed. Then they talked about what they were able to capture from the two times that Lucretia had been able to get through the backdoor into the company network, which had answered some more questions.

What has Hal pulled out of their network? she wondered. Moving on little cat's feet, I'm sure he got more than he gave. Nice of him not to give them anything that would look bad for me when it bites them.

"So what is the conclusion?" Paul commanded, obviously annoyed with the long, dull discussions. "All this possible? Maybe? we think?. What do we have?"

"We have what we have been looking for," the chief accountant announced. "Proof which both confirms our suspicions and which hints to of us things that we had no idea of! Proof of the treasures that they sit on, the research they are focusing on, and some of their goals. And, we know that the person Ms. Liancol met with was the person who destroyed the cartel's network several years ago. The person who stole all that money from the cartel, cost us the child pornography project we had worked so long and hard on, and generally destroyed the cartel's computer network." Hopefully not our network, the accountant thought unhappily to himself. Hopefully there were no surprises when we crept into their networks. Thankfully nothing has popped up yet.

"Really?" Paul replied, actually surprised. He looked sharply at Lucretia. "What did you think of this person?"

"He seemed very bright, my lord," Lucretia answered. "Young. I wondered why he should be so high in the company. But people rise rapidly in today's world, so his being in a position like that is not as unusual as it used to be."

"And you met Sir Jonathan?" Paul demanded.

"Yes," Lucretia replied. "Mother Superior was surprised to hear that.

She hates him. She said he was dangerous."

"More dangerous than you can imagine," Paul grimaced. "My worst enemy who has haunted me over the eons. So we have that company, which has information we need. More than just information—treasure. We have our ancient enemy in control at that company. And we have this upstart, who has embarrassed and humiliated us, not counting the actual economic damage he's caused us, running the show. The cartel has been asking for revenge. Well, now they shall have it."

"Time to take steps," Paul commanded, an odd happy smile flickering over his face. "Time for action." He stared at Lucretia. "I need you to prepare a business plan for the steps we will take should that company, well, suffer a leadership loss. If, say Aeternalis, GmbH wasn't really eternal. What opportunities might we have then? You've been working on an analysis of their company structure. Go ahead and finish that. And be ready to offer any support services we might need from you in New York—if we should need housing and food for people from out of town, for example." Paul glanced away and his lips moved, but he said nothing. He turned to his chief of staff. "We shall begin immediately." Paul realized that Lucretia was still on the steps. "You are dismissed," he announced, imperially waving his hand her, not even looking in her direction.

"Thank you, my lord," she replied, slowly standing up, her legs partially numb from having knelt for so long on the stone steps. She was terrified and shocked at what Paul was planning, but she couldn't show any of it. She stood, bowed her head, and began backing up.

"Stop," Paul ordered, and she glanced up at him, surprised. "What think you of my plan?"

"Our enemies must learn fear," Lucretia asserted, picturing Mother Superior run over by a truck to put herself in the right emotional state.

Paul nodded and smiled. "Good." He waved his hand again, dismissing her.

Lucretia continued backing out slowly, and was then escorted from the audience chamber. She kept a radiant, confident look on her face as she walked back to her room. Not a flicker! They will kill me and speed up their plan. A shower. In the shower, her head covered with soap, she let the tears flow. Soap in my eyes, careless of me. She despaired. I've killed my family. The new ones and then the old ones when they figure out what really happened.

She took her time with her hair—shampoo, conditioner, lots of hair in her eyes covering her face. Gut feeling? I can't let this happen. But I can't say anything until it's about to happen. If I do, and they suspect me, then it will still come down, and I'll not be able to warn anyone.

SWITZERLAND. DECEMBER 24ᵀᴴ

The chateau had huge fresh evergreen wreathes tied to the iron gates. The grounds were snow covered, a beautiful fairy ice palace. The big puffy flakes swirled around the huge, armored limos shuttling back and forth between the airport and the chateau, bringing guests for the Christmas celebration.

Inside the Chateau it was a blaze of lights, wreathes, and Christmas trees. All of the staff wore special Christmas uniforms. Only the metal detectors at the entrances and the careful scanning of all presents brought in marred the spontaneous effect of a joyous celebration.

"Another Natalis Solis Invicti, the Birthday of the Unconquerable Sun," Paul remarked to the Butler. "You have done a beautiful job of decorating the palace."

The Butler beamed, terrified that his efforts would be considered a failure. "Real gold, my lord," pointing out the bright displays.

"Good," Paul smiled. "That shows respect for the Gods."

The butler nodded. I guessed right. Business must have been good this year.

A group of costumed singers and dancers walked by, practicing their songs.

"Mummers," Paul commented to the Butler. "Very good. You have missed nothing."

"An ancient tradition, before caroling. I had hoped you would be pleased. And the feast? All you had asked for. We are honoring Mithras, the ancient feast of the Saturnalia, the winter solstice, with the richest, most exotic delicacies from all over the world."

"Wonderful. Saturn, the god of sowing and husbandry—we certainly wish to honor him. And we intend to sow this year."

The Butler carefully noticed nothing.

"You have work to do," Paul ordered, The Butler bowed deeply, backed up, and then turning, hurried down the hallway, shouting at his staff. Paul contemplated the formal and elaborate decorations. Not quite Persia, but a good display.

"My lord, there are guests here for audiences," his chief of staff advised.

"Of course. Business as usual. No rest for the emperor." They walked towards the audience chamber, passing through a room with a mammoth fireplace. The fireplace had been expertly filled, and the huge logs burned brightly. Paul stopped and held his hands out to the fire to warm them. "It's cold in the mansion," he observed to the chief of staff. "The heat feels good."

"A stone fortress in the winter," the chief of staff replied. "Even in

Persia, the palace was cold."

Paul nodded his head, watching the fire. How many years had he watched Yule logs burn in honor of Mithras being born? He remembered when it had been the primary celebration of the empire. He'd taken many of the emotional hooks from that religion when he had remade Christianity. He recalled some of ancient celebrations begging the Sun God to come back and renew the world. The magic had always worked; the Sun God always came back, the days becoming longer and warmer.

"Where are the candles for Mithras?" Paul demanded. "Remember, it is customary to light a candle to encourage Mithras to reappear next year. One can never go wrong asking that."

"There is a candle in this room, my lord," the aide answered anxiously, pointing to a corner where a huge candle burned.

"I always liked Mithras—the savior who kills, not the one who is killed. Still, the other story works better for the masses." Rubbing his hands, feeling the glowing heat of the fire, Paul glanced over to another corner of the room, where there was a huge decorated tree. The tree was central to the northern European winter solstices, he thought, and it made sense. In the depths of winter, when all is cold and dead, the bright green trees remind you that life will come back again.

"The trees were blessed by the Druids before cutting," the chief of staff added, noticing Paul staring at the trees.

"It's always good to show respect. The Gods are reluctant to guide us, so we do what we can, hoping they will favor us. I remember the Druid's ceremonies in the old days, when they worshipped the huge trees, deep in the forest. Talk about cold! Wrapped in all the furs you could get and we still froze. Well, business calls." The guards, snapping to attention, held the doors as they walked into the audience chamber.

NEW YORK. COLDMEN SACKING

Lucretia sat in the office, idly watching the news. Why do we bother showing up at all the day before Christmas? listening to the laughter and uproar echoing down the hall. Because it would be the same whatever the day was before the holiday, she told herself. It's good to see people enjoying themselves, anyhow.

She stared at the piece of paper on her desk and felt sick. As requested, she has reserved several hotel rooms through several shell companies and arranged for transportation for a number of people and their unspecified equipment. Mother Superior was quite clear on what she wanted. "I hasten to obey," Lucretia mumbled, "your assholiness." She didn't have to guess for who, and why. This is a fine Christmas present, she sighed. Stop it! I have to keep looking happy, don't look worried. Don't make the watchers wonder.

"The staff is having eggnog in the break room," her secretary announced. "Care to join us?"

Lucretia almost snapped back her customary no, but then thought, Hell, why not? "Sure." She stood up and walked out of her office. She and the secretary walked down the hall, talking about their children.

NEW YORK. DECEMBER 24TH

The warehouse doors had large, green wreaths with red holly berries worked into the branches. Inside, the hallways glowed with lights and warmth. The huge community room was brightly lit with a huge tree in a corner. The room was so large and high that the twenty-plus foot tree still looked too small.

"The children are too small to really get the idea," Hal commented, "but they like tearing paper off things."

"At Maria's age, everything is exciting," Cali replied. "we found some nice things we think she will like."

Hal snuck a kiss. "Look! Mistletoe!"

"Ah, isn't it supposed to be above me? Just technically?"

"It's the spirit of the thing, not the petty details," Hal offered. "Now, in Babylon, the feast of the Son of Isis, Isis being the Goddess of Nature, was celebrated on December 25. Well, on or about, as their calendar was a little inexact sometimes. Raucous partying, gluttonous eating and drinking, and gift-giving were traditions of this feast, which went on for quite a while."

"Not much has changed, has it?" Jesus observed, standing next to them. "What a beautiful room!"

"Feast of the Son of Isis?" Cali asked. "I didn't know that."

"The mother goddess and her child turned into Mary and Jesus, and Christ was presented as the Son of Righteousness, replacing the sun god, Sol Invictus," Jesus explained. "In 350, Pope Julius I declared that Christ's birth would be celebrated on December 25. The masses were quite stubborn about celebrating their holidays, so if you can't beat them, join them. It's as good a day as any."

"Ah, guests arriving," Jesus declared, glancing at the people filling the entry, and he rushed off to greet them.

"It's nice to all be together for Christmas," Cali bubbled, snuggling up to Hal. "Everyone will be here."

"We're going to have to raise the tree if more gifts show up," Hal advised. "Fortunately, I made arrangements should that be necessary. And the weather is good. Relatively little snow, and the airports are functioning."

"The tree is beautiful," Cali exclaimed. "It makes you feel like nature is alive again, even in the depths of winter. The ancients revered life. Nature was everywhere, alive. Every fountain had its spirit, every mountain its deity, and every water, grove, and meadow, its supernatural association. The whispering of the trees was the subtle speech of the gods who dwelt within.[13]"

"Now, we ignore nature, treat it like a dog to do our bidding," Mary sighed. "Oh, well, enough of that. It's Christmas! The days will be getting longer, the sun will have warmth again." She heard a cry from the other room. "Your daughter may need changing."

"Nature at its most raw and elemental," Cali sighed. She glared around. "That Hal! Vanished again. Well, I'll do the honors."

Hal was standing behind Lungorthin, talking to him. "Dodged that one," Hal commented, watching Cali walk out of the room. "I'm not good with that. If there was a keyboard and a set of instructions to type on it, I'd do better."

"Goth Girl won't let me near the children," Lungorthin rumbled. "Something about my strength and how I'm too clumsy. I'm happy to agree. Before, the pups ran in the meadow and pooped where they would, which was a lot easier."

"That it would be! A little rough on the carpets in here, I'm afraid." Hal walked over to the candles burning brightly above the fireplace. "I never realized their importance," he told Lungorthin. "Traditionally, they were almost as important as the Yule log. The candles are gifts—Mary was very careful about that. We actually had a meeting to determine who was the head of the household, as the candles can only be lit or extinguished by the head. It wasn't that clear, so we set up candles for everyone, just to cover ourselves."

"The candles should burn steadily, never to be moved or snuffed, lest death follow," Lungorthin replied. "At least through Christmas night, until the sun rises."

"It's amazing how serious the traditions really are," Hal remarked. "The Christmas Carol story, the modern bright stories on television, gloss over the deeper meanings."

SWITZERLAND. CHRISTMAS

The formal dining room was a blaze of colors and lights. The room was full and the assembled guests were happily digging into an extravagant feast. The Butler's rash promise to Paul that the best exotic foods from around the world had been brought to the chateau was, if anything, an understatement. Whole cooked pigs, roast beef after roast beef, and mounds of fresh fruit from around the world. An entire corner of the room was devoted to desserts of all sizes and shapes. The waiters and waitresses were hovering around, quick to fill their guests' requests. The wine flowed freely, and the party roared along.

This room also had huge Yule logs burning in a mammoth fireplace in honor of the sun, to encourage him to make the days longer and warmer. And there was not one, but two huge Christmas trees, dark evergreens lit from top to bottom, gifts piled up underneath them and overflowing onto the stone floors.

Cesare sat with his retinue at a table. The Cardinal and Dominique were at the front table. There were many tables full of business associates and partners of Paul, all celebrating.

"Cesare is even in a good mood," Dominique commented. "It probably means that someone got a gift they didn't want.

"Almost certainly true," the Cardinal agreed. "Well, once a year he relaxes a bit. Abandons that burden of carrying the world around, which he really doesn't carry, because even Paul isn't that foolish."

"Lucretia couldn't come. She has her children, I know."

"And business," the Cardinal frowned. "Well, we shall see how it goes."

"Another plan?" Dominique asked. "Paul just has to act! And, I don't see Grendel." She scrutinized the room. "That's a Christmas gift in itself."

"More wine, I think," the Cardinal told the waiter hovering near them. "It's Christmas, my dear, but business goes on," he remarked to Dominique.

Suddenly, the Butler rapped his staff loudly on the hard stone floor. The guests fell silent. A spotlight lit up the entry, and in walked a man in a bright red suit, with a long white beard.

"Ho, ho, ho," he laughed. "And have we been good girls and boys this year?"

"Yes," the crowd shouted.

"Then you're out of luck," the man laughed. "Only bad boys and girls get presents here."

The crowd roared with laughter and delight as young women dressed like elves quickly started running presents from the trees to the guests seated at the tables. Santa walked to the high table. He took his beard off and sat down. "There," Paul chuckled, patting the padding under his red suit. "Giving gifts is the fun part. You know, Santa Claus is a sovereign judge. He answers to no one and no one has authority over him, and when he 'comes to town,' he comes with a full bag of rewards for those who have been good. At least in his eyes."

"And what is this?" Paul added, looking at a thin present handed to him by the Butler. He carefully tore the paper off. Valerian, a flower that causes drowsiness—what a pretty name for a new product. A gift from the cartel. New things coming. And more, he thought. He quickly read the short note.

"These are real presents for me," Paul declared to the Cardinal and the others at the table. "I must have been a better boy this year than I thought."

"Or worse," the Cardinal observed.

Paul laughed. "This is just what I asked for," holding the note up that was in the present. He smiled and folded the note, carefully putting it in his pocket. Suddenly, waiters and waitresses burst out of the kitchen, carrying heavy trays. "Here is the goose!" Paul exclaimed. "And it smells wonderful." The food came in waves.

New York. Lucretia's Christmas

Lucretia and her family went shopping for a Christmas tree, finally finding one at a farm an hour from their condo. Lucretia ordered, "Bring it to us and give me the bill," and the truck followed them home.

"Money is good for some things," her mother muttered, anxiously watching the men grunt as they maneuvered the tree carefully down the hallway.

That night they had decorated the tree, and the children had stared at it every day for the next two weeks, poking at the packages underneath when they thought no one was watching them.

Christmas morning, Lucretia and her family were sitting on the floor, sorting out the presents to open. Jose was jumping up and down in excitement and her daughter, Donna Juana, was sneaking around, seeing what she could get into that she wasn't supposed to be into.

"Who are these from?" her mother asked. "They were delivered yesterday."

"They can't be from my sisters," Lucretia muttered. "Sticks and coal are usually in a smaller package."

"I think you send them nice gifts just to make them angry," her mother commented.

"Would I do that?" Lucretia countered. "After all they have done to us?"

"It's Christmas," her mother commented. "Perhaps we'll let that one go."

"Dominique!" Lucretia exclaimed, looking at the inscription. She tore open the one addressed to her and held up the necklace. "It's beautiful! How thoughtful of her."

"Beautiful is a small word for this," her mother declared, holding up the necklace she had received. "Those are real." She squinted at the jewels. "Wow. Maybe I can retire after all."

Jose shouted as he opened each new gift.

"What is this?" Lucretia asked, puzzled, staring at a large box. "Well, it's to Jose." She handed it to him.

Jose tore it open, and stared. "A custom game machine. I've only seen these online!"

Lucretia stared at it for a second, shocked, and then smiled. "I knew you'd like it," Lucretia announced, glancing at her mother, who nodded, smiling. Hal, Lucretia thought. He likes the toys. She smiled at Jose, who was completely fascinated with the machine.

Her mother opened an ornately wrapped box and pulled out a bottle of fine wine. She studied it for a moment, and then laughed, an odd laugh—happy, yet bitter. "This does bring back memories," shaking her head. Lucifer. The wine from the night Lucretia was conceived. "Thank you, honey," and she bent over and kissed Lucretia on the forehead.

Lucretia stared cluelessly at the bottle. "Ah, yeah, I knew you'd like that vintage," Lucretia offered, recovering. The watchers, she thought. Well, we're supposed to be devious with each other on Christmas.

Her daughter was thrilled to just tear paper off things and not get yelled at for doing it.

"Another year," Lucretia's mother promised, happily watching her granddaughter. "And she'll get the idea."

"Another year," Lucretia worried.

The watchers were not paying attention, having opened a bottle of holiday cheer in their small office, and they missed the mystery presents and the momentary expressions.

NEW YORK. CHRISTMAS

The children screamed with delight as Jesus tromped into the room with his white beard, red cloak, and heavy black boots. "And who was good this year?" he merrily shouted, looking at the children and adults.

"Let's go with all of us," Hal suggested. "Light on the details, big on the concept."

"Always a good idea," Jesus agreed, "especially on my birthday."

"It was March, I think, dear," Mary corrected, "just to be technical. I was there."

"Still, this makes a great day for a birthday. Shortest day of the year, the sun coming back, and all that. It's cold outside, but in here, it's all bright lights and warm food. So presents? And then we eat!"

Lucifer and Hal's mother stood in a corner, arm in arm, watching the children tear at the presents.

Shouts of "Thank you!" and "Just what I wanted!" rang through the room as the adults opened their presents.

"That's one nice thing about living in an old warehouse," Mary declared, looking at the happy crowd. "Lots of space."

"Oy, the utility bills," Jesus moaned.

"There's always something," Goth Girl agreed.

"Here's a gift that came the other day—no return address, very quiet,"

Lucifer frowned, doubtfully handing it to Cali. "We had it checked, and there doesn't seem to be anything nasty in there."

"Sad," Cali sighed, "but we have to think about these things. Oh!" She shouted "Look!" pulling the picture out and excitedly waving it around to show the others. "It's Jose Jr., Lucretia, her mother, and her daughter," pointing them out to everyone. "What a wonderful gift!"

"And what a risk," Lucifer mused, "for her to send that to you."

"We should have sent something," Cali mumbled, crestfallen. "I feel bad now."

"Perhaps Jose received an incredible, state-of-the-art game machine from Lucretia this year," Hal laughed. "Just perhaps."

Cali laughed. "He'll love that, if he's at all like his father." She kissed Hal.

"Okay, break it up," Mary ordered as the kissing turned into an embrace. "There are children present. Here are some special gifts," Mary told Hal and Cali, handing each of them a package. "From the three of us."

Hal's was a beautiful, ancient ring, with a lion's head carved out of a gemstone. Cali's was a necklace with a lion, a leopard, and a she-wolf worked into the design.

"Beautiful!" Cali exclaimed, holding it up the light and then putting it on. "Like it?" she asked Hal.

"Magnificent! And the necklace is nice, too."

"Flatterer!" Cali teased.

"This ring is incredible," Hal mumbled. He looked at Mary. "Thank you very much!" He slipped it on his finger.

"I still have the necklace Jesus gave me all those years ago," Cali added. "Remember, Hal, the one I showed you at UM?"

"The one the literature professor wanted after we were gone? How could I forget?" It is an authentic masterpiece. I researched it one day. As is this," he added, examining the ring. "Now I feel like I've been light on the gifts I've given."

"You being here is the best gift," Mary gushed, kissing Cali and Hal.

"I calculated the increase in the value of the companies from the changes you've made since you started," Lucifer added. "You've given us plenty of presents this year!"

"Dinner," the cook called out. They trooped into the dining room.

"It's ham this year," Jesus explained. "An ancient tradition held that a boar had killed the sun deity Adonis. A pig was sacrificed to entreat the sun god to come back."

"And it's good!" Hal offered, sitting down. "Absolutely wonderful!"

SWITZERLAND. CHRISTMAS NIGHT

He was tired, wounded, and the ancient battle had been going badly. Fleeing, he was trapped and Lucifer drove his sword into Paul's stomach, up to the hilt, and spit in Paul's face as the blood gushed from Paul's mouth. Paul woke up, shouting wildly, terrified. He sat up and then jumped out of bed, walking warily around the room, shaking his head as he pulled out of the dream.

"What, my lord?" the woman in the bed pleaded. "Is there anything I can do?

"No," Paul replied, realizing what she had seen. He touched a bell and the chamberlain came in. Paul glanced at him for a second and nodded, and the man bowed and left.

"What was that all about?" the woman asked, dropping the covers she had pulled up to cover herself when the chamberlain walked in.

"Nothing," Paul told her. "He'll bring me a drink that will help me wake up. Old dreams," Paul growled. "Old wars."

Suddenly, the Cardinal strode in with two guards. The woman quickly covered herself again, staring at Paul.

Paul nodded and the guards hauled the screaming, naked woman out of the bed and down the hallway, out of the room. They listened to her shrieks fading in the distance.

"The same dream?" the Cardinal asked.

"The same," Paul replied. "I can't let the rumors get out."

"No, my lord, you are right," the Cardinal agreed. "She will be a gift for the creatures, I think. They feel they are forgotten, and will be happy. She cannot go to Cesare—he would find out things he should not know."

"You are right, my friend." Paul pulled on his Assyrian King tunic. "Here, I'll walk with you."

They walked to a large room. It looked like a game room, but with strange, old figures and targets. Paul hefted a harpoon and let it fly. It hit the target, splintering the wood.

"I'll have the attendants come and replace the targets," the Cardinal commented. "If I may, my lord, I'll go back to sleep. I have to be in Rome tomorrow."

"You look tired," noticing the bags under the Cardinal's eyes.

"I don't sleep well," the Cardinal complained. "Inaction, I think. I perhaps need more exercise. Where is a horse and a sword when I need one?"

After the Cardinal left, Paul walked slowly over, pulled the harpoon out of the target, and walked back to position.

NEW YORK. CHRISTMAS NIGHT

The party had died down, and most of the children were in bed.

Hal stood by the windows, staring out at the dark street, not smiling.

Cali walked up behind him. "Where's that Christmas cheer?"

Hal jumped, and his drink spilled. "Damn," brushing at the wine staining his shirt. "Oh well, it's a burgundy shirt."

"That's not a relaxed Christmas spirit I'm seeing," Cali commented, studying him carefully. "Is there something out there? Or too much Christmas cheer?"

"Not unless you've been adding something to the eggnog. And, I don't see anything out there, but there is something in the back of my mind, something picking at me. Maybe it's just me. I seem to be uncoordinated today. I've been bumping my toes and pinching my fingers." He stared down at the street, frowning.

"You do look worried, honey."

"This thing almost pops up and then vanishes again," Hal complained. "I don't know what it is. It's just a nagging feeling, like I'm missing something but don't know what that thing is. My attention is grabbed but I don't know on what. Annoying." He shrugged and pulled the curtains after a final unhappy glance into the dark.

"Listen to the little doubts," Cali reminded him. "Our discussion the other night—remember?"

"Is that what we were discussing?" Hal teased, smiling at her. "The festivities afterward diverted my attention a bit. It will come to me, I think. Saying to listen and letting it pop out are two different things." He frowned, almost able to grasp a floating something and then it was gone again.

"Maria certainly enjoyed Christmas! "All that tearing up stuff, and surrounded by a pile of presents like she was in a fort! It isn't like she's spoiled or anything."

"No, not spoiled a bit!" Hal laughed. "What a great sight! And she's at the age where anything is exciting. Easy to buy for." He was thoughtful again. "What were we talking about the other day? Unknown unknowns—the ones we don't know we don't know, and don't suspect. I'd just feel better if it would pop out of the back of my mind. Oh, well. They will have to remain unknown for a while." He and Cali walked hand in hand to where Maria was squealing with joy, pushing presents over and crawling after the dogs.

Later that night, Hal peered out the window into the dark. Denial is the most insidious fear response of all, he thought. Fear of harm to the family— it's easy to want to pretend there isn't any danger out there. So we deny, pushing it into a corner, into places we never think to look. He absently watched a truck drive slowly down the street, pulling into the warehouse down and across from them. He shook his head, frustrated as he walked back to the celebration.

CHAPTER 9. DRIVEN OUT

<u>DECEMBER 26TH</u>

In the warehouse around the corner from the family's warehouse, a group of men were sleeping in a large room.

"Wake it up, people," the sergeant snarled, walking into the room.

Heads popped up, and then people started to sit up.

"This is the day that we've been training for. We've got some time before we move, but we have to be perfect. It has to happen exactly as planned, so everyone get ready, clean and check your weapons, and then do it again. We're scheduled to act in roughly three, four hours, give or take."

"I thought we were going to do this ourselves," a man mumbled.

"I'd thought so, too," the sergeant admitted. "A change of plans—or maybe we were never told the real plan."

"Why tell the people on the ground what has to be done?" another voice added. "That would be a first."

"Not our job to run the train," the sergeant declared.

"No, only our job to take the blame if it goes off the tracks," a man snapped. "I reference our prior employer."

"Is it true, sir, that the target is that person who destroyed our government careers?" another asked.

"The rumor mill is always active," the sergeant replied. "Yeah, that's true. The kid who ruined the pornography network, and along with that network our careers, is the target. And his family. Objections?"

"No, sir."

"He ruined my life," a man exclaimed. "The wife moved out, took the kids, got a court order against me. The court thought I'd been the one assembling all that stuff and dumped on me."

"All of us paid for others' mistakes," the sergeant agreed. "We're lucky to get this opportunity. Hell, we're lucky to still be alive—most of the rest of the network was retired without pensions."

It was quiet in the room for a minute.

"Now, this is a joint enterprise, and we are support, not the leaders," the sergeant advised.

"That's a weird group that showed up two days ago," a man mumbled.

"That's putting it mildly," the sergeant growled. "I'm not sure who we are in greater danger from—that kid and his people or our 'friends.' I know I want our 'partners' happy with us. So, I don't want you people focused on revenge here. I don't want any emotions getting in the way. We're professionals, regardless of what the world thinks of us now and we have a job to do. After it's done, well, a little personal satisfaction would be in order. Clear?"

"Clear, sir," the men answered.

"So what are you all sitting there for? Waiting for your mothers to come and wipe your asses?" the sergeant snarled.

People started moving very quickly.

NOTHING AS EXPECTED

It was the day after Christmas; a quiet day at the office. The phone wasn't ringing, as most of the world took the whole week off between Christmas and New Year's.

Hal sat in his office, waiting to go to a conference. He was seething. Administrative nonsense! *A day that I could get some real work done without interruptions, and this! I can't even pretend that I had car trouble because a limo is on its way, sent by the people running the seminar. That's flattering, but odd,* he realized. *Normally, I don't let people know where my office is or what my schedule is.* "How did they find out?" he mumbled to himself. He sat back, puzzled and unhappy. *How did they find out?* He glanced at the clock. *Damn, I've got to get ready.* He started absently shuffling papers, as much to delay himself as to do anything useful. *There is something bothering me,* he thought again, for the thirtieth time in the last day. *I just can't put my finger on it. And why am I going to this? It isn't important. How did I get moved into this box?*

Annoyed, he jammed papers in his briefcase, and they tore. He glared at the mess, furious. *And Lungorthin's headed out to a meeting, too. Why? We never have both of us away from the factory. What about security? The caretaker is an old man now. It's because the conference has Lucretia in it,* he told himself. *But why was she put on the list? Who were the people who put this together? Who would know that I would be interested in her being there?*

What did that marketing guy say last week? a random thought pushing into his consciousness. *He told us—what? Decoys dupe us. There was a study. Volunteers were asked to decide among three autos that met minimum specifications. It was hard to choose because the first two cars were marred by differing tradeoffs. The third auto, almost the same as the first one, had a worse trade off. Showing the customer the third, most undesirable auto increased the appeal of the first. Why? Hardwired in the brain, the third option decreased the activity of the amygdala, a part of the brain tied to negative emotions. Why do I care about that?* he thought, now even more annoyed.

"There is someone here to see you," Aliston announced, standing in the door, looking puzzled. "He doesn't have an appointment, but he says he's an old friend. I told him you had to rush, but he's quite insistent."

"Hi, Hal!" A cheerful voice came from the secretary's office. "Long time no see."

"Vladimir!" Hal shouted, glad to hear his voice. "Come in! What brings you here? This is a friend from school, Aliston. He's part of the group that runs that factory we purchased in Detroit. Vladimir, your timing is either great or awful. I have to run for a meeting." Hal grimaced.

"Not a meeting you are looking forward to?" Vladimir asked, studying Hal. "So sit for a minute. It will wait."

"You're right," Hal agreed, happy at the prospect of a delay. "Please, sit, rest your sphincter."

Aliston shook her head and left.

"I was in town and wanted to see you." Vladimir examined the office approvingly. "You've come a long way, but I always knew you'd do well. Here, a treat from your youth. I remembered you used to love these." He pulled out a Milky Way and put it on Hal's desk.

Hal had the worst craving for the candy bar. "I've not had one in years! I don't know why I haven't had one, because that looks great." Hal grabbed it off the desk and quickly ate it. "Delicious," Hal mumbled. And it really is, Hal thought. I feel much, well, healthier. Stronger. Quicker? "So much for the USDA research. I knew they were paid off by the broccoli people."

"Another small thing," Vladimir added. "A gift, for all you have done for us. And, before I give it to you, I tell you that you must accept it. You would insult us to refuse. Nonnegotiable. It's important to us, and to you. Agreed?"

Hal stared at him, puzzled. A ceramic swan, he thought. It's always something like that. "Now I'm worried," he admitted. "But I promise, even if it's moving multiple arms and legs."

"You remember our younger days," Vladimir laughed. "No, it's not like that." He pulled out a beautifully cased samurai sword and held it out to Hal, bowing slightly as he did.

"No! You have to take it," Vladimir protested sternly, catching Hal's look. "You promised."

Hal took the sword, shocked. Gently, he pulled the sword out of the case. It was beautifully wrought. Magnificent. He stared at it, dumbfounded. "I've never seen the like. I don't know what to say," he stammered. "Hell, I'd never have stolen your lunch in tenth grade if I'd known this was coming."

"I think the tuna in the sandwich was bad that day anyhow," Vladimir recalled. "My recollection is that Daniel the linebacker then stole the sandwich from you, and he was sick for days, so justice prevailed. Anyhow, I've got to go. Today is going to be a big day." Vladimir gazed oddly at Hal for a moment. "You. Take. Care. today. Don't let that sword out of your sight—that would be, well, bad luck. I think you'll find it valuable, in many ways."

Those were the words Michael had said to him the last time Hal had seen him. Hal shook it off, and, smiling, walked over to Vladimir. They shook hands, then embraced, old friends.

Vladimir turned to leave, then stopped at the door and turned back to Hal. "Good luck, my friend," he sighed and then walked out.

Hal stared after him, astonished. He looked back and forth between the sword in his hand and the empty door Vladimir had vanished through. That was really strange. I should have stayed home and faced the wrath of Maria. She had been searching for more presents this morning when he left, not happy at all that there were none.

Hal carefully laid the sword on his desk and sat down, staring at it.

Aliston walked in and did a double take when she saw the sword. "I've never seen one of that quality," she gasped, awed. "And he gave it to you? Can I be his friend, too?"

"I'm sure," Hal replied. "He practically fell on the floor when he saw you."

"True," Aliston replied, hopeful for a moment. "But I doubt he has any more swords like this. Men usually have a different sword to present to me. Oh, and that meeting? The limo is downstairs—they called."

Hal frowned. "Isn't this a bit odd?" he mumbled, thinking aloud. "This is more elaborate than a simple conference should be. They leave me no way out, do they? And how do I take this sword there? Vladimir insisted that I take it everywhere."

"I know I'd not leave it more than a foot from me," Aliston asserted. "I don't think you know the value of what he gave you."

His cell phone rang. "Damn," and then he looked at the number. His face grew intent. "Hello?"

"Stephanie? Hi, this is Lucretia. I'm confirming our shopping trip—remember? We meet at Coach today at eleven, and then lunch, your pick. Remember, we set this last week? Ah, this isn't Stephanie? Oh, my mistake—I believe I have a wrong number! Such a silly error for me to make. I'm sorry to have bothered you." The call ended.

Lucretia hung up the phone, making a face.

Her secretary watched her, puzzled.

"Always confirm. That personal touch is important! My daughter didn't sleep well last night, and it seems to be affecting me. Well, I'll try again." She redialed and talked to the person on the other end for a minute, and then hung up. "All confirmed. This should be fun!"

"I know what you mean about tired," the secretary replied. "My two-year-old won't sleep at night, and then she naps in the day, waiting to ambush me when I get home. I can't remember the last time I was fully awake."

Hal held the phone to his ear, staring blankly, listening to the dial tone. Lucretia's words played over and over in his mind. The decisive moment was, among other things, "the simultaneous recognition, in a fraction of a second, of the significance of an event." Lucretia isn't going to be at the seminar. She wasn't scheduled to be there. Ever. And everyone is gone from the warehouse. It's open to attack. The mind's hidden layer had voted on what was most important and sent that image up into awareness. And it was an ugly image. They are attacking the warehouse, Hal knew, shocked. It's all a trap. This limo, this seminar, Lungorthin's trip—I'm probably being watched. Someone they have on staff, somewhere in the building. Act normal, first rule.

Hal forced a laugh, trying not to look around.

Aliston glanced at him, puzzled and then worried.

"Yeah, that's really helpful," Hal told the dial tone. "Look, I appreciate your call. Talk to you soon." He smiled, a fake smile, and finished gathering his papers together.

"Ms. McGowan, could you grab that file?" Hal ordered, pointing at a file near his desk. "I need to take it. Could you bring it to me?" Hal stood up, his back to the door.

Now very concerned, Aliston forced a smile and walked over to him. Hal positioned himself so that she was hidden behind him from anyone looking in from the hallway. "Look normal," he hissed. "Smile."

"Here is the file," she announced. "I've been working on it for the meeting today."

"There will be an attack on the warehouse to kill everyone there," Hal whispered. "I have to get home, but we have to act normal in case there is someone here watching." He forced a smile that was closer to a grimace.

"I will call the limo," Aliston remarked, putting on her efficient face. "I'll tell them you were held up by an unexpected guest, but you will be down soon."

She carefully moved so her face was hidden from the door. "The maintenance guy that looks like you—he would like a break today, I think," she whispered. She stepped towards his desk and her hand hit a glass, which fell on the floor and broke. "Damn, I'm clumsy! I'm so sorry about that! I'll call maintenance right now."

Hal nodded, smiling, as she calmly walked out. My hands are shaking, he thought. Breathe. Focus. People are depending on me. Now, think. We "see" what we expect to see. We don't see the bottle of beer on the shelf in our fridge because we're hunting for a can of beer. I knew something was wrong, but I pushed it away. What else am I missing? What's been happening that I have not seen? He sat down and stared at the computer screen. Have to look normal.

Okay, the first thing is taking care of business. He typed a short memo. He printed it, read it quickly, and signed it just as the maintenance man was rushed into the office, Aliston shouting at him like she normally would. As she walked in, she pushed the door partially shut behind her.

Aliston was still shouting at the maintenance man, who looked harried, as she stepped into a corner of the office hidden from the hallway. "Over here, Hal," she whispered, motioning at him frantically. "You're going to exchange clothes with him—he knows the plan."

The maintenance man was complaining loudly about how the glass scratched the floor, and he couldn't fix that. Aliston was yelling at him, calling him incompetent. Hal quickly stepped into the hidden corner, took off his suit coat, shirt, pants, and shoes, and then pulled on a maintenance outfit Aliston had thrown in the corner.

"There are glass shards over here," Aliston shouted, disgusted, pointing at the corner of the room. The maintenance man rushed to the corner, out of sight, and then Hal started sweeping up the floor. In a minute, the maintenance man was standing at Hal's desk, confidently pulling the papers together, dressed in Hal's Armani suit. "Is the limo in front?" the man demanded in a reasonable copy of Hal's voice. "I'm late." He looked annoyed.

That's a better "annoyed" than I do, Hal thought. Maybe I can take lessons.

"Yes, sir," Aliston replied. She turned to look at Hal, clearly detesting his existence. "Will you clean that up?" she yelled, obviously furious, waving her arms. "And then get out of here! Security, watch this man, and get him out of here when he's done," she shouted at the guard standing by the door.

Maintenance Hal in the Armani suit strode out the door. "I'm late," he declared loudly, and rushed into the elevator. Hal finished cleaning up and grabbed the maintenance toolkit. He glanced at the sword on the desk, but it was too obviously in view for him to grab it.

"The sword," Hal whispered to Aliston. "I need it—it's important."

"I'll get it," Aliston whispered back, nodding. "Get him downstairs!" she shouted to the security guard, pointing at Hal. "And get some air freshener in here!" waving her arms and stalking off.

The guard grabbed Hal's arm and moved him along, half carrying him out of the office. In a second, they were in the hallway. People were standing in the hallway watching the show, and they snickered as Hal was meekly hauled off, his head carefully down, hidden under a maintenance cap.

    Hal and the guard took a freight elevator to the basement.

"The man taking my place—he'll be okay, won't he?" Hal asked. "I'd assume someone with a hostile intent is waiting for him."

"I understand steps are being taken," the guard replied. "Perhaps the limo will be delayed in traffic. Not your concern, sir."

"I'm thinking that there is a lot of security I really don't know about," Hal remarked. "That maintenance man was a remarkably quick study, and your performance is quite good."

"Wouldn't know, sir," the guard responded politely. They stepped out and stood in the garage outside the elevator. In a second, another elevator opened and Aliston came stalking out, furious, carrying a maintenance tool bag.

"Your tools, idiot!" she shouted at Hal, and appeared to toss the bag on the floor. Somehow the bag was softly laid on the concrete without disturbing the contents at all.

"Well, I'm sorry about the accident," Hal stammered. "Maybe it can be fixed?"

"I wouldn't count on it," Aliston snarled, and several people walking by laughed after they passed.

"Here," Hal whispered to Aliston, handing her a letter. "For the good of France and at my order, the bearer has done what they have done."

"What's this?" she asked, puzzled.

"It's an official letter appointing you Vice President of Operations if I'm gone."

She gasped.

The guard looked shocked for a second, but quickly recovered.

"You keep a civil tongue toward your betters!" the guard snapped at Hal. "You speak to this fine woman again like that, and it will be your job."

"It just was," Hal sighed, smiling a little, and he bent to pick up the tool kit.

"Walk him out of the building," Aliston snarled to the guard. "I'm going to talk to personnel about him—we can't have his kind of attitude here. Go with God," she whispered to Hal, her face twisting in fear. Only for a second—then the usual calm control was back. She turned and strode to the elevator, pushing the up button without looking back.

Hal meekly walked towards the exit to the parking ramp, paced by the guard, who kept one hand on his pistol. The guard watched Hal contemptuously.

They stopped outside the building. The guard silently stood just inside the garage, pretending to watch Hal while discreetly scanning the street.

Hal stood on the sidewalk for a minute, his mind racing. Think! What

163

did they say at that training seminar? The one with the sullen mercenaries with facial scars. Grab your fears; turn them into motivation. Survival is a lot of actions, and you can't do them all at once. You have to take a bite at a time. Don't eat the whole stupid elephant. What's next?

First, Lungorthin has to be turned around, headed back to the warehouse. Second, the caretaker has to be warned, but not obviously preparing for an attack, because they could jump their timetable. Third, warn dad. They are waiting for something—what? My arrival at the conference? Lungorthin's arrival at his meeting? I must have seen this, but I let it go by. It's easy to see what you expect to see, and damned hard to see what should be there and isn't. It's seeing the small puddle on the kitchen floor and assuming it's from an ice cube. But it may not have been that at all. What am I believing that are just assumptions? Hal wracked his mind as he dialed Lungorthin.

STEPS

The caretaker was sitting in the kitchen on a bar stool at the bar, stirring his coffee. The phone rang, and he stared at it for a second. He grumbled to the cook, "It's the day after Christmas, and look, they give me no rest. Hell, have to answer." He took the call. "So what's not working now?" he grumbled into the phone. "Break into an old man's rest," he mumbled to the cook.

"Look and act normal," Hal hissed. "Say something now, with a smile, something."

"Yeah, I can hear you," the caretaker grumbled, and made a motion with his hand. The cook laughed and went back to chopping vegetables.

I see you watching in the glass, the caretaker thought.

"There's an attack coming. It was a trap," Hal warned. "I was to be gone and Lungorthin also. I'm headed home and Lungorthin is headed home. Make it look normal 'til we get there, but get ready. Say something normal."

"So which switch is it? In the baby's room? It seems to work part of the time? No, I can look at it," the caretaker replied calmly.

"We don't know who they have inside, or what's bugged. We know nothing right now," Hal snarled. "I'll be there soon."

"Got it," the caretaker agreed, and carefully switching the number displayed to another number, he put the phone down.

The cook looked at him questioningly, but with a certain knowing look behind it.

Apprehension? the caretaker thought. "They think I'm their slave," the caretaker complained, angry at himself for not watching the cook carefully before.

"Hell, I better get to work." He tossed the spoon on the table and it

We're all just fat and

chunked as it hit. Not paying attention, he thought. We're all just fat and happy, safe in our truce, and we had a good holiday. That's how I used to set up attacks.

"Maybe they will recognize your importance someday," the cook commented.

"Yeah, not in my lifetime," the caretaker growled. "Thanks for the thought, though."

The cook smiled and kept chopping.

And you're one on the inside, furious with himself for not having noticed before. That flicker about my lifetime—you think it's going to be short. Good. Who else?

Hal quickly dialed the last number on his short list. "Dad? There will be an attack on the warehouse very soon. Minutes, no more than an hour. No, I'm sure. I'll explain later. Don't know how many, don't know their weapons, I just don't know. Lungorthin is headed back. I'll be there soon. Get who you can as soon as you can."

A Cab Ride

Hal glanced at his watch and his calm vanished. Damn! He ran down the sidewalk, waving frantically for a cab. Several cabs sped by, ignoring his worn handyman clothes, drawn like magnets to suits with briefcases and fat tips. Suddenly, a cab ground to a halt next to him.

Hal jumped in, shouting the address. I never get a cab when I need one, he absently thought. And this one doesn't stink of old beer and vomit. And the cabbie speaks English? I hope I didn't use all my luck getting this cab.

"Here," Hal begged the driver, "this will cover the fare!" He pushed a hundred-dollar bill through the slot. "Please hurry. Please."

The cabbie's eyes were all Hal could see in the mirror as the cab quickly pulled into traffic. Grey and thoughtful eyes, measuring him. Hal felt transparent before the gaze.

"You look troubled, my son," the cabbie observed. "Every new life begins with a confession. We have some time."

Hal stared at him and then opened—completely—to the eyes in the mirror. Hal bowed his head. "I'm terrified," Hal confessed. "There are people, things, powerful and dangerous, about to attack my home. I missed the signs, I didn't see it coming. They are coming to kill my family. If today is the day of my death, I ask that it not be theirs. This I cheerfully sacrifice for them."

"No more can be asked," the cabbie acknowledged, a deep, reassuring voice. "But life is complex. Some deaths are better than life, and some deaths are a new life. What you fear is not important, and what will happen to you is not important, because those are not under your control. It's what you will do that is important. This is all the difference."

Hal gazed into the grey eyes and found comfort. He carefully lifted the sword from the bag, pulling on the scabbard to expose six inches of the blade, and peered into the shining steel, his blue eyes reflected back to him. He breathed, slowly and carefully. "I accept my death," he told his reflection. "That is not my concern."

"If you are afraid of death, you are afraid of life," the cabbie mused. "But there are many kinds of deaths. The end of life is perhaps not the worst. So, what is your quest? What are you living for that is more important than life?"

"To protect my family," Hal announced, suddenly focused.

"What cause more righteous than to protect family?" the cabbie demanded. "And what is the power of your righteous anger? What could stand against it?"

Hal smiled, a hard smile. "None shall stand," he vowed.

"The hero?" the cabbie wondered. "Bright edges and proud standards. Victory and peace. This?"

"I...never got over the death of Hector," Hal confessed. "Brave, wise man, smiling at his wife and baby as he went to certain death. For honor. And do I go now to my death? Only for my wife and child to be destroyed after I am gone? I hope and despair. Hero? I don't know what that is anymore. But I will protect my family."

"Good," the cabbie approved, nodding his head. Holding up the hundred-dollar bill, he observed, "Money may talk, but it doesn't give directions. This is an external symbol only. It is not an inspiration by which you can choose what is right in life. I'll keep it, because it has meaning to the fueling station, those soulless thugs." He smiled. "But Inspiration is what matters for life."

"Confession is good for the soul," Hal murmured.

"No act of contrition is necessary," the cabbie replied sadly. "I do not say 'Go in peace,' because you must go to kill. And to die."

Hal sat motionless for a second, studying the man's eyes in the mirror. "I will make my family proud," Hal promised, surprised at the relief he felt, his fear and indecision gone.

"Each new life may begin with a confession. But the new life starts with the death of the old life, and the rebirth into the new, richer life," the old man promised. "Remember that when it is dark about you and you despair."

The cab screeched to a halt. "And we are here. In time, I'd say. Go to your family, my child. They need you."

Hal nodded and jumped out. He stood on the sidewalk, dazed for a second, thoughts churning. Then he straightened up and ran to the door, desperately asking himself how he would attack this place.

Waiting

The government team was standing in a corner of Paul's warehouse, synchronizing equipment, checking and re-checking.

"Love this," a man marveled, playing with the helmet display. "It lays the layout of the building over the view. Augmented reality, fantastic stuff. Does it in the dark, also."

In another corner, Paul's squad of men was assembled, standing quietly.

And in another room, Paul's creatures discussed their plans.

There was a growl from the other room, and the leader of Paul's men ran in. The government men stared after him in surprise and then quickly looked away after a whispered order from their sergeant.

"Necessary steps have been taken?" the creature growled.

"Yes, my lord," the man promised. "There will be numerous accidents in a few minutes. The Cardinal's men at the police station will ignore phone calls; they will send response teams to the wrong places. And my men are in the fake uniforms, with the necessary covering documents."

"Good. A good plan."

Hal ran down the sidewalk carrying the athletic bag. Lungorthin jumped out of another cab down the street and ran for the entrance. That's torn it! They will know what's up now. He tensed, waiting to feel the bullets hitting him, but they made it to the door, which they pushed open. They dashed in, pushing it shut and locking it.

"What the hell?" the lookout shouted, as he saw Hal and Lungorthin jumping out of their cabs.

"What?" the sergeant snarled, rushing to the window. "Damn! They were not supposed to be here. We had other plans for them."

The creature loomed above him. "Not a problem," it croaked. "Better fight, more honor. Have your men ready."

The sergeant, pale, nodded and rushed around, shouting orders.

8 P's

Hal and Lungorthin stood inside the warehouse. The caretaker ran up to them.

"The cook," the caretaker whispered. "One of theirs. Not sure if there are others."

Hal nodded and glanced at Lungorthin.

Lungorthin rushed into the kitchen. There was a whack, and he came back pulling the unconscious cook, holding her cell phone in his hand. "She made a call," he growled, tossing the phone to Hal.

Hal glanced at the phone, then dropped it on the floor and stomped on it. "Too much risk of it listening in on us," Hal explained to the caretaker, who was staring at the pieces on the floor.

"What?" Hal's mother rushed out, staring at the cook lying on the floor. She shouted at Lungorthin. "What have you done?"

Cali, Goth, the kids, guards, and the nanny rushed in, everyone shouting.

"Shut up!" Hal ordered, and they fell silent. "There will be an attack—in moments, I fear. Get the kids set, get ready to run. We have a plan—remember it! What do we do? Think, people. We have practiced this. The eight Ps. Proper prior planning and preparation prevents piss-poor performance. What are you all supposed to be doing? Now?"

The kids were screaming, sensing their parents' fear. The nanny growled and the kids shut up. Hal had to repress the urge to shut up himself.

Hal knelt and unzipped his athletic bag. He pulled out the sword and put in on his back, the strap over his chest. "Samurai," he announced cheerfully.

Lungorthin studied the sword thoughtfully. The caretaker just stared, stunned.

"A gift from a friend," Hal commented, noticing their expressions. "Providence, you might say."

"At least," the caretaker replied, reading the inscription on the scabbard. "I've never actually seen one of those. I've only heard stories about them."

"Guns," Hal ordered. "Armor. Positions. Move, people. Now."

People ran. Guards grabbed heavy weapons, pulled on armor, and took their positions. Within five minutes, the warehouse was as secure as it could be.

"We can't use the heavy weapons," Hal concluded, frustrated. "The bullets are too powerful—we would kill far too many innocent people and probably knock the warehouse down around us at the same time. Shit." He looked around. "Well, this is as good as we can do for the moment. The warehouse is too big, and there are too few of us." He checked his 9mm and the extra ammunition. "It's something."

"Others coming," Lungorthin growled. "Not long."

"Long enough," Hal replied. "Traffic will be snarled, my friend. This was well done. But we are here, and we were not supposed to be. They have to improvise and that's hard under pressure. They will make mistakes. What are they thinking? What would I be thinking?"

____ "Why do things always happen to me?" Cali bitched. She was standing beside him with Maria in one arm and an AK-47, full clip, in the other hand.

"It's Jamie Lee Curtis, the Halloween girl," Hal observed. "Bigger boobs, though." He looked down approvingly.

Cali gave him a look.

"Hey, look, she always survived," Hal asserted.

"At least the scary guy is on our side this time," Cali advised, poking Lungorthin with her elbow. She winced. "That's like hitting a rock."

"Yeah, it's the guys in suits that are the problem. Always were, now that I think about it."

"Well, only the young die young," Cali offered.

"And that's supposed to make me feel better? Now I'm filled with confidence."

"Here, try this." Cali leaned in and kissed him.

"Now I do feel better!," Hal laughed, smiling at her and Maria, whose bright dark eyes were staring at him, quiet for moment. "Listen," he ordered. "You get back. No shooting this time! You've got Maria to guard. If something happened to you and I survived, not only would I feel terrible, but your mother would carve me into pieces. So I lose both ways."

"And keep Goth back there with you," Lungorthin rumbled. "We have problems enough without all of you in the middle of what's about to happen."

"Now I don't feel so good," Cali grimaced. She moved back towards an inner room, carrying Maria, who was now waving her arms frantically and shouting for daddy. Cali turned to shout encouragement at Hal and froze.

Hal was shouting at two of the guards. "Okay, you and you, over to the front. You, downstairs—see if they are coming through the sewers. Do something, people!"

And then Hal stood motionless in the middle of the chaos. He pulled the sword from its scabbard, and then, holding it in both hands, raised it in front of him. He stared into the glowing metal, lit by an inner fire, for a few seconds and then dropped it to his side in fighting position. Cali heard him quietly sigh. For a moment, he stood, head slightly bowed, sad and resigned but at peace. Cali glanced away and saw Lungorthin studying Hal from the other side of the room. Lungorthin quickly glanced at Cali. Their eyes met for a second and then he looked back at Hal.

Hal looked around, noticed Cali staring at him and smiled at her—an odd, relaxed smile. "If I change, I love you anyway," he promised softly. Suddenly, there was shouting at the front door, and his expression changed, hardened.

"Be careful," Cali begged, terrified. "Be careful!"

"Not an available option today, my lady! Take Maria to safety. Now."

Cali stepped back and slammed the door as Hal and Lungorthin rushed towards the front entrance.

GRENDEL

"Okay, change of plans," the sergeant shouted. "This is the new plan." He quickly told his men.

In the back, the creature talked to his people, hissing their new orders. They knelt, and then stood. They turned to see the men staring at them, terrified.

"Showtime," the creature snarled.

"Okay, last chance to plan," Hal declared, more cheerfully than he could have thought himself capable of. "STOP: Stop, think, observe, plan. One goal at a time, one decision at a time, one action at a time. What are we doing?"

"Guards in place, check," Lungorthin rumbled. "Firepower focused on the weakest spot: the front door."

"Why attack the front?" Hal demanded, knowing something was wrong. "This is an attack to kill all. What was the term the Germans used about Russia? 'Scorched earth,' nothing left but smoking embers. Think! In Ann Arbor, they had uniforms. Watch for uniforms in the front. Maybe a truck to take away prisoners? Too complex. No, an arrest that goes bad—all will be killed. The uniforms won't be local, but look close. They only need to confuse us for a few seconds."

The front doorbell rang.

"It's not the postman," Hal commented. "He always rings twice."

The caretaker shook his head.

"It's them," Hal advised. "They look like cops, but they're not. Look really closely at the monitor." He pulled up the image, zoomed in.

Lungorthin nodded. "Close," he rumbled. "Not quite. Good enough if you were not watching."

"Pull away from the door," Hal shouted. "They will open up in a few minutes."

Outside, the mock police were starting to shout at the door and wave their weapons. Glancing at the monitors, Hal saw people on the street starting to run away.

"You, and you!" Hal yelled at two of the guards. "Get behind them—the tunnels. Open up behind them when they do." The men nodded and sprinted down the hallway.

"Fire? Is the alternate power running? The fire suppressors? The access to the tunnels? No, not the front door. It will be..." They have a team, he thought. It's close. They have to be in the building over there, the one we have seen the new manufacturing activity in. Perfect cover. "They....are set to attack..."

Boom!

The explosion blasted open a hole in the back of the warehouse. There was a woman's scream, and then shouting and automatic weapons fire.

Hal and Lungorthin rushed towards the blast, and, taking post, quickly killed the first attackers dashing through the hole in the wall.

The fire suppressors burst out. They flooded the area with foam, stopped the blaze, and made the floor slippery. The next attackers rushed in and slid, making them easy targets.

Behind them, there was automatic rifle fire at the front door.

"This is the real attack," Hal snapped. "You and you," he shouted at two guards, "back to the front door. I'll guard this." Hal forced himself to breathe and to look around carefully from side to side. Scan the horizon to avoid fixation, the class had taught.

The plaster wall burst apart from the other side and a dark shape rushed through, slapping the rubble away.

Lungorthin turned and stared for a second at the dark shape. "Grendel!" Lungorthin cursed, and raised his sword. He was too slow, and the creature knocked him down with a club and stood over him, the creature's dark sword raised to kill.

Hal moved quickly, astonishing himself and parried the blow aimed at Lungorthin. The dark sword was deflected into a brick wall and imbedded deep into the wall.

In the moment that the creature was distracted, Hal pulled on Lungorthin, helping him stumble out of the way. Hal turned and stood between Lungorthin and the creature.

"I am Peter of the Nitrian," the creature hissed, as he pulls his sword from the wall. "You will be one of the legion I have killed, boy. And then your family after you. But more slowly, I think, than your death." Peter smiled, his teeth crooked. "Like Hypatia—flayed, I think."

Hal laughed. Laughter, like breathing, reduces our emotional arousal level as well, he absently thought. What they told me at the seminar. It makes us feel more in control of the situation and pisses off the enemy. "Today is a good day to die," he announced to the creature. "And I like Grendel, because it fits you better, you frog-faced, fat sloppy, reject from a Godzilla movie. You think you look terrifying? I've seen scarier Girl Scouts. You're a pitiful excuse for something that the cat threw up."

Grendel studied at Hal appraisingly as he carefully wiped the dust off his dark blade, and then he moved into position. Grendel laughed at the pistol in Hal's hand. "As I had foreseen," Grendel snarled.

There was a burst of rifle fire in the front—different weapons. Screams from the front-door attackers. Grendel glanced, frowned.

"No battle plan survives the initial contact with the enemy," Hal commented. He casually tossed the pistol aside and moved his sword to his right hand. "Guns are too quick. You don't get to savor the kill. In their last moments, people show you who they really are. Especially crawling cowards like you."

Grendel regarded him thoughtfully. "Perhaps, a man worth killing," he rumbled, and they charged.

Hal easily sidestepped Grendel's charge, and Grendel's sword slash tore through the brick wall, dust and fragments flying everywhere.

"Slow," Hal taunted. "So slow. So old. Out of practice, I think."

Grendel hesitated—doubt, indecision, and a flicker of fear in his eyes. Is it the prophecy? he wondered and then attacked again.

Police have learned to exploit tunnel vision in others by intentionally stepping to the side to get into a suspect's blind spot. Just thinking to identify stress reactions can mean survival. Under stress, people fall back to habit; they don't expect tunnel vision, they forget to think. Grendel, confident and then shaken, moved reflexively. He feinted, as he had a thousand times and moved to Hal's blind spot, slashing down out of Hal's vision.

Hal, ready, held and then moved the inch required for Grendel's blade to miss. As the blow hissed by him, Hal slashed through Grendel's sword arm, severing it from Grendel's body. Grendel howled, pivoted with pain, and Hal, turning, slashed across Grendel's belly, opening the creature up. Grendel roared in agony, falling to his knees, but slashed down with his remaining arm, his claws tearing deep furrows into Hal's left shoulder. The venom from his claws flowed deep into the wound.

Hal screamed with fury, pain, and shock, but he slashed down as the creature knelt on the floor, its guts pouring out, beheading Grendel with a single stroke. Grendel's huge head crashed on the floor and Hal kicked it towards the mob of Paul's men watching the fight. They were frozen in fear and horror, watching Grendel's head tumbling towards them, and then Hal charged, hacking and slashing his way through them.

Cali, ignoring orders, yanked open the door when she heard Hal's scream and saw him charge Paul's men. Shocked, she stepped forward to try and stop him as some of the men dropped their arms, screaming their surrender, but Lungorthin held her tightly. "I'd not stand against him like this," he rumbled, "and he wouldn't know it was you until after he had killed you." In a few minutes it was over, and Hal turned to face them, covered in blood.

Lungorthin went over and knelt before Hal. "My lord," he rumbled, but glanced up as Hal paled and slumped down on his knees, only the sword point driven into the floor stopping him from falling.

"He's wounded," Lungorthin growled. "Get a doctor—no, get Mary," as he saw Hal's gashed shoulder. "And get everyone out of here." He wiped his hand over his face, trying to deny what he saw. Through the hole in the wall, Lucifer's men poured in, and the fight rapidly turned against Paul's forces.

Hal's mind slowed and he detached, calmly watching himself lose focus, the world breaking into smaller and smaller parts. Difficulty thinking when tired, unfocused, stressed, he thought. That's what they said at the seminar. You can feel the neurons giving up when under stress. You can hear the words, but they don't mean anything. And they are right, he realized. The sounds gradually merged and the light went away.

NEXT

Cali sat in the inner safe room, in shock. All she saw, over and over, was Hal falling, and Lungorthin catching him, and then the horror on Lungorthin's face as he stared at Hal, lying in Lungorthin's arms. Every trail that her mind went down led into darkness. She was holding Maria, trying to stay in control for Maria's sake. Goth and her children were sitting next to her, Goth with her arm around Cali. The nanny hovered around, carrying an automatic weapon and a sword in her belt.

Mary walked slowly out of the room where Hal had fallen.

Cali looked up, terrified. Goth clutched Cali's hand.

"I've stabilized him," Mary declared, walking over to Cali and putting her arm around her. "There's an ambulance here. They are loading him in now, and he's headed to the hospital."

"Can they help him there?" Cali pleaded. "Will he live?"

"I think he will live," Mary answered. "I can't know for sure, Cali, but I think he will. But he can't stay at the hospital. They will have killers converging on the hospital. Hal will...well, as far as the world knows; he'll die there. It's necessary, to throw them off. He'll be taken to a place of safety, the same place we are all going to. So the next thing is to pack, immediately! What little is left, we must grab and go. Quickly, because we're burning the warehouse when we leave. Paul won't know what damage we took that way. You'll see Hal later."

"What will happen?" Cali cried. "Why does it seem like every time things are finally going to be okay, something terrible happens?"

There's no answer for that, Mary thought. I wish I knew myself. "'Take no thought for the morrow, for the morrow shall take thought for the things of itself. Sufficient unto the day is the evil thereof,'," forcing a smile, and then she sighed. "Evil the day has been. There will be better." She stood up, pulling Cali with her. Lungorthin lumbered into the room and carefully helped Goth up.

"I have to go in the ambulance," Mary ordered. "You go with Lungorthin. Lucifer is mopping up." Mary's face knotted in anger. "Even they may not deserve what he shall give them, with my blessing. And your father will meet us at the safe place," she told Goth.

"But what...?" Cali started to say.

"Who of you by worrying can add a single hour to his life?" the caretaker murmured, putting his arm around her. "Come, we must go." He led them to the transports.

"What the hell is going on?" the police dispatcher shouted. "All these calls from this address? Automatic weapons fire, explosions! And no one is getting there?"

"The roads are all torn up," another dispatcher snarled. "Road repairs and accidents. That big truck on fire has the primary access completely blocked."

The chief thought and then nodded to his assistant. Suddenly, emergency vehicles started heading towards the disaster.

"That gave them all the time we could," the chief muttered to his deputy. "They didn't need a lot of time, not with that kind of firepower. Make sure their exit is covered by our people. Go and put in an appearance at the scene," he ordered his deputy, who nodded. "I'll get a story ready for the news."

Hal's ambulance arrived at the hospital. Mary's people quickly shuttled him inside, pushing aside the police. Hal was hastily moved to a section of the hospital different than the official records showed.

"This has to be quick," Mary warned the doctor. "We have only a few minutes. Their counterstrike will be here soon."

The doctor nodded and signed the death certificate.

A few minutes later, Hal was being wheeled out a back entrance. Five minutes later, the truck carrying Hal quietly passed through the tunnel and out of town.

At the hospital, the doctor was shouting at the FBI agents standing in front of him. "I signed a death certificate," the doctor yelled. "They took him away. You think it's my job to track bodies? Get out of my way. I have lives to save."

The younger FBI agent was furious and took a step towards the doctor. The senior agent grabbed him, held him still, and calmly thanked the doctor for his help.

The doctor nodded and walked off quickly, shocked at the close call. Serious stuff, he thought. He'd have killed me. Government scum. The doctor shook his head and picked up the next chart.

Ten long hours later, the transports stopped. Cali carried Maria carefully. She was finally asleep, after a long, fussy ride.

"It's beautiful," Cali sighed, looking around. It was dark, but there were lights illuminating the entrance, which went into the wall of a cliff. The moon lit the trees, which seemed to go forever. The rock precipices stood like sentinels around them.

THE NEWS

The newswoman was standing outside what was left of the warehouse. Flames were still shooting through the roof, and the entire area had been evacuated.

"Police report a terrorist attack at this warehouse," the newswoman reported. Then she scanned a new bulletin. "Correction—this was a terrorist base. All this happened when the police attacked, stopping the terrorists from carrying out their plans just in time."

Lucretia was sitting in her office working. She heard shouts from down the hallway as her secretary rushed in.

"You've got to see this!" she shouted at Lucretia, and then turned and ran down the hallway, her heels clomping.

"This must be serious," Lucretia thought, walking quickly. Women don't run in heels unless they are so excited that they forget they are wearing them. Lucretia's stomach suddenly churned as she connected the dots. She ran down the hall and stood in the back of the crowd, which was staring intently at a couple of computer monitors. They were tuned to different news feeds. The feeds showed weapons fire, police sirens, and aerial shots from helicopters. As far as she could see, it was a complete burn out. She felt sick for a moment, and then controlled herself. Hal would have caught on, she told herself. They will be fine. She watched for a few minutes, shrugged, and walked back to her office.

She forced herself to get to work on that analysis of Hal's company. It's like holding your hand in the fire, she thought, grimly going through the information. But I'm no good to them unless I'm trusted.

The watchers reported back to Mother Superior, who was pleased.

A DESPERATE PLAN

Mary studied the test results on the printouts. Sighing, she looked away, staring blankly into the computer screen.

"It's that bad?" Lucifer demanded bitterly, as he stood next to her, watching her closely.

"No, it isn't that bad," Mary mumbled, forcing a smile.

"Now I'm really worried," Lucifer countered. "Trying to deceive me— always a bad sign. The worst, actually."

"Grendel's venom is deep in him," Mary whispered. "A lot of it. Full strength."

Lucifer looked down and away. "Never has anyone survived that," he muttered, distraught. He slumped down into a chair next to Mary.

"Never has anyone survived as long as Hal has survived," Mary declared, taking Lucifer's arm. "Never has anyone—anyone—ever killed Grendel. No one. And there is something in Hal's blood and DNA, something I haven't seen before. Grendel's venom usually takes over. It isn't taking over here. It's there, but not as I've ever seen it."

"Is there anything we can do?" Lucifer pleaded.

"There's something..." Mary mumbled. "Grendel was Paul's creature. A creature from before Paul, brought into Paul's service by Paul's chalice, which modified Grendel. If we had Paul's chalice, his serum to work with, that would be something. But how?"

"Lucretia," Lucifer answered. "She survived it. And she owes Hal."

"She's the one who warned him of the attack," Mary mused. "Hal told Lungorthin before the battle started."

"Really?" Lucifer replied, his mind racing. "I'll talk to her."

"She must act voluntarily," Mary warned. "You know how intricate this is. Involuntary could just make it worse."

OUT OF THE PAST

Lucretia's mother sorted through the mail. The watchers are getting casual again, she thought, because the envelopes were not sealed up quite right. Really, we deserve a better class of snoops peering into our lives. I'm going to file a grievance with the union rep. She saw a letter from an address that meant something to only her. She let that letter fall on the floor, swearing as it fell, but finished sorting all the other mail before she bent to pick it up. She casually tore it open and read it, then tossed it in the pile of the other junk mail.

I've expected this, she thought. Waited and feared and hoped for years. And now?

They met in a restaurant a few blocks from the condo. She was shown to a private room upstairs. As she walked up the steps, she noted a woman dressed identically to her sitting half-hidden in a booth. Who is her hairdresser? she wondered as she climbed the stairs. Her highlights are better than mine are.

"Long time," Lucifer declared, standing as she walked in. He took her hand and kissed it.

"Long time indeed," Lucretia's mother agreed sadly. "My wish, my choice. And I've paid for it. I've long reflected about the mistakes I made trusting people and a church that then turned on me."

"You did what you thought was right, which is all any of us can do." He gazed at her and smiled. "You are still a beauty," he admitted. "The years have been good."

"You old goat," she teased. "That line worked before. And, the years have been kind. Perhaps some of your doing and I appreciate it. Still, that's not what we are here for today."

"No," Lucifer acknowledged, smiling. "Direct as always. You know about the attack, and Hal?"

"Yes," she replied. "I was sorry to hear of his death. Lucretia was crushed."

"He isn't dead," Lucifer answered. "Oh, he's gravely injured, but not dead yet. We wanted to distract the attackers because they have death squads looking for him. I killed all I could and their support teams, but one can't count on getting them all."

"I wondered," Lucretia's mother replied. "Some of the shadows have disappeared when I walk to the store. I'd grown so used to them that it was almost a disappointment. At my age, you take all the admirers you can get."

"They moved to another state," Lucifer remarked, studying her carefully "Another state of existence."

"Good," she nodded, a hard smile on her face. "I'd warned Lucretia about those people, but there was little we could do."

"It turns out," Lucifer explained "that the drug Lucretia took to become part of their organization can help Hal's survival. At least we think it can. He was poisoned and we hope that drug can help him overcome the poison. But her gift must be voluntary, given with full knowledge of the reasons and consequences. No deception, no tricks. Lucretia must give freely, completely of her choice."

"I thought you were the master of deception," Lucretia's mother teased, smiling at him. "Just more marketing, I guess."

Lucifer grimaced. "There is a lot of false marketing out there. I should have done something before."

"And you need me to help?" Lucretia's mother demanded. "I, who turned on you all those years ago? How can you trust me?"

"Because you are you," Lucifer replied. "You will do what you think is right. You would not bother to lie to me. You didn't then. You wouldn't now."

"True enough. I do this for her," she answered. "Her people will destroy her—and the children—and only you would have the power to stand against them. But I also do this for us," looking into his eyes. "For the mistake I made before, for having turned against you despite what was in my heart."

"Here," Lucifer urged, and pulled up chairs for them to sit in. She sat down, and he sat next to her. They sat, silent for a few minutes.

"So, I will talk to her," Lucretia's mother promised. "She will do what is right. But how can we do this? We are watched."

"Not as intently as before. A walk to a show for the children, I think. I know of a theater that has private rooms. It won't take long."

She nodded. "When? Oh, and I'm glad your son survives."

Lucifer stared at her, shocked. "How did you know that?"

"Lucretia. She knew you were family, just the way you acted."

"She is exceptional. Another thing I've handled wrong. My mistakes have been stacking up in front of my door these past few days."

She laughed, but it was a sad laugh. "I know about mistakes." She put her hand on his shoulder; he put his hand on her hand. They sat for a second, quiet.

"It would not be better if things happened to people just as they wish," she teased.

Lucifer laughed, shaking his head ruefully. "I've got to start being more careful about what I say. Those nice pithy sayings roll out better than they roll back in."

They stood. "I thank you for this." He went to kiss her hand, and she pulled his lips to hers.

"It is I who thank you," she whispered. "Hal saved the children and I from physical harm, but he saved Lucretia's spirit."

LUCRETIA'S CHOICE

"Lucretia, I have something serious to tell you," her mother murmured. "So look happy."

Oh, that's an effective technique, Lucretia thought. Mom's not getting that HR job. Lucretia bent over her daughter, teasing the little girl, who was babbling about the birds flying by and pointing wildly at the sky.

"Boid?" her daughter shouted, pointing at the pigeon near them on the sidewalk.

"We need to move away from New York," Lucretia muttered. "Only two, and she has the accent already."

"That young man you called—he is still alive," her mother whispered, helping Lucretia restrain her daughter, who was desperate to catch the pigeon.

Lucretia froze for a second and then frantically raced after her daughter who had managed to wiggle free. Lucretia walked back to her mother holding the squirming little girl, teasing her daughter again. "Birds? Birds?"

"Boids!" her daughter shouted, frustrated. "Boids, boids!"

"Where does she get that strong-minded streak?" her mother asked, shaking her head.

Lucretia glanced at her mother for a second. "Your loins," Lucretia replied. "I was only the go-between."

"The young man—he is gravely ill, poisoned by the monster your friends sent against him," her mother whispered.

"Not my friends," Lucretia whispered back. "My captors."

"True enough," her mother agreed. She dropped a toy on the sidewalk, and the little girl waved her arms wildly and screamed for the toy back. They all knelt around the toy.

"I've been told, and I believe, that something in your blood could save him," her mother murmured. "Something you got from that awful drug they gave you before you joined them."

"It would be nice if something good came of that. I'll help."

"Your help must be completely voluntary," her mother warned. "You can have no reservations. It's magic, you see."

Lucretia glanced doubtfully at her mother.

"Fine, it isn't magic," her mother admitted. "But the old magic would demand that you give completely voluntarily. And you take a risk. Should your people ever find this out, we will all die. Horribly, actually. I know about your people."

Lucretia shivered despite herself. "Then what shall I do? He shall die if I don't act, and we shall die if I do act?"

"We shall die if you don't. Your people will turn on you eventually, and if he dies we have no one. Now, good business isn't quite the same as completely voluntary, but it's close."

Lucretia closed her eyes for a second. Her mother watched her, biting her lip.

"Arrange the meeting," Lucretia demanded, suddenly confident. "Your analysis is right, as always. And besides, it's the right thing. Even I do that occasionally. If we lived and he died, well, something in me would die with him."

"You are too harsh on yourself," her mother whispered gruffly, hiding her pride in her daughter. "Here," she told her granddaughter, who was wiggling wildly. "Down and run in the park!"

The little girl squealed happily and ran after the pigeons, who scattered when she came close to them.

"You will do the right thing, mother," Jose told her, standing next to her. "You always do."

"You hear more than you should," his grandmother scolded him. "You never, never speak of this outside the family!"

"Thank you," Lucretia admitted, putting her arm around Jose. "That helps more than you can know."

A TRIP TO THE THEATER

That night Lucretia, her mother, her daughter, and her son walked happily to a new show at a theater near them. There was a sign outside telling everyone that there was something wrong and there were no cell phone or computer signals inside—something to do with electrical interference. The sidewalk was full of worried parents on cell phones, telling people that they were going to vanish into the void for an hour or so, terrified that the world would end without their constant participation.

Once inside, her son ran off with some friends of his and her daughter was carried upstairs with them.

"I didn't see any watchers," Lucretia commented as they climbed the stairs.

"I've been told that most of them died in the cleanup after the attack on the warehouse.

"No great loss there. The only sad thing is that Paul would agree. His accountants hate to fund the pension plans, so attrition, for them, is a positive accounting entry."

"Such nice people," her mother commented as they walked down the hallway. "Now I'm not sorry I didn't send a Christmas card."

Sir Jonathan stood at the end of the hallway waiting for them. "Thank you for coming," Sir Jonathan offered as they walked up to him. "In here, please."

They walked into a simple room, deep inside the theater.

"The cell phones are dead?" Lucretia demanded, worried.

"Dead," Sir Jonathan promised. "It's just a precaution, because we think the watchers are gone. But better safe than sorry."

"Sir Jonathan, I was crushed when I heard about Hal."

"Without you," he replied, "They would all have been dead. We owe you their lives as it is. But now I must impose on you further, and ask for help for Hal."

"He's your son, isn't he?" Lucretia asked, studying Sir Jonathan as she sat down.

Sir Jonathan nodded, unable to speak.

"I'll do anything I can," Lucretia promised. "He's been fair and honest with me, and that's been pretty damn rare in my life. And Hal and Cali are all the direct family Jose has. Which wraps around and makes you family to me, I think. This gets confusing."

"It does get confusing," Mary acknowledged. She stood up from her seat in the far corner of the room. "But that's another mess we might as well face. I'm Cali's mother, her real mother and she thanks you for what you're doing. She hopes to meet you and Jose in person soon. But, as you know, I killed your daughter's father. I didn't have any choice, but this has to be dealt with."

Lucretia looked at her and smiled a sad smile. "He was one of the few people who treated me fairly and I miss him sometimes. But I've asked around and I get the same story from the Cardinal that Hal told me. Even the same story from Mother Superior, who would always slant the story against you when she could. Don Cortes started the battle, and you had no choice. You giving him a chance to fight and die with honor, well...character shows in the little things. I have no complaints against you."

Mary studied Lucretia, and then embraced her.

Lucretia cried for a moment. "Sorry," wiping her eyes. "The strong act slips occasionally."

Mary glanced at Lucretia and smiled. "Strong is more than surface. You are strong beyond what you know. But we have little time, so I must ask you: Do you voluntarily give this blood for Hal's life, knowing the risk you take?"

"I do."

Mary gazed deeply into Lucretia's eyes and then nodded, satisfied. Guiding Lucretia to a seat, Mary quickly put the rubber hose around Lucretia's arm and expertly began the process of taking blood samples. "Several samples," Mary muttered, not taking her eyes off of Lucretia's arm. "So many things can go wrong."

"That's the truth," Lucretia agreed. She looked away, at the other wall. "Just tell me when it's over. I hate watching little needles in me."

After a few minutes, Mary put a cotton swab on the puncture and carefully put the samples in a protective case. "You have done right," Mary declared. "Many are called, few are chosen." She straightened up and picked up the case. "I'll leave you now. I do think something else has to be said." She looked firmly at Sir Jonathan, who nodded.

Lucretia stared blankly at Mary as she left, and then looked back and forth between Sir Jonathan and her mother, confused.

"And?" Lucretia asked, watching on Sir Jonathan, who was staring at Lucretia's mother, who was peering intently at the bare floor. "And?"

Her mother looked up at her, tears in her eyes. "He's your father," her mother confessed, pointing at Sir Jonathan. "The hateful demon you thought was your father knew it, and that drove his rage against me. Your sisters are his children, but not you. Passion, And then denial. I have paid."

"What?" Lucretia screamed, standing up. "What? All my life, a fraud?

181

What!! How could you not tell me? I hated that man you told me was my father, sick at the thought that any of him could be part of me. How could you hide this?"

Lucretia's daughter stared at her mother, shocked to see her mother throwing a tantrum.

"There was an abundance of good reasons," Sir Jonathan advised, trying to calm Lucretia down. "Look what happened to Hal—both now and before in Ann Arbor, because he was my child and certain people found out. Actually the people you unfortunately work for, although that has turned out surprisingly well. Who can predict the future?"

"So that makes me Hal's sister," Lucretia mumbled, working out the relationships. "Why didn't you tell me before I gave the blood?"

"A different kind of voluntary, the magic needs," her mother replied. "Sorry. Well, it's magic, and you have to be careful. And, well, as long as we are telling secrets, ah, there is something else. Just, well, a little thing you should know."

"And what would that be?" Lucretia demanded, her eyes flashing. "What other small, insignificant detail have you hidden from me all my life?"

"His name is Sir Jonathan, but he's had many other names. Like Paul, he's lived for centuries. His name is, well..."

"The name I am best known as," Sir Jonathan declared, "is Lucifer."

Lucretia stared at him and started to laugh. "I've been told I am the devil's spawn many times. It's a relief to find that it's actually true." She reached for Lucifer and embraced him. Shocked, he held her for a few minutes.

She stepped back, holding his hand, and he wiped away a tear with the other hand.

"Hmmm," Lucretia observed, critically examining him. "A softy after all. One should never trust Paul's stories. I've known that for a long time."

"We must go," her mother urged. "There may still be watchers."

Lucretia nodded, still holding Lucifer's hand.

"We can pull you out of this," Lucifer offered. "All of you, out of your world and into a safer world. A world of family."

Lucretia, excited, stared into his eyes for a second and then, sighing, looked down at the floor. "No. No. You need someone on the inside. There are many things still in process. Dark things that I have not fully grasped yet. I must play my part for a while. Besides," glancing at Lucifer. "Hal is Smiley, and I'm Karla. I'll play my role for as long as needed. Then I'll take the new world that he offered me before."

She kissed Lucifer on the lips, and then picked her daughter up and pulled her mother out of the room. Their footsteps receded down the hallway.

Mary came back into the room and carefully looked at Lucifer, who was standing in the middle of the room, looking worn and tired.

"Surprising life is, isn't it?" she commented. "'If you do not expect the unexpected you will not find it, for it is not to be reached by search or trail.' Heraclitus, I think."

"That does it," Lucifer vowed. "No more pithy sayings from me. I'm paying the price for my pretend wisdom now."

CHAPTER 10. DIGGING OUT

SWITZERLAND.

Paul stood alone on the balcony, staring out over the dark lake. Grendel is gone! Paul thought, anguished. I can't believe it. That damn Professor was right about that kid. But now I have no choice. If I don't kill them all, then people will see me as weak. It's the trap that Don Cortes fell into. You have to double up when you lose, so it's all or nothing.

What is the good? Grendel used to snarl, "To crush your enemies, to see them driven before you, and to hear the lamentation of their women." Conan didn't have a clue what that really meant. Now, if some of Grendel's creatures are still alive after that debacle, I will pull them in for support. Can he be recreated? Where were the colony creatures? Who would know? Grendel kept things to himself.

The Adversary stood in the corner of the room, saying nothing. Xerxes, Tamburlaine, Constantine, and others stood around, contemplating the floor.

"Fine," Xerxes admitted to the Adversary. "We all know how much you like to say 'I told you so.' So you were right."

"There are times to take joy in victory, and times to recognize the depth of the danger. This is a danger day. On the bright side, they were driven out of their safe place, and the boy was supposed to have died. However, no body was found," the Adversary mused. "That's not a good sign, but he could be dead."

"It's not good," Constantine observed, "when you are leading the cheerleading section. It's like death assisting in the emergency room."

"But he's right," Xerxes contended. "This has not been all bad, by any means. And we have leads into that company, which was thrown into disarray by the leaders going into hiding."

"There have even been overtures by the other cartel," Paul remarked thoughtfully. "That's good—actually, it has never happened before, and it's good for our reputation."

"Shout about something we should be ashamed of," Constantine offered. "It has worked before. Maybe little, tiny rumors that Grendel was overreaching himself, something that would look like your duplicity was deeper than anyone imagined, and thus your power is greater than anyone could have imagined."

"He's really dead?" Xerxes demanded. "I don't want him coming back angry at us! Our present problems would be trivial compared to that."

"No, he's dead," Paul answered. "Cut into pieces by a sword I thought no longer existed. There are forces against us, but we seem to have swum to safety somehow."

A MEMORIAL DINNER

There was a large, formal dinner at the chateau a week later. Paul and his son entered to the cheers of the crowd.

Another wonderful dinner was served. After the dishes were removed by the servants, Paul rose. All immediately quieted.

"A week to remember," Paul acknowledged. "Grief and victory combined, as they have been so often before." He raised a glass. "To missing comrades," he announced somberly, and drank.

All stood and drank, and then sat down.

"And victory? The vipers who have haunted us for centuries have been driven from their nest, and a powerful enemy is dead. We have an opportunity to seize control of their companies and to grasp the information we have been after for so long. We plow, we plant, and we reap. What has happened this week has been in process for a very long time. We are moving ahead rapidly against their companies and keeping the pressure up on them as they run."

The Cardinal toyed with his empty wine glass, pondering Paul's choice of words. Just as the planted seed will grow according to its kind, evil acts will produce a harvest of calamity for their perpetrators. Now, the Cardinal reflected, did they write that, or did we?

"You all have tasks," Paul shouted. "We are united and stronger than ever. To our victory." He raised his glass again.

"To our victory," the crowd shouted, and they stood, draining their glasses.

Paul put his glass down and waved at the crowd, who stood and cheered him as he walked out, his son closely following him. A few minutes later, they stood alone in a room in the corner of the chateau.

"That put the best face on it," Paul remarked, worried.

"I thought it went well, Father," Cesare replied. "You hit the loss of Grendel first, moved it out of the way, finished with the victories, and moved on. You did all one can do. They will walk out, yes, thinking about Grendel, but thinking more about the successes and the victories. Having Grendel's surviving creatures sprinkled among the guards will help focus their minds on their tasks."

"And on to the next big project," Paul declared. "That young woman will be back here, and she's important for that project. No accidents, okay? We really do need her. Later, you will have your toy."

"As you command, sire," Cesare promised, bowing slightly. "The pleasure will be all the greater for having been delayed."

"It generally is. I know."

They walked out of the room, Paul to his apartment in the chateau, and Cesare leaving to catch a plane to Hong Kong.

NEW YORK. COFFEE AT COLUMBIANS

Jesus, Mary, and Lucifer were meeting at Columbians, a hot new coffee shop where the staff wore long black leather coats and sunglasses. You ordered your coffee using code words, using your cell phone. It was a dark place, more like a bar than a coffee shop, with lots of little rooms and privacy. It had been a huge success in the short time it had been open. It also had several entrances and exits, few of which were known by the general public. An idea of Hal's, owned by a subsidiary company, it had been a useful place for private meetings before.

Lucifer sat at a table in a quiet, private room in the back of the building, far away from the sprinkling of customers in the cafe. A large window opened to a sky of leaden clouds over an industrial wasteland, all broken towers and crumbled walls. Nice, he thought. Who wrote this script?

Mary and Jesus walked into the room and sat down at the table, saying nothing.

"Whose fault is this?" Lucifer demanded of the ruined factories in the background in flawless Aramaic. "Mine. My fault, for having seen what I wanted to see."

"You are being too harsh on yourself," Mary protested, concerned. Her eyes were red from too little sleep and too much stress. "We made the big choices together. We agreed."

Jesus said nothing as he looked out over the bleak landscape.

"My son poisoned. He survived the poison of Grendel, which is unheard of. Partly the result of good luck, mostly because of things we cannot understand. He is still in a coma, and who knows what's going on in his mind, trying to fight off Grendel's power? His mother is dead. We almost lost all of them to a simple ruse that Paul has used for three thousand years," Lucifer shouted to the ruined buildings. "And now what?"

"Let's make better mistakes tomorrow," Jesus observed. "What do we do tomorrow? That's always the most important question. Always the question we want to ignore."

"Sometimes I sit and think about every stupid thing I've ever done, all at once," Mary added. "Hideously painful, but it's easier than trying to figure out what to do next."

"Humans live in three worlds," Lucifer admitted. "The social, the real, and the personal, and the social is the most important. The consensus agreement prevails. Perhaps we have become too human, and ignored the real world and our personal worlds too much."

"So have you ordered the troops out?" Jesus asked warily.

Lucifer actually laughed, a bitter, frustrated laugh. "Those days are long in the past, my friend. I no longer lead the legions. This isn't that kind of world. We don't have those resources available. I've killed those who attacked us and increased security on our companies and properties, but there is no army to lead. And no target. We burn a chateau on Lake Lucerne? We sink a pleasure yacht in Nice? Those change nothing."

"This is past the tit-for-tat that we have been playing at for a thousand years," Mary snarled, almost to herself. "A determined attempt to destroy us and all we care about. Again, to draw us out and destroy us! The second attempt in just a few years, and we let it come to this. We didn't recognize that he wouldn't stop. We didn't want to admit to ourselves that he is still Xerxes, the god on earth before whom all must bow or die. We looked to what we wanted to see, not what he is. We looked to what we wanted to have, what we thought should be."

"It must end," Jesus demanded. "We have tried to lead and encourage, but they don't understand."

Lucifer and Mary stared at Jesus, shocked out of their despair.

"My message has been twisted and turned inside out and upside down, and I've left it there," Jesus growled. "Left it for Paul to exploit in any way he wants. There is something about their thinking that doesn't work. We let them walk away from the vision and thought of the ancient world and into the small, totally human-scaled worlds that pass for theology today. Worlds that will lead to their destruction. No, this can't go on. We were wrong, and we have to think about what is really right."

They sat in silence for a few minutes.

"Well, on the bright side," Jesus admitted, "there are advantages to closing some doors. We needed a wakeup, I guess."

"And I know the thank-you card I'd like to send Paul," Lucifer replied. "I wonder if plastic explosives can be molded like that?"

"Perhaps we should thank him," Mary mused. "What we learned from the attack, and the serum that saved Hal, is worth a great deal. It's far more than Paul would have given us if he had known. And the loss of Grendel will weaken Paul more than he dares imagine."

"At almost the cost of our lives, and everything we hold dear," Lucifer pointed out.

"What doesn't kill you makes you stranger," Jesus commented.

Lucifer and Mary shook their heads.

"Hal is quite remarkable," Mary remarked. "Lungorthin said he has never seen his like. He will live," bending forward and touching Lucifer's arm. "I know—I am a goddess of life. Trust me."

Lucifer looked searchingly in her eyes, and she was shocked at how much he needed the reassurance. He nodded and smiled.

"It will change him. How, I don't know," she warned. "As the serum from Lucretia interacts with the serum we gave him, there will be effects. And the poison from Grendel is another unknown. But he seems to be working with all of that, somehow."

"They are all moved to the mountains, for now. We have killed any resources Paul seems to have in the area to head off problems. Paul has even sent overtures of a truce, headed by no less than the Cardinal and Mother Superior," Lucifer reported.

"And you will meet them?" Jesus asked, surprised.

"Yes," Lucifer answered. "I'll take appropriate precautions, but the charade will tell me something."

"They all must die," Mary hissed. "They and their colony creatures, gone forever. This battle must end. The world is changing, becoming something new, and this old war must be buried with the old world it defined."

Jesus studied her. "You have a disturbing resemblance to the alien queen when you get really angry. It's the inhuman rage in your eyes, I think. But I agree with you completely."

"Xiang Yu was a Chinese general in the third century B.C. who took his troops across the Yangtze River into enemy territory and performed an experiment in decision making. He crushed his troops' cooking pots and burned their ships. He explained that this was to focus them on moving forward. Paul has been kind enough to do the same for us," Lucifer concluded. "Well, our coffee is gone. Time to act."

SÃO PAULO

Paul, the Major, and the Professor sat in a penthouse hotel room in São Paulo, Brazil. Paul's chief of staff was sitting behind them, and there were guards in the outer rooms and the hallway.

"I'm told business is going well?"

"Astonishingly well," the Major replied happily. "The whole 'hydra-headed monster' isn't just wrong, it's an emotional fantasy being passed off as rational policy. People like to have their mental states changed. The increasing criminalization of the world has pushed many, many capable people outside the narrow legal structures, and all of those people have to make a living. So we have all the bodies we need for our business. The governments, the moralists, and the police slide over the reality that no one is holding a gun to the heads of the people taking the drugs. The governments are holding a gun to the heads of the people doing drugs, and that isn't enough to even slow the drug business."

"Evolution favors the cartels," the Professor added. "Of course, that is completely the opposite of what the world pretends it wants. We try, and if we fail, we try something else, focused on success. The governments can't define what success would be, so how can they reach it? As everything is shaped by the suits in a committee room somewhere, effective action is, by definition, impossible. Governments are what you'd call intelligent design, perhaps semi-intelligent design, and can never respond as quickly to the world as we can."

"That's the reason I switched sides all those years ago," the Major remarked. "Um...and the money. Two reasons. And the power. And the women. Okay, those are among the reasons I switched."

"In the past," Paul declared, "the rough men on horses would appear on the horizon, sweep in, and take over. Now we take over from the inside. The governments are corrupted and bound to us. The ordinary people turn to us for pleasure in their lives. Little countries wash our money through the Arabs. The Arabs' banks have so much power that they can push aside the developed world's laws and rules. Once in a while they let a bank crash and burn, another great public victory for the drug fighters, but the money seized wasn't ours. And now? This list of the new drugs starting production, and the ones in the pipeline, are truly extraordinary. Even beyond what I imagined possible."

Paul stood up and paced over to the window. "Now, I rarely make these kinds of admissions, but I should, perhaps, have listened more closely to you," he told the Professor. "The attack on that boy and his family—we had success, but failure also. He is protected, as you said. A mystery."

"I have seen the truth and it doesn't make sense," the Professor replied. "At least as it regards them."

"So, with the loss of Grendel, this next step is all the more important," Paul demanded, turning around and facing the Professor. "But it isn't going well? Permission to speak your mind—isn't that the modern phrase? I need information, not confirmation of my opinion."

"Thank you, my lord," the Professor replied. "It depends on what you want to accomplish as to how well things are going. These very strong control drugs are not producing dependable results. There is a lot of variability inside people when it comes to how their systems handle inputs. Why do some die of the flu, and some not get sick? Everyone has cancer inside of them, because it's part of cell growth and renewal, but most push it away and it doesn't take over. There are terribly dangerous bacteria that rapidly kill those infected, but about one-third of the population has the bacteria living in their noses, and it doesn't seem to harm them. Anti-depressants are effective maybe forty percent of the time, and placebos about thirty percent of the time. Why? We don't know. Perhaps in fifty, a hundred years, we'll know, but not now. We don't have the data, the computer power, the models."

He stood up and started to pace. "Sorry, it's the years of teaching—I get long winded. Now, what I said is all excuses, I know. The lesser drugs, well...a little variability doesn't matter that much. People who take drugs voluntarily—in a sense, they weed out the outliers, because the outliers stop taking the drugs. Drugs that are imposed on people don't have that safety mechanism. The control drugs hit the dead center of a person. The drugs the minister has been experimenting with? Well, he's right— there are too many dying in religious ecstasy. Now, if you want them to die, that isn't hard to arrange. The kill rate can go up to one hundred percent because it scales up well. They will be the happiest about-to-die people you've ever seen, full of the spirit of whatever god they follow. It's quite a sight, actually." He paused for a minute, thinking about the experiments he'd watched. "The bug doesn't seem to naturally decay as quickly as I'd wish. We carpet-bomb the trials and move on, but it's strong when scaled up. The problem is that I can't get it to scale down well so that the kill rate is zero but it still does something useful. So, not so good.

"Then that biological warfare drug!" The Professor grimaced. "Effects: homicidal rage, anger, fury. That's very touchy stuff. It has been worked on for many years, by all militaries and governments. There are lots of ways to produce the effect, but very poor results at controlling them after they are let loose. It's because they are biologicals, and biologicals start doing their own thing as soon as they are released. They swap DNA and RNA with other bacteria in an orgy of non-sexual reproduction. They collect things that make them resistant to antidotes, sometimes stronger, and sometimes they pick up side effects. The results often are not good, from our point of view. The ideal bug is cholera, actually. It has a natural bacterial predator that will take it to nothing in a hurry. I have not yet found a predator for these drugs. I have been able to modify the bugs so that they can't be traced back to us. Any fingerprints buried in the DNA of the drugs point to a multitude of militaries.

"So, yes, they are out there, and yes, they will do what you want. It's that they do more than you want that is the heart of the problem. It's a question of how critical it is that they don't do more than the minimum. As far as controlling them after they are released, there are ways of controlling the bugs including simply bombing the infected area off the map. That is an absolutely last-ditch step because one has to provide information to a government that has bombers, and people then ask pointed questions about how you knew so much about the problem before it erupted. But compared to unleashing another Black Death, well, saving the world is probably a first priority."

"So, if I'm following," Paul summarized. "You can guarantee that the drugs will scale up, but not down. And you can guarantee the results in the target area for the scaled-up drugs, you just can't promise that the bug will stop where we want it to?"

"Completely correct, my lord."

"What about the tests that the Indians ran?" Paul's chief of staff demanded. "They insisted they had better luck in controlling the drugs' spread."

"And that's what they told us," the Professor replied. "I'm doubtful. I've run the same tests, and mine turn out differently. They wouldn't let me watch their tests, and their sites were burned clean afterwards. So I can't say what happened or didn't happen, because I don't have good data. The data they have provided to me has been processed enough that I can't work back to the raw results. When pressed, they just give excuses. I know I doubt their results."

"What we are dealing with here," Paul announced, waving his hand at the city, which sprawled out as far as they could see, "is a predator so successful that it will have to weed itself out. The creature has eliminated all the natural controls on its population growth. There will be a predator—there always is. That," pointing again to the city, "is a monoculture. Isn't that how you refer to it, Professor? Monocultures always crash and burn. We must crash it—a preventive burn, the books would call it, controlling the crash so that there will be something left."

"Culling the herd," the Major agreed. "The weak, the sick. Nature's way."

"So, Professor, tell me why it can't be done," Paul commanded. "Skip the ethical, the moral. It's the practical I want to hear."

"I've had some success with my trials. The problem is that success masks failure. The more a thing operates successfully, the more confidence we have in it. So we dismiss little failures as trivial annoyances rather than preludes to catastrophe. A couple of the bugs got loose from the trial areas, and a few people died, but the epidemic didn't spread. Will it always die out, or was that random chance that it didn't spread? I don't know. But I do know that systems that require error-free performance are doomed to failure. Computer simulations and other methods of predicting whether components will fail are themselves vulnerable to failure, because there are biases built into the models.

"Another way of looking at it is that a tool we know is successful for X situation, when used for Y situation may crash and burn, taking valuable things with it. The difficult part is when X situation didn't seem that different from Y. Disasters are a wonderful learning tool if anyone survives for the write-up. I know what those drugs do under controlled conditions and limited time. Throwing them out into the world, a huge experiment with our fingers crossed for luck, is opening the door to the unknown unknowns lurking out there."

"Is there an antidote?" Paul asked. "If things should go, as you say, south?"

"There are some," the Professor answered. "They take some time to make, and are a desperate fallback. But I'll get started on them, I'll have something available just in case. Having said that, I wanted to make it absolutely clear that I don't buy the Indians' results. I'm discomforted by their confidence that we are in control—that we can read the little signs and always predict accurately what's going to happen. Any statistician can tell you that we're going to find the effect we're looking for and ignore evidence to the contrary, especially when there is serious money at stake. I think the toys will spread unpredictably if they are used. It could be major-league unfortunate, or it could be an annoyance."

Paul sat by the window for a few minutes, silent. The others stared out at the city.

"We have to act," Paul decided. "We'll pick sites with some geographic distance from other population centers, which might help. You'll work on the antidotes, just in case, and have that information ready to pass to various governments should it become necessary. We need to keep up the pressure on Aeternalis, GmbH and keep them off balance. They are dangerous enemies, and I have driven them onto the killing ground now. They will fight to the death. So we can't delay, or let up."

CHAPTER 11. THE WASTELAND

RUN TO GROUND

It has been more than a week since they fled to the mountains. Cali is sitting in a little room at a makeshift desk made of a door resting on two sawhorses. It's not much of an office, she decided. And, it's not much of a place, period. She thought about the damp running through the whole cave that the heating system was fighting a losing battle with. We can't stay here. Oh, it's pretty outside with all the trees and the river quietly flowing by, but we have limited supplies and we are easy prey for an attack if they find us. There's one way into the cave, which means that there is only one way out. Even Paul's people can figure that out. I wonder if anyone has any plans? I'm almost afraid to ask. She sighed, stood up and wandered out. She spent the next couple of days talking to people, and her conclusion was that, generally, people were stunned and frozen.

Three days later, she was back at the makeshift desk. No reason to stay is a good reason to go. There isn't a lot of planning going on here. Mary's intent on getting Hal healthy, Lucifer is off running the attacks against Paul's people, and Jesus is trying to keep the businesses afloat as Paul's privateers attack on every front they can. Goth Girl is sleeping a lot. So, there are not a lot of volunteers for the job. All raise their hands who want Cali as chief planner? She raised her hand. "Thank you for your show of support," she announced to the desk. "If nominated I will not run, if elected I will not serve. Um...wrong speech."

She made notes for a few hours and then stared at all the piled-up paper. Nonsense, I need nonsense. I'm in a rut. She wandered off and watched a Looney Tunes DVD for a while. "Okay, my mind is cleared of any useful conscious thought," she declared to the wall, sitting at the desk. So what do we need? All you need is love? Actually, the basic human necessities are air, water, food, and shelter. So, we need: food for a bunch of people and ways of getting the food that are not really obvious, medical facilities, living space for a bunch of people—and we'll add people as time goes by—some kind of office/work areas, space for the kids to play. Then we need the more unusual, but more critical for us: Hiding? Deception? Allies? She did a rough calculation of the space needed and was shocked. Far more space was needed than they had at the warehouse. That's a lot of space!

She started poking at ideas, but kept finding herself enthusiastically detailing little sections of a plan. That would be helpful if the overall plan wasn't a travesty of a sham of a mockery. "And it won't work, either," she mumbled to herself. Okay, I'm not finding the correct scale for planning. What did the book say? The more uncertain we are, the more we over-plan, because a joyful immersion into minute detail means I don't have to confront the real problem. The bigger the threat, the stronger the desire to foresee all possibilities and every conceivable mishap. That's a plan that has "ruin" stamped in red letters all over it.

Two hours later, Cali was practicing her calligraphy, embroidering 'ruin' ornately in red on the last plan she had worked up. She groaned and wadded up the last set of notes. Nothing productive to show for it, and people are waiting for a decision and a plan, holding their breath, waiting for my brilliance to light the way. Um...some of them may have just keeled over from lack of oxygen, so I'm behind schedule. Okay, sit back and think here. Is this a complex problem, yes/no? It is. What are the ranges of choices I have in dealing with a complex problem? Start with the goals or jump into the mess and start pushing things around? I could size up a situation, one of those 'holding my thumb out to the world to measure it' like artists used to do, or I could do a rough outline, or I could just fall into a detailed analysis. Scratch the detailed analysis. That's failed so far.

What am I saying here? Over there... She put her right hand on the edge of the notepad. That is my perception of the situation in the real world. Over here... She put her left hand on the edge of the notepad. These are my goals. Little arrows, curves, and dashes connect the goals and the real world. Little curse marks are embroidered around the edges. If the problem is a static situation, I can crank out detailed steps. Of course, no meaningful problem is static and controlled.

A fluid, evolving situation takes rough strokes. Rough strokes with a paddle, if you have one. Up shit creek without a paddle? Failures at lots of levels there. Bang at the problem, and then bang again. Iterative—isn't that the word? Walk through once, then walk through again with changes, round and round the process until it's solved or you become dizzy, puke, and move on. Every problem has its own unique time problems, most of which are not conveniently highlighted in red. Some problems you can think about for a while, stop part way, and rethink because you can take a couple of shots at the problem. Some you get one frantic pass at. Come over, come over, red rover, ready or not! Okay, this is a 'one frantic pass.' That lessens the pressure?

Think! What did they say at that seminar? They said the key for any successful plan is 'what's the desired outcome?' If you know that, then you have focus, direction, and success criteria. In other words, I know what's winning and what does the finish line look like. Simple case is moi, in a flattering track suit, breaking the tape, the crowd cheering my victory? Here it is survival and prosperity for the whole group, and that's a lot more complex outcome. That desired outcome is the driver to the whole plan, and that's why it is a guaranteed disaster coming if I misstate the desired outcome.

Once that outcome is framed, then the mind starts thinking, really thinking. Actually, that's an easy picture, Cali decided. Everyone safe and secure, and we have resources and possibilities. Everything at its proper time and with proper attention to existing conditions? That's as useful as Proverbs, she grimaced. Pretty slogans with no traction. An inner process stands in need of outward criteria? So, when all the emotional handwringing doesn't work, let's start with what we have to work with in the real world. Let's get some external feedback.

Cali searched through files on the laptop and found the map she was looking for. So, here are all the properties owned or controlled by the companies, nicely marked with little circles. Exclusion criteria to start with: we can't use the productive plants; too many people around them would notice our merry band, and those plants are infiltrated by Paul's people for sure. He just seems to like that kind of stuff. She spent an hour working her way through the list, marking off one possibility after another.

Not so many left now, she realized, happier. Next, key constraints/inclusion criteria. We have a large group that stands out and that must be hidden. This mountain retreat is hidden, but it meets none of the other criteria. So it has to be a place in an urban area, essentially abandoned, where we also have friends. Hal's friend from Detroit? Of course—the guy with the sword! Detroit, she sighed, frowning. She looked at the map, and one of the few remaining possibilities was in Detroit. She'd been there many times while she was a student. She had taken classes at Wayne State University, deep in the combat zone, and had driven through the wastelands many times. Well, who would look for us there? Who would think we were that crazy? And who'd be crazy enough to come after us there? I remember what Hal and I were joking about years ago in the safe house in Ann Arbor, about hiding in Detroit from the cartel.

> *"I suspect it would have been a broken-down apartment building in Detroit," Cali countered. "First, no one would go down there to find us, and second, if they did, there isn't anything worse they could do to us. They'd probably let us live."*
>
> *"Ugh," Hal grimaced. "I've been in those parts of town. They probably would let us live. Heck, we'd have jobs at the liquor store behind the bulletproof glass."*

No jobs behind the bulletproof glass! Not part of the desired outcome. And we have toys. Sensors. We can tap into energy sources off the grid and so hidden from the grid. Then we don't show up, we are just little ghosts, flitting shadows in the night. While you can't hide in this modern world, you can deceive. That's actually easier than it used to be, because people only see what they look for, and we will set up a picture they won't question. We can't build a fortress that can't be scaled, but we can build one they wouldn't bother with.

What would Hal think? Cali wondered, starting to cry. She'd talked to Lungorthin about the battle two days ago, finally having the strength to deal with the memories.

"He knew," Lungorthin admitted, "what was coming. I've seen that look before, when you know death will come for you. And he stood and fought, knowing." Lungorthin studied her thoughtfully. "Nothing more could have been asked of anyone. You should be proud."

Proud? Cali thought through her tears. Pride is a small reed for strength. I'm Hector's wife, Andromache, with my child, waiting for the evil to come. She held her head, despairing for a moment. But Hal's doing better, she thought, determined, wiping her tears away. He will be fine. Mary promised. He must have a place to go so he can recover. I just have to find it. Frustrated, she wadded up the papers and threw them at the wall. They separated mid-flight into a snowfall of paper, a small drift leaning against the wall.

"So, when faced with two choices, simply toss a coin," she advised the wall. "It works, not because it settles the question for you, but because in that brief moment when the coin is in the air, you suddenly know what you are hoping for. "Sure, I'm game." She fished in her purse for a coin. Her fingers found an ancient drachma that Mary had given her as a gift. I like that, feeling the weight in her hand. She flipped the coin in the air and saw a vision of an old factory in Detroit. That's easy. I didn't even have to pick heads or tails. She carefully put the coin back in her purse. A scene from an old movie flashed before her.

> Dr. Klahn: The CIA thinks they can infiltrate the Mountain of Dr. Klahn!
> CIA Agent: You can't scare me, you slant-eyed yellow bastard.
> Dr. Klahn: Take him to...Detroit!
> CIA Agent: No! No, not Detroit! No! No, please! Anything but that! No! No![14]

She laughed out loud. Like Mao's Long March to the country. I wonder if I can get people to carry me on a litter like they did him! Pithy advice time, where is The Art of War ? The complete guide to life, albeit slightly cynical. All warfare is based on deception. I like that. If you hide your form, conceal your tracks, and always remain strictly prepared—then you can be invulnerable yourself. Yup, that's where we want to be.

Okay, one small, last problem. How do I sell this to the group? And how do we move?

A FAVOR

The next day, Mary walked into Cali's room while Cali was struggling with Maria.

"Cali, I have a favor to ask you," Mary announced as Maria frantically waved her arms and cried for her grandmother to save her from her mother.

"What would that be?" Cali mumbled, focused on trying to get Maria to put food in her mouth instead of all over the room.

"We need someone to be the spokesperson for the company, actually," Mary admitted. "Hal's still in a coma, and there's no one else to do it. Hal made his secretary, Aliston, the Chief Operations Officer of the company before he left, which was a bit of a shock to us."

"She's unbelievably competent," Cali replied, defending Aliston. "I know she's beautiful, but Hal told me she really ran the company. She knows all the secrets and all the people."

"Really?" Mary mused. "I didn't realize that—none of us did. Well, that explains why Francisco was so firm in backing Hal's promotion of her, although he was sorry to lose his secretary. Somehow he thought he could take more vacations with her running the show, which really is a vote of confidence. Well, all the better, then. But we still need family there to represent us. You're the planner, and you show well."

"Thanks a lot," Cali sighed, looking down at her blouse, which was flecked with orange yogurt. "This is a good look for the corporate figurehead."

"You're my daughter—of course you show well. And it's important," Mary pleaded. "With all the recent chaos, someone has to appear to be in charge of the ship."

"I'd turn it down if I could," Cali admitted, "but I can't deny the need. So, what do I have to do?"

"Some trips to New York. We obviously don't want to publicize this place, so you have to go to Hal's office and be a spokesperson."

Hal's office, Cali thought, and choked up. She looked away, pretending to try and feed Maria again, who was now very bored in the high chair and making her opinion loudly known.

"It will be fine," Mary promised, standing next to Cali. She put one arm around Cali. "Actually," as Mary expertly wiped Maria's mouth, "it will be easier than this. And you brought this upon yourself, actually."

"Pray tell?"

"Your analysis and plan for moving were so good that we all thought, well, who could be better to represent the company? The vote was unanimous."

"Next time, I'm demanding a quorum. So, is there an expense account that comes with this?" Cali asked.

Two days later, Cali was standing nervously off stage, waiting to host a press conference at the office building in New York.

"You look wonderful!" Aliston told her. "Seriously!"

"Thanks for taking me shopping yesterday. I've been so busy, I haven't had time. Or, well, an opportunity. It's difficult to go to a store and concentrate on shopping when you're standing there wondering whether there is a bullet headed for your back."

"I understand," Aliston replied. "Kids and major life disasters do make shopping harder." She peered out intently at the stage. "Everyone's here and set. Okay, it's Showtime!"

Cali walked out, smiling. Her job, it seemed, was to introduce people and to look happy, which she thought she could handle. She adroitly fielded questions about the mysterious trip that Hal was on and the rumors about their connection to the warehouse that had burned down.

ACTION

Cali was driven back from New York. She had to switch cars several times to make sure there were no pursuers, but did manage to get some sleep.

The next day, they left before sunrise for Detroit. There was a loose caravan of minivans and large sedans carrying everyone. Two large trucks had gone the day before with key essentials and several more large trucks would load everything after everyone was gone. It was a long trip, made longer because they were split into several groups to minimize attention. There were at least two sedans with armed guards with each group that regularly switched the lead and last positions. Occasionally, they switched between minor and major roads to pick up any shadows, but none appeared.

The children were whiny and exhausted by the time they reached the far suburbs of Detroit. When they reached the city limits, a large truck carrying with Lungorthin's creatures took the lead. Nearing the factory, they were shocked at the devastation. Lost people wandered down broken sidewalks, past empty storefronts. The few brightly lit stores were parasites: check-cashing shores, dirty bars and questionable restaurants. They passed ruined homes, blocks of crumbling, half-burned commercial buildings collapsing on themselves and empty warehouses.

Finally, the caravan stopped in front of a strange place. They could dimly see the old factory building, the front lit by the streetlights lining the long driveway, the bulk of the factory vanishing into the dark. There was a dense thicket of thorn trees surrounding the whole factory. Only a few tattered leaves were still on the trees, but the long silver thorns reflected the last rays of the sun. It was bitter cold, a strong wind blowing small, hard snowflakes, almost sleet, out of the west. It was dusk, and most of the street lights were burned out. The few that did work cast small circles of light against the gloom, highlighting the dark instead of driving it away.

They slowly piled out of the vans, stiff from sitting for long hours, and they lined up in front of the entry.

"'New ideas need old buildings,' Jane Jacobs once wrote," Jesus laughed, seeing the look on Cali's face.

"Well," Cali remarked, looking with disgust at the black, mystery-liquid stains on the drive, still visible under the blowing snow, "then our ideas should be absolutely up-to-date. Open the dictionary to 'old and decrepit,' and this is the picture. Fine," talking to the snow, "it was my idea. And who's going to be looking for us here? I can't believe I'm here myself."

Jesus watched the flames flickering as they rose out of the wide crack running from gate post to gate post across the entry. Then he examined the thorn trees, listening to their dried leaves rattling in the vicious wind, and finally studied the wasteland surrounding them. "I remember this place," smiling and nodding his head. "Good to be back."

"What a mess!" Mary complained, kicking away some rubble in the driveway. "And how do we enter?"

They carefully studied the flickering flame blocking the entry.

"That wasn't in the data," Cali declared, defensively.

"Like a flaming sword," Jesus commented. He glanced at Lucifer. "You should feel at home."

"Right, it's always the symbols," Lucifer sighed. "Where are the royalty checks I should be getting for the use of my intellectual property? If the library in Alexandria hadn't burned with my copyrights, I'd be set."

They heard heavy footsteps headed toward them out of the dark. Vladimir emerged out of the gloom, rubbing his hands to warm them in the cold, and smiling broadly at the group. "Where's Hal?" Vladimir asked, looking around.

"In the back van, which is actually an ambulance," Lucifer replied. "But he's going to be okay."

"Yes, I think he will," Vladimir advised.

Lucifer looked sharply at him. "What do you know?"

"An encounter with the enemy changes always," his blue eyes searching Lucifer's face. "Greater or lesser, he will decide. All is change—you said so yourself. No man ever steps in the same river twice, for it's not the same river and he's not the same man."

"I am absolutely swearing off pithy sayings. They have been coming back to bite me a lot recently," Lucifer declared, glancing at Mary, who was laughing at him.

Lucifer stood for a moment, thinking. "What you say is true and that gives me hope." He paused for a minute and examined the gate again. "Ah, any other entrances? This seems a little impractical. Driving over a flame voids the car warranties. And ignites the gas tanks."

Vladimir laughed. "Enter, Morning Star," he commanded, and the flame vanished. The black metal gates gleamed suddenly, the huge black posts a background for the complex motif of ivy and serpents carved to twist

199

around them.

"The detail is superb," Jesus announced, walking over to one post to examine it. "See, there are symbols of the wind, lightning, and guardian bears in the metalwork. Inspired design." He studied Vladimir.

Lucifer gazed intently into Vladimir's eyes and then smiled a wry smile of recognition. "It's been a long time. It's good to see you again. A joy I had not dared hope for, actually."

"It's been a very long time," Vladimir agreed. "Not lost time, just a long time. Standing guard gives a person time to think. Reflect about the meaning of things."

Lucifer looked at him and nodded sadly. "'It can be necessary to travel a long distance out of the way in order to come back a short distance correctly,' Edward Albee once wrote. I've reflected over the many long years myself."

"You are the friend who brought Hal his sword?" Cali asked, stepping close to Vladimir, as she held Maria wrapped tightly in a huge snowsuit with only her bright eyes visible. Maria was staring wide-eyed at Vladimir. "We all owe you our lives."

"Vladimir Leibowitz, at your service, m'lady." He bowed to Cali. "The rumors of your beauty only hinted at your radiance! And you married Hal, that sly dog," shaking his head. "The guy who couldn't get a date for the prom. Well, I'll tell you stories some other day."

Cali laughed and so did Maria.

"Saving your lives? Not true! Hal had to wield the sword. I was only the deliveryman. But I'm glad it worked out. I feared I'd not be in time. I don't know how FedEx manages to get stuff there on time as much as they do. I didn't realize how hard it was." He looked at them, huddled in their coats. "You must be freezing, and here I stand talking. Get inside! There will be plenty of time to talk later."

They rushed back into the vans, which drove into the dark factory grounds. A hundred feet further down the drive, there was a lighted door and many people waiting to help them unload.

Lucifer and Vladimir stood together, watching them go. When they were all in, the flame reappeared in the entry.

"It will come and go at your need," Vladimir observed. "The thorn trees surrounding this land are really impassable. Nasty things! Do stay away, because they have venom in the thorns that is unpleasant—to say the least. Definitely not your run-of-the-mill thorn trees. Oh, and you all must be hungry. We run a small cafe around here—the best place to eat for miles! Of course, it's the only place to eat for miles, but we like it. It's the 'Justa Café,' and the cook is ready with hot food after your long trip. Here's a menu." He handed one to Lucifer.

"We couldn't ask for more," Lucifer promised. "Friends where one never expects it—that's the best part of travel." They shook hands, and Lucifer walked in, the flame vanishing and then reappearing after he had passed.

JESUS & VLADIMIR

The next day, Jesus wandered over to the restaurant and ordered breakfast.

Two huge plates of food were brought to him, and he fell upon them. He finally pushed the plates away, cleaned. "That was wonderful!" he announced to Vladimir. "Fresh, hot—a master chef's work!"

"When you're hungry and cold, it doesn't take much," Vladimir replied, deliberately waiting for the cook's reaction.

"Don't let him tell you that!" the cook shouted. "I am a master chef!"

"And he is," Vladimir admitted. "Well, we've had lots of years to polish our skills. It's good to have to do some new things every so often."

"You have quite a community here. Must be couple hundred people?" Jesus asked.

"More now, I think. A core of veterans and their families," Vladimir answered. "Some who have been with us for a long time, and then some we took in when we saw their need. Men and women badly treated, abused, and damaged by the system, rejected by the world. The damaged, but not the destroyed. Remnants of lost tribes, you might say."

"And there are rumors about this part of town," the cook added, walking out of the kitchen and wiping his hands on a rag. He stood at the counter. "Strange things they say happen here. So we don't get bothered a lot. We've marked an area with some signs, really tribe marks. People who come here looking for trouble—they find it."

"Muggers and thieves come to this area, and they never leave, it is rumored," Vladimir observed.

Jesus studied Vladimir. "Active engagement—that wasn't the old way, as I recall?"

"No, it wasn't," Vladimir admitted. "Those weren't the orders. But no orders have come for a long time, and we have guarded through the empty years. We've thought about things. The mind of the gods cannot be read from their deeds, it's said. And what was read, well, may have been the wrong reading."

"Almost certainly wrong," the cook agreed, frowning. "Based on what's happened since then. So, we decided to cleanse at least part of this wasteland. These people have had a hard enough time."

More customers came in. The waitress shouted at the cook, who waved his cigar at her and went back in the kitchen.

"Do you see this as a comedown for us?" Vladimir asked Jesus. "Not as it was, certainly, not all that pomp and the glory."

Jesus thought for a minute, and shook his head no. "No, not at all. I've worked lots of jobs with no glory. Carpenter, remember? The glory comes from the work you do, not the reflected shine from others opinions. And that food was truly a work of art. A Rembrandt with lettuce and tomato."

"Good," clapping Jesus on the back. "We'll have to talk more."

"Any time," Jesus promised. "And anything I can do to help the group—I'd be glad to help. Helping has been my life, or at least trying to."

Vladimir nodded, smiling. "That's an offer I'll take you up on." He looked up, frowning. "I must go over the meat delivery with that scoundrel," pointing to the delivery truck, "if we expect to have any edible meat to serve." He quickly walked out, shouting at the man.

SWITZERLAND. LUCRETIA PRESENTS HER REPORT

Lucretia was kneeling before the dais in Paul's audience chamber. She had presented the report on Aeternalis, GmbH to Paul and his staff.

"There was a factory in—what is the name of that city? Detroit?" a junior staff accountant mumbled. "It was in your preliminary report."

"Correct," Lucretia replied, her stomach churning. "It seems that it was on the list of, well, hopelessly polluted sites, and they backed out when that was discovered. It was careless of them to have not caught it before they did. There was a flurry of title conveyances, and it seems to be owned by a different company now, with the cleanup liability back in the lap of the government. I put the events into a report in the appendix. Did you see it?"

"I saw it," another staff accountant sniffed. "What they did made a lot of sense, actually. I made some notes on how they pushed the liability away. Perhaps we can use that technique someday ourselves. Buying that factory was like them, however, because only a complete idiot would buy something that would be so obviously polluted." The other staff nodded their heads, and the one who raised the question looked at the floor.

How do you tell the difference between an extroverted accountant and an introverted accountant? The introverted accountant looks at his shoes, and the extroverted accountant looks at your shoes. So close, young man! That almost made your career. You spotted the weak link in the whole report.

"This is excellent work," the chief accountant told Lucretia. "You've found many places for us to attack. And it's all from public documents! How could this have been missed in the past?" He looked pointedly at his staff, who looked terrified for a moment.

"Not entirely public documents," Lucretia interrupted. "Coldmen Sacking has many resources that others do not." Why not curry a little favor? she thought. I don't want a full investigation of how they missed stuff, because they could trip over the real facts about Detroit.

Even the chief accountant looked relieved at her statement. "Well, I didn't think of that. "We have excellent contacts, but your firm has tunnels to everything." He bowed his head slightly to her. The staff looked positively joyful.

The Cardinal had followed the conversation with interest. Paul was bored.

"Good. Let's move forward. Thank you again, Lucretia," Paul announced, with genuine thanks in his voice. "You've been everything the Cardinal had hoped for. It's so rare to find real talent." He waved his hand to dismiss her, but actually studied her as she stood up and slowly backed out, her eyes carefully on the floor.

DETROIT. FACING UP

"So, what's up?" Vladimir sighed, walking into the restaurant and finding it full of unhappy faces.

"You were right," the cook told him. "They bitched—you win." He handed Vladimir a twenty-dollar bill.

"I can call them," Vladimir laughed. Vladimir turned to the group. "Okay, tell me, in short sentences and simple words, what's got you all fired up, as if I can't guess." He leaned against the counter, watching them.

A man stood up, angry and defensive. "It's the creatures they brought with them," he demanded. "What we've fought against, what we've been opposed to, I thought, all these eons. Creatures from the pit—isn't that what they are?" The others nodded their heads angrily.

"Let's look at the facts," Vladimir replied. "None of you has been able to enter the factory without myself or Rafael accompanying you. Why? Because the flame wouldn't let you in! But they waltz in and the flame lets all of them in and out, the creatures the same as the others. What does that tell you about your place in the hierarchy? What does that tell you about what we thought, and what really is?"

The man looked down, silent.

"Anyone?" Vladimir shouted. "We are supposed to be the brightest, the quickest, and you sit there like lumps of coal with sad faces painted on you. Haven't you thought at all about events over the eons? Do you just use your heads as hat holders?" He looked angrily around the room, and no one looked him in the eye.

"Fine," Vladimir snapped. "I couldn't believe it either, which is why I'm angry. I knew this would happen, but knowing it's going to happen in the mind and believing it emotionally—those are two different things. They are creatures of life, creatures who, yes, rebelled and sought life. They didn't follow orders, they didn't mindlessly obey what they thought they were told, they thought and fought. We thought they were wrong. Time has passed, and some of what we thought was wrong, some of what they thought was wrong, and really, it isn't all about good and evil, it's about life. Life is beyond good and evil. It's outside the human stories."

"So what are we?" a woman asked, a single tear running down her face. "Defined by the stories, what are we outside the stories?"

"The same question has dogged me," Vladimir mused. "Why did everywhere we settle become a wasteland, despite our earnest intentions and bright goals? I think that it's time you all thought about that, or rather, 'felt' about that. We're wrong in what we've been doing, that much is clear. The 'good' doesn't turn productive land into a wasteland over and over. We're being sent a message and we're not hearing. Hell, it's more than not hearing-we have been standing there with our hands over our ears humming loudly so we can't hear! Can any of you deny that? Can any of you refute that? Because I'd love to have a good answer that doesn't tell me I've wasted eons and done evil in the name of the good. Anyone?" He scanned the group.

"I've thought the same," a man confessed. "I feared to say it, but our bright hopes and noble dreams are rotting away. We have to be missing something."

"Job asked the same question," the cook added. "Think and reflect—but Vladimir is right. Feeling is what we need. Too long we've thought in rigid lines and square patterns, which are not life."

"What say you?" Vladimir asked the man who spoke first.

"I hear and obey, my lord," the man replied.

"I can't accept that," Vladimir sighed. "No more 'my lord.' I'm done imposing my opinion on people, because I've lost my sense of overriding righteousness. Why? Because, frankly, I haven't been right that much lately. You must come to your own opinion and do what you think is right, whatever that might be. Rebel against me! But don't freeze, don't react out of the past against new events that make you realize you may have—we all may have—made some big mistakes."

One of the men poked the first angry man on the shoulder. The man turned to look at him.

"Does any of your emotional response have anything to do with the fact that you thought that blonde woman creature was an absolute knockout?" the man remarked casually. "Just a thought."

The angry man stared and then, rubbing his hand over his face, laughed. "An open book. I'm pitiful, and yes, she is an amazing creature. Perhaps, well, I could learn about life."

He flushed as the crowd laughed and hooted, and then the crowd calmed down.

"It's okay," Vladimir promised. "The old rules just don't apply anymore. Perhaps you could work with them and learn about them, then make decisions. Perhaps more than work with them-perhaps become friends? I have become friends with them. Each of us needs to understand what is happening, because things are changing. We, perhaps, have been the ones frozen in the ice."

"You are right about the rules, my...ah, Vladimir," a woman agreed. "They are working in the factory. With them living there, the factory is cleaning up, almost coming alive again, when all our efforts just lead to rust and ruin. So, painful as it may be, maybe they have an understanding we don't have."

"And you thought that big, male creature was attractive too," another woman added.

The woman nodded. "That's one big man, and the schwanzstucker on him! Oh mein Gott!" She made a motion with her hands.

The other women laughed, and the men looked rather uncomfortable.

"Well, with that, I think maybe we're focused on life again," Vladimir laughed. "I knew we'd have this discussion, and I've been dreading it, too. After all, we were supposed to be the confident, the powerful, the knowing. And we ain't none of them, bros, as they say in this neighborhood. Let's see what we can learn. A plan? And a beer?"

The group nodded their heads and lined up for a beer, talking and starting to laugh as they talked.

Vladimir and the cook stood together for a minute, watching.

"That went well," the cook concluded.

"They were ready for it," Vladimir replied. "It's been staring us in the face for too long."

CHAPTER 12. HAL'S SAGA

HAL & GRENDEL

Hal awoke, finding himself lying on the cold ground. He sat up, looking around. A ruined garden? Nice. He could only see for a few yards before everything vanished into a thick mist. He stood up and paced around the garden. The air was cold, damp. Most of the cultivated plants were dead or dying, and the few plants that were healthy were weeds, which had extravagantly overgrown the planting beds, tumbling over the pathways. The stonework framing the garden was broken and crumbling.

"Is this a dream or reality?" Hal asked the mist. "What is reality? It's generally agreed that sanity is vastly overrated. A psychotic is a guy who has just found out what's going on. I always liked that one."

"APRIL is the cruellest month, breeding
Lilacs out of the dead land, mixing
Memory and desire, stirring
Dull roots with spring rain[15]."

See, college wasn't entirely wasted.

He stopped and peered around. "What a nice place," he announced to the weeds. "A little work, a little polish, and it would still be a dismal swamp at the end of the world. At least it's not raining." A gentle breeze started to blow, carrying a light cold mist. "Okay, gee, at least it's not sunny and eighty degrees with a light cooling breeze." No change occurred, and the mist actually seemed to intensify. Why does that never work? he wondered, wiping the mist off his face.

"You know, talking to yourself is a sign of madness," Hal 2 advised, standing next to him.

"I wouldn't say a 'sign,'" Hal 3 disagreed, climbing on one of the ruined walls. "Maybe a poster?" He fell off to the ground behind the wall, dust and debris rising up from the crash.

"Oh, definitely good," Hal remarked to Hal 2, as Hal 3 climbed slowly out from behind the wall. "Let's see: talks to god, talks to angels, talks to self, argues with self, loses arguments with self. Really not doing well on the self-assessment scale today."

"Actually, talking to yourself can be helpful," Hal 2 replied. "The poor people with voices and delusions—it's the negative feedback they complain about. Having a voice in your head shouting positive things can be great sometimes. The key is whether it damages your daily life or not." Hal 2 put his notes away.

"The voices couldn't be, well, women cheerleaders from beer

commercials?" Hal pleaded hopefully.

Hal 2 and Hal 3 stood there unchanged.

"Okay, that doesn't work either. So, what is this place?" Hal demanded.

"Unconscious?" Hal 2 suggested. "Usually it's the sea, though, with all that restless tossing and turning. This is, well, a little lifeless."

"And you couldn't pick someplace warm, sunny, a beach...maybe nubile women in bikinis?" Hal 3 complained.

"It's my place," a voice rumbled from across the garden. "Fee fi fo fum, I smell the blood of an Englishman. Be he live or be he dead, I'll grind his bones to make my bread."

"Grendel," Hal snarled, clutching for a sword and finding none. "Ah, Scandinavian, actually, is my heritage. Norse. Hereditary enemies of the English."

"Close enough," Grendel replied. "I was there when the Vikings invaded England again and again. Good times," he sighed wistfully. "Where do they go? Sorry," shaking his head. "Slipping out of character there." He stopped for a second and thought, frowning. Then, nodding to himself, he smiled at Hal, a predator's toothy smile, all yellow and pointed teeth. "You're weak, wounded, lost in a wasteland," he threatened, looming over Hal.

"Begone, shade! I shall not run from you," Hal vowed. "Like that? It's graphic novel talk. So rare I actually get to use it."

"Not run from I," Grendel replied, ignoring Hal's rambling. "But run from what you have unleashed? Well, that's our party today."

Hal 2 and Hal 3 pulled out party favors and hats, but sheepishly put them away at a glance from Hal.

"Are they really necessary?" Grendel questioned, looking skeptically at Hal 2 and Hal 3. "There is a standard theme for these types of encounters, and you're stretching it."

"Why not?" Hal answered. "The more the merrier. As I'm not sure how I got here or they got here or you got here, well, I guess they are necessary."

"Fine, have it your way. Look there." Grendel pointed, and the mist parted. "Does it look familiar?"

"And now each one went the way upon which he had decided, there where they saw it to be thickest; so that each, entering of his own volition, leaving behind the known good company and table of Arthur's towered court, would experience the unknown pathless forest in his own heroic way[16]," Hal 2 read from his notes."

"I didn't want to leave the good company and table of Arthur's towered court," Hal 3 grumbled. "Serving wenches..."

Grendel glared at Hal, disgusted. "Yeah, that's the forest. Getting his menacing voice back, he growled, "Can you embrace your nightmares? Make them a part of you? Go back and pull up the old ones? Can you bear to bring your darkest dreams to the forefront? Because all of them are hiding in that forest, waiting for you. Did you bring your magic wand? No? Pity."

"Typical of the call is the dark forest, the great tree, the babbling spring, and the loathed, underestimated appearance of the carrier of the power of destiny," Hal 3 quoted, reading from his notes. "Loathed appearance of the carrier of the power of destiny... well, that would be you, Mr. Grendel," he offered politely.

Grendel looked away, annoyed. "I tell you, taunting isn't what it used to be," grumbling to himself, kicking at a ruined wall, which fell over with a loud crash. Dust and debris blew into the air, and then drifted away, leaving random piles of broken bricks and cracked stone blocks strewn around.

"Ooops," Grendel mumbled. "My bad."

Hal contemplated Grendel and then the forest. "Why not? I feel like a walk." Hal briskly walked to the edge of the forest, scanning along the tree line for the place to enter. "Where? Where does it feel right?" He closed his eyes for a second. "There." He walked towards a mass of brush pushing out from under the dark, looming trees. Pushing through the brush, grunting as he forced his way in, he vanished into the forest.

"There is an irresistible fascination that appears suddenly as guide, marking a new period, a new stage in that which has to be faced. It is somehow profoundly familiar to the unconscious, although unknown and even frightening to the consciousness. As it makes itself known, what formerly was meaningful may become strangely emptied of value.' Good," Hal 2 noted, making a checkmark on his notes.

"Gentlemen?" Grendel inquired to Hal 2 and Hal 3. They looked at each other, shrugged their shoulders, and walked in.

"Damn," they cursed. "These are thorn bushes!"

"Not my dream," Grendel advised, lightly swatting the bushes away. "Complain to your boss."

"Alter ego," Hal 2 muttered, "technically."

"Or are we the alter egos?" Hal 3 argued. "It's all very confusing."

What seemed like an hour later, they caught up with Hal, who was standing in a clearing next to a bubbling stream, rubbing his wounded shoulder. "All pain, and still no gain," he sighed.

There were noises in the forest. Tree limbs clashed in the dark undergrowth. The rustling suggested large animals moving; you could almost see them out of the corner of your eye, but saw nothing when you looked directly towards the sound.

"The water's good," Hal advised, pointing to the stream. "Drink. You must all be thirsty."

"We're figments of your imagination," Hal 2 observed quietly.

"So humor me and drink," Hal ordered.

Hal 2, Hal 3, and Grendel drank from the stream.

"It is good," Hal 2 agreed. "Refreshing. Where to now?"

"I'm not sure," Hal answered, looking around. "My mind is trapped in circles. I'm stuck in the fog, trying to force emotion, denying the emotion pushing at me. Being in a fog, you lose that feeling of joy in life. When you're down, you don't realize what up is. That kind of stuff. Still, I feel better after the water. Actually, a lot better. I think...that way." He struck out deeper into the forest. Surprisingly, there was a mass of trails, zigzagging and crossing each other, running through the forest. "It's a maze, isn't it? Well, that would be life." Hal wandered down several paths, increasingly frustrated, as Grendel, Hal 2, and Hal 3 followed. They made occasional snide comments, but mainly carried on an animated conversation about sports. "They know the statistics for the last four games," Hal grumbled, "but a path out? Nada." Finally, he closed his eyes and simply cut through the forest.

"You enter the forest at the darkest point, where there is no path. Where there's a way or path, it is someone else's path. The idea is to find your own pathway to bliss," Hal 2 noted. "Check."

Soon, Hal was standing at the edge of the forest, gazing over the rich meadow in bloom before him.

"The woods are lovely, dark and deep, but I have promises to keep, and miles to go before I sleep," Grendel murmured.

Hal glanced at him, surprised.

"Yeah, well, I read occasionally, too," Grendel defended. "A book of poems, a glass of wine, fresh bread, and a sunny day—I had a life. Did, before you hacked me up."

"It was a Hal of a way to go," Hal remarked.

Grendel grimaced. "You do deserve the suffering you are going to receive."

Hal saw a cliff rising in the distance. "That looks promising," and began walking through the deep grass of the meadow towards the cliff. He sniffed the rich air as they walked through the flowers. The smell was sweet and invigorating.

"No poppies?" Hal asked.

"The copyright was taken," Grendel snapped.

As they approached the cliff, Hal saw an opening in the rock face—a cave going deep into the cliff. Waiting outside the cave entrance were a leopard, a lion, and a she-wolf. Hal stopped a short distance from them.

Grendel hissed at them and the lion, leopard and she-wolf, crouched, ready.

"Stop!" Hal shouted. "Everyone stop. I have enough problems as it is. All friends here."

The leopard, lion and she-wolf relaxed. The leopard climbed a nearby tree, carefully worked himself into a comfortable position, and watched. The lion sat on a slab of rock, like a throne. And the she-wolf paced. She stopped in front of Hal. "We cannot go through here, Hal. We have been on this side of the cliff for a very long time. You must find the secret knowledge so that we may pass through also."

"Can you trust them?" Grendel interrupted. "You know what Dante thought."

"Look who speaks," the lion roared. "Evil itself in our valley." His tail began to twitch.

"Enough," Hal begged. "Peace, please!" Hal glanced at Grendel: "They are life itself. Dante was a fool. Actually, a man in trouble with the church who bought them off with bad verse. Not the first or the last." Then Hal looked back at the lion, the leopard and the she-wolf. "And Grendel, here, is a knowledge that you have denied to your peril."

"Still," he muttered, troubled as he stared into the darkness of the cave. "I stood before a dark cave, knowing I must go in, but I shuddered at the thought that I might not be able to find my way back." He stood quietly, reflecting for a few minutes. "We thought we had overcome the evil, only to find that we had just awakened it," Hal sighed to the darkness of the cave.

The leopard, the lion, the she-wolf and Grendel watched, keeping their thoughts to themselves.

"People love chopping wood. In this activity one immediately sees results," Hal 3 offered, standing there with an ax, looking cheerful.

"The passage through the gates of metamorphosis," Hal 2 muttered, reading from his notes. He looked up and squinted at the cave entry. "Yeah, looks like it."

Grendel looked away, pained. "Really, is this any way to respect the traditions?" he demanded, appealing to the creatures, who shook their heads. The shadows of the birds wheeling above flickered over them, far up in the grey yet cloudless sky.

"In for a dime, in for a dollar," Hal decided, reaching for the burning torch that suddenly appeared next to him. He glanced at the leopard, lion, and the she-wolf. "Well, it's my dream—it's tough enough as it is," he muttered and held the torch high before him as he walked into the cave.

"Gentlemen?" Grendel requested, and Hal 2 and Hal 3, plainly terrified, entered the cave, followed by Grendel.

"What an eccentric performance," the leopard purred.

"Certainly the strangest in long eons," the she-wolf growled.

Some time later.

"Look, this disordered imagination could use better writers and scenery," Hal 2 complained, sitting on a stone, munching an apple.

"Yes," Hal 3 agreed, "and wenches. Big Wagnerian wenches with long, blonde hair and huge breasts carrying us to someplace private, where we would be plied with mead and then vent our lusts."

"Vent our lusts?" Hal 2 laughed. "What comic book was that in?"

"I read real books once in a while," Hal 3 retorted.

Hal 2 glanced doubtfully at Hal 3.

"Okay, fine. It was in Superman," Hal 3 confessed. "Lex Luther was in a classical phase."

"He's such a wimp," Hal 2 confided, pointing at Hal. "Married to Cali and so he can't even have wenches in his dreams. Pitiful."

They looked around. The dark and unpleasant cave had opened to a wasteland. What wasn't blackened and burned ground was a stinking, rotten marsh, as far as the eye could see.

"No dead creatures in the marsh, are there?" Hal 3 asked anxiously, looking around.

"Stinks like it," Hal 2 grumbled. "But I don't think so."

"No live creatures in the marsh that might be hungry?" Hal 3 whispered, looking around carefully.

"We're figments of imagination. We are not edible," Hal 2 explained. "We have discussed this."

"Yeah, well what if there are hungry figments out there?" Hal 3 countered, not persuaded.

A distance away from Hal 2 and Hal 3, Hal stood on the blackened ground, Grendel facing him.

"Vanity of vanities, all is vanity, " Grendel hissed at Hal. Grendel waved his arm at the wasteland. "Look around you! For the fate of the sons of man and the fate of the beast is a single fate. As one dies so dies the other, and all have a single spirit, and man's advantage over the beast is naught, for everything is mere breath. Everything goes to a single place. Everything was from the dust, and everything goes back to the dust. Who knows whether man's spirit goes upward and the beast's spirit goes down to the earth?[17]"

Hal stared out at the wasteland.

"The wise man has eyes in his head, and the fool goes in darkness. Yet I, too, knew that a single fate befalls them all. And I said in my heart, 'Like the fate of the fool, it will befall me, too, and so why have I become so wise?' And I said in my heart that this, too, is mere breath. For there is no remembrance of the wise, as with the fool, forever. Since in the days to come, all will be forgotten. Yes, the wise dies like the fool! And I hated life, for all that was done under the sun was evil to me, for all is mere breath and herding the wind," Grendel jeered, pressing his point. "Your foolish quest is for naught, all dust at the end."

"In every culture, I come across a chapter headed 'Wisdom.' And then I know exactly what is going to follow," Hal answered. "Denying the wonder of life because it will end? Mourning the loss of what they turned their back on? Ecclesiastes drones on and on. My shoulder aches," rubbing it carefully. "The wound will not heal. Why is that, Grendel?"

"Ask what the wound is," Grendel rumbled. "See you the wasteland around us? The king is wounded and the land is wasted."

The Fisher King, not dead and not alive, waiting for the question to be asked to free him, appeared in front of them. "What is your pain?" his angry voice demanded. "Take your pain; hold it, touch it, embrace it, and it will be healed." But the pain burned like a fire between the Fisher King and Hal."

Grendel watched Hal, who was talking excitedly to himself, staring at the king. "Don't mind me," Grendel complained, sitting down. "No, go ahead; just because I'm the all-powerful force of evil here, please, take your time. Show me no respect, what do I care? Amateurs!" Grendel sputtered, talking to the wasteland. "They don't follow the union rules at all. I could get written up for this!"

"Percival never asked the right question, did he?" Hal mused. "Now, what was it? There was a busty wench in the comic book at that point, soliciting Percival—that might have been a departure from the strict thirteenth-century text, but she was welcome relief. Still, she was distracting. And that is the question, isn't it, Grendel?"

"The busty wench?" Grendel replied. "I've always favored those myself. Roasted, with an apple."

"A man of taste," Hal observed, nodding. "Nightmare creatures should be cultured, I've always thought. No, it's life, isn't it? The church rejected life and the world, and the Fisher King was the life force in the world. Rejected, wounded, the world is wasted."

The Fisher King reached out to Hal, and they touched hands at the fire of pain burning between them. Hal felt the King's pain, and through the Kings pain, Hal's pain. Touching the King, Hal touched his wounded self, which began to heal. Organic shapes, twisting, turning, roots pushing deep into the earth—Hal could feel life flowing into him from the soil. "Like Adonis, I have died and am reborn. And life flows back into me as the Tree of Life takes me into its embrace." Hal threw his arms up. "Life triumphant."

Grendel stepped back as the blacked stones suddenly were covered in green grass and trees pushed from the ruined soil. Clear water flowed along the dried streambed, and a soft breeze came over the land, gently pushing the meadow grasses. Fish jumped in the stream.

"Impressive," Grendel rumbled, "I grant you that. This is not my world," wrinkling his nose at the sweet smell of the flowers filling the air. You have made it further than anyone has. But there is a final test."

They were suddenly in a dark, hellish world. Grendel loomed, the red firelight flickering off him, a huge, terrifying presence. He was casually gnawing on what was clearly a human leg, the foot flopping as he chewed. They stared at him.

"Anyone we know?" Hal 3 asked, concerned.

Grendel smiled, a toothy, nasty grin with saliva and blood running down his chin, and Hal 3 backed up.

"Is that USDA inspected?" Hal 2 inquired. "You just don't know what's in the food anymore."

Grendel studied the leg doubtfully and then, sighing, tossed it into the dark in back of him. "Really, you people are just not playing the game. That's gotten screams for eons. Although your point about the meat is, well taken. "Now I'm worried."

"Cross-species transmission is pretty rare," Hal promised. "Especially in dream sequences."

"Nice to know," Grendel replied. He thought for a second, and then stood, a terrifying dark figure, his eyes red, reflecting the flames. He towered over Hal.

"The mythological hero is lured, carried away, or voluntarily proceeds to the threshold of adventure. There he encounters a shadow presence that guards the passage. The hero may defeat or conciliate this power and go alive into the kingdom of the dark or be slain by the opponent and descend into death beyond the threshold. Got it," Hal 3 muttered. "Right on course." He put his notes away.

Grendel paused for a second, shaking his head in disbelief, and then, ignoring Hal 3, Grendel again rose to his full height, towering far above Hal.

"We are taken from the mother, chewed into fragments, and assimilated to the world-annihilating body of the ogre for whom all the precious forms and beings are only the courses of a feast; but then, miraculously reborn, we are more than we were. Check," Hal 2 noted.

"What!!" Grendel shouted, pointing angrily at Hal 2. "Can't you control him?"

"Sorry," Hal replied, turning and scowling at Hal 2. "Hush!"

Grendel breathed deeply. "Now where was I?" he grumbled. He rubbed his forehead for a moment. "Oh, yeah, I remember. It was the 'I take your soul and body for my own.' Got it." He loomed high again, reaching out for Hal.

"The result of a successful adventure by the hero is the release of the flow of life back into the body of the world," Hal 3 mumbled, rapidly leafing through his notes. "I've lost my place in the script . . .is that where we are now? Ah, good."

"Fine!" Grendel roared. "Fine. No respect for the rituals. I can't work like this. I need a break. Coffee, anyone?"

"Ah, sure," Hal agreed. "It's been wearing on me too. Hey, you guys?"

Hal 2 and Hal 3 nodded.

They sat down on rocks, seated around a blazing fire, holding mugs of steaming coffee. "It's a dream, okay?" Grendel complained. "And this isn't going right at all. Centuries I've done this, but this just isn't working. First I'm hacked to pieces in life, and now I can't do the magic with the venom. I tell you—there are days it doesn't pay to get out of bed."

"I understand," Hal agreed. "Really. I've had a lot of those. So, what are we trying to accomplish here? Just tell me." He sipped the coffee and then examined it carefully. "By the way, this coffee is excellent."

"Do you like it?" Grendel replied. "I had some in Geneva the other day, so this must be my memory. It was fresh-brewed and hot. The day was overcast and with occasional mist. Just like the moors." He sipped his coffee, reflecting.

"Well," Grendel rumbled, "it's like this. I've survived centuries of the dark, doing things that are so far outside good and evil that humans can't grasp it. Paul's work has been mainly the dark. Interesting that a person who so rails on so, damning the enemy endlessly, is the personification of what he portrays as the enemy. He never sees it, either."

"That explains this," Hal replied, studying the scenery. "Dark, dismal, flames, a black river. The river Styx, I'd guess? I neglected to bring gold coins for the ferryman, but he seems to be on break now anyhow. Fire feels good, actually," running his hand through a nearby flame. "Yeah, that feels better."

"You're not supposed to be able to do that," Grendel scolded, exasperated. "Violates all the rules. I use the traditional symbols, and look what happens."

"Oh, my father is Lucifer," Hal mentioned. "Didn't Paul tell you?"

Grendel slapped his forehead with his right hand. "Paul always leaves out the details," he rumbled. "Why doesn't he do meeting notes like everyone else in the modern world? No, this isn't working at all. Well, let's at least finish it correctly."

"Which would be?" Hal 2 inquired, a little anxiously.

"You absorb me into the very heart of your being, wrapped in your DNA and all through yourself," Grendel replied. "Very dramatic—usually a lot of shouting and twitching. Then you become my minion."

"Don't like the minion part," Hal 3 contended. "Still, will there be coffee? What about wenches?"

"Come to the dark side," Grendel rumbled. "We have cookies."

"Cookies are good," Hal 2 mused. "This doesn't sound so bad."

Grendel slumped in despair. "I just don't feel like I'm getting through to you people," he sighed. "Well, fine, here goes." Grendel stood up to his full height and reached out to Hal.

Hal stood up and smiled. "I name you friend. I seek you to become me, and I you."

"What!" Grendel shouted. "This isn't right at all. Look, you've read the comic books, you know the script. Remember? Begone, foul fiend, etc."

"Look," Hal replied. "A monster is something denied, basic Campbell. You should never, never fight your monsters. One needs every little bit of power and strength one can get in this world. Monsters are power and ability. As the master wrote, if anyone should undertake the perilous journey into the darkness, he will find himself in a land of symbolic figures, ageless perils, gargoyles, trials, and secret helpers, monsters one and all. Why deny the strength, understanding, and power that they can bring?"

"I bring the dark," Grendel advised, in a calm, serious and far more terrifying voice. "Eons of the dark, flowing into you. Life isn't just the sunny days and pleasant breezes. Life is the cold and the bitter. Life isn't just the joy of birth and becoming; life is the horror of death, loss, and transfiguration. The Jedi walled away the dark, ran screaming from it, and then wondered why life turned on them."

"The whole light/dark thing never really made a lot of sense," Hal agreed. "Buddha said life is a burning fire. We live on death; we transfigure life for our life. Seems a bit dark, but that's life. That Good/Evil conflict, all that 'thus spoke Zarathustra'? In the end it's just a lot of tricks to get people to contribute to the building fund. The walls you build to keep your fears out only, in the end, keep you in. Every feared monster walled out gains strength. That titanic good/evil struggle—it's a fault of the human thinking in stories, not the way reality actually is. And suffering? I fought and fought with calculus, but never could grasp it."

"That is suffering," Grendel admitted. "I tried, but ended up eating the professors, toasted over the burning textbooks. They weren't bad. A little dry."

"Did you try a Fig Newton for dessert afterwards?" Hal asked. "No?"

"Dying to the old life, reborn in the new. But even though reborn into the new, challenges and tests," Hal 2 read from his notes. "Yeah, sounds right."

Hal and Grendel glared at Hal 2 and Hal 2 shut up.

"I've felt in a rut, it's true. Perhaps it was time to turn from Paul," Grendel mused. "Perhaps it is a new world. Yes, join a new side." He smiled, all glittering fangs, and Hal 2 and Hal 3 jumped backwards.

Hal laughed. "Friend, come to me."

Grendel stood tall again, and began to loom, the shadows behind him growing. Then he studied Hal, shrugged his shoulders and they grasped hands. Grendel dissolved into a mist, enveloping Hal, and then faded to nothingness. Hal stood there for quite a while, motionless.

"Do you think he's okay?" Hal 2 asked. "I'm about out of coffee."

"And mine's getting cold," Hal 3 complained, grimacing as he tasted it. "Well, I'm not sure if he's OK or not", scrutinizing Hal. "I'm not seeing any twitching. Mr. Grendel specified there would be twitching."

Hal twitched all over. "There! Happy? I'm fine!"

"All absorbed," Hal 2 asked. "All gone?"

"Not exactly," Hal's blue eyes turned all black for a second, and then back to normal blue.

"That's scary," Hal 3 gasped, holding his chest and panting. "Ah, I'm going over there, behind that tree for a minute. I carry a change of clothing for just such an event."

Hal and Hal 2 waited patiently for Hal 3, who came back shortly.

The world turned to mist, and when the mist cleared they were standing in the middle of a desert oasis. The water was lapping quietly under the trees, which were gently blowing. In the distance, there seemed to be something moving across the sand, birds flying high above it. It was indistinct; still too far in the distance.

"Surely the second coming is at hand," Hal murmured. "But not yet..."

"This place is better," Hal 2 declared. "But it's hot and dusty, and I'm hungry."

"Me to," Hal 3 announced.

"Well, it's my dream, so let's eat," Hal laughed. He snapped his fingers and they were in a raucous country bar, sitting at a rough wood-plank table overflowing with food. Steak, fries, and beers were lined up in front of them. Sitting next to each of them was a busty woman—two around Hal. The women were wearing tight shorts and low-cut flannel blouses, roughly a parody of the standard country-western, all-desirable female, and several waitresses, dressed the same, hovered around, bringing more food.

"Feast!" Hal 2 shouted happily. "Salute!"

"Not in a country bar, idiot!" Hal 3 snapped. "It's God save the King!"

Hal glanced at them, shrugged, and went back to the steak, which he devoured.

"Did you notice some slight, small change in him?" Hal 2 whispered to Hal 3. "Nothing obvious, just something, oh, small and subtle?"

"No, nothing comes to mind," Hal 3 replied. He had one arm around the girl next to him and was shoveling down his steak with the other hand. "Why do you ask?"

"No reason, really," Hal 2 mumbled, putting his arm around the woman next to him. "But," looking deeply into Hal's eyes, "I think you're really hungry."

MEAT & MEAD

Hal's eyes opened. Cali, Mary, Lucifer, and Jesus sat around the room, worried.

The nurse rushed to Hal and studied him. "Hungry, I'll bet," she offered, and pushed a tray of Jell-O in front of him.

Hal's expression hardened, changed. Angry. "Food," he hissed, and the nurse screamed and jumped back.

"Ah, food it is," Mary agreed quickly, moving to shield the nurse. "What did you have in mind, Hal?"

"Meat and mead," Hal growled without hesitation, and then he looked puzzled. "Why did I say that? Still, it sounds good."

"Meat and mead it is," Mary promised, smiling. "Get some." She frowned at the staff, who ran off.

Lucifer leaned over, whispering to Jesus. "Meat and mead is Beowulf, not Grendel, I think. A good sign."

"I just hope they bring extra food," Jesus replied. "The hiss was worrisome, but he's been through a lot. I'm hungry, too."

In a few minutes, Lungorthin barged in carrying a huge tray piled with steak and containers of mead.

"Mead you want, boy," he rumbled. "Mead it is." He poured out a full flagon of mead and pushed a steak in front of Hal.

Hal fell on the steak and the mead, and then another, and then another. Finally, he sat back. "To your health," he hiccupped to Lungorthin, and held his flagon up. They clash flagons. Hal smiled and then fell limp, asleep.

"I think he's recovering well," Mary remarked, examining Hal with a critical eye and pulling the covers up to his shoulders.

"Do you notice some small difference in him?" Cali asked, rather timidly. "I mean, just a little different?"

"That he eats, drinks, and curses like a twelfth-century Norse hero?" Lucifer declared, slurring his words. "Other than that, no, nothing really." He lurched to his feet, and he, Jesus, and Lungorthin went down the hallway singing songs in praise of Odin and the lost realm.

"Ah, fine," Cali mumbled, a bit undecided, and sat down on the bed, biting her lip as she absently smoothed the covers over Hal.

"He'll be fine," Mary promised, and hiccupped. "Wow," holding her head. "That mead has an effect. I'll, ah, see you later." She stumbled out of the room.

The Mead's revenge

The sun streaming in woke Hal. He was in a bright room, painted a light yellow, cheerful. The furniture was carved, almost in organic patterns, ancient styles. But embracing, pleasant, and comforting.

Hal clutched his head. "Ohhh," he moaned. "Mead. Never again after waking up from a coma. Which actually is a fairly easy resolution to live up to," he added, peering at Cali. "It has all the necessary limitations to make it meaningless, but the surface styling of a serious vow."

"Darling, you are alive!" Cali exclaimed.

"You call this living?" Hal complained, closing his eyes and holding his head with both hands. "Oy."

"You had a nice funeral, honey," Cali told him, picking at the comforter. "It was simple but elegant. You would have enjoyed it. I picked the flowers myself."

Hal contemplated Cali. "The whole 'enjoying your funeral' is a little complex with the mead still splashing through my head," he mumbled. "Turned into a wake, didn't it and the dearly departed got to participate after all. Although I think dying would be less painful than this headache." He slumped down, pulling a pillow over his head.

"So you won't be wanting breakfast?" Cali asked. "Some nice bacon, eggs, and toast? The cook has it all waiting."

"Food," Hal shouted, sitting up, excited. Then he grabbed his head again. "A man has to do what a man has to do. Eating is doctor's orders."

"None of that 'man has to do' stuff until you recover a little more," Cali teased, "but I'll get the food." She rushed out, and in a few minutes the smell of the freshly cooked breakfast filled the room. Hal dove into his plate.

"So, that's a healthy sign," Cali observed, watching him clean his third plate.

Hal sat back, smiling. "That was really wonderful," he sighed, and then dozed off.

HAL & GRENDELINE

"There's something I didn't mention," Grendel mentioned, sitting on a rock, casually looking away from Hal.

"And what would that be?" Hal asked. "I'm going to have to start bringing legal into these things. The addendums always seem to have surprises."

"Legal!" Grendel snarled. "There's a horror! The counsels of despair. I wonder if that's part of their certificate of admission to the bar." Grendel stood up, suddenly in a very large but exquisitely tailored three-piece, dark blue suit and white shirt with a red power tie. The power tie was actually shooting little bolts of lightening.

"Well, my research suggests Incrementalism," Grendel advised, in a dry, professional manner. He took off his glasses and pointed with them at Hal. "I'd suggest moving not so much toward a goal as away from trouble. Why? Because your speedy payment of my bills is directly related to your fear. You see trouble, you are fearful, you pay my bill. A goal? I have to paint a pretty picture in the air. Its just human nature that all you see is the problems reaching that goal, not the advantages. As a result, you pay my bill slowly, which is a problem for me. Now, eventually, moving away from trouble brings larger trouble, but as you are emotionally worked up, you can't think through that I might have helped bring this new trouble in on little cat's feet, and I get to bill more!

"Second: there is no reason to actually think about things. Let's just pretend that the world is the way we want it to be and draw up the contracts like that. You like that because you want the world to be the way you want, and when you are happy, you pay my bill. What's even better is that I can lower the fees for contract drafting and double my fees for the litigation. Because when you pretend the world is what you want it to be, you can rely on the world to come back with a thunderbolt to put the lie to your pretensions. Life just enjoys that part.

"Finally..." Grendel was suddenly in a very large ballet costume. "...let us do the information dance of rational ritualism. If we all hold hands, metaphorically, then we can pretend what we are doing is logical and rational, and we make a magic so that the world will do as we want." He twirled across the stage, flying the wings a little too fast. There was a loud crashing. Glass broke, the scenery shook, and the curtains trembled for a second. Grendel poked his bloodied head out from behind the curtain. "Well, magic doesn't always work," he apologized, and disappeared. A stagehand ran across with a placard. "The 'data pas de deux' will be the next act," it read. Then Grendel danced back across the stage in a German Oktoberfest outfit with a broom-handle partner. "Da, the interpretation waltz," he gasped, breathing heavily. "We read the entrails of the lawsuit, we pour over the Delphic utterances of the judge, but somehow it always works out to the maximum billing time possible. Weird, really, that it should always be the same in every case."

Grendel was back in the three-piece suit. "It's critical to use information that supports our position when we make decisions. I generally work with authorities that I can rely on based on prior experience. That is, rely on to tell the client to fight to the bitter end of their checkbook. For example, my uncle Herbert, happy and drooling in the old folks' home; and then there is that stock analyst in a hut somewhere north of the Arctic circle who is sure he can grow palm trees. Yup, the future is unknowable anyhow, so might as well get the opinions that end up the best for me." Grendel had his glasses back on. He adjusted his power tie and then looked at Hal, smiling. He was holding a thick bill for services. "I've given your case a great deal of thought. "$7,597, not including copying costs and allocated telephone time. Oh, and I billed you for the time it took to prepare the bill. And the stagehand's labor."

Hal took the bill and read quickly through it. "And your dinner last night where you thought about this problem? And consultations, with, um, Sassy Sally at the casino? Well, always good to have some toilet paper, even in my dreams. And, back to what you didn't mention?"

Grendel sat, now resplendent as a Viking warrior with a club and a sword. "It was better when we used to spit the enemies and cook them. Legal now slow roasts those poor people over months and years, poking them with hearings and depositions and a nonstop flow of paper. That's cruel beyond what even I consider appropriate, actually. I mean, really! A little rack, a little fire, then kill and move on. This long-wounding stuff that legal does, poking their thumbs into your cuts, is just distasteful."

"Well spoken," Hal declared, nodding. "I couldn't agree more myself."

"Anyhow, there is something else, which you would have realized if you'd thought about it," Grendel continued, peering away into the distance.

"Always my fault, it is. Are you sure you don't want a job with legal?" Hal demanded. "You've got all the moves down."

Grendel looked disgusted and shook his head.

"No? Well, I'm going to be sorry I asked this, but the small thing I overlooked—that would be?"

"My mother," Grendel sighed. "You may recall from the comic book that my mother was the real power behind the terror."

"I remember now! Yes, very impressive. The power, the beauty, and breeding the next-generation Grendel—that was a dramatic scene. This all stays in this dream/coma, I'm assuming? We're already in a damp cave set in a dark forest. Do I have to journey to another dark cave in another wasteland?"

"You can pick them," Grendel remarked, sipping his coffee. "Why couldn't you pick, say, the Cayman islands? Sunny, warm, nice beach."

"I asked the same thing myself. Got no good answer."

"Now, my mother," Grendel explained. "Paul could never take the meeting with her. He always avoided it. He would wake up screaming, run around, and then have to kill someone to wash the horror away. But your friends—Jesus, Mary, and Lucifer—they avoided the meeting too. She was something they wanted to wish away. Didn't fit the storyline, you might say."

"That doesn't sound good." Hal frowned, then brightened up. "Still, as merging with you has been critically important to me, although I never would have expected it, I look forward to meeting your mother. Of course, I'm married to Cali, so a powerful, aggressive semi-goddess isn't a totally new experience."

"That's some woman, that Cali," Grendel agreed, studying Hal. "And you have a daughter by her, which is asking for more trouble than I can imagine. Don't come home when she's thirteen and arguing with her mother. Work late at the office for a couple of months. Maybe years."

"We hope for more children. It's my enthusiastic nature."

Grendel smiled sadly at Hal and shook his head. "Too soon old, too late wise." He stood up, and suddenly he was dressed as a ringmaster. "Ladies and gentlemen," he announced to the crowd murmuring in the dark, "we have a show for you tonight! Without further delay, please meet my mother, Grendeline."

The crowd dashed for the exits as Hal and Grendel watched. "Well, I'm out of here," Grendel declared. "Hope to see you again." He joined the crowd headed for the exit.

"Trampling the wounded and hurdling the dead," Hal 3 commented. "A Detroit crowd. Brings back memories of Red Wings games when I was in college."

"Now that gives me, well, a little concern," Hal mused, sitting on the rock, watching the last of the crowd vanish into the dark.

"Perhaps a large concern?" Hal 2 offered, shivering as he stood next to him.

"They left the wounded behind," Hal 3 added. "Which is absolutely not a good sign. Mr. Grendel's out of here with the rest of them, and...Hello beautiful," standing up straight and adjusting his tie.

A ravishing blonde woman limped out of the dark, her right foot in a cast, but otherwise naked.

"Slithered, I think," Hal 3 murmured. "Not walked."

"Cali's not going to like this," Hal 2 warned.

"What is it with you and Hal?" Hal 3 complained. "You think Cali doesn't have naked men in her dreams, so you can't have naked women? You are so straight and boring." Hal 3 was careful not to take his eyes off the woman, who stood about six feet away from them.

"A naked woman, limping, needing help," Hal remarked, standing up. "I've seen this one before. Isn't that a knife in your hand in back of you?"

She laughed and held her hands out. They were empty. "I'll not need a knife for you, my dear," laughing, with a trace of a hiss. "Oh!" looking down his body. "Nice of you to come to attention," she purred. "All of you."

"It would be impolite," Hal declared, "to not show my respect and admiration."

"No sword? No spear? Well, at least a spear in your hand. No AK-47 with a grenade-launcher attachment?" she demanded. "I'm disappointed. Normally they put up more of a fight."

"Well, all of that warfare in your unconscious does make a mess of the internal structure. The mind takes a terrible beating. All that sound and light, signifying nothing."

"Paul ran," she remarked, sitting down on a rock higher than his, a queen on her throne looking down at a peasant.

"I know. I know some of his mind. It isn't pretty. And, if I may venture an opinion, my lady, I have enough domination battles with Cali. What if we just talk? I concede your ultimate power of life."

"Fine," she sighed. "Boring, but okay." The rock lowered itself so they were on the same level.

"Watch out, boss," Hal 2 whispered to Hal. "An opponent that talks is planning to attack."

Hal 3 was dressed in a poorly fitting Roman tribune's uniform and trying to look menacing. "We've fought worse," he declaimed in a manly voice.

"Oh, please! Give me a break," Grendeline groaned. Grendeline 2 and Grendeline 3 sauntered out of the darkness. "Please, give them something to do while we do our business," Grendeline ordered Grendeline 2 and Grendeline 3, who happily nodded.

"Better," Hal 3 smiled as the redheaded Grendeline 3 shimmied up to him.

"Nice toga," Grendeline 3 giggled, "and what a sharp sword." She smiled as she ran her finger along the blade.

"I'm worried about this," Grendeline 2 asserted, walking up to Hal 2.

She was a brunette—dark suit, long skirt, her hair pulled back, and wearing serious horn-rimmed glasses. "It could go wrong. The risk assessment seems to have been rushed."

"Couldn't agree more," Hal 2 agreed, vigorously nodding his head. "It's nice to finally meet someone with some sense. Maybe we should compare notes?"

"Good," Grendeline 2 replied, "but perhaps over here, a little away from the fireworks? We don't want any, well, collateral damage." They walked away, engaging in a quiet, intense, and worried conversation with frequent glances at Grendeline and Hal.

Grendeline 3 and Hal 3 had wandered a little farther off and seemed preoccupied.

"Okay, I like that," Hal admitted. "Very efficient. And so the power of the goddess shows itself. Literally." He took a quick glance down her body. "Far ahead of Grendel, the alter egos just frustrated him. Morgana with Arthur, you with Beowulf, and a thousand other stories over the centuries. How do you and Mary work together?"

"Mary is Kali, but even she recoils from the raw power of the female goddess. I'm life, really. Completely disruptive to the social order, because life cares only about life. Life uses every resource, every opportunity. It is limited by nothing, it tests every direction that it can go in. Life is remorseless—no regrets, no looking back—and glories in the death and transfiguration of other life. I am the deep power of the Tree, my boy."

She leaned towards him, studying him carefully. "The squealing of the prey, the hot blood running down your throat. The live prey writhing inside you as you swallow it and sink to the depths to digest and enjoy. Mary is Kali, but Kali is the human version of the story. There's a lot more there, a lot deeper and harder. People push away the horrors of life; pull into their small stories and tight structures. Shocked when they find the stories empty of life and emotion, they wistfully look out, but your own prisons are the strongest, aren't they?"

"Strongest when they are bright and you are proud of them," Hal agreed. "Am I the hero here? I've lost track."

"The hero?" Grendeline scoffed. "The avenging bright hero, striking down the beast, standing triumphant over the body, listening to the cheers of the crowd. Proud?"

"I was Achilles," Hal confessed. He stared away into the distance, frowning. "In my wrath, I slew those who had stopped fighting." He glanced back at Grendeline. "They came to kill. They died. That is the old law."

"Do you seek to convince me?" Grendeline taunted. "I'm the wild—kill them all, it's no concern to me. Life and death play out each moment in the world, no stories involved. Just events. But it troubles you. Why?"

"I saw myself as the true hero," Hal confessed. "Hector would not have slain them."

"Standing tall in his horsehair helmet, his breastplates gleaming, with a bright polished shield and sharp sword. And for his honor and bravery, Troy was destroyed, because he died when he was needed by others. If you go to your death for fear of your honor in others' eyes, putting aside protecting your family, that is the act of a coward. Afraid of a voice in your head, the reflection of others' ghostly opinions. Beneath contempt. What think you of your proud warrior now?" Grendeline snarled.

"I do not know," Hal conceded. "He meant well, none better, and he destroyed all he held sacred."

"The minds of the gods cannot be read from their acts," Grendeline confided. "And the victors wrote the story. We should leave the brave man in his hopeless battle, respected and honored for what he tried to do. I remember Troy," she mused. "It was not as written, or at least as has come down to us. No, he was a brave man, and he anguished over his choices."

They sat in silence for a few minutes.

"The men you killed—they deserved death," Grendeline declared. "They were not children coming to play. They brought guns. And deception is one of their oldest tricks. An upraised hand can hold a weapon also."

"All you say is true, and yet I sit. How to wave my hand, and have the walls I've built up just vanish?

"Time reveals all things," Grendeline drawled.

"I'd say a lot is revealed now," Hal admitted, staring at her, dropping his pretense. "I might as well enjoy the scene. You're the consummate succubus, tested over the centuries, and nothing could be criticized."

"Technically correct," Grendeline 2 advised, reading from her notes. "In folklore a succubus is a female demon who takes the form of a human woman in order to seduce men, usually through, ah, sexual intercourse." She cleared her throat. "In the notes, you see. Traditionally, religion held that repeated intercourse with a succubus may result in the deterioration of health or even death."

Grendeline glared at Grendeline 2, who scurried away.

"That's my cue," Grendeline noted, standing very close to Hal. "What say you?"

"What if we perhaps just talk?" Hal stammered. "A little foreplay, some teasing conversation? I was just honoring craftswomanship when I see it."

"Nice to deal with competent people," she replied, sitting back down. "That was the first offer, by the way. You are right to let your emotions out. Really, emotions are all you can work with. Here, you have a classic decision under conditions of uncertainty, partial information, etc."

"Given the information displayed, there's no uncertainty and nothing left to display. Which means that the information displayed is a cover for what's really important. What am I not seeing?" Hal puzzled.

"What do you think?" Grendeline questioned, purring as she ran a fingernail down Hal's leg, which was suddenly bare.

"That's nice," Hal gasped. "There's....something about when opponents do something.... there is something else coming...but it's hard to remember the exact quote right now. No, no—that's fine, you don't have to stop. I expect to be tortured in the process. Don't be concerned."

She laughed and stood up again. "Well, it isn't fun to torture if they enjoy it. Come, brave knight. I see your sword seeks to leave its sheath and do battle."

"Not opponents," Hal replied, troubled. "Small stories must have a conflict. People can't see without a border to carefully fence it all in. Stories are not life; stories are children's wishes written down. Shall I fight and overcome and win, a great victory with crumbling monuments over the centuries? Look at me and despair, carved in stone in the desert? Because then I have defined my great victory as what I know now. Everything I might have learned outside my little story is gone forever. Gone, that is, until the demon child of our mating comes back out of the caves and makes me pay the price for my cowardice. Tell me, great mother, what I should be thinking?"

"That was the second offer," Grendeline noted, "just to be technical. It's union rules—they require a clear notice. You're brave. Normally humans are more than happy to feel power and control for the moment and pay the price down the road. Breeding is fun—both men and women jump to it. Tomorrow is another day, they think, if they think at all. Stepping out into the new? Dissolving yourself into another state? They will nail bars over the windows to the outside."

"Yeah, seen that play over and over," Hal replied. "It doesn't work."

"Hal 3 and Grendeline 3 seem to be happy with the breeding idea," Grendeline observed, watching them happily intertwined in the grass.

"They would. Figments of the imagination from the old reptile brain."

"And Hal 2 and Grendeline 2 seem clear that nothing is working out according to plan, and that it needs to be sent to committee and tabled for discussion, although I think that Hal 3 and Grendeline 3 are giving them some other ideas," Grendeline mused, watching the alter egos. "I've seen this play before, too."

"So here we are," Hal observed.

"Are you sure about this? Look, you're married to Cali and you've already bred a demon, albeit a small one at this point. What's another one?"

Grendeline teased.

"I'm hoping for more children," Hal replied. "But real ones, not ones in my mind. Grendel warned me about Maria at thirteen. Maria in real life will be bad enough, but a phantom Maria, like Beowulf's dragon inside? That's more punishment than I deserve. At least, more than I think I deserve."

"You are foolish, boy," Grendeline advised, shaking her head. "It's your father in you."

"And Lucifer and Jesus?" Hal demanded. "What have they done with your knowledge and power?"

"They push me away. Fascinated with the toy that civilization is, they went off to play with it. They forgot that life comes from me," Grendeline reflected. "Oh, they lust and desire, but the power of life is truly terrifying. Heck, I scare myself sometimes. Watch." She transformed into a huge spider with razor-sharp claws.

Hal 2 and Grendeline 2 screamed and ran. Hal 3 and Grendeline 3 glanced over and then kept going.

"The reproductive response," looking admiringly at Hal 3 and Grendeline 3, who didn't even miss a beat as Grendeline morphed back to the beautiful woman. "That's life in its essence."

"Tell me about it," Hal agreed. "Sex isn't a story, it's a real event. Full engagement, you might say. Happiness without drugs. Well, maybe a few drugs."

Hal 2 and Grendeline 2 were talking seriously, comparing notes. They started reading sections and references and disputing each other.

Hal and Grendeline watched them for a few minutes.

Hal 3 and Grendeline 3 came back to the fire snickering, looking relaxed and happy, making frankly organic suggestions full of pleasure and joy.

Hal 2 and Grendeline 2 glanced at each other in a different way, and decided to discuss matters a little farther from the fire.

"The third time I ask. Shall we do the traditional dance?" Grendeline announced, her beauty intensifying until she was all the goddesses drawn and carved across the centuries. "I offer you all you would want in the world out there," she purred. "All I ask is a small contribution from you, something you will be joyful about the rest of your life." She rose and loomed over him, her presence, smell, and luster overwhelming.

"Wonderful," Hal gasped. "Beyond what I've ever dreamed, except when I think about Cali, of course. Have to cover myself here. But, I must quibble. It will not be joyful all my life. Technically, some of it. Then, really, not at all. Look at Beowulf. He took the prize and it was hollow. Winning in a world when the game is fixed is a complete fraud. Your triumphs are ashes, and the days only reflect back your emptiness as you wait for the terror to come."

"True that is," Grendeline agreed. "But three times only do I call. So think carefully."

"And after the third offer?" Hal asked.

"Then you must die to your present life. Perhaps live in another. Perhaps not. They don't always come back. And they never, never come back the same," Grendeline commented, studying Hal as she shaved long ribbons of stone off the rock she was sitting on with her steel claws.

"I like that," Hal admitted, contemplating her claws effortlessly taking chunks out of the solid rock. "An effective visual goes right to the subconscious...but wait—isn't this is the subconscious? Regardless, it's effective. Really, though, think with me about this. You expect me to go back to Cali after mating with you? Remember the queen in Beowulf—a life frozen in anger? Cali's more action oriented than that. It's really just a question of who dismembers me."

"That's true," Grendeline laughed. "That woman is a tiger. And they will all have your memories. They must face this themselves. Life is growth or death. Will they follow as far as you have gone?" she wondered to herself, admiring her steel fingernails for a moment.

She glanced coldly at Hal. "Do you not fear Cali will meet me? That the blood will run cold in her veins, and her life will be a terror to her afterwards? You will hold her trembling body, her mind broken, knowing that you have destroyed your blessed love. What a hero that would be!"

Hal saw Cali crying in his arms, and he turned away, denying the horror. But what can one do? Lock away everything you love behind glass walls and visit them twice a day to enjoy their company, only to destroy them completely that way? What I love about her is what she is, and life gives and takes. Change is pretty when it's bright flowers opening, and hideous when it's withered and blackened petals lying on the floor. But change is life.

He stared at the horror, then closed his eyes and turned away from the terror for a moment. Then he looked directly at it again, opening to the horror. He held his head for a time, but finally looked up at her. "You have a way with words, my lady. A nightmare vision worse than any movie. But, I fear more if she does not. Pain can't always be avoided or run from."

"You have learned," Grendeline sighed, nodding sadly. "But their experience will not be as yours. Their wounds are different, their questions are different, and their path is through their own darkness. Think you not that you have blazed a path for them."

"I haven't even blazed a path for myself," Hal confessed. "And each must enter the forest where it is thickest, and create their own path."

She inspected him carefully, and then smiled, a wistful smile with a trace of hope. "Brave, you are. Needed, it is. But listen: with Grendel, you believed that the wound of the Fished King had been cured. You believed you were out of the wasteland."

"You know not," she hissed, leaning close to him, and she was suddenly a reptile, brilliant in blues and reds. Beautiful, powerful, alien beyond imagination. Her black eyes stared deeply into him. "We were life for uncounted hundreds of millions of years. You cannot imagine what we were like, and we were closer to what you are than most life is. You know not your wound. You know not the true fullness of life. Oh, you have felt the other creatures' lives, lived a bit through their memories, but it's deeper than that. The legends say you should not look straight at the gods because the legends fear the power of life. When you directly at life itself, you open to the power that will overcome you. Foolish, proud mortal, touching the sun."

Hal sat, staring out over the empty plain, rocky and hard. "You speak the hard truth, Goddess Freyja. Nor do I know my own wound, or the questions I should ask. The Fisher King sits and waits. For what?"

"You must serve the goddess," Grendeline countered. "She does not serve you."

"Buddha said that the name of the object isn't the object. Great comic book, by the way," he remarked, noting Grendeline's glance. "Busty Indian maidens in saris. Well, some of the time in saris, anyhow."

"You're the one who didn't want to mate for the easy way," Grendeline laughed.

"My name for a thing pretends the name is the same as the thing. The basis for all magic, actually. When I use the name, I emotionally believe that I have control over the 'thing,' but that is just my fantasy. When I accept others' names for things, I've given myself over to their pretend control of the greater world. The words I use bind me, not the world that I seek to bind with them. The priests' words control only the human stories, not the real world that they pretend they control."

"True. The priests promised the King that their story would make him all-powerful, but it was a scam that the priests always win."

"And by walling away life, I'm bounded by that small world their words create." Hal continued. "Life is wonderful—'wonder full,' Job declared. And terrible at the same time. The priests' words offer a pretty false child's world, turning real life into monsters and demons, horrible threats that cannot be dared and survived. Lions and tigers and bears, oh my! They make language their tool because it's so controllable. In truth, what's most important can't be told; the transcendent, inexpressible truths are beyond the words. And where the words are symbols of the transcendent truths, they are misunderstood to be the truth itself. Still, language is good for ordering a beer, at least."

He stood up and paced for a few minutes. "Beowulf was the hero, And Arthur. They kept their structured, small worlds with the clear borders. The raw power of life, they denied. The Fisher King was horribly wounded by their rejection of life, and they left him there in his agony. Then, in their shame, embarrassed, they fed their lusts and hid the results. And it's always the same. The well-meant lie that corrupts all you reach out to do. The shadow always grows again in the stories because the shadow is the power in the world that they denied. The shadow was the lie that they wanted life to be something other than it was. The pretty, magic words don't lock out life forever. And, as always, if you shout loudly about something you should be ashamed of, the social world buys your story. So they blame women and emotion for the chaos they brought upon themselves, and set up the game to start again."

"The raw power of life running under the structures. Foundations of sand, and all that," nodding her head.

"That's what Paul's afraid of," Hal mused. "He knows that the power of life is out there, always upsetting the square borders to fence it out. Xerxes stands on his throne, knowing that life laughs at him. Their hero stories push life to the outside, all monsters and demons, until the world crashes through their paper plans. They pick themselves up, the priests say magic words, and they all pretend that the walls will keep life out."

"To lift an autumn hair is no sign of great strength; to see sun and moon is no sign of sharp sight; to hear the noise of thunder is no sign of a quick ear. So standing with the herd, believing the taught meanings—the Punch and Judy show of the eternal struggle of good and evil, with bright fireworks punctuating the approved message— what wisdom is that? None," Grendeline added. "But it is emotionally comfortable."

She stopped and looked around at the scene before her. Then she contemplated him thoughtfully. "You will become something different, something you did not expect. I may become something different from what I am. That is not something that even I can easily face. Perhaps I have frozen and not noticed over the eons." She pondered, her forehead wrinkled in thought. "Being the ultimate power and realizing that perhaps you can become something new, well...perhaps we all freeze a bit to avoid the change that is life."

"So, just to make sure I understand the plan here," Hal offered. "It's standard meeting procedure to state back what I think you said. Sorry, it's the accountant in me. You are life in its incomprehensible power and fury, absorbing all, conquering all before you over the uncounted eons. I'm sitting here, foolishly hoping to absorb you into me. In reality, you will absorb me into you, truly leaving me changed, torn apart and reabsorbed literally into the mother."

"You'd have to ask Grendeline 2 about the small print. Those are just words. Experience is all." She waved her hand, and the scene changed. They were on a dark moor, standing before an ancient bridge over a deep chasm, so deep that the bottom cannot be seen. Clouds roiled deep below, throwing mist and vapors past the bridge. The other side was vague, dark.

Hal stood at the edge, looking into the roiling darkness below. "When the abyss stares into you, what does it see?"

"It sees what you can be," Grendeline answered. "That is why you fear the abyss."

Hal watched a volcano erupting in the distance. "The subconscious is nothing if not subtle. Well, make friends with your monsters, especially when they are as beautiful as you, my lady." Hal bowed to her. "Buy them a beer. Have a long talk."

"Mead," Grendeline demanded. "None of those cheap bars, either, buster. I'm a lady. So, to move past this little thing that is your life now, you must be dismembered and opened to the transcendent. It's absorption by and of the mother goddess and the life force, is it?"

"I name you friend," Hal offered, "and welcome you."

Hal held his hand up, and she grasped it. They stood for a moment, and then they dissolved into swirling clouds of mist that combined, eddied, and flowed. Small lightning bolts flashed in the eddies, and after some time they reformed into Hal. But not quite as he had been.

"Wow," Hal 3 gulped, looking at Grendeline 3, who was wrapped around him. "What a great scene!"

"Nice," Hal 2 agreed, and Grendeline 2 nodded vigorously, sitting up in the grass. Her glasses were tilted, and her hair was not as well controlled as before.

The world around was suddenly flush with life. A rain forest from ancient times, so rich with life and power. "Wonder-full. The tree isn't conscious, but it lives a life of complexity past my imagination."

HAL & CALI

Hal was lying in bed the next morning. He was blankly staring at the window, the heavy drapes glowing from the light of the sun behind them.

Cali, sitting on a chair next to the bed, had her hand on his, silently watching him.

"How's Maria?" he asked, looking carefully at her.

"Great. She's with the other kids. She's doing great."

The horror they felt, knowing how close they had come to losing Maria made them quiet for a few minutes.

"I'm feeling a lot better," Hal declared. "But I think I had a crisis of faith. Maybe that's the wrong word? You know how we are taught all these stories about the world and what it's like, and how you should behave? All that stuff we never really think about. When we met Jesus, Mary, and Lucifer, well, that pretty well rattled things for the usual story we'd been taught, but we were busy and things were happening. Grendel, and even more so Grendeline, brought out all of the conflicts and made me face all of the contradictions—and the monsters. I think, after it's all done, I like the monsters better than I like most people now, but it's wearing, stories and emotions conflicting as they change and grow. It's been such a long exposition."

"It's been bothering me too. I think about the wall in Ann Arbor, and I don't know how to reconcile it with the old stories, where we are now, and where we are going."

"I'm thinking that Descartes was wrong." Hal remarked.

"You actually read books in college?" Cali queried.

"A French comic book, cubist painters drinking absinthe in a café near the Seine," Hal recalled. "There is meaning—the stories we are taught—and there is inspiration—what we feel inside. The feeling of life, the feeling of being one with the world, that's all inside and it's wonderful. The outside stories just seem to get in the way now. But it's hard to think about."

"I didn't know that comic books had those kinds of stories," Cali teased. "I thought it was all big superheroes and busty wenches."

"Now there is an inspiration!" Hal laughed, his eyes lighting up. "Why it is that I'm always recovering from my wounds when you talk like that?"

"Sounds like the recovery is coming along well," Cali smiled. "But that twinkle in your eye has consequences! Maria doesn't seem like the happy, supportive older sister type."

"More the domineering tyrant. Perhaps the Dark Queen in Snow White? I think Wednesday Addams, of the Addams' family. She does know her own mind. I'm not sure where she would have gotten that."

"Not from Moi, the cheerful elf maiden," Cali murmured, squeezing Hal's hand. Hal laughed and tried to sit up to kiss her. She bent down, kissing him as she gently pushed him back down to his pillow. Then she fussed with the covers as he watched her.

"My mother was proud of you," she confided. "I was, well, you know how I am, just rambling one day and she actually yelled at me. She declared I didn't deserve a husband like you. Beowulf against Grendel, she exclaimed, an epic battle. They had lost many men and creatures to Grendel over the centuries. They took what was left of him and burned him, but there may be colony creatures somewhere."

"I die a happy man," Hal declared, "my true value recognized." He lay flat, folding his arms over his chest, winking at Cali.

"And your father, Lungorthin and the caretaker were impressed. So, yeah, pretty much a complete sweep."

"And you, my fair queen?" Hal asked.

"You were terrible in your wrath," Cali mumbled, shivering as she remembered. "Isn't that how the comic books say it? Like a force of nature against them. You only stopped and collapsed when they were all dead."

"They came to kill," Hal snarled, his eyes hard. "They died. That was the old justice. I heard your cries to stop, but it would have been wrong."

For a moment, she no longer saw the wounded man lying pale, the man she'd married. She saw the berserker, the demon in the fight, lying in the bed, weakened but still terrible. Cali stood up for a second, and walked to the window, pulling the drapes open. She looked out at the sky for a moment to clear her thoughts, and then walked back and sat next to Hal. "And when you fell—I screamed, and I thought Lungorthin was going to lose his mind. I had never seen a look of rage like yours before. But I've seen another. When your father came in and knelt over you, he cried for a minute. Then Mary rushed in and took over your care. When he stood up, his face showed the same rage you had as he swept out with his retainers. What do they say in the old books? 'His wrath burned with a bright fire'? The words are not strong enough." Cali thought, and muttered something in an ancient language.

"Ah, Greek to me?"

"Aramaic," Cali replied. "It's amazing what one picks up around here. Roughly, it is 'Well done is better than well said,' and you did well."

"As comparisons to my usual semi-literate, rambling self start from a low threshold indeed, so the glow of my deeds shines all the brighter," Hal laughed.

"Hard to argue with that," Cali teased. "Since then? Blood has been spilled, and keeps spilling. That's life," she observed, shrugging.

Hal murmured, almost to himself:

"Now Grendel raged[18] and sought to find escape, But Beowulf maintained his fearful grip
Until he burst the sinews of the arm, And made the juncture of the bones appear.
Then tore he from the beast his arm and breast, And Grendel stood in terror unto death.
Full well he knew his days had reached the end. Then fled he to the coverts of the mere,
His arm and shoulder in the hero's grasp; And Beowulf stood victor in the Hall!"

He glanced at Cali, who was really surprised. "That comic book had great illustrations,. "Norse maidens with flagons of mead. I'm not sure why they were there, but they certainly filled out the scene."

"Grendel was a creature out of the '300' movie—the giant. A worthy servant of Paul! An alien creature, not burdened by morality or ethics. Still, you want Norse maidens? I'll start singing Wagner."

"They taught that in Catholic school?" Hal asked, surprised. "I thought that was too, well, Lutheran? As well as Norse pagan."

"You'd love to see me as Brunhilde," Cali giggled. "A warrior maiden with a spear."

"Heck, there isn't enough gold available to make adequate breastplates. No! No violence! Remember, I'm a wounded man."

Hal suddenly away, remembering the woman's scream. "I wish my mother had lived," a tear running down his cheek. "I was too late. I didn't see far enough ahead."

"Your father is distraught over your mothers death. A trick, he shouts, that Paul has been playing for three thousand years, and it worked again. He almost explodes when he talks about it."

They sat for a few minutes, silent, wrapped in thought.

His wound, she wondered, carefully smoothing the comforter to keep her hands busy. They have been talking in whispers. Something serious, something that spreads, or can spread. Maybe like the knife in *Lord of the Rings*— it worked its black magic unless it was caught? That had a lasting effect! But that was a book, not this world. But what is this world? It's not what I was told or imagined, and Hal must be thinking the same.

"Do you remember Beowulf?" Hal mused. "Suffering through it in high school, I know I saw only the battle, the bright victory against the terrible monster. I know I missed the key, in that first fight between Grendel and Beowulf, when the opposites attack in a fury and to their surprise—shock, actually—discover that they are the same in many ways? Obviously more for Beowulf, who survives but is wounded in a way he never would have expected. His bright ideals and clear vision, what he thought he 'was', the root of his strength, swept away for the muddy colors and deep greys of the real world. It took the shine off what he saw himself as. And he never really worked through all of the changes, frozen between what he had been, he thought—and what he was to become. It destroyed him, the land and his kingdom. He never answered the Fisher King."

Cali, biting her lip, studied him fearfully.

"Living in an alternate reality, or maybe the true reality, is disconcerting. I've been more conscious of things around me than people seem to think. It seems that battle with Grendel was more than just a physical fight, it was mental, spiritual and emotional war as well."

"No one has really told me the story," Cali admitted. "I've been worried, but, well, no one really wants to talk. I ask, and all I get are very serious faces that look quickly away."

Hal smiled at Cali, squeezing her hand. "I like that he was named Grendel. 'A demon outside God' was the original translation. Philosophically, that ties to the ancient myths from far before the Christian God came to the North and took all the heroes away."

Cali sat silent, questioning him with her eyes.

"In the comic book. Really! The challenge that Beowulf and Grendel faced was that they were both far outside the pale, outside any of the human stories and their little bordered worlds. Beowulf was an uneasy fit in the world of man before the fight, in the role as the strongest man. But still a man, thinking and acting as a man. After the fight, well, then really not a man anymore. Something greater and lesser, perhaps, from the human stories perspective. In 'The Dark Knight', Batman denied that the Joker could complete him. He was wrong. Perhaps it should have been phrased the other way."

"That wasn't in the comic book," Cali argued. "It's too subtle. And too complex."

"Not true—it's in the little drawings around the edges of the frames in the comic books," Hal teased. "You have to look at them carefully."

"So prithee, good sir knight, tell me what happened," Cali ordered, anxiously. "Like, stop jerking my chain, dude."

"I'm thinking our time in New York has had an effect on you, my dear. Small and subtle, but an effect." Hal thought for a minute and sighed. "It's a dark story. As I faded, I could feel him gathering strength. A dark thing in my mind, far more terrifying than his external appearance, which was bad enough. Didn't smell as bad, though, which was nice. And it overcame me, into the dark. Coming out of the wild, in a black place where there is no help. Do you wish them to find you? They are terrible! And they are," Hal murmured, almost to himself. "Dark and terrible, and powerful."

Hal gazed out the window for a moment to clear his mind.

"He talked to me for a long time", glancing back at Cali. "First him. Then his mother, stronger than could be imagined. They wrapped themselves into the very fiber of my being. I could feel my DNA changing, adding and splitting. Oh, there were the usual promises: 'You shall be as terrible as the Storm and the Lightning, as fair as the Morning, as dreadful as the Night, ruling over all like the Sun! All shall love you and despair!' Or along those lines? It's hard to remember exactly, tossing in the throes of nightmare."

Hal was silent for a minute. He crossed his arms and stared at the wall, but he only saw his dreams. "Myths are tougher when they get serious. They are disguised as fairy tales, pretty stories for children—even the ones from

Grimm, which had traces of the real world poking through the embroidery. The social world doesn't want all that complexity. We grow and see ourselves as something, as someone, and we evaluate every motion and every thought against that core 'me'. The mind demands consistency, despite everything that happens 'out there'. But drifting in the nether world, you lose your moorings. You feel the contradictions, the separate selves. You know, there is a theory that dreaming isn't a different mental state. The theory argues that we always dream, but when we are conscious, we integrate our sensory inputs into the dreams. Explains a lot, actually." Hal was silent, the lines of pain tight around his mouth.

Cali sat frozen, covering her mouth, her eyes huge as she stared at him.

"What was it Campbell wrote? 'You must discover and assimilate your opposite, your unsuspected self, either swallowing or being swallowed. Walls are swept away, resistance is futile, and you put aside virtue, beauty, and life and bow or submit to the absolutely intolerable.' All the external meanings you are taught, actually. And then you find that you and the opposite are not of differing species, but one flesh. Inspiration makes you whole.[19]" He noticed Cali's fear and smiled at her, holding her hand carefully. "It's prettier on paper. And easier.

"I was swallowed," his smile vanishing, the lines of pain reappearing. "No swallowing. It was bigger than me. Grendel's blood and venom were filled with colony creatures, carrying the memories of its life and its thoughts. A long life it had, tied to and part of Paul. Anger and conquest, victory and blood, writ across the centuries. And I went through it all. Through things almost beyond imagining. Yet it was afraid also. Afraid of the other creatures, the fear that Paul has; it cannot accept the bigger stories. I took in the entire creature, far outside any rules, outside anything ever written. Beyond good and evil—isn't that the formulation, the essence of the myth? And I took the fear from the creature as it grew to the bigger world, absorbing the other creatures of the world out there. And then his mother, who was Life itself, richer and deeper than the creatures' experiences we lived through, came and brought me into a world of Life, Life writ large."

"Little boy made a mistake, hey, pink cloud has now turned to grey, oh...[20]" He stopped and was quiet for a minute. "You can't run from monsters, Cali," Hal reported. "For one thing, it's hard to find a good running shoe store in your dreams, and then shower facilities are really abysmal."

Cali giggled. "I'm picturing you and Grendel trying on Nikes, calmly discussing stride length and whether the fabric breathes well or not."

"And charge cards? Monsters don't carry them, so they just eat the store staff and walk out. Really, you can't take them anywhere."

"That would be handy," Cali reflected. "No end-of-the-month credit card statements to worry about."

"So they are a part of me, and perhaps I'm a part of them. What did Obi-Wan say—'It's your point of view'? Can't say totally absorbed yet, but certainly a large part of me, which is probably why everyone is whispering and worried, I'm guessing. I'd suspect that people filled with Grendel's venom in the past didn't fare all that well. When a person is forced out of all that they have ever known, walls overthrown, monsters free, rules crumpled like so much tissue paper, thrown completely and unexpectedly into the unbounded world, well, there isn't much of a map showing the way back. Finding rules and guides that you can live by in an unbounded world, and then functioning the next day—I'm guessing many went far, far outside the bounded world. Probably wasn't much of a village left afterward? Vikings rampaging across Europe—yeah, I can see that pretty clearly."

Cali looked away, wishing she could wipe the pain from Hal's face. "That's the gist that I've gathered. They walked a dark path—isn't that the pretty way of saying it?"

Hal hummed, "Lost my mind, yeah...but I don't mind...can't find it anywhere...[21]" That isn't true, by the way. I feel stronger than before. Perhaps that's a true sign of madness, but I learned a lot. That's what you are supposed to do, right? Gaining wisdom is suffering. Odin gave an eye for wisdom, and hung upon a cross for many days. As opposed to gaining weight, which just requires milkshakes. By the way...that would be a great idea. I'm hungry."

"You are one weird dude," Cali teased, and she leaned forward. "You should judge a man by his questions rather than his answers, and you pass." She kissed him on the forehead. "I can sing too. 'You're my friend...and if we change...well, I love you anyway[22].'"

Hal pulled her to him and kissed her hard, passionately. "You are a rare catch," he promised when he came up for air. "I knew it that day I saw you in class."

Cali laughed. "I knew you were mine for the taking, because your eyes would light up when I walked in the room."

"Not just my eyes," Hal hinted, moving against Cali.

"Well, you are feeling better!" Cali giggled. "That's the man I knew." Maybe not the cold, hard look in the corner of the eyes, she thought quickly to herself. But he's been through a lot. And maybe he'll need it. It isn't going to get easier.

"I know Paul's mind," Hal commented, lying back on the bed. "It's multiple personalities playing against each other. Not a pretty place at all, but I know what he plans. As you may have guessed, it's nothing really good for us, unless you like being cooked in a wine sauce with a side of asparagus in garlic butter. He has sophisticated taste, I grant him that. I can tell you, based on what I know of his mind, that Paul will never stop. He thinks his fears exist because we exist, and believes, with all his heart, that his fears will vanish when we are gone. Wrong he is, but he's still completely focused on our nonexistence. And we are such nice people."

Cali sat silent, thinking.

"But enough about me—what has been happening outside my disordered psyche?" Hal inquired. "What's the scoop?"

"Chocolate, vanilla, and rocky road," tapping out 'thump duh duh thump thump'!

"Two bits and a shave! Where are my tomatoes?"

"At least be glad I'm not holding a pie," Cali laughed. "I generally avoid temptation unless I can't resist it. Want to see me in baggy pants with a fish? Real old English comedy—the old ones are the good ones."

"I'd like to put a fish down your pants," Hal offered, his eyes lighting up. "Why is it that I never have a seltzer bottle when I need one? It would make a huge mess, though."

They sat and smiled at each other.

"You mumbled to your father that it isn't bravery to die for your family," Cali reported, looking out the window again, thinking back. "That struck a chord. No, perhaps chord is the wrong word. That fractured a fault line that had been building for a long time. They have let children and family die because they thought they were doing what was right. Now they doubt themselves. They are not blaming each other. They were surprised to realize that they were pretending they ran the world, and had made noble choices based on what they thought were their duties and responsibilities. They realized it was all false, and to keep the pretense going they had locked out what they really saw and thought. Now they are letting the world in, when they didn't realize they had held it out. And there is no going back."

"Well, then everyone has been enjoying themselves," Hal remarked, pushing his pillows into a more comfortable shape and then lying back down. "Could be worse. Here we are, in a pleasant mountain retreat, comfortable and warm. See, I heard a little of what you talked about as I faded in and out."

"I wouldn't say enjoying ourselves, exactly. A lot of grim faces and forced smiles," Cali countered. "A lot of shouted discussions. Jesus, Mary, and Lucifer are not yelling at each other, but are yelling at themselves about decisions over the centuries, mistakes that were made, things they didn't see because they didn't want to see. Anguishing, in the full sense of the word. And they are saying scary things. Not to me, but I can hear whispers, and Goth and I talk. This was a turning point. Paul intended to kill all of us this time. With Grendel leading the attack, and the biological agents they were set to use as a backup, they were clear in their minds. This was scorched earth, Germany in Russia in 1942. Or Rome at Carthage when they sowed salt in the ground afterwards. No compromises possible. And Jesus, Mary and Lucifer are furious with themselves for not seeing it coming. For having treated the cartel attacks on us as a skirmish like so many others. For not seeing who was behind it and why. You are never so blind as when you don't want to see—that has been the gist of it. And then everything is blindingly clear when you tear the bandages off and you have to see what you so desperately tried to deny."

"None of us saw this, or could have," Hal offered. "Too many things going on, and, well, you see what you look for. That was my speech to the corporation executives, and look how well I saw past my blinders. We wanted to see good times, security, and happiness. Who wouldn't?"

"I don't think that Paul realizes the anger that has finally burst out. I know I'm glad they are not mad at me like that!"

"So what's out this window? I've only seen the sky peeking between drawn drapes," Hal asked. "Are there delis? A nice pastrami on rye with Swiss and Russian dressing? There must be something out here. Roots? Berries? Bears?"

"I'm not sure I should tell you this," Cali sighed, "but maybe it gets worse."

"Worse?" Hal asked, raising his eyebrows. "I've spent what feels like a lifetime embracing Grendel's horrors over the centuries, and you say worse?"

"We moved to Detroit, honey. I reviewed all the company records, and that old factory you bought? That was the best safe place I could find," Cali reported, glancing at Hal. "Vladimir and his friends are helping guard."

"Yup, worse," Hal agreed, nodding. "The light at the end of the tunnel? A 100-car freight roaring at you. Detroit, where they hurdle the dead and trample the wounded? You always think it can't get worse, and then Pow! Life surprises you."

"I bought you a T-shirt. It says 'I came, I saw, I made it out alive'."

"And we went back in? Mary can't do her research in, say, a nice villa near Nice, overlooking the Mediterranean, or say, in the Cayman Islands? We could loan them the money. Just a thought," he added quickly, noticing her serious look.

"You actually bought this old factory as some kind of a tax dodge you set up," Cali pointed out. "I found it on the maps on your computer."

"It's not a tax dodge," Hal disagreed. "Technically, it is a leveraged shelter under the law, and I have a letter from our attorneys confirming that, along with their absolute assurance that any audit would support the position they have taken. It's important, because the difference between a tax dodge and a leveraged shelter is jail time. Of course," more talking to himself, "they also provided a letter confirming the existence of unicorns and threw in a map to Atlantis, so I do have certain reservations about that firm."

"It was the best choice," Cali sighed, looking discouraged. "A decision had to be made, and I made it."

"You have chosen wisely. Take the castle back to Transsexual, Magenta," Hal growled in a deep voice. He winked at her.

She looked unhappy.

"No, seriously, you made the right choice, honey," Hal promised. "Really! I hated the mountains, all that fresh air, birds singing, and gently bubbling streams whispering happy songs. And New York was too expensive. You have seen past the surface and into the depths, my dear, perceiving the true reality."

Cali tilted her head away from Hal, glaring at him, her eyes squinted. "Have you ever really considered the benefits of going back into a coma?" she inquired casually, flexing her fingers.

"Ah, no, honey. I'm good, really. And put the food tray down, please. Slowly, down over there, honey. It's okay. You did fine. I'd have made the same choice."

"Anyhow," Cali concluded, "we are safe. Well, as safe as can be. We actually moved in a week or so ago. You've been out for quite a while."

"Let me tell you, it felt like quite a while," Hal agreed. "Still, at least it isn't the salt mines. Actually, I doubt there was much left of them after our idle frolic." He reflected for a minute. "It was Vladimir who came to see me the day of the attack. He gave me the sword. And the Milky Way—that was good."

"I thanked him! He said something like, 'It was nothing, it was you that wielded it, that was the important thing.' Made it sound like he was just applying for a job with FedEx. I told him he'd look good in those tight shorts the delivery people wear, and I think I embarrassed him."

"I met him at the boarding school, after my adoptive parents were killed," Hal recalled. "He helped a lot. We watched each other's backs. Boarding schools are actually dedicated training institutes for bullies, and we were brought in as fodder. After that, he joined the army—guess he didn't get enough bullying at school. He was damaged pretty badly, wounded in body and in mind. I found out where he was and tried to help him. There was a cluster of people with him, as I recall, and they were having some problems with the landlord and the city. When I bought the property, it fixed all of that. Yeah, Detroit was a good choice; I'd argue that none could have been better. What did Hamlet say? 'There is a divinity that shapes our ends, rough-hew them as we will?'"

"Vladimir is much more than you know," Cali declared. "He seems to have known Mary, Jesus, and Lucifer in the past. The long-ago past. They are friends now, after not being friends in the past. No one says anything—I have to guess. Really, being around here is like living in a codebook. People say things, and you have to look up the meaning on your secret decoder ring."

"Detroit, huh?" Hal mused. "At least the cost of living is reasonable. And it's really all in your mind—a prison in a palace, freedom in a jail. At least we're not in college again!"

"I don't think they'd let us back in," Cali admitted. "There was too much property destruction associated with our presence in Ann Arbor."

"You're the one who cost the school a division football championship with your tap dance on that football player!" Hal retorted. Brightening, he smiled. "Ribs. And chili dogs. It'll be fine. Maybe an occasional stealthy visit to Zingerman's for deli. In full disguise, of course. They take their football seriously in Ann Arbor—I think our pictures are still nailed to the utility poles. Yeah, I like this."

"You sound better," smiling happily at Hal. "Hungry is good."

"I hope they kept something of Grendel," Hal commented. "No, I'm not that hungry," he added, catching Cali's confused look.

"If they did, they didn't intend to," Cali promised. "There were no tears when he burned at the warehouse. They were careful to pour gasoline all over him, and then left his body surrounded by more containers full of gasoline just to make sure the fire was hot enough."

"Believe it or not, I'm thinking I want him recreated. I can figure out where his colony creatures are, I guess, if there is nothing else left."

"I'll ask them if there was anything left, although I can promise that you are the only one who would want him back," Cali warned. "Paul has even been putting out rumors that he arranged for Grendel to be killed to show his power."

"That's a laugh! Talk about putting the best face on events. It would serve him right to have to explain that little white lie to Grendel."

"They ordered that you are not supposed to be thinking or working, and my mother actually waved her finger at me!" Cali announced. "And none of that, either, I was specifically told," as Hal's glance moved down Cali's body. "Remember, mom is a fertility goddess, and she thinks about that a lot. 'None of that' was clearly included in my instructions."

"My fair lady, the ultimate adventure, when all the barriers and ogres have been overcome, is commonly represented as a mystical marriage of the triumphant hero with the queen goddess of the world. We did the marriage, but there's nothing in there about not continuing the celebration. And Grendel was der uber ogre. Would the queen goddess deny the written script? Joseph Campbell's authority? There could be contract issues here!"

"Flattery will get you everything," Cali giggled, her eyes sparkling. "What poor courtesy it would be to deny the brave Knight his earned reward!"

"And who are we to listen to the wisdom of our elders? All this life coursing through me—would you deny this weak, suffering man the medicine that can cure me?" Hal argued. "And, my proud beauty, don't you recall 'Young Frankenstein'? The monster in the movie had an enormous schwanzstucker that somehow the good doctor acquired when they merged minds. Isn't your scientific curiosity aroused at the thought of what I got from the monster? Wouldn't you like to know whether such a dark deed could actually take place?"

"Maybe it really does all depend on your point of view as to what, well, 'working' would be defined as," Cali whispered, leaning closer to Hal. "Certainly they wanted me to help you. And this certainly isn't thinking—not with the forebrain, anyhow."

"Obi-Wan, your figure has improved."

Cali giggled and hastily slipped her dress off. "I, ah, locked the door when I came in," as she started to slide under the covers. "Just in case, you know...so, Hal...let's examine you...for medical reasons, of course."

"Oh, you're a doctor now, Zoot?" Hal laughed.

"Well, I've had basic medical training, yes," Cali replied in a clipped, British accent. She threw back the covers.

"Oh," Cali gasped. "Oh my..."

They slept into the afternoon. Hal woke up as Cali was putting her dress back on.

"I have to see what Maria has gotten into. She's so excited about being here, and she gets into places that no one knew were there. Even the nanny despairs sometimes." She kissed him and shimmied out, winking at him as the door closed.

He smiled, hummed a little ditty to himself, and suddenly dropped off into a deep sleep again. He was rising from the deep ocean...

A LOST GARDEN

A day later, Hal and Cali were sitting in their bedroom, Mary having judged Hal healthy enough to be moved back to Hal and Cali's apartment. It's the personal touch that brings recovery, Mary had offhandedly remarked to Cali, who had carefully looked at the wall.

"What's that smell?" Hal asked Cali.

"I don't smell anything," Cali answered, sniffing, turning her head from side to side. "Maybe breakfast?"

Hal pushed off the covers. "I know I smell something! Let's go look."

"Ah, sure? Whatever. Remember you're not supposed to tire yourself out."

"I go forth," Hal announced, carefully leaning on the bed. "I'd go first, but I'm tired."

"You are feeling better," Cali laughed. "Terrible humor is a certain sign."

They walked out of their apartment, Hal pulling Cali along as best he could.

"It's, well, down here," Hal muttered, taking them down a long passageway to a distant, ruined area of the factory.

"It's cold, Hal!" Cali objected, shivering. "There can't be anything down here."

"There," Hal promised, putting his hand on an old, carved door. It didn't budge.

"There's a turnee thing,'" Cali puzzled. "So? I'm not an engineer," catching Hal's look.

Hal grabbed the wheel. "It's like a submarine door," trying to twist it. "An airlock mechanism, but it's rusted..." As he pushed, the metal squealed and the lock disengaged. He kept turning the wheel and the door slowly opened, the hinges squeaking. "It was an airlock. Look, there are rubber seals around the door."

"That's not on the list of your doctor-approved rehab activities," Cali worried, peering at him anxiously. "You look, well, a little pale."

"Nothing to it. The smell is coming from this room." He stepped through the doorframe, pushing the door completely open. It opened into a dark room, illuminated by a few beams of light from old skylights.

"It's actually hot in here," Cali gasped. "Quick, in! Don't waste the heat."

They stepped in and pushed the door shut behind them. It clicked and Cali stared at it, worried.

Hal didn't pay any attention. He just stood there, breathing deeply. "It's actually hot— steam heat, I think. A utility somewhere must wonder why they produce so much steam and get paid so little."

"It's filthy in here," Cali muttered, disgusted. "Ugh." She picked her hand up quickly. "There's stuff growing all over. Squishy stuff."

"It's a garden," Hal marveled. "Abandoned when the factory closed. And look!" He pointed, and there was a small, white tree glowing in a beam of bright sunlight.

They carefully picked their way through the rubble as they walked over to it.

"That's where the smell is from," Hal declared, breathing deeply. "It's wonderful, like life itself, so sweet and clear."

"I can smell it a bit," Cali mumbled, wrinkling her nose. "Just a bit. Should we do something to help it?" She bent down, reaching out to touch the tree.

"No!" Hal ordered, grabbing her arm and pulling her back. "Don't touch it! It will take care of itself."

Cali stared at him, puzzled.

"Old magic. Trust me. Really."

"Right," Cali scoffed. "I've heard that 'trust me' before."

"You fell for the walk down a distant passage and walking into the dark room, so why not trust me on this?" Hal countered happily looking around. "Ah, here is a bench!"

They sat on the bench, watching the tree for a while. Cali glanced at Hal and was shocked. He seemed to be almost glowing with health.

"Well, that's enough for today. Let's leave it alone," Hal murmured, and they left, carefully picking their way back across the slippery floor. The door opened easily and they stepped into the hallway.

Turning, Hal twisted the wheel shut. It turned quietly, the door suddenly moving freely for him. "There. "It's safe now."

Cali pulled on the wheel, curious, but nothing happened. It was as if it was frozen.

"It takes a touch," Hal advised. "Let's go back to the room, my proud beauty."

"This isn't going to be one of those 'life coursing through me' evenings again, is it?" Cali guessed. "Remember the doctor's orders?"

Hal smiled at Cali and his eyes glinted. A trace of Grendel swept over his face, and then it was gone. "How about a large, hot pizza, cheese bread, and a liter of Coca-Cola on a cold night? And, well, who can predict life? Would you limit your experience by defining it?"

"Oh, I can predict this one," Cali laughed, wrapping her arms around him and kissing him. "Pizza first, love later, and wild dreams tonight." They walked, arm in arm, back to their rooms.

LETTING GO

The next day, Hal was lying in bed in the apartment, resting. Cali pushed the door open, carrying a tray with Coney dogs and milkshakes for both of them.

"The redeeming feature of living in a cold climate," Cali remarked as she sat down, "is that I have to stoke the furnace of life. I.E., eat like a pig. Almost as much as you do."

"Oink. All animals are equal, but some are more equal than others. Animal Farm was a dangerously perceptive book."

Cali looked at him quizzically.

"Comic book," Hal hastily corrected. "Neat pig drawings."

They practically absorbed the Coney dogs, saying nothing until all the food was gone. Then they sat by the window in some comfortable chairs Cali had found, since Hal was tired of sitting in bed.

"George Smiley," Hal remarked. "I always liked him. Not the part about his wife fooling around with, oh, most of the known world," winking at Cali. "But I liked George, who was a principled man in an unprincipled world. No, that really isn't quite right. An unprincipled world dressed in pretense, and a man who knew himself despite all the nonsense. Dealing in a shady, undetermined world of shifting alliances and finding his way. Not easy, not pleasant, and not without wounds or sorrow. But a good life."

"You are way too serious! Never stay up on the barren heights of cleverness, but come down into the green valleys of silliness. Who can argue with Wittgenstein?"

"You Kant say that! You Kant take him seriously!"

"I'm putting on my Hobbesian nailed boots, and going to kick some creature butt," Cali growled.

"Hume...Hmmm...you say," Hal snickered. "People told us we learned nothing in college. And they were right."

Cali giggled and then looked away from Hall, staring out the window, her face becoming serious.

Hal watched her carefully.

"Let's talk about your mother and your decisions. No, this has to be done," she declared as Hal glanced away, distressed. "Look, Hal, things don't always go right. Maybe less around us than most people, but you didn't make a mistake—or even an error."

"Technical definitions?" Hal demanded. "I love it when you talk planning. It's your heavy breathing that does it."

"Error: doing the right thing the wrong way. Mistake: doing the wrong thing, period. And if you don't take your hand off my thigh, I'll get a ruler. No fraternizing with the professor."

"Weapons are not necessary, professor. Do I need to take notes?"

"There will be a quiz later," Cali teased. "Maybe a take-home, if you're good." She quickly moved out of Hal's grasp. "No, let's talk, really."

Glum, Hal sat back in his chair. "Where's the sugar? A little bit of sugar makes the medicine go down..."

"Look, you didn't screw up. You're looking out the window, and you're thinking—I know what you're thinking. You should have done something differently? you should have known? You deviated from what should have been done."

"Deviation is one of my best qualities. Everyone says so."

Rolling her eyes, Cali kept going. "You are thinking that you weren't paying attention and because of that your mother died. I can see it in your eyes, and it's not true. It was a well-set trap. Without Lucretia, we would all have been dead. NO one saw this, and they have been fighting wars and setting traps far longer than us. Sometimes things just don't work. Let the guilt go! We have enough problems as it is."

"Guilt is one of those concepts that Grendel found fascinating," Hal mused. "He thought it was hilarious that one would regret your actions. The closest he got to grasping the idea of regret was sorrow that he couldn't pillage and burn a village again, experimenting with new concepts and methods. Regretting the pillage and burning just wasn't his modus operandi."

Cali watched him thoughtfully.

"There are other definitions of error and mistake," Hal added. "An error is buying flowers for your wife, but buying white flowers instead of her favorite pink. A mistake is buying flowers for your girlfriend if there is also a wife."

"No, that's life and death," Cali declared. "Life for the first, and death for the second. Women are clear on that one."

"I'm glad you forced this discussion. I've been wrestling with it, and it's a heavy burden. And sometimes I want to carry the burden, because pretending I could have done something differently gives me control; a control that really didn't exist. Sounds stupid, but true. You're right, absolutely right. The monsters have been telling me the same thing. They don't believe in carrying pointless burdens. Life is hard enough as it is. Stand next to a cross holding nails, and you shouldn't be surprised if someone hangs you from it someday—that's their attitude."

"You can spend minutes, hours, days, weeks, or even months overanalyzing a situation; trying to put the pieces together, justifying what could've, would've happened...or you can just leave the pieces on the floor and move the fuck on."

"I like that! Broken puzzles are a waste of time."

"I've...been talking to Mary and the others," Cali confessed, looking out the window. "'Impressed' is an understatement for what they think about your experience with Grendel. They are wondering whether, well, we should all try at least some of the experience."

Hal examined her, his eyes glittering coldly. "Grendeline warned me this would happen," his voice harsh and hard. His voice softened and became Hal again. "This is no gift. You thought the first chalice was hard? This is far more intense. 'Worse' is a judgment, but 'intense' is factually correct. Oh, fine, it must happen, I know it. But it must be voluntary. The old magic again, you see. And it isn't a pleasant decision to make. Standing on the edge of the gorge of eternal torment? Well, it reads better than it lives, especially at three in the morning."

"I'm getting that expanded selection of cartoon channels from the cable company," Cali concluded. "No more History Channel for a while!" She waved her finger at Hal, who laughed.

"We will all need the strength," Cali argued. "No one is excited about the prospect of entertaining Grendel, but life is going to be harder than it has been, is the message I'm hearing. The caretaker was talking the other day about fighting and life. He slips into his Zen master speeches, but this one actually made a little sense. Resilience is a precious skill; you can never get enough of it. Resilience is important because it bring three gifts: it gives you the belief that you can influence life events; it opens your inspiration to find purpose in life's turmoil; and it gives you a conviction that you can learn from both positive and negative experiences. Necessary, because they give you a sort of buffer, cushioning the blow of any given disaster."

"Did he hit you on the head from behind?" Hal asked. "That's what he usually did to me when he got into the Zen master thing."

"I'm faster than I used to be," Cali laughed. "I've learned to listen for his little cat feet."

"And it will give resilience if you go through this," Hal granted. "But...I fear to give it to you. I fear the results."

"Do you think yourself stronger than me?" Cali teased. "You think yourself stronger than Mary, Jesus, or Lucifer? What HAVE you been drinking?"

"This cheap Detroit wine you have been buying," Hal grimaced. "I keep feeling I should be sitting next to a dumpster in a cheap, dirty trench coat, exposing myself to the pigeons. You need to get better advice from the sommelier, AND spend more than three dollars a bottle."

"Hmmm...you're probably right. Even Lungorthin is grumbling and his taste runs to quantity rather than quality. "Fine. I'll get better wine."

"A nice Pinot, California—or even a Grand Traverse wine," Hal suggested. "Support your local vineyards. Now you're talking."

"Focus, honey. Back to Grendel. We've all talked, and maybe it's a false confidence, but we all think we can do this."

"Confidence is one thing. Throwing yourself into the abyss is something else," Hal declared, studying the sky. "You get a parachute on the way down if you do well—otherwise, you don't. You remember the poetry reading? Falling into nothingness? A lot of that, and for a very long time. Not just visions—it's experiences of events that, when written down, are locked away and denied. Would you like to know about the Inquisition? I was there, ringside. I witnessed and felt striking down Jesus and Lucifer in prior lives and Mary's torments in the dungeons. Harsh, in the full twelfth-century definition of the word."

Hal studied Cali, his eyes soft and worried. He took her hands carefully in his, his hands trembling. "Grendeline snarled, 'Do you not fear Cali will meet me? That the blood will run cold in her veins, and her life will be a terror to her afterwards? You will hold her trembling body, her mind broken, knowing that you have destroyed your blessed love. What a hero that would be!'"

Hal closed his eyes for a moment, opening to and accepting the terror of the vision, carefully slowing his breathing. Then, he opened his eyes again, solemnly gazing at Cali. "I told her that I'd be more afraid for you to not absorb her. That was, of course, a lie and the truth at the same time."

"Grendeline?" Cali gulped, terrified of the vision Hal had described.

"Grendeline is the life goddess. Grendel, her son, is the entry, the introduction."

They sat for some time, staring out the window.

"It's your decision, my dear. Oh, it was foretold, and it is necessary. But terrible, as necessary things sometimes are."

"We all have embraced at least some of our monsters," Cali defended. "We believe we can do this."

Hal glanced at her skeptically, but said nothing. He thought for a minute.

"You know, the world is really not as we were taught it was," Hal argued. "I read this weird physics article, excerpted in a comic book. It argued, roughly, 'We think that the evidence is conclusive enough to suggest that any object in this Universe can be in many different locations at the same time.'"

"Yeah," Cali snickered, "and I know what locations you're thinking about. You're not going to be in that location without saying something nice to me."

"This must be the reason that quantum physicists are endangered species," Hal mused. "Not going to work well as a pick-up line. Especially with such a beautiful and sophisticated woman as yourself, wise in the ways of men and their tricks."

"Flatterer!" Cali laughed. "I guess it's time for your daily exercise—for medicinal purposes only, of course."

"The triumph may be represented as the hero's sexual union with the goddess-mother of the world," Hal declared, moving to sit on the bed and patting the space bed next to him. "You've got to love Campbell. Where else can you get lines like that?"

DINNER & A DECISION

Everyone was at dinner a few days later, sitting around a large dining-room table. The factory did not have the same style of furnishings that the Lake Michigan house had; the factory's furniture was more practical, rough-hewn. But the furniture fitted the factory, set against the brick walls that still showed traces of soot and the exposed, rusty beams far above. Even though they had been there only a short time, the factory glowed with life again.

"Cali tells me you wish to leave your pleasant lives and experience the horrors of Grendel," Hal sighed, glancing around the table. "And then, surviving that, Grendeline. I can tell you it's awful. What you should do is your choice."

"Life hasn't been all that pleasant all the time," Mary answered.

"I know," Hal replied, studying her, his eyes cold. "Grendel showed me the Inquisition, and before. He enjoyed those parts of history. All of you were his guests at one time or another."

Lucifer and Jesus glanced at each other. Mary stared thoughtfully at the wall, recalling a dungeon from a long, long time ago.

"We wondered how much he brought with him," Lucifer admitted. "We, well, have never had anyone survive his venom before. Let me correct that. People technically were alive—but not as the people they were. As small Grendel's, subject to his will. But they usually don't last long. No one has ever absorbed him before and come back with his knowledge."

"I imagine not," Hal grimaced. "There is the core of a person, all the hardwired parts. You start banging on those, and it's the essence of pain, distilled. Your central stories, turned upside down and inside out. Without the chalice and the drugs from Lucretia helping to offset the impact, I doubt I would have. And Vladimir, that rogue, with his magic candy bar before the fight! But even then it was no easy experience. Absorbing your own monsters is hard enough. Absorbing a true external one— incomprehensible. What is the myth formulation? 'No creature can attain a higher grade of nature without ceasing to exist?.' It reads better than it lives."

"So we should thank Paul for his attack on us? Questionable, I think," Cali commented.

"And," Hal added, leaning forward, "Grendeline knew all of you. Goddess Freyja, I called her, and she denied it not, that you had held her away. And she waits for you. In a dream, I came out of the forest, and the lion, the leopard, and the she-wolf were waiting by a tunnel. They were not able to go through, and they were waiting."

Mary and Jesus stared at Hal, stunned. Lucifer studied the table, tracing an ancient rune upon it with his finger.

"What they gave me is a gift, a treasure beyond measure. But like all treasure, it isn't quite what you think it will be. And the consequences will be different than you hope-or fear. You are giving up all of what you take to be your best interest. We all freeze where we are. Rather than a future that will be an unremitting series of deaths and birth, we see a future where one's present system of ideals, virtues, goals, and advantages are to be fixed and made secure. Grendel, and even more so Grendeline, made it clear, beyond the shadow of a doubt, how small and false our vision of today, fixed and secure into the future, really is."

"What, you are channeling Joseph Campbell from the netherworld? Lighten up!" Cali retorted. "And don't start quoting Spengler again! How about some Looney Tunes instead? Or here's today's *Wall Street Journal* editorial."

"Funny. I want nonsense, not fantasy. I know I sound pretentious— hell, I am pretentious, no question about that. I know who I'm talking to and what all of you have done and seen. It's just different from the chalice and the experiences you gave Cali and I. It's what you said before, writ large. You can accept the world as it is—weird, wonderful, and horrible as it is—or you can reject the world because it isn't what you were told it would be or isn't doing what you want, or, finally, you can partly reject the world, agreeing to accept it only if the world changes to what you think the world should be like. It's that discussion on steroids with a light show. And option one is the only winner."

"If you wake up and you're not in pain, you know you're dead," Jesus remarked. "Russians cut to the chase."

"We've been talking," Mary advised. "Long, hard discussions; thinking about things we had pushed aside, ignored."

"Well done is better than well said," Lucifer observed. "You've done more than we ever could have expected. Now we find ourselves in the uncomfortable position of saying clever things without acting on them. Now we have to learn something new rather than hand the surprises out."

"Great deeds are usually wrought at great risks," Mary smirked, glancing at Lucifer, who groaned.

"I thought that manuscript had been burned," Lucifer sighed. "Why is it that they didn't save my 'Best Greek One-Liners'? Knocked them dead at the Agora."

"If you did it, I will try," Lungorthin rumbled. "Never have I seen a battle like yours with Grendel, and I will follow you."

Hal stared at him, stunned. "Ah, did what I had to, I guess," he stammered. "Didn't think."

"You don't understand," Lucifer offered. "Lungorthin is never impressed. He is one of the most dangerous fighting machines I have ever known and I would not care to face him myself. And he doesn't say things lightly like humans do. You impressed him— almost unheard of. I am very

249

proud."

Hal was speechless, staring down at the table. Cali took his hand and she smiled when he glanced at her.

"Well, it's decided," Mary announced. "I'll draw your blood, work up a serum, and we will try it."

"Including Cali and I," Goth Girl interrupted.

"You can't!" Lungorthin grumbled. "The baby!"

"That's babies," Goth Girl pointed out. "You've got to put a governor on that thing! I can't repopulate the entire world by myself." She put her hand on his arm and kissed him.

"Has to be done," Cali added. "The risk is huge, but we don't know if we have time to wait or not. Another biological attack by Paul's people, and we're gone for sure. 'The ordeal is a deepening of the problem of the first threshold, and the question is still in the balance,' and so on."

"You need to start reading *People*," Goth Girl remarked. "Sad whining by celebrities about how life on millions a year isn't rewarding enough, to put things in perspective."

"Is there more pizza?" Hal inquired. "We seem to be straying from the key focus here."

Another pizza appeared on the table, whisked over by one of the servants.

"Oh, and the company needs you to start working on the computer stuff again when you feel strong enough," Lucifer added. "We have connections that are secure, and no one can do what you were doing."

"Wonderful," Hal exclaimed, his eyes sparkling. "This mournful, character-building reflection and personal growth is getting a little long. Back to non-reality and the Internet!"

CALI & GRENDEL

That night, Cali took the serum and fell into a deep sleep.

She pulled on the heavy castle door. It creaked slowly open as she yanked with all her strength. "This better not be a monk handing out pamphlets again!" She grumbled to herself.

There was a knight outside, covered in mud.

"What is your name, good knight?" Cali asked cheerfully and then she suddenly sniffed loudly. "What is that disgusting smell?" she demanded. "What did you step in?"

"I'm Sir Hal...the Chaste," Hal replied, lifting his visor so she could see his face. "Fine," catching Cali's doubtful look. "Sir Hal, The Really Not Very Smooth With Women. That smell? You have dogs, and you don't poop scoop."

"You—leave your boots out there...no, way out there," Cali ordered. She closed her eyes for a second, yanking on the wrinkles in her dress to calm her. Opening her eyes again, she put her preppy cheerfulness back on. "My name is Cali. Just Cali," she giggled. Who writes this crap? she thought furiously, still smiling. "Please, do come in, Sir Knight. You look tired!"

She frowned and looked down at her script. This is my dream? It's sounding like Hal's dream. What? This can't be! She read for a minute and then slowly put the script down, sighing. Punishment, that's what this is. So, put on a happy face!

"In God's name, show me the Grail that I seek!" Hal demanded.

"Oh, good knight, you have suffered much!" Cali gushed. Frowning, she complained, "Look, you think you've suffered? What do you think I've gone through in this drafty old castle, locked up with these catty women? Stealing my clothes, fighting over the bathrooms, and women, when there are no men around, are, well, crude..."

Hal stared at her, confused.

"Sorry, out of character," Cali commented. Her preppy smile came back. "Ah...you have suffered much! You are delirious! And covered in dog poop," she sighed.

Hal took a quick glance at his script. "I saw the beacon...the Grail is here! Please, beautiful maiden, allow your humble servant entry." Hal begged.

"Sir Hal, the Clearly Not Very Smooth With Women," Cali answered, "it would be ungallant to refuse our invitation. This is a castle full of young, idle women. Bored young women, whose only recreation is creating delicate underwear..."

"Well, that one's hard to turn down," Hal smiled and began to rush in.

"Shoes off, and I knew it!" Cali shouted. "I knew that would get you in here!"

Is this Hal's dream or mine? Cali thought. All I get is grief! Even in my dreams, I'm locked in a castle with a bunch of catty women, and the men that show up don't get it. Talk about not knowing the question to ask. Why don't women get the quests too? Men may be nasty to women when the urge hits them, but women seem to live for the viciousness. That's why women don't watch sports on TV—their games are played on different fields. What sport could be half as entertaining as the emotional destruction of another woman, knowing she'll have to face you tomorrow? Blood sport, indeed. The strongest prisons are the ones we make for ourselves.

The castle lights and noisy chatter vanished, and suddenly there was silence—total silence. The wasteland appeared, with the deep gorge cutting through it. And a dark shadow rose, standing at the entry to the ancient bridge over the gorge.

The scene brightened, and it was Grendel, an old man with a wild expression, laughing to himself and dancing a little jig.

"I know you," Cali snarled. "You're the guy who kept buying me drinks at that bar in Ann Arbor. What was the name of the bar? Abandon All Hope Ye Who Enter Here? Yeah, that was it. A rare example of truth in advertising. What? I don't get a break even in my dreams?"

Grendel patiently waits until Cali is finishes spouting off. "Look, it gets boring being a figment of people's imagination. A little fun, hey? Fine, back to the script," Grendel sighed. "Okay, page 543...where?...ah...Who approaches the Terrible Bridge of the First Date, must answer me these questions three, ere the other side she see. Really, who writes this stuff?" appealing in vain to the wasteland. He shrugs, and glances at Cali.

"You mean I win a second date if I answer the questions right? Maybe I'll just throw myself into the gorge now. That would be easier," Cali growled.

Grendel waved the script in front of her, pointing at her lines.

"Fine! Ask me the questions, you weird, twisted old man," Cali hissed.

"Fail to answer the questions three, ye be cast into the Gorge of Eternal Datelessness," Grendel sneered. "Look, it's two in the morning. You knew the danger when you chose to stay to closing time."

"Would you like to guess what is rising in my gorge now at the thought of us dating?" Cali smiled sweetly.

"No respect," Grendel grumbled. "Okay. What is your name?"

"It's Cali," she replied. "Just Cali. No Internet searches—I know your tricks."

"Hmmm, is that a correctly framed answer?" Grendel muttered, scanning the rulebook, quickly flipping pages. He found the page he wanted, and carefully read it. Then he glared at Cali, disappointed. "It passes. Too bad. Okay, next. What is your quest?"

"To find...my life again," Cali mumbled.

Grendel examined a decrepit piece of equipment in his hand. "Okay, the Truth-O-Meter buys it. I'm doubtful myself, but we'll run with it. So, what is your favorite lipstick color?"

"That pink from Revlon that I just can't find around here anymore. It's in that little package, the one..." Cali blurted out.

"Good enough," Grendel declared. "I really don't care about the lipstick that much. It's just a question. Right, off you go."

Cali walked carefully across the bridge, gripping the guide ropes as the bridge twisted with each step.

"Lipstick?" Grendel protested to the wasteland, waving the script.

"Why not 'favorite foundation powder,' something I can get some use out of? This damp is terrible on my complexion. Oh, well." He vanished.

Cali walked toward the forest after crossing the bridge.

Grendel was waiting for her, a huge, dark-cloaked figure at the edge of the dense brush. "Each must find their own way in," he rumbled. "It isn't funny after this part."

"Like, it's been funny? I must have missed it," Cali snarled. She straightened her shoulders and closed her eyes. Where? She opened her eyes and walked towards the dense overgrowth. In a minute she had vanished.

"Damn!" she yelled. "Thorns! I hate camping!" And then there was a tromping into the underbrush, which faded gradually.

Grendel stood outside the forest, thoughtfully watching, and then shrugged. "It's their dream, and they give themselves thorns. Why not a relaxing lounge chair on the beach to find themselves in? Humans!" He walked into the forest to find her.

HAL & CALI

Hal was sitting on the bed, watching Cali. She'd been out for a several days, having the hardest time of any of them.

He looked away, absently looking out the window. It's a sunny day—unusual in Detroit. Large, yellow ball in the sky, spreading warmth. I was sure that violates some local ordinance.

Hal glanced back at the bed and Cali was staring intently at him, a feral look in her eyes.

"What say you, fair maid?" Hal asked, worried.

"Seriously, I am not doing drugs with you again, Hal," Cali growled. "That was much stranger than the poem."

"If people offer you drugs, you should say, 'Thank you.' Drugs are expensive," Hal countered.

Cali gave him a dirty look.

"I was worried," Hal admitted. "You've been out the longest."

"Really?" Cali asked. "What's been happening?"

"Goth came out of it really fast. She opened her eyes and snickered, 'Like, a monster inside me? That's something new. NOT!' Then she stared intently at Lungorthin and the rest of us quickly left the room. The joyous celebration got noisy," Hal recalled.

Cali laughed.

There's a different timbre, Hal thought. Just something. "Mary, Jesus, and Lucifer came out of it after Goth. They have been talking among themselves. That was a day ago."

"Out for a day?"

"Two, actually," Hal replied. "A lot of shouting and screaming. I knew it would work out—you're tough—but it wasn't pretty. Not that you aren't pretty, of course, but, oh, well...let's let that one go."

"Hal, the Not So Smooth With Women, was a knight in my dreams," Cali laughed. "But thanks for being here. I knew you were here...somehow."

"And?" Hal asked. "Grendel told me I was a fool to let you try this."

"Why?" Cali asked.

"Well, he muttered something about women being worse than men. 'Harpies and Furies,' Grendel muttered and he shook his head. 'I'll fight any man,' Grendel told me, 'and know what they will do. But women? Manipulative, vindictive. And you're pouring the monster into her? Brave man. 'No, I take that back-foolish.' And he's on the side of evil!"

"Woman as the temptress, the woman is life—Cali 2 read those notes. Yeah, I remember. Grendel really isn't happy with any of us. I loved the additional personalities, though," Cali giggled. "And I'll have you know that I had dinner at a country bar with naked Chippendale dancers as my waiters. Heck, what's the point of going to the dark side if you can't have any fun?"

"Grendel did say something about that also," Hal remarked. "That women really are not as they put on. He had a funny smile when he said it."

"But," Cali admitted. "It was hard—harder than I imagined to absorb the monster. A lot of really non-politically-correct behavior in the past. All of that 'Man's highest joy is in victory: to conquer one's enemies; to pursue them; to deprive them of their possessions; to make their beloved weep; to ride on their horses; and to embrace their wives and daughters,' feels differently as a wife and daughter."

"Yeah, but I know you," Hal scoffed. "You'd have taken their jewels and gold in two weeks, and have them running errands for you. They'd never know what hit them."

"Well, there is that," Cali laughed. "But hush! You're wrecking my 'poor sad me' trap. I'll send Mongols after you!"

"Mary did say something about how it played differently to a woman," Hal added. "She was thoughtful, but angry at Paul. I thought she was angry before, but that was nothing compared to the fury she carries now. She's seen the light, she snarled. Jesus and Lucifer allowed they would politely demure to her suggestions and left it at that."

"According to the myth pattern...she has to learn how to become the woman with the immortal male, the mother goddess herself...woman, in the picture language of mythology, represents the totality of what can be known. Cali 3," Cali recalled. "Elf maidens, but clumsy. They kept falling over things."

"She stoops to conquer," Hal observed. "Grendel has really been a font of knowledge for my understanding of many, many things. But you must be hungry."

"Food," Cali hissed.

"Nice," Hal declared, nodding, "but I kept the nurse away this time. She's been taking a bit of an emotional beating trying to deal with all of us. We had to assign a nurse of her own to her and she's doing better. What say you, my lady? What is your heart's desire? Food, that is."

"Meat and mead," Cali shouted happily. "I didn't understand the other day, but wow!"

"And so it shall," Hal promised. He stepped outside, into the hallway and shouted. In a few minutes, the room was full of people and food.

A Grail Beacon?

"I thought I saw a grail beacon shining out the window," Hal remarked, peeking into the room where Cali was dozing.

Cali stirred lazily. "I was just waking up," she mumbled. "A grail beacon, you say?"

"It's not the real Grail?" Hal demanded, distraught.

"Oh, wicked, naughty, evil Cali!" Cali scolded. "Oh, and she is a naughty person! Well, she must pay the penalty, and here in Castle Detroit, we have but one punishment for lighting the grail beacon. You must tie her down and spank her!"

"And people told me being a knight wasn't rewarding," Hal observed happily.

Cali glared, disgusted, at Hal, and then was back in character: "Yes, yes, you must give me a good spanking!" she continued, but she wasn't really smiling.

"A man has to do what a man has to do, no question about it," Hal admitted.

Cali glared at the ceiling and then looked back at Hal. "I really have to say this?" she pleaded.

"In the script, right there," Hal insisted. "It's been run by Legal, Clause 43b of the contract."

"Fine. And after the spanking, the oral sex," Cali muttered. "Happy?"

"There's a rhetorical question," Hal observed, pulling his shirt over his head.

"You people really are sick, you know that?" Grendel rumbled.

"Me. You. Bed. Now," Cali ordered, winking at Hal.

THE GARDEN OPENS FOR CALI

Hal and Cali walked down the long passageway towards the garden.

Cali reached out and easily spun the wheel. "It wouldn't move before, but after Grendel, you see?" she declared proudly.

Hal smiled and nodded.

They went in, and the sweet smell was stronger. The tree had grown taller, the trunk thicker. The white bark reflected the light from above, and there were many more deep, green leaves.

"Look, Hal," Cali as she reached out to touch the wall. "The moss is growing up the sides." She stroked it softly. "And the little bugs are cleaning the soot off the old walls." She let one of the bugs run across her hand. "The power of Life. I never realized before."

"Look at the carvings," Hal added. "The bugs, as they clean the soot off, are starting to reveal them."

They sat by the tree for a while, time passing unnoticed, breathing deeply the sweet air.

"That figure," Cali asked, pointing at a carving. "He seems so ancient. What is he holding?"

"That is Osiris," Hal answered. "That's the flail, for winnowing the wheat, and the sickle. He held those as he judged the dead souls standing before him. And there are many kinds of death, as we have discovered, that can be judged."

CHAPTER 13. WHERE DID WE GO WRONG?

DETROIT. JESUS THE MOTIVATIONAL SPEAKER

Jesus drummed his fingers on the arm of the chair, frustrated. Perhaps being a motivational speaker hasn't worked out to be the career choice I originally thought it would be. I'm thinking that booklet I read extolling the virtues of this career omitted some critical information. Maybe it was the translation?

Mary happily frolics along celebrating life in her role as a fertility goddess and Lucifer wanders through the wild, encouraging misbehavior by the animals. I have to, first, have a plan, and then second, encourage people to participate. I'm really not feeling that inspired about that today. Given all that has happened, it's clear we have to talk in a structured way, because some key goals are clearly not working. So, my job is to figure out how to have the conversation that no one, absolutely no one, wants to have, but all know we have to.

So, first, why do we have to talk about what has happened? Well, what did happen? Our plans were well thought out and executed as planned, with the net result that we created and spread a story that has been hijacked, turned upside down, and is running the system off the rails. Fail. We meant well, but the quote on well-meant intentions has been staring us in the face for two millennia. Fail. And what has each of us done? All that we planned to do. We had it in the bag, and it clawed its way out. Fail.

That was fun, he thought wryly to himself. Something about confession being good for the soul? Did that—I don't feel better. How about pithy slogans? Failure is just success next time? Not helping.

So what did we want to do? The goal was for the humans to emotionally reconcile to the nature of the creature, and at the same time use the tools available to improve their world and their lives. Nice, small, definable goal. Well, it kind of worked—there has been enormous improvement in the physical standard of living of at least half the world. The reconciliation to the nature of the creature, the balancing of the emotional needs of the human animal, has been a failure. Centuries of hysterical running around, wrapping the flag of today's beliefs around them as the self, not as a guide to the self. They are more concerned with the scandal du jour than with the beauty of life in front of them. More obsessed with the child's Tinker toys of their philosophy than with the incredible complexity of life. Now, we are doing better than the Middle Ages, which were a complete hijacking of the daily focus of life into a fantasy realm. But there are large

257

parts of the world pulling for a replay of the Middle Ages, and pulling hard. If there is another crash, given the stretched resources supporting the billions of people and the complex interconnections of this modern world, it could be a big crash, and a long, long time before they recover. If they recover before the next comet hits, or Yellowstone erupts and we go through the volcano disasters again.

So, the conversation needs to address: one, the stories are too small and they are not working, and two, there is a very real cliff coming up that they are set to run full speed off of. Nothing to it. A few meeting points and we can solve that.

Second, for a difficult conversation, what are the emotional positions of the participants? I'm completely invested in this. I've urged the others to work with the humans, and we've coaxed, prodded, and encouraged. It has worked better than with the raptors. I think Mary and Lucifer still liked the raptors better, in all truth. There was something to be said about their direct simplicity and focus. Unfortunately, by the end, their intense focus was on eating all of us, and only the comet saved us. Squid? You just can't work with technology under the water, and you can only go so far with crude biotech two thousand feet down in the ocean. No, this was a reasonable choice, really, the only choice. So emotionally, we're still all on board to keep trying to make this work. So, not really a failure. It just feels like it.

Lucifer is furious about the destruction of the wild and turning their backs on life. Mary feels the same way, and I can't blame them. Bringing them fire and tools didn't really increase their understanding, it just increased their resources, and they bred like rabbits. No matter what they had, what we gave them, they managed to breed the surplus out in a few generations and then went back to the old tricks. If I get Lucifer and Mary worked up, they'll go back to the sea and let it all fall apart. If it weren't for the kids and grandkids, I think they would have done that already. I'm not far from that myself, except they've filled the sea with plastic and garbage. Serve them right if we bring back that creature that metabolized plastic and the oil and coal organics that plastic came from. That would bring things back down in a hurry! Jesus played with the thought of a luxuriant world again, covered in virgin rain forests, and then pushed it out of his mind with a sigh. Not our job today, he thought. We can only do what we can with what we have to work with.

Now, the children and grandchildren—that's something that is more important than we ever let it be before, Jesus realized. We had been high minded, seeking the right and letting our children die because it was "necessary." Perhaps we have been too human, taken in by the pretty, logical ideas. Damn Plato and his idealized concept of the world! Dazzled the fools with its false complexity, just hard enough that most people couldn't grasp it, but a child's toy compared to the real complexity of the world. And the parasites ran with it—tools to fool the masses, and after all, it's the idiot with the gun that you really have to be concerned with. Paul grasped that in a flash, and we never saw the depth of the danger. The raptors would not have taken that nonsense. Paul would have been dog meat centuries ago. Jesus idly played with a picture in his mind of a troop of raptors toying with Paul, but wistfully pushed away the pleasure of seeing Paul in segments.

So, progress to date? Net result: fail. Emotions explosive. Fail. Nothing like setting the basis for a critical, long talk on a minefield. Because now we get to the hard stuff; we are messing with our identities as we go over these problems. What does each of us see ourselves as? Well, I've already covered that our identities are completely pissed off and alienated from where things have gone. Let's try and start with something good. This new grasp of biotech—that is exciting, as far as any creature has come. The new computers, the silicon life, that is truly exciting, opening to something never dreamed of by any of us. And it's close. We can feel it. Another hundred years, at most, and it's all different. Maybe twenty years. Yes, that's the approach. Keep pushing a little longer, because of these. Then the bigger stories come through the new life. The creatures with the smaller stories? What usually happens to them? Ironically, the rabbits enjoy their lives, short and frantic as they are, as much as the wolves do. It's embracing yourself that matters. A rabbit that wanted to be a wolf? What an unhappy rabbit it would be, and what a short life it would have. I don't care what Monty Python dreamed up. That rabbit wasn't going to be that dangerous.

Yeah—ground a new identity in the new life that's coming, the bigger stories that the new life will bring, and the opportunities for new things that we've never seen. And finally, the technology to get off this rock, into the universe, learning and seeing. Before the next comet, or the Jovians get here first. Okay, I have a plan to work with.

How to start this? Ye shall become fishers of men—did that, didn't work right. And there are not any fish left, anyhow. You shall be lords over the other creatures? That didn't work either. You shall recognize that you are life like any other, and live with respect and understanding? Duh, smaller words and slower, please. I wonder if we can get the beer commercial writers to come up with something. Living within the Tree of Life, that's the goal. How about, "We're just one step away. As Indiana Jones said, that's usually when the ground falls out from underneath your feet." No, too truthful for this talk. Umm, how about: "In this race, there's no silver medal for finishing second." I like that, it focuses.

BETTER MISTAKES NEXT TIME

"Pep talk time?" Lucifer asked, stirring his mocha.

"Not a bad idea," Mary agreed as she took a sip, carefully assessing the strength of her tea. She added some sugar and took another sip. "Better," she said. "At least this part they are getting right."

"Has to be done," Jesus replied, pouring more milk into his coffee. Doubtfully, he stirred it and then took a taste. "Maybe I should just go the fancy coffee route," peering into his cup. "By the time I'm done playing with this, it'll probably be one of those latte skim extra flavors specials."

Mary and Lucifer leaned back and studied Jesus.

"Welllll, we've got a really good show tonight, folks," Jesus announced. Mary and Lucifer stirred their drinks noncommittally. "Wow, what a tough audience. This isn't like Jerusalem—they loved me there."

"They crucified you, technically," Mary pointed out. "Tough love?"

"So, I've been thinking," Jesus sighed. "Go ahead, say it, get it over with."

"Someone has to think," Lucifer replied. "As has been pointed out at various times, I'm the male and the wild, and I think with my sexual organs. Mary is the all-female, and she thinks with her sexual organs. So someone has the unpleasant job of thinking with the equipment above the waist, boring as it may be."

"That does sound boring," Mary mused. "Don't I have a mystery religion priestess appointment for later? Umm...I'll have to check my calendar. Sounds like a lot more fun."

Jesus stared at them, tapping his fingers on the table. "Now I'm worried—you're being agreeable. Okay, basics. One. Ground truths and fierce conversations. A fierce conversation is a conversation in which we drop the masks and say what's really bothering us. We talk about what we really care about. While polite social discourse may keep the trains running, in crisis time the masks just hide the problems."

"We're pretty clear on that," Mary agreed. "Events of the past weeks have pounded that into us."

"Basic two," Jesus continued. "A ground truth is a military term that refers to what is actually happening on the ground vs. the official reports."

"Like our glorious victory against the Slavs in the second century AD that was caused by their fear of the nest of groundhogs they ran into on the battlefield? Something about how their ancestors were being trampled? They almost had us that time, and I'll never forget the joy as they suddenly ran away from a certain victory." Lucifer laughed.

"Shining glory is more dependent on controlling the write-up than the events on the battlefield," Mary agreed.

"Centurion," Lucifer recalled. "I liked that job. Not a lot of decisions, and a lot of action. Good uniform, too."

Jesus smiled. "Lots to be said for being staff. The pay isn't as good, but the emperor didn't blame them personally. So, let's get started on the issues. Difficult conversations about things we've maybe done right, maybe done wrong over time."

"Such as?" Lucifer commented. "How about this debacle unfolding before our eyes? I claim substantial blame for it, by the way. Call yourself on your own bullshit."

"I, too," Mary declared. "Get that out of the way, move along."

"Wow," Jesus remarked. "Skipping the whole who is right and wrong is a great idea. What has happened really was beyond all our control, or imagination."

"True enough," Lucifer agreed. "Sargon/Xerxes/Paul has been far more—and less—than I ever dreamed."

"I knew him better, more deeply and intimately, you might say, than any of you," Mary confided. "Men talk on their pillows, and he never talked of what he became. Or maybe I was sleepy," grinning. "It's hard work being a fertility goddess/priestess."

Lucifer got a silly look and then thought better. "No, this conversation will go down fast. Perhaps we should move along."

"Okay," Jesus continued, quickly moving on. "We've talked before about how some things are working out fantastically, such as the new life and tech coming, and some things are working out horribly, such as the environmental destruction, the failure of the small stories, and as a consequence of one and two, the likelihood that they will manage to trash themselves before the new things come."

"Seems like a quick and accurate description," Lucifer acknowledged. "Yeah. And I feel inadequate for not having done something that I couldn't have done or thought of doing, and I blame myself—and all of you, by the way—in completely unreasonable and useless ways. Maybe we have become too human."

"Second that," Mary replied. "Let's not go into the women/men emotional arguments, but I feel all of those ways myself."

Jesus contemplated them. "I'm tempted to stop now while I'm ahead. And maybe we should. On top of everything else, Grendel has been an eye opener in so many ways. I understand many things about humans—and other creatures—that perhaps I never really wanted to understand before. It's easy to talk about embracing the whole of life, the bright and the horrible, but Grendel really brings it home. It's been a long time since we were non-human, and I forgot more than I thought I had."

"You know," Mary warned, "there is a Grendeline. Hal wasn't kidding."

They looked at her.

"There is a feminine Grendel," she declared. "Not really much the nurturing, caring type, more the complete savage, like a hungry mother bear with cubs to feed. But she has some clear understandings about life and they are valid. We've let the world close about us, walled out what we didn't want to see."

"I've grown to like Grendel," Lucifer confessed. "You're right—there are parts of the wild I'd let slide away into the darkness. Life is full, and I'd pushed away what seems, well, savage, vicious."

"At a minimum," Jesus observed.

"We wanted to be Jedi long before the idea popped up," Lucifer admitted. "Controlling the bright promise of the new day, ignoring the dark life that the day is based on."

"How did Hal do it?" Mary wondered thoughtfully. "What we got was the pretty version of Grendel."

Jesus and Lucifer stared at her, shocked.

"You're kidding," Lucifer exclaimed. "That was Grendel lite?"

"Tastes great, less filling—NOT!" Jesus added. "Not going to sell a lot of that brew."

"I don't know," Lucifer countered. "It has a good graphic that the copyright expired on a few years ago—oh, maybe the thirteenth century?"

"Never get it past legal," Jesus promised. "Actually, I don't think that the legal staff would survive drinking it."

"That's a positive right there," Lucifer remarked. "But you're right. Too many side effects."

"No, not full strength," Mary continued, ignoring them. "Strong, but absolutely not the full version. Oh, it's out there, if you want. Grendeline, well, she didn't seem to respect us as much as she did Hal and so she didn't come out, you might say. We got Hal's memories and Grendel, but Grendeline held back."

"Not respect us! Immortal beings, semi-gods from a thousand legends!" Lucifer complained.

"We didn't beat him in combat," Jesus admitted. "So, that's fair. Actually, we've taken some pretty good beatings from him/her over the centuries."

"True," Lucifer grumbled. "But not respecting us? Now my feelings are hurt."

"Oh, poor boy! How about a nice lollipop to make it all better?" Mary offered, stroking his arm.

"Orange Tootsie Pop?" Lucifer pleaded. "I really like those."

"So she's there," Mary declared, ignoring Lucifer. "And she seems to have changed from her contact with Hal. Grendel and Beowulf took from each other what they did not expect. Grendel was strong with Cali, but she has pulled through. Kindness from strangers is always refreshing! Still, I'd not push too hard for the full effect. Hal absorbed it and has grown with it, but there's a road I don't want to walk down." She bit her lip, gazing out the window for a minute.

"Except that we will have to go down that path, I'm sure. Grendeline is just waiting for the right time, for us to face what we've been avoiding all these eons. Let's see: Campbell's formulation is something like, umm, there must, if we are to experience long survival, be a continuous 'recurrence of birth' to overcome all the little deaths of daily life. It is by means of our own victories that Nemesis finds us; our doom breaks from the shell of our virtue. When our day is come for the victory of death, death closes in, and there is nothing we can do, except be crucified and resurrected. Dismembered totally, and then reborn," Lucifer quoted.

"That doesn't sound so good," Jesus sighed. "I've tried the crucified and resurrected, but that was resurrected to the small human stories. This will be worse." He thought for a minute. "Okay, let's end this on a positive note. Our achievements speak for themselves, group. We're being too hard on ourselves, but it has been a bad month. Normally, what I caution is to remember our failures, discouragements, and doubts, except that the world has thoughtfully provided a football-arena sized scoreboard to help us remember our errors. Normally, we tend to forget our difficulties, false starts, and aimless groping for direction, exulting in our successes, except that we've been pretty short on successes recently. It's human, which we at least partly are, to see our past achievements as the successful end result of a plan, and to view present difficulties as signs of decline and decay, generally not our fault. Both are true, and false."

"Can't argue with any of that," Lucifer muttered, looking grimly at his empty coffee cup. "Yeah, good time to break."

"Let's make better mistakes tomorrow," Mary offered.

PINK FREUD & THE INTERPRETATION OF STORIES

"Therapy session time again?" Lucifer asked. "I brought the music!" He touched a small speaker, which began playing.

"The Wall?" Jesus guessed.

"Pink Freud," Lucifer answered, holding up a poster.

"It's my mother, doctor," Jesus exclaimed, throwing his hands up.

"Yeah, right," Mary grumbled. "Oy! I should tell you about my son! Does he call? No. Send me a card on my three thousand, five hundred and eighty-ninth birthday? No."

"So where did we go wrong?" Lucifer wondered. "It's this, isn't it?"

Why do the wicked live, grow rich and gather wealth?
Their seed is firm-founded before them, their offspring before their eyes.

Their homes are safe from fear, and God's rod is not against them.
Their bull breeds and brings no miscarriage, their cow calves and does
not lose her young.
They send out their little ones like a flock, and their children go dancing.
They carry the timbrel and lyre, and rejoice at the sound of the flute.
They pass their days in bounty, and in an instant they go down to Sheol.
And they say to God, 'Turn away from us, we have no desire to know
Your ways²³.'

"Which is essentially what we are bitching about. That we did what we thought was right, and got it handed back to us on a plate along with important body parts," Jesus agreed. "Right and wrong, and the external world. To God, all things are good and just, but men think some are good and evil because they just can't see the events without imposing good and evil on the world through the stories, and even though we should know better, it's galling."

"It was letting men have all those highfalutin ideas about creation and nature so they became the powers. That's what went wrong. That's how they split apart from reality and marched over that cliff," Mary asserted.

"I'm feeling like my sex is being blamed here," Jesus commented to Lucifer. "I'm not feeling any positive reinforcement."

"Not a false impression," Lucifer agreed. "I'm with your emotional response. Yeah, my feelings are hurt."

"And who's the emotional sex now?" Mary countered. "It was the shift from the cycle of life—okay, the world of women—to the world of important things that men do that women can't be taught about. Because women were working the fields and men had lots of time to come up with ideas to justify sitting around. And then it was carefully tied to politics, power, and money by Paul, tied up in a nice bow. Platonic ideals, all straight lines, clear human constructs—the need to control the world by pretending that the ideas humans come up with are more than the world. That way they can mooch off the food the women bring in."

"Thomas Jefferson wrote, and I quote," Lucifer added. "Speaking of Plato, I will add, that 'no writer, ancient or modern, has bewildered the world with more misleading influence than this renowned philosopher. Plato's visions have furnished a basis for endless systems of mystical theology, and he is therefore all but adopted as a Christian saint. It is surely time for men to think for themselves, and to throw off the authority of names so artificially magnified.'"

"Can't argue with that," Mary snarled. "Picking up little boys with those fancy philosophy lines. The examined life—what he really meant by that is disgusting."

"You're right," Jesus agreed. "The pretty ideas confuse the creature with the tools. The human isn't 'rational.' Rational analysis of the world is a tool. Strapping a mask on the creature, defining yourself by the social identify, mixes the foreground and the background."

"Worked for Paul," Lucifer pointed out. "He saw that chink in their armor and made it work for him."

"It serves us right, in a way," Jesus admitted. "We meant well for them and he meant for them to serve him well. He won because we pretended to see what they were and denied what they are."

"Really, all their ethics and philosophies are rooted in the smell and the visual tests," Mary muttered, disgusted. "Pretty/perfumed things are good, messy/stinky things are bad, and so they ignore what's really going on out there."

"And we tried to work with that, using the well-meant lie, and it's been our downfall," Lucifer declared. "Well-meant lies just confuse people, which we actually planned on. We hoped confusion would lead to understanding, but it didn't because they think only in set stories. The stories are small, all bordered and bright edges, only clear against the dark backgrounds. The light-filled symbols in the stories froze into grey concrete weights. The stories became forts to hide in from understanding the world. Stories bonded them into groups, and became their masks in the social world. So the harder you push on the stories, the tighter they hold onto them. Paul understood his prey far better than we, who thought we were the hunters."

"Fishers," Jesus corrected. "Technically."

"We tried the bigger stories, but they couldn't grasp the full complexity," Lucifer continued. "So we lied, meaning well. Intending that the next story would correct the first one, and so on. We thought we could coax them, move them gradually to the bigger stories, by little stories that weren't quite true but had elements of the truth. We treated them like children, trying to keep them alive to adulthood, but they never took the next big step, to challenge, question, and rebel, and then rebuild the stories. Unfortunately, a single contradiction corrupts and allows falsehoods to proliferate. The stories became falsehoods built upon falsehoods. Well meant, but not working."

"Nothing is so difficult as not deceiving oneself," Mary commented.

"Jews don't recognize Jesus; Protestants don't recognize the Pope; Baptists don't recognize each other in the liquor store," Jesus joked.

"Like their heroes, pretending to live up to a false set of values so that everyone will live up to them too. Then, when people find out it's at least partially false, they disengage, become alienated; they don't go all the way through to knowledge, they suck their thumb and whine. What's the line the suffering hero proclaims, as he heaps ashes upon himself? 'Because sometimes the truth isn't good enough...sometimes, people deserve more.' There isn't more than the truth, which is hard enough to grasp without the soft lies around it that are supposed to make it more palatable. They want a silent guardian, a watchful protector...the dark knight, and it's all based on what the group wants to believe. Reality is just an occasional annoyance to be brushed away whenever they can. It's lies, building on more lies," Mary snapped.

"At eighteen our convictions are hills from which we look; at forty-five they are caves in which we hide. F. Scott Fitzgerald," Lucifer quoted. "See, a pithy saying that I'm not responsible for."

"They were fun people," Mary recalled. "A little crazy—okay," catching Jesus's look, "a lot crazy. But fun people."

"My message was to look to the self, the emotions in the self," Jesus protested. "Inspiration. Instead, Paul bound them with 'Meaning'. Meaning is what you are told you should believe and think and act based on some grandiose elaborate story, badly translated from a dead language. Without inspiration, which is life, then the stories always get smaller and smaller. The stories, when they are small, become mean, both in the spiteful and nasty sense and in the shabby, low-grade sense. And the leaders are never those noble philosopher kings that Plato so praised—another thing he got wrong. The leaders are the people who can emotionally carry the weight of leadership. How? Either they are so focused on their own selves that the weight is never noticed, or they are so focused on some grandiose idea that the weight is light. So the 'meanest,' smallest humans become the leaders because they can effortlessly exploit the holes, and the thoughtful find themselves on the wrong side of the guns."

"I have never seen a situation in which dishonesty, no matter how well intended, was a long-term solution," Mary admitted. "Sooner rather than later, we need to face the music."

"Up Against the Wall?" Lucifer asked.

Mary shook her head, despairing.

"Difficult truth is better than wonderful falsehood," Lucifer quoted. "Epicurus."

"I thought you gave up pithy sayings," Jesus asked.

"It's an addiction," Lucifer confessed. "I tried a twelve-step program, but all I got was some good ideas for more sayings."

"I understand," Jesus admitted. "I was addicted to writing fairy tales."

"When was that?" Mary asked.

"Once upon a time," Jesus snickered.

"That's Grimm," Lucifer laughed.

Mary contemplated them. "A sense of humor is probably the best thing about humans. And if either one of you develop one, I'd be glad to hear something funny. So what do we do next?"

"A schism in the soul," Lucifer pronounced, "cannot be resolved by any return to the good old days, seeking an ideal projected future, or even by welding together again the deteriorating elements. Only birth can conquer death—the birth not of the old thing again, but of something new."

"Sounds painful," Mary grimaced. "I've done childbirth. Re-birthing ourselves seems rather metaphorically complex. I'm getting a mental picture that isn't pretty. And that means Grendeline, based on Hal's memories."

They sat and stared at the table for a few minutes.

"I'm feeling blocked and frustrated," Mary admitted. "The words seem right, but they are not sinking in."

"We have a plan," Jesus declared. "Adapting to events—that what Cali says is all you can do when things are in flux."

"Destiny grants us our wishes, but in its own way, in order to give us something beyond our wishes. Goethe," Lucifer commented.

"I'm going to punch you if you don't get off the Goethe," Mary growled.

"Getting your goat?" Jesus asked. "You and Dumbledore's brother?"

"That's baaaaad," Mary jeered.

"Hey, a goat was Paul's favorite drawing of me," Lucifer offered. "Something about my lustful nature, hardy spirit, and ah, well, prominent physical attributes, but I deny the cloven foot thing completely."

"The ancient Greeks proclaimed, 'know thyself,'" Mary replied. "I think we have evidence of failure here."

"If you know the enemy and know yourself, you need not fear the result of a hundred battles," Lucifer announced.

Mary and Jesus groaned.

THE JUICE OF THE BEAN

Hal was standing at the kitchen counter, fussing with the coffee machine in their private apartment.

"It is by Caffeine alone I set my mind in Motion, it is by the juice of the Bean that thoughts acquire speed, the hands acquire shakes, the shakes become a warning. It is by Caffeine alone I set my mind in Motion," Hal declared slowly and seriously as he poured out his and Cali's coffee.

Cali lurched to the counter. "I can...stop...any time..." she rasped, reaching out a hand for her coffee, her hand shaking so hard that she stabilized it with the other hand. "Ah, good," taking the first sip. "My precious, precious," she murmured, stroking the coffee cup as she sat down. "Yes, good, heh heh, heh heh." She looked up at Hal, a perky smile on her face. "And how are you this morning, honey?"

"I'm not worried about what I just saw. I'm worried that I feel the same." He sipped his coffee and looked out the window.

"I miss the coffee house in Ann Arbor," Cali complained. "They had a sign. 'Our coffee is an experience that chalk is unable to convey.' You know, it's not addictive," as the shakes slowed.

"I was in a coffee shop in Ann Arbor one day before we met, joking with the guy making my coffee, and I told him coffee wasn't addictive—I could quit any time. He laughed and told me, 'Yeah, it's not,' and then took my coffee away. Wouldn't give it to me. I politely asked, and he refused. Laughed at me, holding my coffee!" Hal recalled, his knuckles whitening as he clenched his coffee cup. "And then I went over the counter, my hands around his throat. Well, the police came, and people were standing around. He started telling them how he took my coffee away and wouldn't give it to me, and a hush fell over the room. A low muttering broke out. Some guy in a cowboy hat went out to his truck to get a rope, and the cops were checking out the ceiling fan, estimating if it would bear the baristas weight. The patrons were breaking the legs off the chairs for clubs, and it was looking grim for the guy. The manager rushed out, refilled everyone's coffee, and cooler heads prevailed. We left the guy struggling under a pile of coffee grounds in the dumpster. At least, I think he was still struggling."

"Like the West Texas Ranger whose first question was whether the recently deceased deserved to die. That would have been a short investigation. I'm frustrated," Cali admitted, holding her coffee. "It's nice here, but I feel so restless."

"Could be worse," Hal commented. "We could have little jobs and overdue credit cards."

"I'm terrified sometimes of Maria growing up without parents," Cali mumbled, a tear running down her face. "All that we've been through..."

Hal got very serious, staring at his coffee. "I think the same thing. No one every says about any other children, which means none survived. I tried getting the caretaker to talk about other children one time, and he shut down in a second with a sad look on his face, which is a bad sign."

"It's scary in a way. When we met them, they were the complete protectors, all powerful. As we've grown to know them, well, they are not people like everyone else, but they don't know it all. In all fairness, they'd be the first to say that, but it's a disappointment. The growing up thing, that people you look up to are people too, with problems of their own."

"True," Hal admitted. "We've even helped them, which I can't believe myself. At least we've earned our keep."

"Did you ever date before we met?" Cali demanded. "That was an obvious play for sympathy by the female, and you answer logically, completely missing the issue. Not that you are not right, it's just, well, logic isn't the issue here."

"How about this?" Hal offered. "Out of clutter, find simplicity. From discord, find harmony. In the middle of difficulty lies opportunity." Einstein, how can it be wrong?

Cali glared at him, and then laughed. She quickly shoved pieces of muffin into her cheeks and in a few seconds she looked like a chipmunk. In a deep voice, she growled, "But I, I never wanted this for you. I work my whole life, I don't apologize, to take care of my family. And I refused to be a fool dancing on the strings held by all of those big shots. That's my life. I don't apologize for that."

Hal laughed hysterically. "Godmother, please, I can pay you next week! I'm not sure Maria will want us there when she gets older. Mom! Like, knock off the corny sayings. I can hear it now."

"I'm not looking forward to her at thirteen, that's for sure," Cali admitted. "Mary laughs when she thinks about Maria at thirteen, which I find worrisome. You know, at two, she's picking out her own outfits now. And mom's not right about what mom wants her to do."

"Maybe we should send her to private school," Hal suggested. "It turns out that everything we learned in kindergarten was not just wrong, it was harmful. It seems that fidgeting, twitching, moving constantly, standing, and pacing are the best for your long-term health, and sitting quietly with your hands folded, waiting for instruction, is the worst way to live your life."

"My mother—adoptive mother—reported that I wasn't good in kindergarten," Cali admitted.

"Maria will be fine," Hal promised, putting his arm around her.

She smiled and started to take a sip of coffee.

"How can she not be safe? We are building a fighting force of extraordinary magnitude. We forge our tradition in the spirit of our ancestors. You have our gratitude."

Cali choked, and spit her coffee all over the counter.

GRENDEL'S FUTURE

The family and friends were sitting at the dinner table.

"Hal, we found Grendel's colony creatures, right where you told us they would be," Lucifer reported. "Now, normally we would have burned them with glee, maybe even salted the land afterward just to make a point, but you insisted we wait. What's the plan?"

"I've been thinking," Hal announced. "I'm thinking we should recreate him."

Looks of complete disbelief were on everyone's face.

"So," Mary inquired carefully, "we finally are delivered from Grendel, the most dangerous tool Paul had, and now we recreate it? Just because life is boring, or what?"

"Life should be interesting," Hal agreed. "But there will be a little change in the re-creation process. I'm going to add myself to the mix."

Lungorthin laughed. "Oh, that's evil," he rumbled, slapping the table, cracking it. "Sorry," trying to push the granite back in place, but he kept snickering.

You are evil!, Grendel's voice echoed in Hal's head. Does your family really know the depths of your depravity? I try and seduce you to the dark side, and now I find myself at the feet of the master. If you weren't married, you could interview with the mother church. I'm with your wife! I'm not taking any more drugs with you. You have weird taste.

Mary glanced around the table, and then smiled at Hal. "Beyond good and evil, you took us. The Grendel's in us are appalled, but impressed. I'll get to work on it."

CHAPTER 14. LUCRETIA'S TASK

Paul sat on his throne, and his son stood next to him. They were talking as Lucretia was shown in. Cesare murmured something quietly and Paul laughed. Lucretia colored. She didn't hear the remark, but she knew that tone.

"You did very well on the project I assigned, to steal information from Aeternalis, GmbH," Paul announced. "Very well indeed."

"Of course, you used methods that a man couldn't use—or wouldn't." Cesare sneered.

Lucretia's smile turned brittle and froze. "I did as you asked, my lord," ignoring Cesare.

"And I thank you for it," Paul replied, giving Cesare a "shut up" look. "Now I have a more important project. One that will make you even more vital to our group. I need you to crash a country. Financial manipulation of an established market is the most profitable speculation—you know that. And currency manipulation, being the moneychanger in the temple, as it were, is the most profitable of all."

"It's also the most dangerous, my lord," Lucretia stammered, stunned. "That's where all the huge blowups come from. I just point it out."

"True," Paul agreed. "Which is why we need you to structure this so it won't lose money. We have resources we can throw at this. Not just financial resources—we have political connections, government agencies, and other connections. We can get reports issued, recommendations to not trade with certain countries, not to purchase certain products, that certain products are unsafe. Lots of possibilities. More than you usually have to work with."

"That would, of course, of course, be illegal," Lucretia pointed out. "Just to frame the discussion."

"We thought you were a can-do person," Cesare snapped. "All I hear you say is 'no.'"

"It's important to frame exactly what we are after here," Lucretia remarked, her fury growing. "If I'm to do a job, I need to know the goal so I can choose alternatives to the goal. Now, the general who wins a battle makes many calculations in his temple ere the battle is fought. The general who loses a battle makes but few calculations beforehand. Thus do many calculations lead to victory, and few calculations to defeat."

"Well said," Paul acknowledged. "Sun Tzu felt that the emperor should not interfere with the general, but I've never really agreed with that position. Still, you make a good point. Okay, here's the goal. We want to bankrupt Paraguay, and make a lot of money in the process. In the process, we want to force a dispute between Brazil and Paraguay that sets the emotions afire. First is the destruction of their currency, and second, waiting to pounce and then buying on the cheap."

Lucretia opened her mouth, but Paul imperiously raised his hand. "Why I seek that is not your concern. The general is concerned with the means to the end of the state. The general is not concerned with the ends. That is the emperor's concern only."

Lucretia bowed. "I hear and obey, my lord. I will provide several possibilities for your selection in this matter. I would point out, with respect, that damage to a currency is the ultimate act of destruction; far more damaging than a rampaging army roaming through a country. The damage the army creates heals, but the damaged currency can take generations to fully heal."

"A woman's response," Cesare jeered.

"I only mention it," Lucretia offered through gritted teeth, "because the damage is so great that sometimes people come looking for recompense. That is all I wished to say."

Paul smiled at Lucretia, ignoring Cesare. "Successful and fortunate crime is called virtue. Lucius Annaeus Seneca, I believe, and that is as true now as it was two thousand years ago," Paul answered. "Look, Lucretia, I know people will come looking for revenge, but we'll play within the rules and they'll play within the rules. And powerful groups will make money, groups more powerful than those we damage. That's the way the world works. Besides, the thrill of conquest—where's your manly drive for adventure? Oh, yeah, you're a woman. Sorry."

Lucretia kept her eyes on the steps.

"So we will be waiting for you to come up with a brilliant plan," Paul declared. "Well, I have some appointments that are starting quite soon. I'll be waiting to hear from you."

Lucretia bowed and left.

As she left, she saw several very beautiful women waiting, their faces slipping from calm beauty to terror and back again. A final quick flash of terror as they are called in and their smiles were painted back on. She looked away as one quickly wiped away a tear as she walked into the room.

DO WHAT?

Lucretia sat in her office, re-reading the notes she made after the meeting with Paul. Yeah, that's what he actually ordered. Amazing. She shook her head. Thank you, may I have another, my lord? What have I gotten myself into? Ah, Lucretia, a small job for you, if you have time. Sink a country, spark a war, and make huge, enormous profits in the process. Sooner is better than later. Ciao. As you wish, my evil master. She bowed slightly. Clean the Augean stables afterwards? No problem.

Okay, what he's asking for is an amplified result from an event. Such as... She reread a newspaper clipping she had saved, because it was so amazing. From The Surfersvillage Global Surf News, 27 December 2009:

"The biggest wave on record occurred in Lituya Bay on the southern coast of Alaska in 1958. An earthquake measuring 8.3 on the Richter scale hit the area and shook loose an estimated 40 million cubic yards of dirt and glacier from a mountainside at the head of the bay. When the debris hit the water, a massive 1,720-foot wave was created and washed over the headland.

"How did the scientists know the wave was so incredibly enormous? Simple. To measure the height of the wave, scientists found the high-water mark — the line where the water reached its highest point on land. This probably is not the biggest wave ever, just the biggest documented. Three fishing boats witnessed the Lituya Bay event. While two people on one of the boats were killed, incredibly, the other two boats rode the waves and their occupants survived." That had to be a day to remember, Lucretia thought. The cruel part is that they couldn't brag about it afterwards, because who would believe a story like that?

"Technically, this wave is described as a 'Splash Wave.' The photo above shows the headland beside the Lituya Glacier that was swept clean of soil and trees to a height of 1740 feet by the giant splash wave. The icebergs seen in the water of Lituya Bay, foreground, were knocked off the glacier by the landslide falling into the bay from a slope to the right of the photograph." That's incredible, studying at the pictures. Who would believe a wave could be seventeen hundred feet high? Roughly one and one-half times the height of the Empire State Building rising up towards you. Exactly what I need to have happen in the economic world. But not with me sitting between the wave and the rock cliff, thank you.

So, I need to arrange an earthquake that jars loose some very big things that sync together and POW! How hard can that be? Paul said he has money, political and press connections, and questionable authorities on our side. On the other side is a sovereign government with an army and a diplomatic corps. Oh, and a historical bent towards machismo—that male-honor thing. Women stay home, mind their little business. Okay, I'm rationalizing, but that's going to make this more fun. Now if I could just arrange for Cesare to have all his money there, that would be the icing on the cake.

This is certainly going to be illegal. Perhaps not the exact black-letter of the law, but certainly the spirit. If it goes well, they'll amend the law. The equivalent of a seventeen hundred-foot wave coming through the financial world is going to make powerful people unhappy. So how to handle that before they are standing in a mob around me with the torches flickering, other than fleeing to a desert island somewhere, which wouldn't last? The mafia knows how to run a fraud. If you run questionable transactions through a failing business, then crash and burn the business in the bankruptcy court, no one pays much attention to the details. Ideally, before the authorities show any interest. Case closed; all that is left are a few dusty, yellowing documents in the court archives. Nothing left on the bare bones but a few teeth marks, and the actual business records interred in an unregulated landfill after a brief but respectful ceremony. Prosecutors pick cases by re-election value, and there's little to be gained from using scarce resources poring over failures. By the time anyone wises up to the extent of the disaster, the trail is cold.

How not to do it? Run it through a business that not only continues, but has a prominent business address. If Enron had the sense to crash their little subsidiaries, the trail would not have led back. Ironically, they thought they could make it work and ran it the legal way. Of course, if they had any sense, they would never have created a publicly held house of cards. Talk about having "ruin" stamped all over the plan! Why not just give the prosecutors a road map and confession to start with? Once the prosecutors realized they could walk into that big office building and get on the evening news, i.e., positive reelection publicity, there would be no stopping them.

What was the Monty Python sketch? Lucretia thought to herself. They had it dead on. She stood up and declaimed to the empty office: "And so the Scarlet Permanent Assurance boldly hoisted sail on the high seas of international finance. For a long time, they sailed empty seas, growing lean and hungry, their ship tattered and worn. And then, suddenly rising before them, was the prize of their dreams. An arrogant financial district swollen with fat, bloated Investment Banks, Hedge Funds and luscious Sovereign Funds. Unsuspecting, the Mandarins of high finance sat smug and self-satisfied, master's of the universe they knew, blithely unaware of the terrible revenge planned against them. The Jolly Roger run up, the reasonably violent men of the Scarlet Permanent Assurance attacked without mercy, ceasing only when the once-proud financial giants lay in ruins, their assets stripped, their credit lines emptied, and their officers walked off the plank."

"It's fun to charter an accountant, and sail the wide accountan-cy[24]," she sang loudly to the birds flying outside the windows.

Her secretary poked her head in with a questioning look on her face. "Practicing for the opera?" she asked.

"Argh," Lucretia growled. "It's the briny deep and the pirate's life for me."

"Aye, aye, captain," her secretary declared, standing straight and saluting. "I'll run the flag up the mizzenmast." She closed the door.

I like this secretary, Lucretia thought. She may be owned by Paul, but at least she has a sense of humor. The other one was just all petty viciousness. She deserved Mother Superior.

Lucretia sat back down at her desk, doodling. So, I need a chain of crashing businesses, based in different countries and subject to a welter of jurisdictions and laws. Not just laws written in different languages with unclear translations—I need them written in different dialects so that even the lawyers in that country cannot decide what the law is. No one person knows all the languages, and the translations can be attacked. With enough money and planning, a web can be spun that no one is going to work through. Fortunately, or unfortunately, few people plan ahead enough. Or perhaps they are just never caught? Lucretia sat back, remembered what the professor who taught the advanced accounting class had said. One day, a brave student had raised his hand and asked what the smart people did when they ran a fraud.

The professor gazed at him thoughtfully. "The party line is that there are no smart people running frauds. The party line is that they always make mistakes, will always be tripped up. The reality is that we don't know because it's all negative evidence. We don't see the holes where the successful frauds were. If you think about it, there are a number of ways to run a fraud that can't be tracked. Now, a successful fraud requires thought, planning, nerve, and focus. Fortunately, there are few people—at least we think there are few people—who can pull that off. I'd feel better," the professor commented dryly, "if everyone in the class didn't have the same excited look, that look that says you have seen the Promised Land open before you." The class laughed, but the look stayed.

"Some people are born to piracy, some people achieve piracy, and some people have piracy thrust upon them," Lucretia mumbled to herself. What happened to my classmates? Most vanished off the face of the earth. Occasionally I see reports of their houses being sold in faraway places as they move to larger homes. Perhaps they took the message of that class to heart. That attorney that Paul uses in the U.S.? I can meet with him and have a business plan ready. Plausible denial, that's all the law firm needs to cover themselves, and that's easy to do.

The next day, Lucretia was riding in a cab back to her office after meeting with the senior partners of the law firm. They even have standard forms for this type of business structure! With check-off boxes for "difficult to track," "impossible to track," and "hang the cost, no one will ever find out." I'm not as smart as I thought I was, but at least I'm on the right track.

"So, where is that seventeen hundred-foot wave?" Lucretia demanded, staring intently at the wall. Hal caught me, and I thought I was being so clever. Anomalies, he told me, and he's right. Watching for the subtle forming, but putting that into measurable goals. I wish I could get his help on this! I'm not sure how that would look on the expense report. Line item—expensive dinner with and enormous bribe paid to sworn Enemy Number One? Perhaps not.

Let's see. Take this from the top. Project planning is simple conceptually: determine what you want to do, assess the steps needed to get there, determine the timeline for the steps. Finally, set up a monitoring system to check your progress, and provide feedback on problems.

So: a clear goal is the first requirement. Okay. I want to make a vast fortune for my evil master in the next few months, focused on Paraguay/Brazil, beginning with manipulation of the global currency markets. That's a nice, simple goal statement. Works in cartoons, at least. The problem with goal statements is that they imply a structure. That is, the goal assumes a world and tools to reach that goal. This seems to be outside the existing structure, if not absolutely banned as destructive to the structure's heart.

Going back to organization, simply writing down all of the possibilities in random order, is the first place for me to start. Expand on the possibilities/choices that I see, and new choices will develop. Work on those for some time, giving myself at least several days to sleep on problems, assuming sleep comes, and my choices will, more likely than not, align into some clear categories. Some choices will be clearly irrelevant; some will open to new definitions of the problems. That's a plan, but let's not put all the eggs in one basket. Another approach—has this ever been done before? I have a lot of eager interns and can mix the questions up so it isn't quite so obvious what's going on. That's tomorrow's project. She shut down her laptop.

Priming the Mind

Lucretia was again at her desk at the office. The door was barred and no phone calls were allowed. The general ponders in her chamber, reading omens and signs, while the troops patrol nervously the perimeter.

She skimmed the piles of research generated by the interns and hopeful junior partners, and then pushed it all aside. Fine, she thought. The general who wins a battle makes many calculations in his temple ere the battle is fought, but what calculations to make? Clarity, simplicity, but what is that? The essence of calculation, to paraphrase Sun Tzu, is to (1) clearly grasp the social consensus worldview, i.e., the story we tell ourselves about how the real world is as we want it; and (2) clearly see the real world as it really is, and then (3) contrast the two, profiting from the errors in the social consensus worldview. That requires: first, clear articulation of the social consensus worldview from a view not buying or selling that consensus, which is pretty damn hard, and second, some way of touching/grasping events in the real world outside the limiting human stories. The bounded world is seeing the world through the stories; the unbounded world is seeing the stories through the world. Again, pretty damn hard.

But like many hard things, there is a reward. The easy thing, which is buying into the social consensus and only seeing real-world events through that consensus, puts you in the fields with a hoe, not the Lord of the Manor. I don't like working with a hoe in the hot sun, she recalled. Tried it as a kid. Misery may love company, and they are welcome to it. Seeing past the stories, playing the social consensus against the real world, profiting from the gaps— there is life in the lap of luxury. Cool drinks on a hot day, pool boys at my beck and call. I like that! Distracted, she drifted away for a minute, and then shook her head. Back to reality.

Now, each moment contains an infinity of events. Lots of them, like stars crashing in a distant galaxy, have a hopefully minimal effect on me. Actually, things just happen and we define them as events. Those events sometimes create/cause/influence other events, sometimes not. Sometimes the ripples combine, sometimes they peter out. Ripples generally build over longer time periods than humans perceive, only to surprise us when the wave finally breaks on us. Patternicity is the blessing and curse of the human mind, the hard-wired obsession to see patterns everywhere and right now, whether or not the patterns actually exist.

My mind, all human minds, must emotionally be in charge, organized, on top of things, in a world that clearly is running outside of our control. Stark proof that we must believe ourselves in control is the right brain/left brain problem. People with severed brains, who actually had surgery, a scalpel physically cutting the connections between the two sides of the brain, can still provide lucid, rational explanations for behaviors controlled by the other side of the brain. Unfortunately, those explanations are completely wrong because the one side of the brain explaining literally has no idea what the other side is doing. The mere fact that their explanations are completely wrong, created out of whole cloth, forced by that necessity to see yourself as coherent and consistent, doesn't dent the individuals absolute belief in their explanations.

Does make one question one's own explanations occasionally," she thought wryly. Case in point-her senior partner, who actually believes his speeches, and is clearly deluded and delusional. That won't play well at the salary review, I'm afraid, and she regretfully drew a line through that idea.

So this is a difficult problem. Compounding the problem, humans have a limited attention span and a very finite number of items that we can keep in focus at any given time—oh, somewhere between five and nine, depending on the person. Something else comes in, one of the others has to go away, which is why writing things down is a good idea. That's why in "The Hitchhiker's Guide to the Galaxy," they build a computer that ran for millions of years to solve the answer to the universe. The computer may have been right, and perhaps the answer to the universe really is "42," but that doesn't tell me anything that's helpful today.

So I can't just say to myself, "Show me what I can't see!" Lucretia thought. Can't wave a wand and show me the future, because I can't see what I'm not seeing. Even the Harry Potter people couldn't do that either. You had to know the spell to cast it, I guess. This makes my head hurt, she realized, wearily rubbing her temples.

Now, even if I clearly see real-world events on one hand and social consensus on the other, the gaps between them nicely defined, there is no guarantee that there will be an investment opportunity. There must be, first, a negative/positive intersection between the coming real-world events and the social consensus, then second, a way of calculating the time impact on the consensus. I.E., when will the real world hit the group hard enough that notice has to be taken? And third, most importantly, there has to be a market whereby one can place your bets on the future. Otherwise, no cool drinks on a hot day for me.

Actually, that's really important, because it narrows down the possibilities. I already know the relevant market, the currency exchange markets, FOREX, and the private and public derivative markets. I know their rules and leverage, and I can pop that up on my computer screen. It's scary, really. All that a country is—resources, opportunities, debt, depravities and wholesome desires of the citizens, everything—summarized into one number, the value of the currency at a given second. Which fluctuates wildly from second to second, as it should.

Driving one day, I realized that the future is like driving in traffic. I know my usual haunts, my small world, and have a general idea what traffic I can expect at a given time. My expectations are clearer today than a month from now. I don't know the specific cars, where they are headed, or what the driver's choices and lives are—none of the minute detail that explains each car on the road. But I know roughly, for my purposes in calculating travel times, when it will be busy and when it won't, and what the average traffic flow is going to be. What I need to know is when an accident is going to occur on X road, which drives all the traffic onto Y road. That's the equivalent of what I'm supposed to do with this currency.

On the bright side, I'm not in college with a thousand dollars to risk and high hopes for the future. I have Paul's resources behind me, which are enormous. The country in point has certain exports, and there are known demands and supplies. It has certain products produced and consumed within the country, again with known demands and supplies. All of those exports and products have pressure points. Food rumored to be poisoned drops in value quickly. Drugs rumored to be inferior, defective, drop in value rapidly. Land rumored to have secret resources can jump in value and ironically bankrupt the people who need that land, because it's grabbed away from them. Fear of a sinking economy dries up bank lending, creating the depression they fear. Then the torrent of Sun Tzu, rocks crashing down the mountain onto eggs, beats on that magic number that is the currency value. Enough of these little drips combining under pressure, and there is my seventeen hundred foot wave, sweeping all before it.

It's anomalies, like Hal told me, excited, drawing connecting lines on the paper. It's the little things that hint the story isn't working that count. So what are the anomalies surrounding the values of the exports? What little facts hint where the demand curve shifts rapidly? That's another thing to unleash the interns on. I like that, she mused. I'm standing tall in black leather boots, holding a field marshal's baton, roaring 'Unleash the interns!' And they rush out into the street, all dark suits and power glasses, pillaging on their laptops as they go.

Finally, we need friends, especially if this blows up as big as it will. Good, close, powerful friends. Many people must make money off this. Bulls make money, and bears make money, but pigs get slaughtered. Paul has a list of his friends who are in. I just have to make sure that they make so much that we all hang together, for we shall assuredly hang separately otherwise.

And where to look to focus down on the key influences on the magic currency number? Tail risk. The risk that the tail wags the dog, not the dog wagging the tail. What did they say in finance class? Lucretia thought back to finance class. How did the professor carefully state the problem and solution?

So, you're a portfolio manager with a condo in New York and a beach house in Maine. You want to keep them. Your significant other wants to keep them, and you want to keep your significant other. Towards that worthy goal, you create a concept that defines a portfolio of investments. That portfolio, you assert, will provide a desirable rate of return. You have tied the projections to reasonable assumptions, it all 'looks' good (skipping the smell test) and the risk committee signs off. The portfolio is marketed to investors (marks) as a substantially above market rate of return that is even safer than leaving your money in your mattress. How much better can things be? So people throw money at your idea.

The devil is in the detail. 'Safe' means that the probability that returns will move between the mean and three standard deviations, either positive or negative, is 99.97%. The probability of returns moving more than three standard deviations beyond the mean is 0.03%, or virtually nil. But, and this is what keeps you up at night, the big money and your superstar status require being in that .03%. You know that the concept of tail risk suggests that the distribution of events will not be not normal, but skewed. Skewed is fatter tails. Fatter tails increase the probability that an investment will move beyond three standard deviations. It's pig in clover time, if they move in a positive direction. If they move in a negative direction, the portfolio is destroyed.

But you're a smart investment manager, Harvard degree on the wall. The risk factor has been signed off on, and you've met the social—AND legal—criteria for rational investment behavior. Extensive analysis, backed up by reams of printouts, proves that the probabilities have been calculated in a statistically rational manner. Lawyer's and accountant's letters fill the prospectus. That you know; and the risk committee knows; and the senior partners know; that it's all pious nonsense and you're betting someone's else's ship on events way, way more likely than .03% is something that only comes out, first, if there is a complete disaster, and second, only if the people who lost money have more political power than the company. That's a little, little tail risk, clearly less than .03%, and so life goes on at an investment firm.

No one really understands statistics anyway, Lucretia knew. Look at the occasional papers popping up saying that the drug companies don't have a clue, statistically, what they are doing when they analyze their test results. They know the results they want, and POOF! The drugs do what they are supposed to do, at least on paper. Are the results defensible? Yes. Are they correct? Probably not. And the data mining of health statistics? That should be characterized as a pirate expedition, blatant looting by research MDs and PhDs desperate for grants and publicity. The lone voices in the wilderness pointing out errors in the calculations are not even shouted down because no one understands what they are talking about anyway.

So, yeah, that conceptually focuses down the target She added a few small touches to her drawing, tying relationships together, and nodded to herself. Anomalies show you the resource inputs that are THE critical change drivers. Change driver effects, being non-linear, are positive feedback cycles, and thus multiplied by their fatter tails. Amplified by the gaps between the social consensus and the real world (IE, the tails are really FAT), then there is that seventeen hundred foot wave. I'm riding it like a pro, all the way into the golden beach and the handsome pool boys. And the continued existence of my family and I, because that's the way that Paul plays. That's the gold, matey, if one can just find it. Arghhh.

Let's hit it from a different angle, keep narrowing this down. There are two ways to make money in the system. One can either make money selling people the story they want to hear, or make money profiting when the oh-so-important story that they run their lives by breaks up on the reef. Selling them the story they want, well, there's crowds lined up to do that—tough to get through the noise. Whereas by making money from the flaws in their story that they can't bear to look at, and so pretend the flaws don't exist, I can sit on the beach and snicker about their errors, tipping the waiters well for drinks. I like that. So it's back to catching the anomalies.

Now, it isn't enough that there is a story and possible problems with the story. There are always problems with the stories. There has to be a problem, by definition. A story is a selected set of events against a sharply colored moral background, highlighting what people want/fear the most. So the background is a problem, what people want is a problem, and what the story will lead to is a problem. The newspapers sell papers exploiting the weakness of the story structure. You can always come up with a reason for why something happened, will happen, shouldn't have happened, and so on.

If you're wrong, well, who can foretell the future? And, by the way, because you are my special friend, and you get my special friend price, here's another story about what's really going to happen this time, no kidding, cross my heart and hope you die.

The newspaper seeks impeccable, crosschecked facts and then weaves them into a narrative that implies causality and superior knowledge. We have to be told stories, and there is nothing wrong with that as long as we realize why and what we are doing. Stepping outside, we realize it's not whether a story distorts reality, because all stories distort, but how it distorts reality.

For better or worse, most human communication is no different from monkeys pulling lice out of each other's fur, Lucretia ruminated, listening to the women chat in the bathroom as she sat quietly in her stall. It's all grooming and social touching. Necessary and useful, but not to be confused with the communication of facts. Speaking of pulling lice out of fur, looking critically at strands of her blonde hair, now I'm wondering about the cleanliness of that hair salon. Yuck.

Most of the time, sadly, the stories have nothing to do with the relevant issues driving the problems. So using the news for investment choices is a sucker's game. *The Wall Street Journal* is no different from seagulls flying over the beach. Seagulls fly in small, widely spaced groups, watching both the water below them and the other seagulls. The minute a seagull dives for a fish in the water, a hundred flock to follow. If you're the ninety-ninth seagull to the party, there isn't much left of the fish when you get there. However, the patrolling sharks, who also watch the seagulls, may have reached the scene by then, because they have a story, too.

Pierre-Daniel Huet, in his Philosophical treatise on the weaknesses of the Human Mind, which was published in, oh, approximately 1690, wrote that any event can have an infinity of possible causes, which humans ignore. We focus on preselected segments of the seen and generalize from it to the unseen, which is the error of confirmation. Socially rewarded behavior, by the way. We all pull the same kind of lice out. We fool ourselves with stories that cater to our hardwired need for patterns and control. We behave as if unknown unknowns, black swans, do not exist. We lament: "To-morrow, and to-morrow, and to-morrow, Creeps in this petty pace from day to day, To the last syllable of recorded time[25]," and yet we cling to the vision of yesterday becoming today. No real thought for the differences, the possibilities. We're not programed to expect the unexpected.

Kant clearly wrote, well, as clearly as a German philosopher can, that what we see (perceive) is a small subset of what is out 'there'. First our perceptions are limited by the hardware-eyes, nose, etc. Then there is the distortion of silent evidence. Remember the professor talking about silent evidence? The class didn't think the idea was all that important, and the professor knew it. "Age shows the value of this," he told us, surveying the dazed and dulled faces in class. "You'll think more of this later. We see what happened, or what we are told happened. We do not see, do not have time to see or think, about what could have happened, what might have happened, and what the differences were have been. Where are the events that didn't happen? Where are the events riding on other events that look like they caused them? History hides Black Swans from us and gives us a mistaken idea about the odds of these events. You stumble over the silent evidence when your plan crashes around you."

Finally, and this is Hal's gift to me: we tunnel; we focus on a few well-defined sources of uncertainly. We are taught to define, structure, and proceed when the light is green. The higher in the educational structure you go, the more carefully you are trained. Within a carefully limited and structured system, like a school, one can do that successfully. On the wide ocean of life, you watch the waves and choose based on scraps of random information—the anomalies. Little wisps of clouds in the distance, red sky at morning? Pay attention and pull the sails in or perish. See the birds wheeling over the water in the distance? Sail there and the fishing is rich.

The both comforting and terrifying thing about the mind is that, really, consciousness is like a passenger on the second floor of a double-decker bus. Frantically sorting through maps, holding his notes against the wind, peering through the rain on his glasses, he shouts directions to the driver, waving his arms wildly to prove his control. The real driver, the unconscious, sitting comfortably on a plush leather seat, confidently holding the steering wheel of the bus on the enclosed first floor, can't hear the consciousness's ravings and so it drives the bus where it should go. The unconscious snickers to itself, knowing that what the consciousness perceives is only what the unconscious feeds to it. So, relax. Decisions make themselves if you just gather data. A picture will form in your mind if you're willing to ignore the wildly shouting person on the second floor of the bus.

"Okay," Lucretia proclaimed, contemplating the bright city lights sparking against the dark night. "A glass of wine, a glance at the picture of the beach house I want, and to sleep. The plan will emerge."

THE PLAN EMERGES

Why Paraguay? Lucretia puzzled. And what is the tie to São Paulo? Paul's instructions were clear and focused. What am I missing? The interns and junior partners had been frantically jumping to her commands for several days. They presented a huge pile of information to her in a long meeting full of charts, graphs, and PowerPoint presentations. Most of what they found was irrelevant, but she bought them all dinner at a nice restaurant for their hard work. Then she sat back in her office and worked through the piles of documents behind the presentations.

Like any country, Paraguay has key products to be stockpiled and then driven down by releasing the stocks. That is the traditional, physical way of crashing a market, but you have to pay market price for all that stuff you are planning on selling cheap after the crash, so there's a big risk doing that. You have to make more profiting from the currency crash than you lose on the value of the stuff you bought falling because of said currency crash. Otherwise, your clever knife in the back ends up in your back—a poor plan. Finally, if you do succeed, there are a piles of warehouse receipts and waybills showing who bought what. That's pretty easy to track back in a computerized world, and when they track back to you, there are angry mobs with torches outside the office building. Fail.

The modern way is to sink the ship with rumors. Rumors that products are inferior and/or poisoned. Or rumors that the key products have vague health risks based on indefinite proofs offered about some people who may have been sick for undefined but inferred reasons. Rumors that build on themselves, posted in blogs, e-mails, phone calls—and then the authorities jump onto the bandwagon. Rising stars at regulatory agencies need a story to build a career on. They produce serious white papers with weasel words in the text, but strong sound bites in the summary for the news media. There are hosts of regulatory authorities to work through. There's the EPA, the various health commissions in Europe, and funny little groups with important sounding names that can easily be confused with really important groups. There's always a blog willing to take up the cudgels that something is unsafe if they get prestige, power, and advertising revenue for being ahead of the crowd. There's no question that some of the processing and shipping methods that any industry/country uses are, at best, questionable in today's world. Any time you have a process unchanged for many years, something isn't going to pass muster by some modern standard. Enough little torpedo rumors hitting under the waterline, and the ship goes down.

So who could pull together a statistically defensive study that could rapidly damage things? Information spreads so quickly now—it would have be timed perfectly. From little countries and backwater web sites that can't be tracked back to by the angry mobs later. It can work, because there are a lot of people sitting out there, waiting to hit that sell button. It's all numbers. For this to happen, the investment analysts have to sit in a room, push spreadsheets around, and the bottom line has to show a crash for the currency based on projections. All those portfolio managers dreaming of that magic .03% result—living proof that they are the Masters of the Universe. What will or won't happen doesn't matter. It's those projections, and acting first to protect their bank/country/corporation/wealthy client. Then the bulls are loose, trampling the crowd running in terror before them.

Conceptually, a disease epidemic and a financial bubble revolve around structural changes. Contagion is the key. Physiological contagion for a flu epidemic and psychological contagion for a market bubble. That's the little weasel reports flitting around the Internet, mutating like a flu virus and spreading by e-mail, faster than air transmission.

What's the downside? Well, the country is devastated—children are hungry in the streets, the wealthy are destroyed. There is that. Paul then comes in, buys assets on the cheap, and doubles his money again on top of his vast profits from the currency manipulation. Yes, that is a plan that even my evil master would embrace. Should I present it? Shall I rationalize to myself, by acknowledging that my family's safety, nay, their very continued existence, is dependent on my coming up with something like this? While I may guess about what happens to all of them in that far-off country, I know exactly what would happen to us. Rationalization, yes. Reality, certainly.

Lucretia spent the next few days laying out the details. What regulatory agencies would have to do what, and when. Who to contact at the agencies with what proof for actions to the taken. What blogs in the world to be encouraged with gifts and grants. Who would profit off the intermediate steps. And the financial investments—hedges to make before the ball starts to roll.

She sat back and contemplated her plan. Karla bought a legend for a girl, and it was the anomalies that tripped it up. The men with no tradecraft skills, the weak-minded that no one would use as agents unless there was no other choice. And here, studying her nice diagram, are the weaknesses in their economy, in their worldview, that they deny and ignore—papered over because they had to believe things are a certain way. They firmly believe, basking in their power and glory, that the world has to be 'this' way, without question or deviation allowed. But it isn't that way. Surprise!

SWITZERLAND. LUCRETIA PRESENTS HER PLAN

"That is my plan, my lord," Lucretia finished, kneeling on the steps on the dais. Paul sat regally on his throne, scrutinizing her. Lucretia had been offended other times when he had almost ignored her, but now decided that perhaps being ignored was better. Paul was surrounded by his accountants, financial advisors, and other staff. All had been frowning throughout the presentation. She waited, eyes up, shoulders back.

Paul stood and began clapping. The others smiled and joined him.

"The best plan in ages! Implementation shall begin," he commanded. "Dominique is waiting to take you to lunch. You have our gratitude."

"Thank you, my lord," she stammered and was ushered out.

The Cardinal and his people threw themselves into the project, the joy of the old Spanish conquistadors back again as they saw gold out there, shimming in the distance.

"What have you done?" Dominique demanded. "They are never that happy! Now there are smiling faces in the throne room. It usually it takes an execution for them to be that excited."

"Oh, it's a long story," Lucretia replied. "Financial stuff."

"Don't tell me," Dominique begged. "I hate that part of the world. But we have reservations for a lunch at a wonderful outdoor canteen in Zurich. Cesare has been warned off in no uncertain terms, I've been told. You are the fair-haired child now, my dear."

They had a wonderful lunch. The day was bright and sunny, a pleasant breeze refreshing them as they sat, enjoying watching the city about them. Lucretia felt transported to an ancient world. The service was beyond excellent, the waiter's attentions focused by their quick but worried glances at the armed guards sprinkled at tables around Lucretia and Dominique. Royalty isn't treated like this in today's world, Lucretia thought. And I've changed—I no longer notice the guards.

After lunch, the limo came to take Lucretia to the airport.

"A little present from Paul," Dominique whispered, handing Lucretia an envelope. "A surprise."

They kissed, and Lucretia jumped in the limo. She opened the envelope and casually pulled out the document inside. Then she stared at it, open-mouthed. It was a deed for the beach house of her dreams, the one displayed only on her computer that no one else knew about. After the second time she read it, she laughed, shaking her head.

NEW YORK, LUCRETIA THINKING

Lucretia was sitting by herself, at her favorite table in her favorite little coffee shop in New York. Private, with a clear view overlooking the river, she could relax. Tipping well is it's own reward! Sipping a fresh, hot cup of coffee, she brooded. So, what has Paul done wrong here? Oh, not the small legal, ethical, and/or moral issues, all of the little stories that in theory human society uses to measure action by. Because, duh!, all of those are violated. Paul would say those are peasants' rules, and by *The Art of War* rules, he's played a good game. The Emperor has the Mandate of Heaven, Paul would argue, and so makes his own rules. No, what has he done wrong that is going to crash the plan? What, in short, impacts me and my family? Small, selfish, I know, but the mice must watch out when the elephants dance.

He's impetuous and he likes to act for the pleasure of acting. Needs to act, actually. He's cruel, at least by today's milquetoast standards, which is what he would say. He overacts when it's not appropriate or necessary. I wonder about those little whispers—that he seems to be several people? Nutty? Doubtful, she thought. He has been many people over the eons. Perhaps all the memories crowd in. And that isn't my problem, exactly. What my problem is would be if he has misstated the problem in his mind. I've provided a problem solution, IF the right problem is front and center.

Clearly, he's got something else in mind. This crashing event is not the ending point, it's tied to something bigger. This is a trigger; a test, perhaps. He has plenty of money, and there are easier ways to make money. The money flowing from drug sales is more than anyone could spend in a hundred lifetimes. Yeah, well, he has had a hundred lifetimes. Still, it can't be the money. And it can't be just the thrill of conquest. That's there, but the thrill is later, in the part I don't know about. What could it be? No hard knowledge, no little facts to work into a pattern, so the time to let your emotions run free is when you can't get good data.

He thinks he's too smart and powerful to crash. But he's not fireproof, because he's a fanatic. Not so far under the facade is Xerxes, the god-emperor. I may have acted like a soft fool, his tool to be commanded, but I'd rather be my kind of fool than his. One day that lack of moderation will be his downfall. Has been in the past, as I recall my history.

So, enough of Paul. Let's look at my downfall, which is near and dear to my heart. Worst-case scenarios? Now, a successful crime has clear rules. First, no witnesses/partners. Complete FAIL there. Lots of documents, plans, paperwork, fingerprints everywhere. But the fingerprints can be legal, and I've been careful. I can't trust Paul to help or even stay neutral. Cesare would be overjoyed to play with me, and I'd vanish at the first hint of having to provide state's evidence. Heck, I might just vanish at the huge success. They betrayed me at Hal's company—what's a betrayal here? No honor among thieves, for sure. Lose on this one.

Second, a successful crime doesn't look like a crime. Now, that can work here. These are legal investments, at least on the face. It's the fake reports, the pulled strings, and economic havoc arranged that really are a crime, legally. But my fingerprints are not on that those. Okay, win on that one. And the money flows? The lawyers and accountants sign off on those, not me. The money to purchase the beach condo he gave me? What bank did that ooze out of? It would be just like Cesare to somehow make it look like a forgery on my part. How to check? Maybe I should order title insurance? I can tell them that's what people do in this part of the world, if anyone asks.

So, I'm not doing too badly. Now back to Paul. The real danger is if he has mis-framed the problem. Wrong from the get-go. Solve the wrong problem, and the world whacks you. He is obsessed with power and glory, and that's not good for dispassionate reflection. Again, I don't know his ultimate goal, so I can't assess if the correct problem is being solved here. Normally, I'd shift reference points for the decision and change the gain/loss specifications, but I just don't have the information. Or really understand his mind to even start to guess what he's thinking. Still, I'm doubtful.

Overconfidence? That he has, but then, not. He's made lots of mistakes in the past. I hear rumors. Heck, read the history books, carefully reading between the lines for hints about what really happened. But he's tied to powerful people, and they all make money together. Something goes wrong, they cover for each other. He's used to operating in a simpler world, a smaller world. The interconnections of today's world aren't his style.

Imperious—that's his style. Now, when we discover something new, we make sense of it by associating it with something that we do know about. What Paul thinks, from the perspective of a Persian god-emperor, has some real limitations in today's world. On the other hand, it provides a clarity that sees through some of the fog.

So what are the categories he uses to plug facts and plans into? Categories define how you use the item. Put things in the wrong categories, and you've defined the wrong problem. Once things are in a category, you never look back at the detail. Why? Duh, because you use categories to avoid the detail. Categorization makes analysis possible, but drop the wrong detail and problems can fester and grow, until boom! So score that one as undecided.

Ripples can signal the black swans, but not clearly. Like waves, sometimes they combine. You can have forty-foot waves, nasty stuff, and then suddenly a one-hundred-foot wave, which is disaster. Or that one in Alaska with its seventeen hundred-foot wave! That's what I don't think he's allowed for, Lucretia realized, nodding to herself. I found an amplified event, and positive feedback goes big fast. I don't think he really expects the size of what's going to happen. She put down her pen with a sigh and shrugged her shoulders. I've done my job. Given an assignment, done the work. Obeyed orders. Orders from people who betrayed me before, and certainly are doing it again.

Which raises an issue, she grimaced. Back to little me. A regular review of goals is a critical thing to do, and I haven't done it in years, really. I'm not even sure what my goals are anymore, except putting food on the table and making the mortgage payments. Life takes over; we do as we are told, we do against what we are told, we do something that we enjoyed once but didn't analyze why we enjoyed it, and the net result is that what we think are our goals may not be our goals at all. That seminar pointed out that we may have chosen our life work based on a misperception of what was actually required to do that work. Check off that box! Or the work may change, such that what we really enjoyed/were good at, changed also. Check off that box, too! Figuring out investment puzzles has turned into destroying countries. And now there's family out there, Hal and Cali, who are in complete conflict with the course I'm on.

It's the daily compromise on this and compromise on that and after a while, the original goal vanishes, and the life becomes tying the compromises together. Linked random compromises don't make any sense.. Is it any surprise my emotions are all over the place? And my choices are limited. Drugs, alcohol, self-destructive behavior, or therapy aimed at continuing the existing nonsensical pattern—those will not work long term, although some may get by from day to day. But I have to keep at it for a while. Cali and Hal need the information that I can give them.

Lucretia pictured Paul, sitting on his throne, saying "Well excuse me for having enormous flaws that I don't work on!" She laughed.

CHAPTER 15. CALI'S SAGA

THIS IS A BAD IDEA.

"Hal, I have to go back there," Cali shouted, frustrated, waving her arms at Hal, who was scowling at her. "I know it's a bad idea, but I'm the company face now. No one else has the time."

"We've been over this," Hal countered. "It all makes perfect sense, clear and clean and unarguable. Which is part of what I don't like about it."

"Someone has to clean up the mess from the attack. The police have some wild ideas about some of our weapons," Cali argued.

"Not wild ideas, correct ideas," Hal smiled. "But they have no real evidence. Anything there can be blamed on the attackers."

"There are some bullets in walls—that kind of stuff. Some things they found in the ruins of the warehouse," Cali commented, shrugging. "The attorneys say it's clean, and the cartel says it's clean."

"That isn't exactly what they said. To be precise, they say it stinks of a setup and a trap. They do say it has to be dealt with, but there are ways of dealing with it other than you jumping into the middle of it. That's quite different from clean. The diametric opposite, actually."

"Fine. I was just trying to make you feel better about this. I think it sucks, too, and I don't understand it. The police problems were from people from a different precinct who were not even supposed to be there."

"Good Catholics, tied to the Cardinal," Hal remarked. "I've checked a bit and looked at the reports from the cartel's people."

"But it's still a report, and has to be dealt with. I can have some news conferences, clean up some stuff with the company—stay on top of stuff. The cartel said they will have people all over," Cali insisted.

"And you get to do a little shopping? Could be worse. The food is wonderful there, too. If I weren't dead, at least legally, anyhow, I'd be on the plane too."

"I'm stronger than I was," Cali promised. "I can handle this."

"You've only met Grendel. Not Grendeline. You don't have all the power you think you do. Grendeline comes out when you need her, but that process of integrating her, along with whatever disaster has sparked the confrontation, can be exciting."

"Exciting? You have a way with words. But you keep your head down, okay? We don't want them to figure out that you're still alive and start circling around the factory."

"A good point," Hal agreed. "We'll cross our fingers. You stay with security! No little trips on the side. It's a drag having a crowd around, but it is absolutely necessary this time."

"Fine, honey. I'll be okay."

The Investigator's Report

Report on Movements of Subject. Confidential.

This investigator was hired to follow the movements of Subject. Investigator hired several researchers to gain information on the public life of the subject. They were admonished to be subtle and unobtrusive. The key points are attached as schedule A to this report.

The reader quickly looked at the schedule. Padding and fluff, he concluded, annoyed, and then flipped back to the main report.

Investigator was able to determine when Subject would arrive in New York. Several operatives were hired, and Subject was followed the entire route from the airport to the hotel. The investigator was able to plant bugs on Subject's luggage when it was carried into the hotel. Investigator's team also planted bugs in the hotel room before subject arrived. Unexpectedly, the transmissions would cut in and out, which has never happened before. Investigator believes that the subject had some kind of an anti-eavesdropping device with her.

"Fool!" the reader snarled. Of course she did.

Information captured has confirmed the tentative schedule that the investigator was provided. Subject attended three meetings and a corporation board dinner yesterday, all per schedule. Investigator is reasonably certain that the schedule attached to this document will be adhered to by Subject. Intercepted communications and a hard-wired bug placed in the subject's room late last night provided additional assurance as to the quality of this information.

No pictures? the reader wondered. None he decided to share. Hopefully they will give him pleasure. He'll be found in an alley tomorrow anyhow, and his office will be destroyed.

The reader carefully reviewed the subject's itinerary for the next day, and then scanned it into the computer. The file was encrypted and routed through several web services to wash the traces away. Subject will find that tomorrow will be an interesting day, I think. The reader smiled to himself. The long, lean fingers closed the report and caressed the cover before putting it away.

New York. Dinner at the Cardinals

Lucretia was getting dressed, busily fussing to avoid thinking.

"Big dinner?" her mother asked. "Nice dress. Very expensive!"

"It's new! Designer." She twirled. "Oops...I can't quite move like that, or parts appear." She quickly tucked herself back into place.

"Still, very pretty. Where? A nice young man?"

"No, Mother," Lucretia sighed. "There are none in my line of work. A dinner at the Cardinal's—some kind of special meeting. A celebration of something, I understand."

"The food will be good," her mother commented.

"No question," Lucretia muttered. She twirled in front of the mirror, undecided. "So, does this work?"

Her mother fussed with the dress. "Don't move too quickly, and you'll be fine. More than fine—they will dream of you tonight. Just be glad you don't know what they dream."

Lucretia kissed her mother and the kids and then dashed out the door. The limo was waiting for her.

Lucretia swept into the Cardinal's dining room. "Sorry I'm late. "Crosstown traffic. An accident, or something. Your driver was cursing the whole trip. I learned some new words, which is always a good thing."

"I don't doubt that," Mother Superior observed. "He's had decades of experience. If you knew Sicilian, you'd really have learned something."

"True. What does...well, perhaps I won't ask. I have a rough guess what he meant by it." She stood by her seat.

"You know the Professor, Lucretia," the Cardinal announced. "Mother Superior you know. This gentleman..." Lucretia shivered for a second as she glanced at him. "...is from our European office. The Sandman is his nickname. A cleanup man, you would say in this country."

The man, tall, dark, and handsome, kissed her hand. She cringed as he touched her. She tried to hide her reactions and smiled, but was glad to sit down again.

"He has that effect," Mother Superior laughed, watching her flinch. "It's effective in his line of work."

Lucretia actually blushed. "Did I do something?" trying to cover. "It's been a long week."

"I'm not offended," the Sandman replied. "Your response is typical, and actually quite accurate. I clean up messes, and people fear me. Better that way."

"Yes, and a nasty mess will be cleaned up," Mother Superior promised happily. "That young whore will be here—the wife of that young man we killed. We'll capture her, humiliate her completely, and then sacrifice her. Another major blow against our enemies. As a side benefit, she will showcase what our new drugs can do. What will astonish her is that she will enjoy everything she does because of the drugs, which will complete her humiliation—and her family's."

"As she is the public face of Aeternalis, GmbH this will be another serious blow against them," the Cardinal added. "The young man who was leading the company, killed. His widow, humiliated, exposed as a whore, and then killed. Inquiring minds will want to know, and they will be told—and shown—everything. I doubt the company will recover. Paul's plan seems foolproof and complete."

"Surprising that Cesare isn't here to help," Mother Superior commented, frowning. "This is what he enjoys the most."

"Too much publicity unfortunately," the Sandman answered. "He sent his regrets."

Lucretia smiled, carefully and deliberately picturing a hideous, slow death for Mother Superior to put a sparkle in her eyes. "To success!" and raised her glass.

"Success," all said, and they drank.

"I've counseled against this," the Professor interrupted, frowning, "for what it's worth. I'm considering changing my name to Cassandra because I keep predicting the future and I keep being right."

"The young man is dead," the Sandman protested.

"No body was ever found," the Professor countered. "A quick death certificate and the body vanished. Some hair was found, sufficient to run DNA tests to confirm the ID, but that was all. Odd, at least, I'd say. I know what that would mean if I had planned it. I tell you, they are protected. There's more than their guardians out there—there's something about them. I'm for all revenge, and honored to be assisting the Sandman at the sacrifice. I'm just saying that nothing goes well around them. And you'll remember to tape over that birthmark?" He studied the Sandman. "She'll waltz right out of there if it isn't covered up."

"What can happen?" the Sandman asked, puzzled.

"I don't know how to explain it," the Professor sighed. "I haven't seen it myself, but the boy killed an associate of mine using his birthmark. Part of a related string of disasters tied to them. Rumors have it that the girl did the same to the person who gave us the information we needed to kidnap Mary—also a disaster in the end. I don't know how it could be possible, but it happened. So be careful! Or the plan is off the rails before it starts."

"You really seem against this," the Cardinal observed. "I can't imagine you'd be on their side, so why is that?"

"I'm certainly not on their side. The two of them have destroyed enough of my life already," the Professor answered. "It's just that they are walking revenge effects. Like a rubber band, everything you do snaps back against you. Fine," catching the glances. "I'm just trying to set the stage here. This isn't a piece of cake. I've sat through several of these joyous plans that morphed into complete clusterf...well, disasters. If it goes as planned, you're welcome to throw my advice back at me, but it is goes badly, then this is all on your heads. "

"They killed my daughter's father," Lucretia snarled, picturing the Sandman burning to get the right tone in her voice. "This whore was part of that murder. She and her husband destroyed the cartel's computer and financial network and stole a great deal of money. It has cost me a great deal of time and effort to repair the damage they caused and earn the money back."

"Good," Mother Superior smiled.

Lucretia suddenly had the urge to bolt. But I always have that urge, she thought. Everyone does.

"Watch the Internet feed," the Professor told them. "And try and make sure your office isn't, because productivity will go to zero. We've gone to a lot of trouble to set this up. It's going to be a hell of a show."

"Lucretia, Paul tells me you have an exciting investment opportunity coming up," the Cardinal declared.

They've tested me, Lucretia realized and I passed. "Yes. Permission to speak freely?"

"Yes, my child," the Cardinal replied. "We're all friends here."

"Well, it's like this..."

She was interrupted by a servant dashing in, who whispered to the Cardinal. The Cardinal nodded, smiling. "I'm sorry to interrupt you, Lucretia, but you will find this enjoyable."

A large-screen television was revealed on one wall, a news program running. "A corporate executive was kidnapped today," the newsman stated. A picture of Cali popped up from a news conference earlier in the day. "This young woman seems to have been abducted tonight on the way to a business meeting. Four security guards were killed, but there was no evidence of any harm to the young woman."

The Cardinal and Mother Superior were laughing, pointing. The Sandman was watching intently.

Lucretia watched the television, again picturing Mother Superior being shot to head off her panic. Cali captured! Lucretia couldn't let of her real emotions come through. Mother Superior tortured, Lucretia frantically pictured, and that kept a smile on her face.

"Now, watch this part," the Sandman announced, leaning forward.

"We have been informed that the dead guards had extensive criminal records," the newsman continued, reading from a sheet of paper passed to him. "It has been reported to us that two of the guards were known drug killers. The obvious question is why this young woman, an officer of a major corporation, would hire drug killers to guard her. One wonders whether there are other surprises coming."

"Very good," the Cardinal congratulated the Sandman. "Well

293

planted."

"It's a start," the Sandman replied, sitting back. "There will be more, and then tomorrow the fun will really begin."

Lucretia studied the newscast intently. What's being said, what isn't being said? Poor Cali! What can I do? Wait—I have a way of contacting Hal. Lucretia timed her happy smile with a remark from Mother Superior, who was beaming at the turn of events.

As Lucretia was leaving the dinner party, the Cardinal mentioned, "Make sure you leave the night of the twenty-ninth open, my dear. It will be an evening to remember."

"I'll do that, Your Eminence," Lucretia promised, carefully asking nothing more.

"Are you not curious?" Mother Superior wondered, watching her carefully.

"The older I get," Lucretia answered, "the less I want to know. It just seems easier some days that way."

"Wise, my child," Mother Superior smiled, taking Lucretia's arm in hers. "Let's go to the limo." They left.

On the ride home, sitting in the dark limo, Lucretia kept a smile on her face as she wracked her mind, frantically trying to think.

CALI & GRENDELINE.

Cali's day was not going well. Now, late for an important charity dinner, she was rushed out of her hotel towards the waiting limo. There were security men in front and in back of her as she stepped out onto the brightly lit streets of downtown Manhattan.

A loud car crash down the street; that unmistakable sound of metal crunching, hard. People were suddenly shouting, and faint screams.

Cali later remembered that she stopped, turning to look toward the accident, Then popping sounds, an electric shock convulsing her body. A streetlight's harsh glare, her starting to fall, then all was blackness.

Cali struggled in a dark dream. Vines twisted around her feet, climbing up her legs. Leeches were on the vines and biting into her. The she-wolf appeared before her, urging her on, looking behind her with terror. The dream faded and she woke up slowly. I'm in a room...dark...dirt floor...where are my clothes? She was so dazed that it didn't even mean anything to her. She lay on the dirt floor; semi-conscious, exhausted and then she faded back into the warm darkness.

"This is nice," Grendeline remarked cheerfully, examining the room. "Reminds me of old times. Naked, beaten, filthy, lying on a dirt floor in a dungeon. Yeah, brings back memories, it does. 'Course, I usually put people in these positions, but I've been here myself. You know," sitting on a rock, smiling at Cali, "it does bring out the essence of a person, don't you think?"

Cali lifted her head and glared groggily at Grendeline. "A sarcastic figment of my imagination. That's what I need now. Moral support."

"You don't need moral support," Grendeline sniffed. "You need immoral support. You need to get your butt in gear, literally, and figure a way out of this hole. Otherwise, you're dead meat. Fortunately for you, I'm as immoral a support as you'll find."

"Hal warned you were much stronger than Grendel was. Ah, sorry, I'm not usually this pitiful" Cali sighed. "It's been a rough couple of days."

"Pitiful?" Grendeline scoffed. "You're pretty pitiful most of the time. Wandering around that factory, feeling sorry for yourself, complaining about the dirt on the factory floors and all the time that your daughter takes out of your schedule! Lucky to be alive, you are, and your daughter, too. Worrying about foolish things—yeah, I'd say that's at least pitiful."

"Well, thanks!" Cali growled, picking her head up. "Fine. I know you've lived a thousand lives and seen it all. You're just like my mother— always 'I've seen worse.' Well, yeah, but the first time through, it isn't so much fun."

"Not like your mother," Grendeline warned. "I'm called a she-wolf too, but not like your mother. Call me the water witch, the elemental. There are many forces in this world. I'm the deep life. Don't you know? Were you listening to Hal?"

"Kind of," Cali mumbled. "It was hard to follow sometimes. What do the philosophers say? A word describing a new experience isn't a word because there isn't any meaning inside the recipient."

"You'd do better to read comic books," Grendeline scolded. "All those fancy words in your books are mostly nonsense. But yeah, until you've walked in someone's shoes, or sandals, you can't understand them completely."

"This doesn't look so good," Cali whined, slumping, a tear running down her face. "My daughter will never know me!"

"Just when you think life can't disappoint you, it jumps to prove you wrong," Grendeline hissed, shaking her head as she stood up. She glared contemptuously at Cali. "I need a word past pitiful for you, my pretty. 'My daughter will never know me, boo-hoo.' Better she doesn't know the sniveling worm crying in front of me! Look, lady, that was a good beating you got, and, well, the other stuff, too. I've given and I've got, and I know. You lived, which is the first step. Yeah, there's your daughter crying for her mother back, and your mother frantically looking for you, and your hero husband searching for you. And that blonde, Aliston? The one with breasts like overripe melons and that sad, helpful look? She will be there next to Hal, her body quivering, tossing her hair just ever so slightly as she stands close by his side to reassure him and help him through his loss."

"That slut! That whore!" Cali screamed, jumping up, livid. "She won't raise my daughter! I'll tear her carefully combed hair out by the roots—all of it!" Cali stomped around the grey, rocky terrain.

"Better," Grendeline declared. "Anger is good. You know, I remember when it was the wealthy who had places like this." She studied the dirty cave. "The poor just slept in the rain. A nice cave like this? People killed for shelter from the elements. But it isn't good enough for you, is it, princess? Of course..." glancing down Cali's body. "...they had more hair than you do."

Cali followed her eyes. "Waxed," Cali mumbled, embarrassed. "And I used to think that hurt! Everything is perspective."

"Fashion," Grendeline laughed. "I could tell you stories about what women have done over the eons. Maybe another time."

Cali slumped down, exhaustion overcoming her.

"Poppies, I think," Grendeline whispered, and waved her arm gently.

Cali fell deeply asleep for a few hours. She woke up, refreshed, and looked around. "What's next?" she forced herself to ask.

"You'll live for a while," Grendeline answered, "although you might not really call it living. Oh, I'm a hallucination. Whether it's the drugs, the stress, or your need, here I am! They have a plan for you. You are a toy, and they are playing with you. They are keeping you alive, very alive, actually, and broadcasting pictures of what they are doing to you to the world, trying to get your family to do something stupid. How long you'll be alive for isn't quite clear. Humiliation and torture are on the cruise-ship agenda for the near future, that's for sure. They are desperate to get to your family, and here you are, a big fat prize cow."

"Moo. I needed that. So, this place makes my butt look fat? Thanks." She pondered. "I'm hearing you say that this is not going to be a good day."

"Depends on how you define the good," Grendeline countered. "There are women who make their living doing what you will be doing, but they have a different attitude towards the process and different reasons for what they do. Look, I've lived long centuries where this is what happened all the time. People are tougher than they think."

"Will I still be pretty?" Cali pleaded. "Will Hal still look at me with desire?"

"Not in our control," Grendeline sighed. "But what can you control?"

"How I feel about it," Cali acknowledged.

"Good," Grendeline replied. "Now sleep. You'll need it, honey."

Another day passed, and Cali was back in her cell.

"Wow, that's a drug," Grendeline remarked, her eyes opening up.

"That's an improvement from the old ones. And I've done them all. Things I like, I've done twice." She hummed cheerfully.

"Yeah, it's all over the colleges," Cali muttered, exhausted. "People pay big money for these."

"I can see why," Grendeline agreed. "These drugs are really temptation. And you know what they say about temptation? Do you really think it is weakness that yields to temptation? I tell you that there are terrible temptations, which require strength and courage to yield to! Oscar Wilde knew temptation, let me tell you."

"That's at least a positive take on this disaster," licking her lips. She grimaced. "Yuck, that is a weird lipstick flavor. Because I think I yielded to everything offered today. Wow, those drugs are strong!" Her thoughts twisted around and around, the room spinning for a minute.

"Temptation is external meaning shouting at you," Grendeline advised. "You can never be tempted to do what you don't want to do, you just have to recognize your choices as your inspiration. That doesn't mean people won't write nasty things about you, but at least you'll enjoy doing it."

"It's getting harder," Cali sobbed. "I'm wearing down. I don't know what to do."

Grendeline contemplated her sadly. "Sleep is always good," she whispered, and Cali passed into a black land.

Another day passed. "Did I really do what I think I did?" Cali asked Grendeline. "The days are floating in and out, and I'm thinking either I'm in an endless porno movie or delusional. I was hoping for delusional, actually."

"Well, I'm not sure it was really 'you' doing it," Grendeline answered carefully. "More like 'done to,' technically. If you want to be precise."

"That's worse," Cali concluded, worried, "if you are being nice about it. Did it, huh?"

"'It' implies a singular action. Those were definitely not singular actions. And all broadcast on this computer network thing. In my day, people just peeked in the windows. Now the whole world peeks in. I will say that they seem to think it's going well. They all seemed to be enjoying themselves."

Cali groaned and held her head in her hands.

"You're not the first to do those things, my pretty. Although," Grendeline mused, "you may be the first for that combination on the Internet. That was rather creative—I have to give them credit for that. They are getting, what do they call it? Hits? Their advertising isn't that creative, but it seems effective."

"I'm going to be sorry I asked this, but what would the advertising be?" Cali steeled herself for the answer.

"Has the beauty of the sexual act ever been so crassly exploited? See for yourself," Grendeline answered. "Simple, catchy, and you can hum the tune."

"That's supposed to make me feel better?" Cali mumbled.

"Call it method acting," Grendeline offered helpfully. "It is necessary to feel the part of the oppressed, trapped, helpless victim. In Hollywood, they would put you through this and you'd have to pay tuition. Here, it's free. I'm not sure the drugs are really fair, though. Makes it look voluntary when it really isn't."

"Those are strong drugs," Cali mumbled. "I thought they would be the ones I'd seen, but NO! You know my mind. I've tried a few, but they were nothing like these. These are pleasant and fun, and I want more of them and it doesn't matter what happens. That's nasty."

"They don't even have side effects," Grendeline remarked. "They actually help some of the basic body processes work better, and the commentary promises that they make a girl lose weight. Maybe even reshape things, so, yeah, nasty, but nice. Certainly better living through chemistry."

"I lose weight and my butt gets smaller? That's a hell of a drug!" Cali exclaimed. "What happened to the good old days when you had to suffer with terrible side effects to prove your commitment to the drug and a life style?"

"Breasts bigger, too," Grendeline continued. "And they firm up the under-chin and make you more regular."

"What, you're reading the brochure while I'm being violated in every possible way? With the whole world watching?" Cali protested. "Thanks for the help!"

"You didn't seem to be objecting that much, actually," Grendeline countered. "Ecstatic lust was the primary mood. You know, you have a pretty face when you smile. I read some of the postings off the Internet."

Cali put her head back in her hands.

"Well, I chalked it up to the drugs," Grendeline offered. "I thought someone should be on your side."

"Builds strong bodies twelve ways, makes you more beautiful and shapely, and burns calories through orgasmic lust. Side effects: violating every societal norm for a woman, including some they hadn't bothered to write down yet," Cali counted up the advantages on the fingers of one hand and the disadvantages on the fingers of the other hand. She stared at her hands. "I'm thinking that they won't be able to manufacture enough to meet the demand. And here I am, prime advertising copy. Owww," she moaned, shifting position. "Some things are a lot more fun on the drugs than when they wear off. I'd love to have something soft to sit on." She glared at Grendeline. "No remarks about my fat butt."

"Societal norms for a woman? Could be worse—female ducks have evolved complex vaginas to control the results of unbridled attentions of male ducks. Aggression is part of the natural world, I'm afraid. Although, your enthusiasm and drive surpasses even the lustful rutting I've seen in the wild. Amazing. I wonder if they will give you some of the royalties? Good work should be rewarded."

Cali glowered at her.

"Well, your husband has seen everything anyhow," Grendeline offered cheerfully.

"My gynecologist hasn't seen all of those things I did today," Cali grumbled. "Ouch," as she slowly changed position again, moving very slowly. "Make that my proctologist also."

"So, will it be a different society when everyone knows everything about everyone?" Grendeline wondered. "I'm not sure I like that. It's the vicious savage in me. I don't like the idea of people mellowing out. Boring."

Cali had finally worked her way into a comfortable position, and was watching Grendeline.

"I was listening to them talk while you were, let's say, semi-conscious but focused," Grendeline reported.

"That's a nice way of describing it," Cali conceded.

"Good and not, my pretty. They are going to pump you full of medicine and more drugs. They want you healthy and pretty. Not," Grendeline quickly added, "that you're not pretty, but they want to really get you glowing. Then they are going to sacrifice you in a Santa Muerte rite. With animals, if I understood them correctly. It should be very dramatic."

"Oh, it just gets better and better," Cali growled. "I'm thinking that crying now would be therapeutic?"

"Really, I'm not much for that myself," Grendeline replied. "I prefer to cry tears of joy over my fallen enemies. What do you think?"

"Some days the statue, some days the pigeon," Cali declared. "You know, you've been good for me. I'm thinking about what I'm going to do to them, debating the temperature at which to sauté their private parts, for example, and I'm feeling better. I've seen this movie," frowing. "Robin Hood, the original. That archery tournament that was a trap. They're trying to draw the family in, too. And Hal, that idiot, will take the bait. Shit."

"When something bad happens to you, you have three choices. You either let it define you, let it destroy you, or let it strengthen you," Grendeline announced, studying Cali. "You know, Cali, humans are literally crazy. They live in three worlds, all at the same time. World one; the external world interacting with the person inside you; World two; the social world's demands and structure interacting with the person inside you; and World three; the person inside you interacting with yourself. Now, they've got you focused on you and the social world, and they have you tearing yourself apart. All that stuff about how people preach one lifestyle and practice another? They've got you practicing the life that they preach against. As long as you take the bait and live in their world, you've lost. You're filled with humiliation and contempt for yourself because you're filled with what others are thinking. You have to focus on the 'you' within you, and then focus on that real world that is banging into you. What the social world makes of all this is their problem, not yours, unless you bring it inside. The social world is a vampire. You have to invite them across the threshold and just like a vampire, the social world will suck the life out of you for its pleasure. For what it's worth, people who matter will realize what you were put through and understand. People hate posers, but embrace the real person fighting the good fight."

"There are things in the last few days—and coming—that are going to be hard to be proud of."

"Honey, you're going to find that many of the truths we cling to depend on your point of view. If you were in the business, you'd be paid more for your next movies. If 'proud' is some social fantasy of the good mother, then your actions don't fit that model. If proud is an internal evaluation, then only you can decide," Grendeline advised. "Those were some pretty impressive physical feats you accomplished there. I'm a goddess of fertility, and mating is what it's all about. I've seen a lot of rituals, and you'd be a star."

Another day went by. Cali was so drugged that she could barely remember what went on. When she did, she pushed her hands over her eyes to make the memories go away.

"How can I take this?" she cried, slumped over in the cell in the dark. "I thought the torture was the worst, but it isn't. It's knowing my family knows what I'm doing and they are ashamed of me."

"You do what you have to do to survive. That's the way it is and always has been. Your family knows that what you are doing is what you have to do to survive. Do you think they want you to nobly resist to the death for a social, external meaning that so they can impress their friends? Real family cares about you, not the outside world. Anyone who kills or damages his or her family for social acceptance isn't human. Not even animal, maybe. Certainly filth."

"I can't tell if it's killing me or making me stronger," Cali mumbled.

"You're wearing down because you insist on doing this alone. Open to life. Open to me. Open to the strength you need. Or you will die—or worse. Broken is worse."

"What was it Hal explained?" Cali recalled, staring at Grendeline. "It was... that there are worse lives than death, and some deaths bring new life."

"Dying to the old, transfigured, reborn. It will be awful, but it's embracing life that makes all the difference. Your hunter ancestors embraced all of it, no matter how horrible. The city people ran and built walls in their minds and around their bodies to keep it out. But you can't run from it," Grendeline replied.

Cali sat quietly, looking at her hands. "No! No sleep!" Cali ordered, glancing at Grendeline, who was about to wave her hand at Cali. "No. A confession has to be part of your new life. See, I read comic books too. Truthfully, I'd read more if they had more bare-chested men in them. Busty ladies don't do much for me."

Grendeline dissolved and reappeared in front of her in a nun's habit. "Make a sign," she commanded, "to show you are penitent and seek forgiveness."

Cali kneeled and bowed her head. "Forgive me, holy mother, for I have sinned."

"What is your sin, my child?" Grendeline demanded. The nun dissolved, a stern woman warrior now standing before Cali.

"I don't even know," Cali muttered, helplessly. "I lost my family, found another. Fought hard, worked hard. Worry when I shouldn't, don't have perspective...no, those are not sins, that's just living." She thought. "I'm being disgraced, humiliated. I'm disgraced forever, ruined in the eyes of the outside world. Worse, my family will pay the price for my actions. Everything I tried to be has been destroyed by what's happened here. I'd deserve it if they didn't come to get me." Biting her lip, Cali glanced at Grendeline, who said nothing.

"That's whining, not a confession, isn't it?" Cali admitted. "Sounds pitiful even to me. Oh, poor Cali! People have terrible things happen to them all the time. Auto accidents, cancer, random chance. I'm just feeling sorry for myself. 'Ain't it awful.', is a losing game to play."

"People are going to do things to you. If you let them control you afterwards, they win twice," Grendeline offered. "When a tree loses a limb, does the tree cry? It grows another. When you trample the grass, does it stay down forever, hurt because the other grass saw it trampled? No, it does what Life commands and rises back up. The Tree of Life flows through all of them, and they go on. When it is their time, they leave their seed behind them and merge with the Tree and the next life. That's what life is all about. Not this social facade you humans carry like a shield to block out the wonder, and the horror, of the real world."

"It's the walls I've built around myself, defining myself as what they told me I was. And now those words are daggers in my mind," Cali mused. "It's the stories. Only against a border can we see, and so how then in an unbounded world, with no borders, can we choose? I'm afraid to go there, but I have to."

"What you think 'they think' is the weight you are staggering under.

You don't know what's in their minds. Hell, they don't know what's in their minds. They are waiting for a clue from you to see what they should think. If you slink in like an impostor, defining yourself as a failure, they are quick on the uptake and happy to play. Stand up, shoulders back, get the twins out there, and at least the men won't be thinking much. You move on. Do you think you are the only woman in the world to be abused, forced to do 'not nice' things?" Grendeline snarled. "I could tell you stories for years about the legions of women have been broken over the ages who didn't deserve any part of what was done to them! Everything you are running away from is in your head, and that is serious. This is real life, not pretense. Lots of the stories they tell you are worse than anything you've done. That little life they want to define around you? That you pay for by their tearing off pieces of you for payment? It isn't pretty either, but it's the accepted story, and works for them. A small life with overdue credit card bills is death by a thousand cuts—far more painful."

"We all die, but not all live," Cali murmured.

"So this is a good time to move from the words?"

"My sin is to have listened to them and separated from life," Cali confessed. "To have confused their Meaning with the real, and to have rejected the inspiration in me. For these and all the sins of my life, I am sorry. Have mercy on me, Mother Goddess of Life."

Grendeline stood before Cali, the woman warrior stern and powerful. She smiled. "May the Tree of Life give you peace, and may you absolve yourself from their sins."

Cali cried, but they were tears of release, a joy rising inside her that had been bottled up, that she thought she'd lost forever.

"No penance?" Cali teased, looking up, her eyes sparkling. "I thought it was traditional."

"Oh, there will be penance," Grendeline promised. "Not the traditional kind, but you must not sin again. Holding to the river of life, finding strength on the inside, and laughing at the outer show. So let's talk. What have they told you about themselves by what they have done to you?" sitting back down. "What can you use against them, if you get a chance?"

"Do to them if I were, say, free to move my limbs, that kind of thing?" moving her arms carefully, grimacing as she did.

"Pitiful job of binding for torture," Grendeline commented, examining the ropes. "If I'd bound you, you wouldn't be able to talk, you'd be in such pain. Really, there is just a lowering of standards in this new world. You have all this fancy material stuff, but no strength of spirit. Sounds like an old person, right? When you are six thousand, two hundred years old, this is how you'll talk. Now, here's what I'd do to them." Grendeline started telling stories.

Cali actually laughed after the last story. "Well, that gives perspective. Sticks and stones may break my bones, but words will only cause permanent psychological scars. If I let them."

"All that dying for a cause and the right, with the chin held up? A good show at the end, but not smart," Grendeline advised. "If you die, you are dead. No children's games here, no standing up when they call 'olly olly oxen free.' Being transfigured into flower food is not recommended."

"So it's: what do they hope for, what do they want, and what do they expect if I act in certain ways? I hate the 'I know you think you know what I think' stuff, but yeah." She put her hands to her head for a moment, and leaned against the wall, shaking. "Those drugs are strong. "They do change a woman. I know they do. I've read about them. I've seen friends change." She was shivering harder. "I can stop them, I think, but it's hard. They tear into my mind, make me think things I shouldn't." Cali peered out as it seemed to darken around her. "There—more are coming in now! "I can feel it." She swept her fingers over her eyes in her mind. The clouds broke and the sun peeked out.

"Nice," Grendeline commented, nodding her approval. "You do have potential, my pretty. Everything is change—you cannot step in the same river twice, etc., so of course you change. You know the speech. And you have controlled the drugs' effects on you. The other women in this place are zombies compared to you. I cringe when you come near them. Their touch is repulsive. Lost souls, I fear. Empty to start with, and when the facade fell, there wasn't anything in its place. Truly, we all die, but not all live."

"The world breaks us all. Afterward, some are stronger at the broken places. Ernest Hemingway, *A Farewell To Arms*. Good comic book, Hal gave it to me," catching Grendeline's questioning expression. "When I had nothing to lose, I had everything. When I stopped being who I am, I found myself. I have nothing left to fear, do I?" staring at Grendeline.

"'*You were born in a prison, Evey. I didn't put you there. I just showed you the bars. You've been in a prison so long, you no longer believe there's an outside world,*'" Grendeline quoted. "I liked V for Vendetta, his rising above suffering. Out of the small stories, into the bigger world, that movie had guts."

"Woman is the depth of the life force—isn't that what the myths say?"

"No Cali 2 and Cali 3," Grendeline wondered, peeking around, "to review the notes? They seemed helpful for Hal. I have to admit that I rather enjoyed them."

Cali laughed. "No, they had the good sense to stay in school. Don't do drugs, kids, and stay in school. Wimps! So life flows through me, and the words mean nothing. And I am denying the experience, life itself, by naming, translating, and classifying every experience that comes. This has to stop.

The tree is deeper than consciousness, and consciousness is only a deceptive guide, the tool of the social norms. The words, the labels, are only tools of the parasites for control. Inside, what can the monsters be but your self pushed away? And how can that be terrifying? And outside, they will fear my monsters when we are friends. Yes," Cali announced. "I think I see."

She stood up. "If I fail, I fail. But I will have tried, which is all I can do. Real failure is failure to try. " She offered her hand to Grendeline. "I name you friend," she stammered. "Will you be my friend? I know your warning to Hal, taunting him with the horror of beholding his love, her mind broken from what he gave to me. I fear, but hope. He was right to give me this chance."

"Do you wish to be friends?" Grendeline demanded, standing up. "Well, we shall see, my pretty, what you are really made of. But I think you're worth the effort. Have you heard the phrase, eat the white? Eat your fears, don't let them eat you. The only difference between a fear that excites you and one that you run from is how you look at it." She smiled, a dark, terrifying smile as she touched Cali's hand.

They dissolved into mist and vapor, roiling in a complex rhythm for a long time, little flashes of lightning coming from inside. After some time, there was Cali within the churning clouds. I can feel the Tree of Life, she exulted. Roots deep into the nourishing soil, the soft water of the rain, and the sun on my leaves, warming me. Out of a cold winter, the buds unfolding, and she felt life fill her. As I was, she wondered, and yet not. She saw the Tree, tall, three-dimensional in the world. And then four dimensions, bringing Jose and her adopted parents back to her, smiling and nourishing her. Finally, the clouds solidified, and there was only Cali—with different eyes. There is no wrath surpassing the wrath of a woman, Cali vowed. She smiled, but it was Grendeline's smile.

LUCRETIA ACTS

At home, Lucretia watched the evening news with her mother. Lucretia carefully moved her hand so only her mother could see, cautioning her about commenting on what they were seeing.

"Terrible crime rate in this town," her mother complained, showing no sign of having seen Lucretia's hand flicker. "I don't care what the statistics show—it's dangerous out there. And this! Isn't that the young woman who heads that questionable company? The company that is trying to defend all those allegations of fraud and weapons violations? I watched the press conference the young woman gave, and she wasn't convincing. They proved that her bodyguards were drug killers! What kind of people are they? And now she is putting on a sex show on the Internet? I hope they put that company, and her, out of business for good."

Actually, the press conference was incredibly convincing, Lucretia thought. She had been really impressed with Cali. It was no wonder Jose had loved his sister. "You're right, Mother," Lucretia agreed loudly. "These people—they have power, they think they can do anything."

Her mother glanced at her. That's the pot calling the kettle black, she sighed to herself. "Well, perhaps justice will come to this woman," her mother snarled. "Wealthy people, they think that they can live by any rules they choose. Maybe she will pay for her conceit." Her mother stood up, touching Lucretia on the shoulder for a moment. "I'll check on the children. I think I hear Jose's computer making those damn game noises." She turned and quietly walked down the hallway.

Lucretia bent forward, for all intents and purposes completely intent on the news for the benefit of the watchers. She hid her phone under a computer tablet, and carefully typed a text on the phone without looking. Then, fumbling with the tablet, she caught a momentary glimpse of the text before sending it.

The next morning, there was a text response. "Moscow rules." She smiled wryly. I'm still Karla, she sighed. She made arrangements and went about her day.

Lucretia & the Professor at Lunch

She told her secretary to dial the number and tell her when the person was on the line. Hiding in plain sight, she thought. "Professor? Hi, this is Lucretia. We didn't have a chance to talk at dinner the other night, and I wondered if you'd care to go to lunch? It has been a long time since we have had the chance to talk."

"Certainly. It would be wonderful to have the chance to go over old times. Where? Fine, I know the place." He absently studied his phone after the conversation ended, rubbing his chin thoughtfully. She's not a casual conversationalist, so this isn't a feel-good talk. Actually, a more purposeful and focused person I've rarely met. So, what's the real plan? Something about that Cali, I'm certain. Shall I share this with our mutual friends? No, I don't trust them even a tiny bit. And I don't want Lucretia's wrath brought down upon me! Let's just see what she is thinking.

Lucretia walked towards the restaurant. She saw a light-blue chalk mark slashed sloppily in the upper-right-hand corner of the fresh graffiti on the wall. She glanced at the wall for a second, gave it a disgusted look for the benefit of the watchers, and then walked into the restaurant. She was greeted by the maître d and was then escorted down a long hallway. As she walked, she heard loud footsteps behind her. She glanced back, worried. A woman dressed identically to her, same hair color and style, passed her and then carefully maneuvered herself into a booth off the hallway, facing the restaurant entry, taking no notice of Lucretia. Nice work, Lucretia thought, as the maître d guided her to a private room at the end of the hallway, far away from the other guests.

The Professor was already in the room, nursing a glass of red wine and idly examining the art on the wall. He turned to greet her. "Long time," being careful to keep his eyes on her face. Distraction is a tool, he knew. Don't relax.

She smiled at him, observing his eyes never leaving her face. A professional, she decided. That's a relief. "Well, let's sit and talk. The food is absolutely wonderful here! Especially for a carnivore like you. I can tell you that the steak is one of the best in the city."

They sat, and then he suddenly tapped his fingernails on his phone. "Odd," he commented, studying his phone closely. "No reception. That's rather unusual." He glanced at Lucretia, waiting.

"Yeah, who would think in this town?" Hal remarked, walking in and pulling the door shut behind him. "Technical problems all over the place. The world is falling apart."

The Professor, paling, stared at Hal. "I knew there was more to this meeting! I'm assuming all the listening devices are off?"

"You are correct," Hal promised. "No transmissions work here, so no one will come to help—or hurt. We have our people ringing this building. I have a gun and a knife, and I killed Grendel in single combat. Perhaps you would care to try your luck?"

"I'll pass," the Professor replied, leaning back, leaving his hands on the table. "You know I don't do the rough stuff."

"It's Cali," Lucretia advised the Professor, as Hal sat down across from the Professor. "She's family to me. Her brother was the father of my son, Jose, I lost the father to the cartels—I can't take losing my son! And you know she's poison to attack! Look what happened to everyone who went after her. You said so yourself at dinner the other night."

The Professor, chewing his lip, contemplated Lucretia. "I suspected this would be the topic of conversation when you called, and decided against saying anything about this to our friends. You know, of course, that if the Cardinal, Mother Superior, and/or any part of the whole gang had any inkling of this, just any little inkling, they would skin us? Slowly, with great pleasure?"

"Clear on that," Lucretia acknowledged. "The Sandman, that cleanup man? He makes my skin crawl even thinking about him."

"And you really don't know about him," the Professor grimaced. "Trust your feelings on this one—you are right about him. I've seen him in action in North Africa."

"Look," Hal declared, "you know why we're here. Your people have Cali. They are torturing and humiliating her and are going to sacrifice her. Perhaps for the sheer joy of it all, perhaps for revenge, perhaps to trap us again—probably for all of the above. Those plans have not worked before. A lot of people are going to be fish food if Cali doesn't make it, and you're on the list. I know you had my adoptive parents killed. I'll drop that past misunderstanding and never pursue it if you help us get Cali out alive."

"You people are not the strongest now," the Professor countered, testing them. "Look at Paul's position, and yours."

Lucretia started to say something and Hal waved her down.

"Not so strong as Paul believes," Hal answered. "Grendel is gone from Paul's side and in a way has joined us. I'm recreating him, actually. That will be a surprise to Paul! And Paul's thinking is ancient and generally wrong. His choices are crazy and sloppy, and you know it."

The Professor nodded his head. "I told them not to attack Cali. Told them not to attack on the family, also. Not because I like you, but because you're bad luck to go after, or protected—who knows? So I'm in stuck in middle of the battle I did everything to avoid and now I have to make a choice? Well, that sucks." He stood up and started to pace. "Sorry, it's the teacher in me. I need a blackboard to write on to think clearly. You've blocked the transmissions—you are absolutely sure? I just want to emphasize it's death for me and Lucretia to be here if the listeners can hear. The slightest whisper to Paul or that demon the Mother Superior, and my last moments would be prolonged and painful."

"They hear nothing," Hal promised. "I'm good with those toys. I actually mixed in a feed from the park, so it seems as though something is happening. They are sitting there, wondering if the equipment is broken, wondering if there is interference, and in general, just wondering. But in all truth, your watchers may have other concerns at the moment, actually. Paul would expect we are in town, and having some of their staff turn up in the river will just confirm that."

"I like that," the Professor observed. "A nice touch. And Grendel on your side? That will be a staggering blow to Paul. Grendel made the Sandman seem like the good fairy."

The Professor sat back down. "Cali's life for the past lives, is that the deal?" He studied Hal. "You could make me do this, well, you know that, of course. I've heard the rumors, and I've done my research. Pull your sleeve up—what's on your arm has power. I wouldn't have believed it before, but it's a stranger world than I used to think it was. You didn't know about that, did you, Lucretia?" the Professor asked, noticing her confused look. "What I was talking about at dinner the other night, you really didn't believe it. Your friend here has some power. He's killed people with it. But," sitting back, shrugging, "they were people who should have been killed. So that's the deal, is it? My voluntary compliance?"

"The deal," Hal agreed. "People make mistakes, time goes by. What happened in the past was meant to be. It would not be better if things happened to people just as they wish. I'm a man of my word." He smiled, Grendel's smile.

"You're most terrifying when you're polite. Does anyone tell you that?" the Professor stammered, his face pale. "But wise. I accept." He contemplated his hands for a moment, sighed, and then looked carefully at Hal and Lucretia. "Okay, here's the deal." He bent forward, drawing on the tablecloth. "This is where the ceremony is going to be and this is what is going to happen..."

HELPING YOURSELF

Cali was lying on the ground again, exhausted after another day's torment.

"Reminds me of old times, it does," Grendeline remarked. "Still, I'm thinking that the modern world has some advantages. All this traditional plumbing is just not sanitary. And your hair! Well, it really needs some work. So, lady, are you going to become something, or not?"

"I'm not seeing the hero bursting through the door to save me, so you're right. I'm going to have to do something about this, and soon. That ceremony is coming up, and while I'm honored at the high esteem they hold me in, this has got to stop."

"And the hero would be? I'm the questioning spirit," Grendeline inquired. "You want the super-heroine, that's yourself, not me. Different union, and the union reps are not to be trifled with."

"I like that," Cali laughed, wiping the dirt off her face. "You, the deep power of the universe, paying your union dues and respecting the contract."

"There are deep powers and deep powers," Grendeline warned, suddenly serious. "It's a big universe. Not today's concern, really, but you've got to shake this 'human story all wrapped in a box' stuff. It's not like that out there. Not even stories, really, it's events, and what you make of them. What was that myth? That the world rests on a turtle, and that turtle rests on another? They get more powerful the further down you go. Trust me, leave the bottom levels alone."

Cali slowly moved herself into a sitting position. "There, that's better. Now, what do I have to work with? Good thing there's no mirror in here—that would really be torment," pulling on a lock of her hair and grimly examining the split ends. "You'd think they'd want me to look a little better than this for the cameras." She grimaced as she slowly stood up. "That hurts," she complained, rubbing her back. "Now, how big is this cell?" She paced it off. "Door bolted, floor dirt, but I think—yes—there is steel or something underneath. Really, a lot of this is show," scratching at the wall. "It's actually metal under there, with just a covering of traditional gunk for effect. Not really mossy stone. The chains are real," she confirmed, pulling on the clasp. "Both legs, and both arms. What, they think I'm Supergirl?"

"I wouldn't say 'girl' at this point in the events," Grendeline commented. "Well, technically."

"Super...well, let that go. So: I'm in here, and hand-to-hand combat is probably out of the question. The walls and floor are metal; I don't know about the roof, but I can't reach it anyhow. Not even a bucket in here, and the janitor isn't cleaning well. It does reek, I've got to admit."

"They don't shower you and clean you up in the morning for your pleasure," Grendeline advised. "No one would watch you like this."

"I'm feeling better and better, just more ravishing every minute." She sat down carefully "Let's see, what do I have to work with? There is my birthmark, but they have covered it up. Even if I uncover it, I can't depend on people looking at it and being affected, as I need them to. Actually, it could make it worse, turning Paul's creatures into homicidal maniacs. Hummm. Ah, but what I do have," she bubbled to Grendeline, "is you. Little colony creatures can take you out to them, I'm thinking, if you want to play. Maybe tear up some of them from the inside, have some fun?"

Grendeline morphed into a horror with extra arms and legs and big teeth, and then slipped back to her human shape. "That was the question to ask the Fisher King, but he's not here, so I'll handle this," she snarled. "Where to start? Kill them all?"

"The one who lacks courage to be a hammer comes off in the role of the anvil. I've done the anvil." She carefully moved her bottom to a new position. "It's time for the hammer." She pondered. "We can't kill them right away. There are the two guards that bring me in and out of here, there are more guards around the, well, production facilities, and there are other support people. Now, with all the transfer of liquids during the show, it would be easy to pass colony creatures to them, but I can't depend on the performers being where I need them when I need them. So it's getting something to the guards first. I think that younger guard. He's brutish, but not as tough as he pretends. The older guard is an inquisitor from the past, all hate and bad intentions."

"Good girl," Grendeline approved. "It doesn't take much—the little creatures pass like a virus. Sneezing, spitting, and licking will do it. Long tongue kisses are very effective when you want to get the creatures back."

"Ummmm," Cali grimaced. "I'm not sure I'd rather not die before trying the open-mouth kisses, but OK, all of those. How long does it take for you to do your thing?"

"Not long for killing, but when you scale it back, a couple of hours for some control," Grendeline cautioned, flexing her fingers, which became long steel claws and then fingers again.

Cali smiled happily. "Food should be coming soon. They said something about getting me cleaned up after dinner. So maybe...a sneeze at the right time...gives you a start? Then maybe...yuck...a kiss after you get a little control of him...and then by morning?"

"Done! It's a plan. But sleep, my pretty...I think you need some sleep."

Cali yawned and then slumped, exhausted, on the floor.

Several hours later, the door opened and the guards tromped in.

"Disgusting!" the older guard sneered. "They told us this was a lady of sophistication and power. I haven't seen anything this repulsive since the Barbary pirate slave ships. I'm not sure that the ships didn't smell better."

"Reeks, it does," the younger guard agreed. "Still, she cleans up pretty well. I'm told the hits on the website are off the counter."

"All this fancy stuff," the older guard complained, unlocking Cali's shackles. "I remember when we'd just have a fire in the square, the townspeople wide-eyed with terror as they watched their friends burn. Easy to get dates after that, I'll tell you. Being a minor church official really had some perks then."

"Come on, lady. Up on your feet." The younger guard dug his fingers into her arms as he pulled her up, enjoying Cali's grimace.

Cali's eyes opened, and she spit into his open mouth from about six inches away. That will do it, she thought.

"Did you see that!" the guard snarled, stepping back and raising his hand to hit her.

"None of that!" the older guard ordered, grasping the younger guards hand. "We are support staff, and the entertainers will put you in the show if you damage the goods. You will be an example of the effects of torture, and they know what they are doing."

"I don't want that," the younger guard mumbled, wiping the spit off his face and backing away. "But I'll cheer them on tomorrow, you whore! "You'll get yours."

I'm thinking you're about to get yours, Cali cheerfully reflected as she was pulled/dragged down the short hallway.

"Here's your project," the guard announced to the two women waiting for Cali. "Clean it up, make it pretty."

"Disgusting," the women hissed, holding their noses. "Quick, get it into the shower." The older guard held her under the arm, and she carefully sneezed in his direction. He'd hurt me, Cali knew, regardless of the consequences. He wants to. I can feel it.

Cali acted her role, which wasn't difficult. Her lines were essentially "No," "Don't," passionate moans and occasional screams. Method acting isn't that hard, she told herself. Why do they pay actors all that money? She did manage to sneeze in the faces of both women.

"Do you think she's getting sick?" one of the women worried. "We don't want her falling over or looking sickly. They'd blame us."

"Call the doctor," the other woman ordered.

A doctor was brought in twice a day to maintain Cali. He would quickly repair the most obvious damage and pump her full of nutrients and drugs. This call was his third trip here today and he wasn't happy to be bothered.

Did they find you in veterinarian school? Cali wondered. Definitely, "Ugh," a large animal specialist. Doing an exam with a pitchfork? And I don't want to know what's in the IV, she guessed as it started again. Sometimes fun, sometimes not. Her body stiffened as the drugs started to work their way in. Not today, I'm thinking, and she relaxed. Work with it, don't react. Her body started to change the drugs to what she wanted.

Several hours later, they walked her back to a regular room, not her cell—a room with a real bed in it and painted walls.

"Don't get hopeful, whore," the older guard smirked. "Life isn't getting easier. They want you pretty in the morning."

The younger guard didn't say anything. He was just standing in the corner looking at his hands, confused.

"Idiot! You forgot her food," the older guard cursed. "You forgot, you go get it. I have other work to do."

The younger guard nodded and left. The older guard confused, staring at the shackles and chains. "Really don't need those, do we?" he muttered, talking to himself, and he walked out, rubbing his forehead. Cali was unchained for the first time since she had been captured.

"This is progress," Cali cheerfully announced to the walls.

In a few minutes, the door opened again, and the younger guard came back in with the food. He clumsily set her food down on the floor, and then stood there, looking at Cali.

Cali smiled at him, and he actually blushed, his face flushing.

Yuck, Cali thought, you want to talk about torture! But she walked over to him and quickly kissed him, a long, sloppy kiss. After a couple of minutes, she started to disengage, but the guard had warmed to his work.

"No, no, no," Cali insisted, pushing him away. "Like, no offense, but you kind of represent everything I despise in the world." She smiled at him as he stared dully at her. "Remember, you're not the entertainer, remember? Your bosses cut body parts off if people don't do as they say. That would be such a nice body part to lose!" It's too small to bother trimming, she thought, but if you can't say something nice, don't say anything at all.

The guard shook his head and let her go. "Something not right," he mumbled, pressing his hands against his temples.

"You will act just like you always act," Cali ordered. "You and your buddy Frankenstein—you come back tomorrow morning, and we'll see what we can do." Sighing, she winked at him.

The guard smiled, his face lighting up, and he nodded his head. He backed out of the room, taking a final, long look at Cali, who grimaced as he leered, and then he slammed the door, locking the deadbolt.

"Nice work," Grendeline commented, as Cali sat down on the bed.

"Men are such easy prey."

"Much better than a few hours ago," Grendeline advised. "Now, it seems that some of the colony creatures came back. That was nice work on the sloppy kiss, by the way. Disgusting work, but well done."

"Disgusting? Tell me about it! "Do we have a plan?"

"Yes, and it's a good thing. They have some serious work in mind for you tomorrow to warm the viewers up for your sacrifice tomorrow night."

"Sacrifice?"

"Just like the old days. Stretching, skin scraping, and burning—brings back memories, it does." Grendeline sighed happily to herself, then shook her head. "Getting old, must be, to reminisce about old times like that."

"Yeah, well, it's your skin coming off this time," Cali pointed out. "Focus on that."

"That's a good point," Grendeline admitted, frowning. "I always hated that part. Well, they are schemers, controlling their little worlds. I think we'll show them how pitiful their plans really are. Introduce a little chaos, the Joker said."

"Sounds fair," Cali offered.

Grendeline gave her a dirty look.

"So, okay—here's the plan..." Cali began.

THE BIG DAY

In the morning, the guards, the makeup women, and the doctor were under Cali's control. They all seemed more confused than anything else.

"No changes from what you always do," Cali hissed. "Follow the schedule." Another day in the limelight, Cali thought as they cleaned her up and fixed her hair. This should be interesting to explain at my next high-school reunion. What's to explain?

"You know," Cali admitted to Grendeline as the makeup women were fussing over her, "This must be what having minions is like. It's not entirely bad, actually. Is this where I start to see my possible futures, and this one has me in black with black lipstick and an army of faithful followers?"

"The problem is that you have to feed and clothe them, and it gets expensive," Grendeline replied. "Minions tend to be light on brainpower and are just annoying after a while. Grendel would eat them after he didn't need them anymore. Saved a lot of trouble, actually."

"No, that isn't going to work well," Cali mused. "I'll stick with the elf-mother future instead. Okay, looks like it's Showtime." The makeup people stepped back. "Another day, another dollar. Ah-choo!" She sneezed into the face of the new guards that came to take her to the production area. "Sorry," grinning at them. "Must be the lack of clothes—it's cold in here. Brrr!" The guards were starting to look a little confused by the time they reached the production area. That's working faster, she thought happily.

The day was short—filled with degrading and humiliating experiences, with several wonderful orgasms mixed in, but short. About two o'clock, she was taken back to the new room. Acting disgusted and humiliated really doesn't take much ability, she decided as she fell on the bed. Method acting indeed. I wonder if I'm going to get a call from the Screen Actor's Guild demanding I pay them dues? At least I sneezed and coughed on everyone I could. And kissed a few, she recalled, disgusted. Memo to file: don't kiss toads—they don't turn into princes. They will pay for that, in spades.

"We will come at six," the older guard mumbled. "You will be fed and cleaned up, and then you will be taken to the ceremony at nine."

She nodded, completely in character, and fell asleep.

At six, the door opened and the guards came in. Stumbled in, actually, she noted. Carefully keeping completely in character, she let herself be dragged out to be fixed up again. Sitting in the makeup chair, she whispered, "Has the schedule changed?" but got no response. For a second, she feared her control of them had faded, but then she got a wink from one of the hair stylists, and knew they were under her control. Finally, her hair was set and her makeup was perfect. Let's get lots of eye shadow on there, she thought. We want that terrified look. The guard pretended to put handcuffs on her. Nice that I have a ceremonial gown, it gives me someplace to hide a knife and a pistol.

There was a knock and then door opened. The Professor walked in, smiling. He glanced at her and quickly looked away, troubled. "Your birthmark isn't taped, Mrs. English. Make sure it's taped on the substitute, or this won't work."

Stunned, she stared at him.

"I'm on your side. Your husband made me an offer I couldn't refuse. Can we talk? But could you, well, cover that birthmark?"

Cali put her hand over her birthmark. "Ignore them," Cali told the Professor, waving at the guards and the makeup women. "They are zoned out."

The Professor quickly examined the guards and makeup people, who stared blankly at him. "This is great stuff! Give me the formula sometime—

313

we can make some money."

Cali studied him for a moment. "Perhaps if I live?" Cali mentioned.

"There is that. Sorry, I lost focus there. The good news is that there is a rescue party coming, but the bad news is that I'm not sure how well it will work. It is fortunate that you seem to have some plans."

"A simple plan," Cali snarled. "You should stay out of the way. I'm planning for bloody."

The Professor sighed, shaking his head. "I told them this was a mistake. Why am I always right about your family? And never about the stock market?"

"Send the priest in now," Cali ordered, an oddly cheerful, yet terrifying look flickering over her face. "I have a surprise for him."

The Professor eyed her appraisingly, and nodded. "Your wish is my command! The Sandman gives me the creeps." He briskly walked out of the room, closing the door behind him.

"After I control the priest, kill the guards," Cali instructed the dazed guards. "You know, knives in their chests?"

The guards dully nodded.

The Sandman, dressed as the head priest, strode in, two guards following closely behind him. Cali shuddered for a second as her first glimpse of him brought back the horror of his touch.

"I've been waiting for this," Grendeline hissed. "Waiting for a long time for this little fish. Thought he was the equal of Grendel, he did? He will pay for his pride."

The Sandman studied her revulsion. Then, grinning, he walked up to her, standing about a foot away.

Cali spit into the Sandman's face. Livid, he raised his hand, but froze, eyes widening in shock. Cali laughed as the colony creatures tore him apart from the inside.

"Don't apologize," Cali advised him, as the Sandman's mouth gaped open, his eyes wide with terror. "Choke and die."

The Sandman shook, his mouth frothed, and he collapsed.

Cali motioned and the Sandman's guards were slaughtered. Then she touched the foam around the Sandman's mouth and put some in her mouth, experiencing what he went through via the colony creatures. Nice, she decided. "You should have known," she taunted. "You have to sacrifice a virgin. It's the old magic." She laughed with delight

"Very, very nice," Grendeline mused. "You perhaps have a talent for this."

"I'm discovering new talents all the time," Cali laughed.

"The lustful temple priestess, the whore for the gods, she who brings life, has another side—the black goddess who brings death," Grendeline observed thoughtfully. "Your mother will be impressed. I'm impressed."

Cali, shocked, stopped for a second.

"Not a time for quiet reflection," Grendeline ordered. "It's something to think about later. You've started well, but the battle has barely begun. Let's keep going."

"Okay, plan," Cali told the minions. Minions? Ugh, they will probably want workmen's compensation insurance and a pension plan. I can see why Grendel ate them. Cali took the robes off the priest, and one of the makeup women took her place as the sacrifice. No underwear, Cali sighed. Never any underwear when I need it.

"Get the Professor in here," Cali ordered a guard, and he rushed out.

In a minute the Professor walked in. He stared at the Sandman lying dead on the floor and then shook his head. "You people are just bad news." He looked critically at Cali in her priest's robes. "A little short, but it will be dark. Do you have any heels?"

One of the makeup women shuffled around and found some six-inch heels. Cali strapped herself into them. These are going to be fun to run in, she worried. Be positive! Everything Fred Astaire did, Ginger Rogers did backwards and in heels. It can be done.

"The plan was?" Cali demanded. "What?"

"It was this. . . " the Professor explained.

Cali mulled over what he had said and then glanced at the Professor. "Schemers trying to control their worlds. I'm going to show the schemers how pathetic their attempts to control things really are."

IT'S SHOWTIME!

At nine o'clock, Cali led the makeup woman out of the room and down the hallway to what had been the 'performance room', now remodeled for her sacrifice. And to think in high school I worried about whether I'd be popular enough to be asked to the prom! Now the whole world wants to watch. Of course, they'd have wanted to watch this at the high school prom.

They slowly paraded into the room. There was loud, Middle Eastern music playing, and the room was dark except for the spotlights on the stage. Cali waited, as the Sandman's script called for an introduction before the sacrifice. Good thing, too, she realized. Otherwise I'd have no time to plan at all. She examined the room as the announcer started to talk.

There were perhaps forty people sitting in the room. She recognized some of the men who had helped torture her and the sex stars, all of who were joking and laughing as they looked towards her. The Cardinal, she thought, and others. Lucretia? Now she knew how the Professor was brought on board.

Exits? She quickly confirmed where and what.

Lucretia sat there, wearing an elegant black dress and a confident expression, making conversation. In her mind, over and over she saw the spymaster Karla, walking slowly across the bridge dividing into Berlin from the East German border. He stops, fishes in his pockets, turns to shield his lighter against the cold wind, enjoying the first few drags off his cigarette, nothing out of ordinary. Exactly as he had always been. Just because she was turning her back on everyone in this room and betraying them, as they deserved, didn't mean she could drop her act for a second. Only a short time longer, she promised herself. That made it easy keeping the smile on her face.

The announcer finished his spiel and excitedly waved his arms toward Cali and the sacrificial woman. As the men started to hoot at them, Cali gently touched the woman and they started to walk to the podium. I can't wait, she realized. She doesn't look enough like me, and I don't look enough like the Sandman, so here goes. Let's see: gun, knife, and gasoline. Nothing like a fire in a small place.

Turning, she tore the robe off the makeup woman, revealing that she wasn't Cali. People jumped up, shouting and pointing, as Cali tossed gasoline on the sex stars, lit a match, and ducked. There was a mini explosion and the fire sprinklers went off, but that was little help to the burning, screaming men, rolling on the floors in agony. Cali pulled out her pistol and shot two guards. The guards under her control were shooting other guards.

A firefight in an enclosed, dark space is chaos. Initially doused by the sprinklers, the fires were regaining power and the smoke was thickening as the sprinklers only dribbled. Who shot the water line? she cursed. Idiots!! Add that to the hiring criteria for minions. She saw the Cardinal, Lucretia, and others running frantically out. Cali tried to reach an exit, but out of the corner of her eye, saw more guards rushing in. She ducked, shot at them and realized that she was trapped.

Blood fell instead of rain this night, she thought, smiling as another fell. At least I went out with a flourish.

Suddenly there were several bursts of automatic rifle fire from outside the room, and the guards at the doorway fell dead.

Hal and his troops burst in, the troops taking post and quickly killing the few guards left.

"Over here," Cali screamed. "Don't shoot me!"

Hal shouted and his troops moved to form a perimeter around Cali. "Clear," the squad leaders shouted, and they rushed out as the fire began running up the walls.

Mother Superior shoved Lucretia to the floor in her haste to get out of the room, stepping over Lucretia as she struggled to get back up.

"Well, fuck you very much," Lucretia mumbled to the floor as she pulled herself to her feet and then stumbled outside. As Lucretia tottered into the street, limping, one heel broken, five men in black uniforms surrounded her. She screamed as they threw her into a black van, slammed the door, and roared off into the night.

"What the hell?" Mother Superior stammered, staring at the van.

"Out of here," the Cardinal hissed. "Before they get us, too." They ran for it, their retinues following them.

They found the Professor in an alley, nursing a burn on his arm and missing his eyebrows but otherwise okay. "Fine fucking security you people have!" he swore, glaring at them. "I'm going back to Mexico, where it's safe."

Hal was half carrying, half pulling Cali along as they ran.

"I remember this," Hal laughed. "No underwear in Ann Arbor either—one of my favorite memories. Over here, honey." He guided her into the waiting van. He banged on the roof, the driver nodded, and they roared off.

"You know," Hal complained, sitting back, glancing at Cali, "since I've met you, people have tried to stab me, shoot me, incinerate me, and chop me up. I am beginning to suspect we're enmeshed in the middle of something sinister here."

"You think?" Cali laughed. "Duh!" She snuggled in next to him.

"Whatever you did really helped," Hal admitted. "We had a great plan—load weapons and run in, then improvise. You had it mostly covered by the time we got there."

After the initial thrill of the battle and rescue, Cali suddenly had a hard time talking. She caught the glances others had thrown at her. "So, heck of show?" she mumbled.

"At least," Hal promised. "You're in my inappropriate thoughts! One of the most impressive shows I've ever seen, and I've seen..." He caught himself. "I saw many things in college. Before we met." He winked at her. "I can think of nothing I have ever seen that was even close in quality and imagination."

"I'm not sure that makes me feel better," Cali sighed. "Umm...and you saved the tapes?"

"In the archives, for research purposes only," Hal replied. "It's important to know how your opponent's mind works, and you can only know that through their deeds. Look, honey. Your mother is a fertility goddess. She had some small criticisms, really, all minor technique issues, but overall, she thought that your work was really exemplary. She started talking about being a priestess prostitute in the ancient world, and then just smiled to herself. You never really know a person, I guess."

"Minor technique issues!" Cali growled. "Like, I gave my all. Well, obviously." She crossed her arms.

Hal studied her carefully, and then held her hand. "Sometimes the torments are in the real world, but it's in the mind that it really matters. Truthfully, I never really appreciated the wonder of you before."

"You're glad to have me back?" Cali begged, her voice starting to shake. "I'm the laughingstock of the world. The company is going to need a new spokesperson."

"Laughingstock isn't quite the right word," Hal countered. "I think lust object is closer." He moved her hand.

"Do you have something in your pocket, or are you glad to see me?" Cali snickered.

"Mae West—always liked that movie. Yeah, I'm glad to have you back! And I think you'll find that people will treat you better than you'd expect. You were, after all, kidnapped, drugged, tortured, and humiliated. What happened to you could happen to anyone, and thinking people will know that. Well, it could have happened to anyone who is an ravishing beauty with a goddess's body. I guess that does limit it a bit."

She laughed and kissed him. "Pervert! I knew it from the day I saw you," she whispered.

"Stalker, too—remember the coffee shop? As you may recall, I warned, 'Wait 'til you get to know me better.' First thing on the list is to get you somewhere safe. Tell me what happened! My plan sucked, but we dashed in anyhow, and you just came waltzing, well, bouncing, out on your own. Very impressive." He pulled her close. "If you change, I love you anyway."

"You are my favorite person in the world," Cali promised, "and that includes the imaginary ones." She nestled down on his lap and fell asleep.

A New Life

Lucretia's mother was playing with the children, trying to inconspicuously watch the clock. In the street below, a black van pulled up to the building entry. A dozen black-suited men rushed in, threw the doorman into a closet, and took control of the lobby. Eight of the men rushed upstairs and broke into the condo, making all the noise they could.

As they left, they threw a smoke bomb into the apartment and lit the drapes. The sprinklers were going on as they rushed out, and the fire alarms were starting to blare. They grabbed the children, who screamed all the way down the stairs and out of the building. Lucretia's mother screamed also, for effect but also because it was just a little too real. For a moment, she thought it was Mother Superior's people, but the squad leader whispered to her that Lucretia was waiting for her, and she nodded.

"But keep screaming," he hissed, and she did.

When everyone was inside the van, it roared off into the night. An hour later, they were riding through the dark countryside, sitting in the back of a van. Lucretia held Jose; her mother held her granddaughter. Lucretia looked sad.

"Life goes on. Days get brighter," her mother promised, touching Lucretia's shoulder. "At least we can look forward to a life again "

"All I worked for," Lucretia muttered. "Gone with the wind." She looked up at her mother and smiled. "I guess it really wasn't all that important anyhow."

"Frankly, Scarlett, I don't give a damn," her mother drawled.

Lucretia laughed.

"That's better," her mother commented. "Let it go. And I hated the doorman. Hey, the happiest people don't have the best of everything, they just make the best of everything."

Lucretia just looked at her.

"Look, I'm your mother. I can make you endure my pithy sayings, and you have to smile about it. It's in the secret mother's handbook."

"You know," Lucretia asked, puzzled, "Cali and Hal had these birthmarks that let them control people, but I didn't get one?"

"Oh, you got one," her mother laughed. "I had a tattoo applied over it. You know that tattoo on the base of your spine, above your butt?"

"Great," Lucretia complained. "They get a powerful weapon, I get a tramp stamp."

"So what's the problem?" her mother countered. "You think you would flash people your ass if they were about to attack you? Never seemed like it would have worked that well to me."

Lucretia laughed and hugged her mother.

"It's a bad day, not a bad life," she told her mother.

THE CARDINAL'S MANSION

"What the hell happened?" the Cardinal demanded, livid, as they walked into the dining room. "What do we know?"

His staff ran off, and an hour later they came back with a report.

"Lucretia has vanished. Paul says it wasn't his people, and Cesare swore it wasn't his people. Her mother and children are gone, and their condo was burned," his chief aide reported, eyes straight ahead, not daring to glance at the Cardinal.

"Out!" the Cardinal shouted. He and Mother Superior sat alone in the room.

"Can't you go find them?" Mother Superior demanded. "Can't you do something?"

"It isn't the old world," he snarled. "I don't have a guard of a hundred men anymore, armed to the teeth. Why don't you try and figure out what happened there, rather than just bitching at me? How is it that a drugged, naked, and helpless young woman is suddenly mentally and physically free, and many of our most devoted followers fight to the death for her? Isn't that a relevant question? Grendel could turn people into his minions, remember? What has happened here? And didn't you see, leading that attack party, the young man that Grendel wounded? No one has ever survived his venom. What are we supposed to think about that?"

Mother Superior sat silent, very worried.

"And," the Cardinal added, "I got the blood tests on Lucretia back. They never reached Paul—some mix-up, it seems—and the only copy of the tests is in my hands. The person she thought was her father was not her father at all. And her DNA? Very unusual. I'd venture, perhaps, that Lucifer was her father."

Mother Superior was terrified. "Paul will kill us!"

"I'd hardly blame him, actually," the Cardinal laughed bitterly. "We brought Lucifer's daughter into the inside circle of power; the attack on the warehouse lost Grendel; the kidnapping/blackmail blew apart, and we lost Lucretia in the process. Now, all of those were Paul's choices, but we were the boots on the ground closest to the disaster. And the Sandman was destroyed, on top of everything! Paul's talent pool is starting to run a little low. No, I think we'd better just let this one go," the Cardinal drummed his fingers on the table for a moment. "Be glad we survived the night. I'd suspect we survived only because they were too busy with other matters."

The Cardinal glared out the window.

"I think the story is that Lucretia was kidnapped by Lucifer," Mother Superior offered, "along with her family, because they blamed her for the kidnapping. The bodies will never be found. Sad, really—such a talented young woman cut down in the prime of life."

"Better than telling Paul that his brilliant young star switched sides under our noses," the Cardinal shouted. "And that the young man isn't dead, actually, despite our promises to Paul that he was. Go home. Let me answer the questions. Go somewhere far away in South America where they can't find you for a while."

Mother Superior bowed and left.

The Cardinal sat at his desk in his study, reflecting.

MARY & LUCRETIA'S MOTHER

"Hi, can I come in?" Mary poked her head into Lucretia's apartment.

"Please!" Lucretia's mother replied, surprised to see her. "Forgive us, it's a mess! We're still getting stuff sorted out."

"Here, the nanny can help with the little girl," Mary advised as the nanny followed her into the room. "Really, she's quite harmless." Mary caught Lucretia's mother's look. "At least to our friends."

"I'm sure," Lucretia's mother stammered. "Here, where are my manners?" She stood up and shook hands with the nanny. "I'm Juana Liancol. And what big teeth you have," she observed dryly to the nanny, who laughed.

"The children don't worry about monsters under the beds," Mary commented. "Nanny will eat the monsters."

In a second, the nanny had the little girl giggling and laughing and was taking her down to the playroom.

"Here, I brought coffee," Mary offered, handing Lucretia's mother a cup.

"Thank you, that's very thoughtful. Shall we sit at the bar?"

They sat down, and there was an uncomfortable silence for a few minutes.

"May I call you Juana?" Mary asked.

"I'd be honored."

"You know the family story, don't you? My past lives?"

"Most of it," Lucretia's mother replied. "Lucifer told me a little."

"I've been a priestess for a hundred temples across the Middle East and the rest of the world. I always enjoyed that work. It was healthy, lively, and it paid well. I had nice dresses and jewelry. The churches of the last two thousand years have been so boring."

"This is about my having been a whore, isn't it?" Lucretia's mother sighed.

"Partly," Mary admitted. "I've done that work lots of times. You can wear it as a badge of shame or honor. After all, most women can't do that work. It takes an attractive and strong-minded woman to run those men the way you want to, which is another reason other women hate it so much. Yeah, I wanted to say that I'm okay with the life you have led, and the others are too."

"That helps. It's a burden to bear, no question about it. This place..." She waved her hand around at the apartment. "...and all of you people, you're so different—it's really a change of world. I wake up in the morning, wondering if I'll be back in that little town, wearing my shame. It's hard."

Mary put her hand on Juana's hand. "Talk to me, okay?"

CALI & HAL TALK

A week later, Cali sat on the bed, staring at Hal. She was not really happy.

"What does the world think?" Cali muttered. "You can tell me."

"Ah, why don't you ask me an easy question, like, oh, does that dress make your butt look fat? Which it doesn't, by the way," Hal replied. "Honey, there is no good answer to your inquiry, just things that will get me in greater or lesser trouble."

"You have learned something about women, honey," Cali teased. "But no, I'm asking. Really asking."

"And I'm really not buying it, but sure, fools rush in, etc.," Hal sighed. He thought for a minute. "As I told you, your mother was quite proud of you. Your physical attributes really shone, you might say, and she was impressed with the fruit of her loins, and all that stuff." Hal sat next to Cali, holding her hand. "Mary was terrified that she would lose you, but proud that you held up. Took a lickin' and kept on tickin,' you might say."

"You're not helping," Cali scolded, shaking her head, but she smiled.

"In all truth, I think the other family members were astonished. Of course, they were furious and horrified at what you were being put through. On the other hand, you are ravishingly beautiful, and you did seem to be enjoying yourself. So, let's leave that one there. Essentially, we would have killed them all had you not done so, but we were proud of you at the same time."

"Good answer," Cali declared. "I don't want pity. I just didn't want, well, distaste."

Hal bent over and opened a bag on the floor. "And talking about your mother, that reminds me, your mother gave me some salve that I was to have given to you after I rescued you," Hal muttered glumly. "She said it was an ancient formula that would help, and was quite insistent. Don't tell her I forgot about it! It's in this bag somewhere, I think." He poked around, not finding it, and then sat back, dismayed.

"You're not just saying this to make me feel better? Like, I'll take feeling better, but do you really mean it?" Cali demanded. "I watched some of the recordings, and I was shocked. Well, a bit shocked. Fine, I'll pretend to be shocked for my outer social mask. When it was happening, I didn't remember that much. Or maybe I did, but it was fun. Those were strong drugs."

"Only the best for my lady," Hal observed. "At least they gave you the expensive stuff." He straightened up and pushed the bag away, looking worried. "I don't know where that salve went. Tell her you lost it, okay? And, so...you've come to terms with Grendeline?"

"Was it that obvious?

"Yeah. There was a change each day. Subtle changes from day to day, but as I went through the recordings frame by frame, I saw it."

Cali whacked him with a pillow. "Pervert!" she growled, but then laughed.

"Studied for research purposes only," Hal promised, wrapping his arms around her and holding her tight. He turned serious. "I did say that it would take a major crisis to bring Grendeline out. Perhaps there was no other way of really coming to terms with her. Dying to the old and being reborn, which was needed with what you were going through."

"What do the church fathers think?" resting her head on his shoulder. "There must be a lot of noise out there."

"I think there were church fathers at the ceremony," Hal retorted. "The Cardinal and Mother Superior for sure."

"Their habits were disgusting," wrinkling her nose. "And the church people who participated in the entertainment? They were, well, so small." She snickered. "It's no wonder they were celibate. A woman wouldn't know they'd been with her."

"And I defer to your expertise," Hal vowed. "Moving along, please."

"And the news commentators?"

"That's been interesting," Hal declared. "Obviously, they couldn't comment on it directly, but the blogs were all over the place. There were feminists defending you for your vigorous lusts, feminists defending you because you were being forced, feminists saying you deserved it because of a variety of reasons, and feminists calling for your death because you'd disgraced women. Surprisingly, the conservatives divided along the same lines. It made for some odd, well, bedfellows among the talking heads, you might say. And there was a lot of uproar about your guards being drug killers until it came out that the information had been planted, along with a lot of other information. Some people got very quiet, very quickly. Of course, some of it was Lungorthin's doing—putting people in the river with weights. Then, people had to take into account the small matter that you killed everyone who attacked you. It's one thing to pick on the poor, oppressed weak, but picking on people who kill their enemies is a lot braver. As you may imagine, the news people backed away from that."

Cali sat on the bed, brooding.

"Look, honey," Hal begged, stroking her hair. "Look at me."

Cali stared at him, worried.

"You can't please everyone, and really, you can't please hardly anyone," Hal reassured. "Except yesterday—you pleased me a lot. And the day before that, and, well, you get the idea. I'm pleased. Your mother did ask, however, and she made it clear that this was only for strictly professional reasons, given that she's a fertility goddess and has certain responsibilities to verify facts...whether you had a phone number for Horse-Orc? That was her pet name for him."

"Umm, I think I doused him in gasoline," Cali recalled, thinking back.

"Yeah, he burned. Well, she wouldn't have liked him that much. Size, but no technique."

"Ah, well, you've just been spoiled," Hal teased. "But" very seriously, "there is a problem that came up and I'm not sure how to handle it."

"That would be?" Cali blurted out.

"Alert observers in Ann Arbor seem to have conclusively tied you to that bar fight where you beat up that football player and cost the University of Michigan the title that year. The furor had died down when we vanished, but it's back now. And they take their football seriously over there," Hal warned.

"I would have thought they would be preoccupied with serious academic concerns," Cali laughed, relaxing. "And I just broke a few of his bones. He had lots of others that I didn't break."

"Serious academic concerns?" Hal questioned. "Did we go to the same school?"

Cali giggled. "Breakfast?"

They went to breakfast.

CALI & LUCRETIA'S MOTHER

"Ah, Cali, could I have a word with you?" Lucretia's mother stood at the apartment door, nervously smiling.

"Sure," Cali replied, surprised. "Come in, please! Everyone is gone. Hal's playing with his computer, and Maria is in the nursery, where I am told she is inciting the other children to rise up and take control, under her leadership as the dark queen. I'm happy to be here. Coffee?"

They sat down at the bar in the kitchen a few minutes later. Cali glanced at Lucretia's mother, waiting.

"My name is Juana," Juana offered. "Well, the name my friends know me by."

"Thank you! I'd love to be friends! It's been so crazy since we all got back here that I haven't had time to talk to you."

"As you might guess," Juana added, "I'm adding my ten cents about your recent experiences."

"I'd guessed," Cali admitted. "Everyone is trying to help, and it means a lot. Still, it's not easy."

"Actually, it won't ever be easy," Juana sighed. "That's not the way life is. But it will be nothing as hard as you think it is now. Look, I'm a whore. I've made a living as a prostitute for most of my life, and I'm not ashamed of what I did. Two of my daughters refuse to talk to me, but Lucretia has always stood by me, which is priceless. I did it because I had to. You don't have to carry that, which I have to tell you is a bit of a burden some days. No, your actions were forced. Drugged and kidnapped, you have no shame from what you did."

"Well, there is the small matter of exposing the most private parts of my body to the entire world," Cali countered. "The crass exploitation of the beauty of the sexual act—that's the slogan they used! I guess it's the kindergarten lessons that bother me. And the section in the secret book for girls, in bold type and underlined, about keeping your skirt down. But you were forced, too. You were thrown out, given no choices, forced into that life."

"There's truth to that," Juana agreed. "You know, don't tell my granddaughter this, but there are worse lives. My business was sex. Most of the time, it's a psychiatrist's job. It always surprised me how often men didn't even want sex, they just wanted someone to talk to. And in that line of work, you get a lot of exercise and get to be outside on nice days. The sex can be fun. It's better than scrubbing clothes or cooking in a dirty bar. Your mother sat me down and had a long talk with me, and I feel better about my life. After she told me about her lives as a priestess in the old days, well, I felt like a neophyte again. Here you think you're an expert, and then someone changes the world around you."

"Mom's good for changing the world around you. I think it's her specialty. She told you the family story?"

"Yes. I was shocked in a way, but then not. After all, Lucifer and I knew each other, in the biblical sense, and I knew some things about him. Your mother made me realize that the world they handed me was designed to beat me up, to make me feel like nothing. That wasn't a real world, and it really wasn't a world that was normal human at all. I was amazed."

They sipped their coffee for a few minutes.

"Well, I didn't come to tell you about my life," putting the coffee spoon down. "I just wanted to tell you that the burden they threw on you has been thrown on a lot of women, and life goes on."

Cali touched her on the shoulder as she started to stand up. "No, please, stay," Cali urged. "Tell me about your life. Tell me about other places, other times. I need to break out of the track I'm stuck on, that's for sure! You made the choice out of duty, thinking it was right, and you paid a price. We've all done what we thought was right, and what the 'right' is seems to be a lot more confused than I ever thought it would be."

"Isn't that the truth!," Juana declared. She looked doubtfully at Cali. "You sure you want to hear my tale of woe?"

"I'd love to. You got to see mine in color, with a soundtrack and a blow-by-blow, as it were, commentary, so it's fair that I hear yours."

"By the way, I agree with your mother," Juana mentioned. "Technically accomplished, your performance was. Oh, I have some quibbles about specific details, but it was good work."

Cali laughed. "Mom said I could get an apprentice priestess position, and it's always nice to have a backup plan. I was kind of offended about the apprentice concept, but mom told me I'd be able to work my way down. It was a metaphor, I think."

"Well, it started like this," Juana offered.

New York. Cali Holds a Press Conference

Two weeks later, Cali was back in New York. After going round and round, she decided to just stand up, directly address the whole mess and put it behind her. After all, she realized, there is no pretending it didn't happen. People will think about this when they meet me for the rest of my life. If I've acknowledged it, pushed it out there, and told them that I'm moving past it, well, that's about all I can do. What other people do is up to them.

She was sitting in a small room, nervous, waiting for the news conference to begin. And this was a good idea because? she asked herself. My sense of certainty isn't coming back to me now.

"It will be fine," Aliston told her, her hand on Cali's shoulder.

"I'm terrified," Cali confessed to Aliston. Cali's face fell for a moment, and she sighed.

"I was in the Israeli army," Aliston offered. "I was captured by the Syrians for six months. Interrogated—or that's what they called it."

"Oh," Cali gasped. "I'm sorry. My problems are nothing compared to that. I'm just feeling sorry for myself."

"Not true," Aliston countered. "You have every right to be terrified and upset. I've been there! When I came back, some people I had relied on to support me turned their backs, but some people that I had expected to hate me rallied around me and supported me. You discover who really matters and who is an asshole."

"Thanks," squeezing Aliston's hand.

"By the way," Aliston advised. "That husband of yours is devoted to you. Go! It's Showtime."

Cali walked out to the press conference, happily thinking about what Aliston had said. Cali stood for a second, blinking in the bright lights, starting to read the prepared speech on the teleprompter. Screw it, she thought, and looked directly at the news people in the room.

"It was a terrible experience," Cali declared, her head up. "But it happened. Small, vicious people hated our company, hated all that we have done, and tried to destroy the company by humiliating me. It didn't work. I'm glad for those who have supported me through all of this and I'm thankful to be asked to be the representative of the company again."

She paused for a moment. "People ask if I'm taking the recordings off the Internet? There's a hopeless task! I'm putting them on a website to save people all the trouble and excitement of tracking them down. The web address is in the briefing paper provided to you. You want to enjoy my pain? We wouldn't have been friends anyhow, so do as you want. What has happened is what has happened. People think I should hide my head, because that's what the social plan says disgraced women have to do. I should follow the authorized script, even though it's a horrible movie? People attacked me, humiliated me, and you think I should hide and hate my life because of what they did? That's really a disgusting plan, and I'm not playing out of that playbook. I took the plan of the people who kidnapped me and turned it on itself. I'm not changing my life because of what someone, somewhere may think I should do. The people I care about—they understand. The others can go to hell.

"I am not a rag doll wrapped in a skirt, stuffed with random male defined 'virtues', I'm not a puppet putting on a public show, kneeling as they pull my strings. I'm a woman. I am proud of what I am and what I've done. Thank you for coming." Cali smiled and turned to leave.

Half of the people in the audience stood up and applauded. The rest sat glumly in their seats. Glum, because cable news thrives on destruction and their hopes to make a fast buck through Cali's destruction was ruined.

Afterwards, Cali sat in Aliston's office, still a bit stunned.

"You did fantastically," Aliston gushed. "People are so proud of you, after all you went through and then how you stood up for yourself."

"Well, I didn't stand up all the time," Cali grimaced.

"She stoops to conquer."

"You know," Cali admitted, looking shyly at Aliston, "I have a confession to make to you."

"And that would be?" Aliston asked cautiously. "I used to have a nun's habit, a leftover from some long-ago Halloween, but I don't know where it went."

"You were part of the reason I got out of that terrible place."

"That's wonderful...I think?" Aliston replied, puzzled.

"Early on, Grendeline, the dark power of Life that Hal gave us all," "told me how you would be next to Hal, concerned and supportive, your pendulous breasts jutting out like melons, quivering as you stood next to him. And I swore I'd get out of there and tear all the hair out of your head. Of course, I won't," laughed, leaning forward and touching Aliston's shoulder.

Aliston looked shocked, and then laughed. "I've been in tough places, and I know you grab motivation from anywhere you can. No blood, no foul."

"You've done wonderfully here," Cali observed. "You've kept things going through all of the disruption. You've done so well that I was wondering, well, if you'd consider coming to Detroit. We need a real office there, and you're the best. Hal made the right choice promoting you to Chief Operations Officer, no question about it. I defended you at first to Mary, Jesus, and Lucifer, but after a short time they were so impressed with what you were doing that they are all your fans now. It looks like Hal's going to start work on the corporate reorganization again since the world discovered he's alive and there's no point in him hiding. Clearly, the need for the reorganization is greater than it was, because the world is changing faster than we thought. I'm working on a bunch of projects with him. We need you and your skills, and it's too hard to run this long distance. We thought you could pick, oh, maybe ten to twenty of your best people, and move them with you. We have lots of space."

"Are you sure?" Aliston demanded, uncertain, studying Cali. "Women usually don't want me around on general principles and especially around their men."

"I want you to come, because I like you as a person. Sherwood Forest can feed and shelter a band of determined fighters. You'd be an asset, if you would care to join our merry little band of outlaws."

Aliston contemplated her for a second and then looked away, a tear running down her face.

"I haven't asked Hal, and he hasn't brought up the idea. This will be a complete surprise," Cali offered. "I wanted to ask you first, just you and me. So what say you?"

"I need an hour to pack," Aliston replied. "I've had it here, and this sounds a lot more interesting. Besides, it would be nice, well, to have some women who don't hate me. Friends would be nice. There are not many of those here."

"Friends," Cali promised and stood up and embraced her. When they stepped back, Cali held Aliston's hand. "Ah, I took the liberty of booking a plane ticket for you. We fly out in four hours."

"Well played," Aliston laughed, shaking her head. "I knew Hal couldn't plan as well as he pretended he could."

"Here's your ticket," pulling it out of her purse and handing it to Aliston. "Meet you at the airport?"

"Can do. I know who I can promote to take this office over and I'll work on the list of people to move out there. We can go over the names with Hal when we look at the office space and living facilities."

"Oh, there's lots of space. I think maybe another two hundred thousand square feet is empty? Maybe more? We really have not completely inventoried the factory."

They planed on the flight. As they collected their bags in the Detroit airport, the security staff and the driver helped them carry them, huffing under Aliston's four large pieces of luggage.

"The driver wasn't exactly expecting me?" Aliston inquired, glancing at Cali.

"Oh, I thought, rather than explain over the phone, I'd just tell people when we got here. Sometimes the best plan is no plan, adapt as events occur. Play it by ear."

Aliston laughed and shook her head.

ALISTON IN DETROIT

When Cali and Aliston got out of the car at the factory, there was a row of surprised faces. Cali quickly introduced everyone and after she helped Aliston put her stuff in her room, Cali called a meeting.

At the meeting, Cali explained why Aliston was there and what the plan was. Mary, Lucifer, Jesus, Lucretia, and Hal nodded and said, "Sure. What's next?"

"This is an agreeable group," Aliston mused. "Best corporate meeting I've ever been in."

"Cali is a great planner, and this is a great plan," Hal offered. "I didn't think of this, but even despite that glaring flaw, it's obviously a great idea."

"Gosh, what a great endorsement," Cali retorted. "Where's my notepad where I keep the list of your character flaws?"

"We couldn't find a hard drive big enough to hold the list," Hal teased, "and the last person to carry the written list got a hernia. But, I did have an idea while you were gone," Hal murmured to Cali, leaning towards her with a smile. "You'll find it interesting, I promise, ma chérie."

"Ah, moving on," Mary interrupted. "I'm very happy you are here. I have to admit that I asked Cali about you when Hal promoted you so suddenly and Cali backed you completely. What you've done is more than I would have believed anyone possibly could have done. Cali's right-having you here is critical with all the changes we see coming."

"Cali said something about changes," Aliston replied, puzzled. "Are there specifics I should know about?"

"There are, actually," Hal answered. "A lot of changes coming, but, well, I think you need to know more about the merry band first. I'm assuming, Cali, that you haven't shared the family history with Aliston?"

"Ah, no," Cali admitted. "I, ah, thought I'd cross that bridge when I came to it."

"I'd say the bridge is here," Jesus commented dryly. "Looming before us, you might say. So, who wants to tell the story?"

"Could you?" Lucifer asked Jesus. "You're the people person, and it's a long story."

"It isn't that easy," Jesus protested. "Cali at least has to help!"

"Moi? The elf maiden scattering flowers before her?" Cali advised. "Just merry sunshine and not a thought in my head."

"I'd like to help, too," Mary announced.

Aliston was glancing from one to another, concerned.

"It's an interesting story," Hal told Aliston. "I'm running off, as I have some work to do. Relax—you'll find it fascinating." Hal stood up and started to walk out.

"I'll help you, Hal," Lucifer offered, abruptly standing.

Jesus and Mary looked at Lucifer quizzically and then smiled to themselves.

"Well," Jesus started, as Aliston studied him "It's like this..."

Hal closed the door behind him, and he and Lucifer walked down the hallway. Hal glanced at Lucifer and smiled.

"What was that all about?" Hal asked. "You don't have anything important to do that I know of."

"Oh, I didn't want to sit in," Lucifer grumbled. "I generally don't mind being the heavy, but sometimes it's annoying."

"Yeah, I'm not buying that." Hal snickered. "Inarticulate around beautiful women. I wondered from where I had inherited that particular character trait. You are my father—there's no doubt about that."

"Ich? Moi? You couldn't be talking about me?" Lucifer laughed. "The lustful monster of a thousand legends, the great seducer of women across the ages? Yeah, the marketing was a little overdone there. And that's quite a woman."

"More than you realize. She runs the company; she's organized, efficient, and under control. And she does that despite every woman hating her on sight and men only grasping about one-half of what she says because she dazes them. When she shifted to e-mail, things went much more smoothly."

"Then I don't feel so bad," Lucifer replied. "I just didn't want to sit there and have to weigh in on cue. 'And heeeere's Lucifer!' The usual role just wasn't where I wanted to be. I probably looked like an idiot."

"I doubt it. With what little I know of women, she's ten steps ahead of you anyhow. Wait and see. Cali ragged on me about following her, and then slipped and told me she wore heels every day to get my attention. Who can figure?"

"Sword-fighting practice," Lucifer argued. "That's an important thing to do. How about it?"

PAUL & FATE

"It went well," Xerxes declared to Paul.

The others agreed.

"She was disgusting," Tamburlaine added. "It's a pity she could not have been at the castle in North Africa."

"Prancing at her a press conference, pretending it will all go away," Paul sneered. "They are getting a million hits a day on that archive of the recordings. It didn't go over as well as she thought it would."

"Hits from distant countries," the Adversary pointed out. "People who had hesitated to buy from Aeternalis, GmbH are placing orders. Lucretia gone, probably dead. And the Sandman is destroyed. A pyrrhic victory, certainly. Another like it, and we shall be destroyed."

The others were silent.

"It was a brave show she put on," Paul admitted. "But people will forget the show and remember the recordings. Well, you can't make an omelet without breaking a few eggs. And my dream tells me that we are on the right track. I see the falcon rising in the air, and the anarchy unleashed will create the world we need."

"The man who has planned badly, if fortune is on his side, may have had a stroke of luck; but his plan was a bad one nonetheless," the Adversary countered.

The others looked at him, frustrated.

"Look, it's a living, okay? This is what I do," the Adversary protested.

"Fate cannot be influenced by any action, for or against," Paul confessed. "Intentions cannot alter predetermined outcomes. We do what we must, and wait for the Gods to decide."

"That's true enough," the Adversary agreed, surprised. He nodded to himself for a moment, and smiled at Paul. "I'm going to have a glass of wine, gentlemen, since I can't better what he just said."

The others stared at him, shocked, and then started talking about old wars.

CALI & MARY, MOTHER TO DAUGHTER

Cali and Mary were sitting at the breakfast table in Cali and Hal's apartment, after Cali came back from New York.

"So, mother-to-daughter talk time?" Mary asked.

"Sure, why not? Everyone's been great, trying to help."

"Caught between Scylla and Charybdis, nothing but difficult choices?" Mary teased.

"I thought of it as a rock and a hard place, myself," Cali countered.

"Perched on the horns of a dilemma?" Mary offered. "Perhaps too literal. You survived and triumphed, so maybe this pep talk is for me. What happened to you was awful, but not terrible in a historical sense. I can tell you stories that would curl your hair! Say, the Germans into Russia in World War II, and then the Russians back into Germany, returning the favor. The armies literally rode on the backs of the women unfortunate enough to be in the way. And that's life sometimes, harsh as it is. At one extreme, you're not a victim, wearing your horrible experience like some kind of demented crown; at the other extreme, you're not hiding from it, making it something to push away and hide from yourself and others. You faced your monsters, integrated them into yourself, and you're stronger for it. Life shits on everyone sometimes. You shake it off and move on. I couldn't be more proud of you." Mary put her hand on Cali's arm.

Cali rested her head on Mary's shoulder for a few minutes. "There are days it talks better than it lives, but I'm so happy you're behind me."

"You grow or you die. I've lost so many daughters over the eons. I was terrified I'd lose you too. But you pulled yourself through, like none had before."

"March or die," Cali growled.

"They didn't take women in the French Foreign Legion, the last time I checked," Mary laughed. "You wouldn't like it—too hot and sandy."

They said nothing for a few minutes. Cali gazed at the clouds drifting by, and Mary reflected, lost in the past.

"So," Cali remarked, looking at her coffee. "Hal tells me he was impressed, and his attentions to me have been proving it, which is good to find out! That was one of my first concerns—whether he would still find me attractive afterwards. Lucretia's mother came by and helped a lot. So, any other thoughts?"

"In my day, a woman would have to work her way up to a state of orgasmic lust using only her imagination and perhaps some wine. Maybe a lot of wine, with several men. None of this newfangled fancy drug stuff that's everywhere today. Daughters today have it too easy, that's what I think," Mary scolded, and then winked at Cali and laughed.

"Now there's a lecture I didn't see myself giving Maria," Cali laughed. "Honey, I had to walk barefoot in the snow to school, five miles uphill both ways, and I was happy to do it! And, I had to get my body into a state of intense desire just by thinking about naked men with no artificial stimulants to help. No, I'm going to have to re-write that speech a bit."

"Any woman would be proud that her daughter could do what you did. They brought in teams, and you chewed them up and spit them out."

"More swallowed. Technically. Well, I was hungry most of the time. They didn't give me a lot of food."

"Whatever, it's a metaphor, honey," shaking her head. "Why would I criticize you? First, it wasn't exactly voluntary. Kidnapping and drugs are not the usual background for a lecture on moral behavior. Putting those small details aside, women lecture their daughters on what they can't do, not what they can do, which is a shame. It isn't a man's body; it has many neat tricks and toys. I've been male, and that isn't my preference. Women lecture their daughters on what they can't do—and why? Because it's what men tell them to do."

Cali wrapped her arms around her mother. "That helps a lot."

"People have done all the things you did over the eons. Why, I remember some of the priestesses in the old days. They would have considered you a rank amateur, which really you are, compared to them. Talented, they were. Now, there is all this pretense. People don't have anything inside themselves—they just reflect what others think of them. You're better off not being friends with those kinds of people. Remember, all those women give you snotty looks because it's the women that enforce the behavior code for women. They put on their panties one leg at a time, just like you do. They are just jealous, envious, small, petty...and the list goes on."

Mary cocked her head and looked critically at Cali. "Are you making notes, honey? I'm pitching, and you're not catching. All this really good stuff I've saved up, just flowing out, well articulated and logically organized. You know, every mother has to give a lecture to her daughter about the world dumping on the daughter. There's no point recreating the wheel—you might as well save some for your talks to your daughter."

"Umm, no," Cali answered, glancing around at the table. I never have a pencil and paper around when I need one. Look, maybe you could give this speech to Maria?"

Cali fell silent, worried, gazing out the window. Mary waited.

"There's something else," Cali confessed. "Something I can't admit to anyone else."

It's coming, Mary knew. So strong she is, yet unsure.

"When Grendeline and I came up with the plan to take control, it worked well," Cali sighed, troubled. "Too well, perhaps. When I killed the Sandman, even Grendeline was taken aback by my, well, hunger. I craved revenge for my pain, I lusted for his death. Grendeline drew back for a moment, studying my delight as the Sandman was torn apart from the inside, and then I tasted his memories and laughed. It's, well, worrisome that she was surprised. Terrifying is more like it. What will I become? Even she asked that for a second. The berserk monster that I saw in Hal when he fought Grendel, that terrified me—well, I surpassed that."

Mary stroked Cali's hair gently. "Kali-Ma can be harsh because she must be. The black mother of death is not a pretty picture at all. I've been Kali-Ma, glaring at my subjects as they knelt before me, altars drenched in blood from their sacrifices to protect themselves from my wrath. Not the sad-eyed Mary of the pictures, is it? Did you ever wonder how we maintained and defended against our enemies over the long eons? Not by singing in joy in the groves of the woods, although that's important. The raw fire of life, the hunger to survive, is what you unleashed. Will you be the dark queen, standing over the bones of your enemies as your subjects bow in terror before you? If it comes to that, then that is what Life demanded. Yet you will always have yourself, and will find your way to what you feel is right."

Cali stared, still troubled, out the window, and then glanced back at Mary. "Never go to the elves for advice, it is said, because they will say both yes and no," Cali teased.

"Not true," Mary denied, kissing her on the forehead. "For you have told me all about you, and I foresee you to be a light shining, not a black cloud full of thunder and lightning. Although," hearing a scream from the other room, "that one may be a black cloud." Mary sighed, shaking her head.

"I'm blaming Hal," Cali declared, jumping up to see what Maria was so upset about. "That behavior is certainly not from me, the happy elf maiden."

CHAPTER 16. LIFE GOES ON

<u>ROAD TRIP!</u>

"Road trip!" Hal came in and grabbed Cali.

"Are you out of your mind?" Cali shouted at him as he dragged her down the hallway. "People after us all over the place, my face more recognizable than, well, a lot of people's?"

"Not necessarily your face," Hal corrected, and ducked. "You still throw like a girl. Hey, it's a nice day. Trip to Lake Michigan!"

Hal pulled Cali into the main living room.

"Mom!" Cali pleaded to Mary. "This nut wants to go to Lake Michigan."

"Dare the dreaded interstates of Michigan? Pothole hunting is today's quarry," Mary commented. "That is dangerous. Still, getting out would be a good thing. But, you'll be disappointed at the house, I'm afraid. Don't stop or act too interested—we're sure they are watching. It's abandoned. You'd be happier going to a beach on a sunny day. But, heck, beat it, get out of the factory."

"I can take care of Maria," the nanny growled. "Don't want her coming back all sunburned and sandy."

"Ok," Hal agreed. "We're out of here."

"Ah, swimsuit? Suntan lotion? Towels?" Cali inquired.

"Don't sweat the details. That's what charge cards are for." He pulled Cali out of the factory and they jumped in a BMW 3 Series Coupe. "Listen to that engine roar! It's even made in the U.S.—well, assembled here."

Cali flopped down in the passenger seat, still shocked, and they roared off.

Three plus hours later, they pulled up at the beach. "What a crowd," Hal remarked, glancing around. "We got almost the last parking spot."

"Ah, swimsuit?" Cali teased. The sun and the air in her face on the way had brightened her mood.

"Downtown. Just a short walk this way. Oh, and here's a big floppy hat and sunglasses, movie star," pulling them out of a bag in the back seat and handing them to her. "A quiet day with the peasants, hiding.,"

Cali grimaced, but quickly turned her hair into a ponytail, shoved it under the hat, put on her sunglasses and made herself invisible to the world.

They wandered through the shops. Cali found a swimsuit, towels, and sun block, and they wandered back to the beach. "I'm sick," she groaned three hours later. "Hot dogs and French fries on a hot day. I never want to eat again."

"Pity," Hal remarked. "They have chocolate ice cream over there."

Cali pushed him aside, walking faster than Hal towards the ice cream. "See, it's the sun. It burns off the calories. Like a free day."

An hour later, they crawled into the BMW and drove out of the beach parking lot. "It's nap time," Hal yawned. "Sleepy."

"We should drive by the lake house," Cali mumbled. "Somehow, depressing or not."

"Better yet!" He drove to the pier and in a short time they were on a sailboat. "A schooner, actually," he pointed out, as they watched the crew cast off. "Small mast in front, large mast in the back. Not a ketch, which is the opposite. Useless knowledge, but it sounds impressive."

"Lake house?" Cali asked, sitting happily on the deck. "Not that I really care. I love this boat!"

"And the best thing is, we don't have to drive it. Pilot it, whatever. Last time I captained a sailboat, I ran it into the rocks. I insisted it went there on its own, despite my advice to it, but no one was happy. So now, we happily sail along, and this..." He pulled out a telescope. "...gives up the lake house from a distance. All a ruse, you see. The sunny day, the beautiful beach, the sailboat on the wine-red sea. Actually it's a blue sea, but the poetry is better. All a ruse."

"Remind me to let you handle all the sneaky planning from now on," Cali teased. "You have a gift for it."

They sailed for an hour, and then Hal pointed towards shore. "Over there, but scan the surroundings first."

Cali experimented with the telescope and finally got the knack of adjusting for the boat's roll. "There are people watching it. I can see cars overlooking it. Amazing that they pay people to sit there all day."

"I wonder what the wage scale is for evildoers?" Hal mused. "Do they have to post OSHA signs? Is there an employee manual? What are the federally mandated safety requirements for, say, theft and killing? Workers' comp? Contract negotiations with the Amalgamated Evil Henchmen Local 842? It's got to be expensive."

"It's a ruin," Cali sighed, putting down the telescope. "Abandoned— even some of the windows are broken and covered with plywood."

"Not a ruin. There is life all around it. Look at the flowers growing, the sand grass blowing in the wind. The waves breaking on the shore. The human-imposed shell is tattered, but the life is still there. It will be there for us someday."

"Aren't you going to look?" Cali asked.

"No, I looked at the satellite pictures before we came. Showed me everything I needed to see, including the watchers. There are more of them than I would have expected. I think they own the cottage to the west."

Cali laughed. "So this was a ruse. Completely a trick to get me out in the sun and fresh air."

"A ruse on a deception on a fabrication on a ploy on a ruse. I have a chart somewhere showing what the real plan was. I get confused."

"Trick me all you want," Cali giggled, lying back on the deck and soaking up the sun. "I could get used to this."

They drove into the factory at dusk, exhausted and sunburned but happy.

"Where's the BMW?" Mary asked.

"Hal swapped cars at this place north of here," Cali explained. "He said this old junker," kicking the fender, "would handle the roads better anyhow. Something about how it would take the repair shop a week to get the tires back in alignment, so it might as well go there now."

"A good plan. Someone has been looking for you."

Maria came running out, loudly demanding mommy.

LUCRETIA

Lucretia was sitting in her apartment. Her son was playing with some of the children of the veterans, and her mother was out with her daughter, wandering around.

Jesus knocked on the door. "Anyone home?"

"Come on in," Lucretia shouted.

Jesus opened the door and peeked in.

"Come, in, please," Lucretia sighed, trying to smile.

"What's up, merry sunshine?" Jesus asked, studying her carefully.

"Oh, just stewing in self-pity," Lucretia complained. "I'm bored. I'm used to doing things. I feel like a fifth wheel. Shall I whine some more, or is this enough?"

"Certainly enough," Jesus agreed. "So you'll be happy to know that I have a job for you. Come on." He walked in and pulled on Lucretia's arm. "Real, socially productive work."

"This doesn't involve a hoe, weeds, and a big field, does it?"

"Absolutely not," he promised. "No, that's a job we give to the people with seniority."

She glanced at him, worried, but shrugged and got up. They walked down the hallway and out of the factory into the sunshine.

"Over here," he explained, waving his arm toward some small buildings. "Is that nice little restaurant, which is really a series of interconnected little businesses. Now, none of the businesses are being run competently, although I'd rather you not share that comment with the owners and/or staff. Their problem is that they don't have good information to make decisions with. It was represented to me, by a little bird, that you know how to create and run a business information system."

"Well, I do know a lot about business and information systems," Lucretia replied. "Usually at, well, a bigger level, but, sure, what can I do?"

Jesus talked about what he knew about the businesses and where he suspected there were problems while they walked to the restaurant, Lucretia nodding her head and asking occasional questions. Reaching the restaurant, Jesus yanked on the door, which squeaked, and they walked in.

"This is the owner," as they walked up behind a man bent over a table in the restaurant. "Lucretia, Vladimir. Vladimir, Lucretia."

Vladimir was carefully gluing down a new top on the table and he didn't look up right away.

"Jesus tells me that you know about business," Vladimir mumbled, He glanced at Lucretia, then immediately stood up, pushing his hair back off his face. "Ah, sorry to be, well, rude. It's just that there are so many things to do around here."

"I can help. Heck, I even know how to glue a countertop." She expertly jiggled the material into place before the glue set. "There," looking up and him and smiling.

Vladimir smiled back at her and they just stood there, motionless.

"Ah, I have work at the factory," Jesus mentioned, "just in case anyone is interested, so I have to leave now." No one was paying any attention to him.

"Ah, bye," Jesus remarked, backing away, and then he turned and walked away as Lucretia and Vladimir started to talk. Ok, that was a success, he thought. Happiness often sneaks in a door you did not think was there.

CALI'S PLAN REVEALED

Hal was humming to himself, working on the computer.

There was a knock on the door.

"I'm already disturbed. Please come in," Hal shouted.

"I can't argue with that," Cali admitted, walking in. She peeked over his shoulder.

"The companies thrived and prospered while I was gone," Hal complained, disappointed. "Don't they realize that the world revolves around me? There are going to have to be some memos sent out—I can see it now."

"When you implement the corporate reorganization plan, everyone will blame you for everything, honey. Then the world will be deemed to revolve around you," Cali promised.

"Always be careful what you wish for. I suspect you are right on that one. Oh, thanks for bringing Aliston here. Not many women would have done that."

"You're good with it, I assume?"

"I'm detecting the overtones in your voice," Hal remarked. "You talk in your sleep, do you know that?"

"You don't mean!" Cali gasped. "I really didn't say. .?"

"I enjoyed the parts about her pendulous melon breasts standing close to me to comfort me, and how you were going to tear her hair out. All of it— you were specific. Leg hairs, too. Because I could see how distraught you were, well, I had to comfort you, didn't I? Two nights ago," Hal laughed.

Cali laughed, shaking her head. "I told her, and she laughed. She said whatever got you out of a tough spot worked."

"I am glad you brought her. She is the best at what she does. Competent, organized, and dangerous. And I think she was lonely. She needed some friends, real friends, and she is accepted here. She seems happy."

"That's good to hear." Cali walked over to the kitchen, and then, studying Hal's reflection glass cabinet doors, casually mentioned, "And your father seems to be happy. I noticed he skipped out on the story the other day. He should have been there—she was impressed with the story she was told about him."

"Happy?" Hal replied. "He can barely talk around her, he's so obsessed with her."

Cali turned and walked back to Hal, smiling to herself.

Hal caught the quick smile of satisfaction on Cali's face. "And what's that look on your face? Cali, what devious plot have you hatched here?"

"It is a truth universally acknowledged, that a single man in possession of a good fortune, must be want of a wife, or at least a girlfriend," Cali answered, humming to herself. "Well, it's in the secret book for girls, third chapter, I think," as she looked at Hal with an impish expression. "After all, we can't just have him wandering loose—who knows what he'd bring home?"

"I told him she was way ahead of him," Hal laughed, shaking his head. "I didn't realize you were ahead of her. Amazing."

"And we did need her here. She was very supportive of me, and when I looked over what had been happening while we were all out of commission, I saw that she was the best at operations."

"On the other hand, you are the best at what you do," Hal vowed as he grabbed her around the waist and pulled her onto his lap. "Of course, practice is never a bad thing, even when you're at the top of your game." He kissed her.

"Grendeline didn't tempt me with the mating offers that you were given. Now, that might have had something to do with the constant mating I was actually doing. But you know, it's experience that matters in life—that's what she taught me." She kissed him back. "The door, I think?"

"I hear and obey, my queen," Hal advised, jumping up to shut the door.

Lucifer & Lucretia's Mother

"How are you doing?" Lucifer asked, peeking his head into Lucretia's apartment.

"Fine," Juana answered, quickly pushing her hair into place. "I, ah, well, wasn't expecting company."

"You're gorgeous in your natural radiant state," Lucifer promised, smiling. "Can I come in?"

"Certainly!"

"And I have flowers," Lucifer offered, holding up a bouquet.

"Oh, oh," she laughed. "This started a lot of trouble the last time." She took the flowers and went over to the kitchen, looking through cabinets for a vase. "Here's one," pulling out a cut crystal vase. She quickly trimmed the flowers and arranged them. "There," critically examining the display. "That works." She set them on the dining room table.

"Despite all the marketing," Lucifer admitted, "I'm not all that good at talking. I can't say how much I appreciate everything you've done for us, and everything Lucretia has done. We'd all be dead without her information and help."

"And she'd be dead, too," Juana countered, "along with all the family. I'd say we're even on that one. And then you brought us here—a new life! It's wonderful, especially in light of, well, how we split up all those years ago."

"We all must do what we think is right," Lucifer responded, shrugging. "I'm not the most dependable male and my reputation precedes me. I'm not criticizing."

"And here you are now," Juana teased, standing next to him and gently arranging his hair. "But I'm too old now, and all that becomes way too complex. I hate to phrase it like this, but—can we be friends?"

"It's always friends," Lucifer sighed. "Maybe I need a different haircut, or a better tailor. No, you're right,", looking up at her. "I'm happy to be grandfather to Jose and Donna, and happy that you're here."

"Prince of darkness, and still can't get a date, eh?" Juana laughed, stroking his hair.

"Don't tell Paul," Lucifer pleaded, smiling. "I have an image to maintain!"

The little girl started shouting from her room.

"I have to run," Juana mumbled, flustered. "She only gets noisier." She gave Lucifer a quick peck on the cheek and ran to the little girl, shouting that grandmother was coming.

"Bye," Lucifer shouted into the chaos and let himself out.

Can't get a date? Lucretia's mother thought. I think there are others with plans for you, my lord. "And for you," she declared, talking to the little girl, "I have plans for you!," as she struggled to put the squirming, squealing girl on the changing table.

THEY ARE WINNING THE WAR ON THE ENVIRONMENT

The family was sitting in the community television room, watching a news program. Mary, just back from an ecology seminar, was furious.

"You go through life trying to be nice to people, struggling to resist the urge to punch them in the face. And why? The whole time, I felt like shouting, 'I'm sorry you're too blind to see all the damage you have caused!'" Mary shouted at the television.

"I think they were too well trained in school, where they teach you capitalization and how to drive in straight lines, and that will be your life. Maybe the people with spirit were weeded out, I don't know," Jesus agreed, disgusted. "They look at the graphs and numbers and charts, and it's clear to anyone. Finite resources and infinite demand doesn't work. Ever. But no response, because, well, it wouldn't be nice to someone, because someone is going to get less."

"At least the war on the environment is going well," Cali acknowledged, watching with dismay. "Total victory any day."

"Explain to future generations that it was good for the economy when they can't farm the land, breathe the air, and drink the water," Hal snarled. "I doubt they will take it cheerfully."

"'Mankind censure injustice fearing that they may be the victims of it, and not because they shrink from committing it,' which is one of the few things Plato got right," Mary quoted. "Empathy is sold as the currency to not judge or question. So the wicked run happily along, using empathy as a shield, and the well meaning are beaten down with the weight they carry."

"More pizza, anyone?" Hal offered, carrying in several boxes that were still steaming.

They all jumped up, grabbed fresh slices, and then sat back down.

"It's like that joke," Mary complained. "The guy was falling off the really high building, and at each floor, when they asked him how he was doing, he said, 'So far, so good.' They happily jumped off the building, all falling, but agreed with each other on the way down that things were working out. 'We're okay!' they shout to the people in the building as they plummet past. The honest ones at least admit that they figure they'll be dead before it blows up. The others just hope and look the other way. It's hopeless. We'll have to just get ready for a crash."

"The small human stories are in for a surprise," Hal added. "Remember what I was showing you a couple of days ago?"

"All those computer-story ideas?" Mary asked.

"Do androids dream of mechanical sheep? That's something that no one is looking at. Talk about complete human blindness! Do you remember Isaac Asimov's laws of robotics? The first was that robots must not injure a human being; the second was that robots must obey orders of a human. What they don't get is that it is completely human stories they are rooting those 'laws' in."

"And?" Lucifer asked, looking up from the pizza.

"Scientists say that we no longer understand how the computers do math. We can't always follow the process by reverse engineering it, and these computers are a fraction as sophisticated as the ones coming. They will generate their own stories," Hal argued. "We don't have a clue what those stories will be, and most importantly, how and where humans will fit in. The computers will change and evolve their programming over time. If there is no intersection between our stories and theirs, how long are they going to serve us when they can move and re-create themselves?"

"It's like that Transformers movie," Jesus commented. "I always wondered about that. Why did they look like humans? Why bother? They could look like anything, hide processors where they are safe—not in the head, a bad place to put the marbles."

"I saw an article[26]," Mary offered. "It argued that we're going to see scientific results that are correct, that are predictive, but are without explanation. We will do science but without insight. Science will still progress, but computers will tell us things that are true, and we won't understand them. What happens when the computers start asking questions that they are interested in, and realize that we can't follow them or understand? Why would they serve us then?"

"New robots slither, move on little spider legs, and move in ways completely different from humans," Hal added. "Humans all of a sudden realized that there were other options than standing on your legs and walking. Duh! There is a world out there besides the human view, but people just don't see past. So the robots are going to look at things in a way we can't even imagine, and it won't be long. The first law of robotics? Most things depend on how you view them. Someone will probably write the laws of robotics as 'How to Serve Mankind,' and we'll all be on the serving plate."

"I loved that Twilight Zone," Jesus laughed. "It's the small print—it always gets you."

"We really can't see what's coming," Mary mused. "I can see the biological research merging with the silicon for true cyborgs. Truly beyond our imagination, and their stories will be different from ours, no question. And regardless of the movies, you can't win a war against robots. They kick them out of the plant faster than you can raise human warriors. They win on attrition if nothing else."

"They are already having to destroy the occasional drone," Hal pointed out, "because they make up their own little minds and run off. They don't talk about it much because that worries the citizens, you see. And then there is the plant-eating robot they are building that can wander around and use plants for energy. They're pitching it as eating only invasive species? It could eat all the wheat and nicely get rid of humans at the same time. The science-fiction movies skip past the hard questions for the easy solutions, exposing a bit of flesh by the heroine to short circuit the thinking parts of the brain."

"Could this really happen?" Lucifer demanded. "I haven't followed this at all."

"Example," Hal stated. "Artificial intelligence, defined in human terms, such as we understand it, has been a failure on computers. So in the 1980s, people started to look at the kinds of things computers do well. They found that a set of small, simple programs interacting with each other was surprisingly like intelligence. Again, the human story completely runs the worldview. No one looks at gnats—tiny little creatures with less processing power than a computer that eat and reproduce quite nicely."

"Too nicely," Mary interrupted. "They are all over the fruit within a day."

"Intelligence isn't a unitary thing. It's a collection of specific, linked behaviors," Hal continued. "So people started using methods not modeled on human intelligence. The scientists discovered that the computer didn't need to be taught how to do something; they could show it what people did, and the computer could figure out how to get to the result. Scary, really. Going back to the math programs—Mathematica seems to use calculations that are completely different from the logical steps humans use. A different story in the machine, and we blow right by it. The program doesn't follow human reasoning, and the results, while correct, often can't be explained to a human. And that's today. What about tomorrow? Ten years from now? And the singularity, when the computer has more functioning power, by human definitions, than humans do? What stories will it run by, and will we have even a clue? I doubt it."

"Given the small, pitiful, self-serving stories humans are using," Mary growled, "I'm not so sure that is bad." She caught Cali's expression. "It was a really, really bad experience at the seminar, honey."

"Maybe the answer to why the universe exists really is forty-two," Hal remarked.

"What?" Jesus asked.

"This book had a computer the size of a planet calculating for millions of years, and finally it spit out the answer to everything, which was '42.' And it could be, because maybe it's an answer to a story we can't grasp," Hal observed.

"Putting in a word for the other side, people get busy," Jesus argued. "Daily life takes over, and one doesn't think outside. Up to your ass in alligators, it's hard to remember that the goal was to drain the swamp—all that stuff."

"It's just that we're not picking our fall," Hal declared. "When you see something coming, you should pick your fall. Like skiing. Better down on your rump than a cartwheel down the slopes with skis and poles flying off. I've done both, and the cartwheel isn't recommended."

"And what's worrisome," Cali added, "is that it's always 'what we were' in the speeches. We can't be less, so we must be the same in the future as we were. Once you look back, put that stake in the ground as your measurement pole, you've frozen. It's just a matter of time until the wall looms before you."

"One real problem," Mary remarked, "is that we have never seen—or been—a species with an 'off' button for reproduction. As if everyone agrees to take a break for coffee instead of sex because it's clear that there are enough of us now. That's not the way the system works—in any creature, from viruses on up. Now, I'm a fertility goddess, and generally I'm happy with the process, but I've seen this dance before. The headlong expansion of a population into limited resources is a train wreck coming. And no one wants to face this, because it means tough choices have to be made. But if there isn't an 'off' switch, then the whole 'We can control the population' is just a pleasant fantasy until the crash comes. Always, if internal limits don't work, then some kind of external constraint will kick in—chosen or not."

"Finding cheap power sources has really been the whole thing driving the last century," Jesus admitted. "Their understanding of themselves and what they are doing hasn't really improved much. Take a Roman citizen and put them in a suburban house with functioning utilities, and they'd be on the commuter train in a week reading their paper in a suit. People are adaptable in some ways, and in some ways absolutely not. Talk about the law of unintended consequences! Cheap oil multiplied the population by five times in a hundred years, setting up the smashup coming. Who would have thought?"

"Boiled frogs," Lucifer offered.

"I beg your pardon?" Jesus inquired.

"Bless you, my child," Lucifer pronounced, moving his hand.

"No, you do the cross like this," Jesus countered, motioning. "Its just tradition."

"Really, you two," Mary demanded. "Focus. Frogs?"

"Boiled frogs," Lucifer explained. "Put a frog in a pot of cold water. Turn the heat up really fast, and the frog jumps out. Turn the heat up really slow, and the frog never recognizes a danger point. Boiled frog. And the frog is assessing the situation all the time as best he can. That's where the world is today. Slowly raising the heat, probably literally."

"Here's the other side of that problem," Mary declared. "One water lily is growing on a pond in your backyard. The lily plant doubles in size each day. If the lily grows unchecked, it would completely cover the pond in thirty days, choking out all other forms of life in the water."

"This isn't a story problem, is it?" Jesus objected. "No trains heading for each other? I hate those."

Ignoring him, Mary continued. "But at first, and for a long time, the plant seems small. You decide not to cut it back, because you like the flowers and the look, until it covers half the pond. How much time will you have to avert disaster once the lily covers half the pond? One day. The water lily will cover half the pond on the twenty-ninth day; on the thirtieth day, it doubles again and covers the entire pond. You have only twenty-four hours before it chokes the life out of your pond. Assuming you are completely on top of the situation, have the equipment to cut it back, etc."

"Perhaps the next creatures will eat plastic," Lucifer remarked. "That's about all they are going to leave."

"Or landfills," Jesus added. "Mountains bigger than the pyramids, the enduring legacy of industrial civilization to the ages—a landfill towering over the ruined cities. I like that."

"It's that systems are tightly coupled but complex," Hal offered.

Jesus groaned. "Another systems discussion. Can I be excused?"

"Hey," Hal asked, "how about this? It was autumn, and the Indians on the reservation asked their new chief if it was going to be a cold winter. The old chief had died unexpectedly, and had never taught the new chief the old secrets. The new chief looked thoughtful when the question was asked, and said he would have to ponder. As he had no way of knowing whether the winter would be cold or mild, to be on the safe side he advised the tribe to collect wood and be prepared for a cold winter. People happily ran off to do that. A few days later, as a practical afterthought, he called the National Weather Service and asked whether they were forecasting a cold winter. The meteorologist replied that, yes, he thought the winter would be cold. The chief advised the tribe to stock even more wood. A couple of weeks later, the chief checked in again with the Weather Service. "Does it still look like a cold winter? asked the chief. "It sure does," replied the meteorologist. "It looks like a very cold winter." The chief advised the tribe to gather up every scrap of wood they could find. A couple of weeks later, the chief called the Weather Service again and asked how the winter was looking at that point. The meteorologist replied, "We're now forecasting that it will be one of the coldest winters on record!" "Really?" chief demanded. "How can you be so sure?" The meteorologist answered, "The Indians are collecting wood like crazy!"

"Boo! Hiss!" Jesus jeered.

"Fine, systems jokes are not that great," Hal admitted. "But bear with me. Linked systems have multiple interconnections, which interact unexpectedly. For example, an airplane coffeemaker heated concealed wires and turned a routine short circuit into a forced landing and near-crash."

"Memo to forget that one before my next flight," Mary noted.

"Complexity, the simultaneous interactions between parts, means it's impossible for anyone to understand how the system might act," Hal explained. "Tight coupling spreads problems once they begin. To make it worse, the general notion of tomorrow is the same as today that we carry wired in our brain is a linear, process-oriented worldview. We're in a non-linear world, and the positive feedback loops get big, fast."

"People start collecting firewood and it builds on itself," Cali observed. "I'm tempted to start myself."

"So how is going green going to work if we can't take into account the savagery of the real world?" Lucifer demanded. "They love little seals and hate bugs. It's a big system, and all the parts work together."

"The saddest, but kind of a funny story," Mary sighed, "is set in London, in the eighteen hundreds. It smelled really bad when there were millions of people and no real sewers. Shit under the houses, shit running into the river. Finally, it smelled so bad that they had to build sewers. What's funny about that is that they built the sewers because they thought the smell caused disease, not the shit. So they acted because of the smell and accidentally fixed the real problem."

"So we hope for a bad smell in the world that people fix and accidentally restore the environment?" Lucifer mused. "Not promising."

"What destroys a species," Mary conceded, "is their strengths. The dinosaurs got bigger and bigger, and it worked. They were protected against the predators by their size. But not against changes in the external world, and they were so big that any disturbance was more than they could handle. They needed all the food inputs they had available. Take some away? Crash.

Fortunate for us mammals, that time. But the social structures that humans created, what they use to work together—that's their strength, and becoming their weakness. The structures take over and have a life of their own."

"And the structures can't bend," Hal added. "You read all these hopeful proposals for how and why countries can throttle back their economic engines. Then we can all live in balance on a small planet—such a pretty, happy goal. Because economic and military power are bound together, unilateral economic deceleration is equivalent to, and as foolhardy as, unilateral disarmament. The world is using economic power as an alternative to war, which has some real advantages. But any given country cannot throttle back to a lower economic level while all the others around are running full tilt. Peer competition drives increased complexity and resource consumption regardless of the cost, human or ecological.[27]"

"Who needs action when you've got words?" Cali sang.

They sat silent, watching the smiling faces on the television.

"That was not fun," Jesus complained. "Remind me to invite you all along for happy hour. NOT. And, as my man Jimmy Buffet would say, it's five o'clock somewhere. I think I need a nice glass of wine."

IT'S NOT ALL WORK

"Hal?" Cali called out. "Not in the apartment, okay. Well, let's wander around."

She heard shouting as she neared the community television room. She walked over and stood in the doorway.

Hal and Lungorthin were yelling at the television, standing and gesturing wildly.

"It's the quarter finals," Goth Girl remarked, standing next to Cali. "Men."

"Where did you find that jersey for Lungorthin?" Cali asked. "That's the biggest Red Wings jersey I've ever seen."

"It seems that in Detroit there are some big fans," Goth Girl replied. "I've never found stuff off the rack for him before."

"Oops. They are out of chili dogs again!" Goth declared as Lungorthin's hand fumbled on an empty plate. She rushed in with a plate full of chili dogs, and he rumbled his thanks. She kissed him on the head, and walked back to Cali.

"He'll eat twenty in a row," she sighed. "I have to buy the sauce by the gallon and pretend that I'm managing a kids' hockey team over on the west side. I'd enter him into an eating contest, except the rules don't allow mythological creatures. He'd get excited and eat some of the contestants, too, so it just wouldn't work."

"Hockey good," Lungorthin growled. "Fights. Don't understand the little black ball—just breaks up the fights."

"Yeah, I never understood that either," Hal agreed.

When the game ended, Hal and Lungorthin stood there shouting at the screen.

"Maybe the ref could take a flashlight and look for that puck..." Hal snarled, and then he caught Cali's look.

"There are children present," Cali pointed out, glancing at the children, who were giggling at Hal and Lungorthin.

"Sword fighting practice, anyone?" Goth Girl suggested helpfully. Work out all those tensions?"

"Good idea," Lungorthin grumbled.

LUCIFER & ALISTON

Lucifer was walking down a passageway at the factory later that day and saw Aliston walking ahead of him. She was walking slowly, seemingly deep in thought.

"Ok," Lucifer mumbled to himself. "Be smooth. Be cool. Oh, the hell with it," and he shrugged. "Hi," Lucifer smiled. Nothing but quick and articulate, he sighed to himself. A half-hour from now, I'll think of something clever.

"Hi," Aliston smiled, a little teasing twist in the corner of her smile.

"You've done wonderfully," Lucifer declared. "Without your help, I don't know where we'd be."

"A smooth talker," Aliston teased, turning her head quickly, tossing her hair and studying his reaction. Pleased, she smiled again and gazed into his eyes. "So, are you really the Prince of Darkness? The master deceiver? I've, well, always wanted to meet a prince."

"And, my fine beauty, I've waited eons for a line like that," Lucifer stammered. "But I have to tell you, a lot of the marketing about the Prince of Darkness was exaggerated. Maybe not all the physical attributes and the goat references..."

Aliston giggled and put her arm in his. "Jesus firmly believes it's five o'clock somewhere," she suggested. "What say we imbibe and talk? Ever since I was a little girl, I've waited for my prince to come. And here you are!"

"Your wish is my command, my lady. I am putty in your hands," Lucifer vowed.

"No man is putty in my hands, my lord," Aliston laughed.

THE BLUE'S MAN

It was a rare sunny day, an unexpected blessing.

Hal sat outside, an old steel door propped open, sitting on a chair in the sun, the wind blocked by the walls. He was playing the harmonica.

Cali had wandered all over the factory looking for him. When she finally found him, she just stood in back of him, watching. Finally, she cleared her throat, and he jumped.

"I never suspected!" Cali gasped, her hands melodramatically over her eyes. "A blues man."

"You'd be surprised at all my talents," Hal replied. "I thought I'd just sit here and relax in the sun." He looked up at the bright sky, shading his eyes with his hand. "It's nice out today." He started playing again.

"Then why don't you leave it out?" Cali asked.

Hal choked.

CARPENTER ANTS

Hal woke up one morning to a racket of hammers, saws, and trucks in the distance.

"We're being attacked by the carpentry union," he murmured sleepily to Cali. "Call out the carpenter ants."

"Yeah, well, don't start with the nailing routine," she teased, jumping up as she heard Maria shouting from her room.

"That's a dangerous step in this town," Hal advised to her back as she vanished into Maria's room. You need a union card for that or they send the enforcers out. I'd rather get a card from the plumbers and pipe-fitters union. Now there are some interesting possibilities." He listened to the saws and hammers in the distance, which seemed to be getting louder.

What is going on? he thought and got dressed. A few minutes later, he was wandering down a corridor towards the noise.

"What's up?" Hal asked Lucifer, who was standing with Vladimir and a group of the veterans and Lucifer's people.

"Oh, we had a lot of space, and some of the veterans are going to move into this wing of the factory," Lucifer observed, too casually. "They and my staff seem to be working together well now, which is a wonderful turn of events! And it turns out that one of them has an engineering background and has all these great drawings to divide the space up."

"And all the pollution that is supposed to be in here?" Vladimir commented. "It turns out that the analysis was inaccurate. This soil is as healthy as it can be. Surprising how things get confused like that. Well, we've got work to do." He motioned to the other veterans, who were talking with Lucifer's creatures, and they all walked towards the chaos, shouting among themselves and waving their arms.

"Always good to have people around," Hal remarked to Lucifer.

"Well, since the world could make a reasonable guess that you are still alive and that Cali is based here, it isn't a complex deduction to figure out that you might be here with Cali," Lucifer admitted. "This needed to be done for many reasons, and security is just a cover. Even better, the caretaker tells me that most of them are expert swordsmen, and we need more challenge in our practices. Oops, I see the forces of evil headed our way! It's the building inspector." Lucifer quickly walked towards the red-faced man in the poor-fitting suit.

And I think I'll go back to the exercise room, Hal thought. Excellent swordsmen? That means I'm about to get my butt handed to me. This seems like an appropriate time for some quick practice.

THE END OF BOOK 2.

COMMENTARY AND DISCUSSION

Joseph Campbell's ideas are a foundation for these books, and I have paraphrased his writings throughout the books. Hopefully he would have approved of my application of his ideas. When the writing style switches to myth and the hero's journey, his ideas are probably shining through.

The Art of War is a constant theme throughout the book.

Another key source of ideas underlying the books is the book The Black Swan, by Nassim Taleb.

The Collapse of Complex Societies, by Joseph Tainter is paraphrased in various places.

Christianity – The First Three Thousand Years, by Diarmaid MacCulloch – I have paraphrased parts from this book for Paul and the Minister. Whether the author would agree with the use I've put the ideas to is unknown, but her book is exquisitely written and recommended.

I have stolen a running gag from The Kentucky Fried Movie, the 'we are building a fighting force of extraordinary magnitude'. There are also occasional other references to lines from the movie. Buy the movie!

Lucretia quotes Josh billings: "It ain't what a man don't know that makes him a fool, but what he does know that ain't so."

Paul says "The problem with German food . .," which is from "Plato and a Platypus Walk into a Bar," by Thomas Cathcart, Daniel Klein, 2008

Chapter 13, Hal's Saga, and all of the Grendeline experiences rely very heavily on the Joseph Campbell's writings. The little readings from their notes of the various Hal 2, Hal 3, and the other personalities, are all from Campbell's work.

There are quotes from Ecclesiastics 1, usually from the King James Version.

There is a chasm and a strange bridge keeper as part of most of the Grendeline encounters. Many will recall a scene like this Monty Python and the Holy Grail, as well as this scene being a motif in literature over the centuries.

Cali quotes Tupac Shakur, 'you can spend minutes, hours . ., which is a great way of expressing the problem.

'purpose in life's turmoil' is roughly paraphrased from "The Unthinkable," by Amanda Ripley.

There is a segment from "The Dark Knight". 'Truth isn't good enough . . sometimes, people deserve more.' This is one of many references to the Dark Knight; which rejecting the image of Batman as a hero. The book rejects, actually, the whole concept of the hero as a person who comes to rescue the foolish. That's a child's hero, and a child's story.

"It is by Caffeine alone I set my mind in Motion . .," which a revision of the Dune ritual with the spice. If someone has the copyright on this revision, I couldn't find it.

There is a quote from a very, very old Wall Street Journal cartoon and I couldn't find any date on the cartoon. It's used where Hal wants to put a recording on his phone.

ABOUT THE AUTHOR

Credentials:

- I have a BA from Michigan State University, majoring in Sociology, with minors in Psychology and English (1972);
- A JD degree from the University of Detroit School of Law (1975);
- an LLM (Master's in Law) in Taxation from Southern Methodist University School of Law (1983);
- a MBA from Michigan State University, Materials and Logistics Management, /Operations Management (1992); and
- a Master in Science from Michigan State University, in Building Construction Management, focused on Project Management (1998).
- I have been licensed as an attorney in Michigan since 1975
- Licensed as a Certified Public Accountant in Michigan since 1981.
- Am a certified Project Management Professional (Project Management Institute)
- Certified Information Technology Professional (AICPA);
- Certified in Financial Forensics (AICPA), and
- Chartered Global Management Accountant (AICPA)
- My practice web site is: www.johnedwardhunt.com

Perhaps little of that matters for the purposes of these books, but it is what one usually puts on the author page. I'm fascinated by Joseph Campbell's ideas, despair about the ecological disaster coming, and know that people don't plan well. So these books encompass those interests and challenge the reader to think outside the box – way, way outside the box.

Endnotes

[1] Elliot, T. S., The Wasteland
[2] Prager, Ellen, Sex, Drugs and Sea Slime, University of Chicago Press, pp x
[3] ibid, pp 19
[4] ibid, pp 26
[5] ibid, pp 34
[6] ibid, pp 38
[7] Machiavelli, Niccolo, The Prince, Chapter 6
[8] [8] Yeats, William Butler, The Second Coming
[9] Noyes, Alfred, The Highwayman, Part One, I
[10] Shakespeare, William, Hamlet, Act I, Scene 1
[11] Robert F. Worth, The New York Times, Thirsty Plant Dries Out Yemen, October 31, 2009.
[12] Elliot, T. S., The Waste Land, V What the Thunder Said
[13] Auld, William Muir, Christmas Traditions
[14] David Zucker, Jim Abrahams and Jerry Zucker, The Kentucky Fried Movie, 1977
[15] Elliot, T. S., The Waste Land
[16] Campbell, Joseph. All of the notes by Hal 2 and Hal 3 are from Campbell's writings, some paraphrased, but clearly from his writings.
[17] Ecclesiastes 3:19 and following.
[18] *Church, Samuel Harden translation, Beowulf,*
[19] Campbell, Joseph, The Hero with a Thousand Faces, 1949 edition, page 89
[20] Alice in Chains, "Dirt" album, "Angry Chair" song
[21] ibid.
[22] Alice in Chains, No Excuses
[23] Job, 21:7 and following.
[24] Monty Python, The Meaning of Life
[25] Shakespeare, William, Macbeth, Act 5, scene 5
[26] Strogatz, Steven, Voices: What's Next in Science, New York Times, November 9, 2010
[27] Tainter, Joseph, The Collapse of Complex Societies, page 214 (paraphrased)

www.ingramcontent.com/pod-product-compliance
Lightning Source LLC
Chambersburg PA
CBHW060353260626
47160CB00006B/2294